OLD COWBOYS
NEVER DIE

OLD COWBOYS
NEVER DIE

WILLIAM W. JOHNSTONE
AND J. A. JOHNSTONE

WHEELER PUBLISHING
A part of Gale, a Cengage Company

Wheeler Publishing Large Print Softcover Western.
The text of this Large Print edition is unabridged.
Other aspects of the book may vary from the original edition.
Set in 16 pt. Plantin.

**LIBRARY OF CONGRESS CIP DATA ON FILE.
CATALOGUING IN PUBLICATION FOR THIS BOOK
IS AVAILABLE FROM THE LIBRARY OF CONGRESS.**

ISBN-13: 979-8-88578-959-2 (softcover alk. paper)

Published in 2023 by arrangement with Pinnacle Books, an imprint of Kensington Publishing Corp.

OLD COWBOYS NEVER DIE

CHAPTER 1

"Well, I reckon that about ties a knot in it," Casey Tubbs announced as he joined the little group of eight men sprawled on their bedrolls around the chuckwagon. "Any coffee left in that pot, Smiley?"

"Yeah," Smiley said, and poured a cup for him.

Like the rest of the crew, Smiley was anxious to hear what Casey had found out when he went to look for Ronald Dorsey. They had driven the last of the two thousand cows into the holding pens at the Abilene rail yards. Dorsey, a lawyer for Whitmore Brothers Cattle Company, was responsible for collecting the money when the cattle were sold. He was also the man who would pay the crew their wages.

"Did you find Dorsey?" Smiley asked.

"Yep, I found him," Casey said.

"Well, what did he say?" Eli Doolin asked impatiently. "When are we gonna get paid?"

7

"He said he figured it all up and we owe the company money for our horses and such," Casey said.

"Damn it, Casey," Eli said, "when's he gonna pay us?"

Eli, along with Casey, was one of the older cowhands for Whitmore Brothers. The two of them had been working cattle together for so long that each one knew when the other was joking. The rest of the crew, all but two were young men in their teens, anxiously waited to hear what Casey had found out.

"Dorsey said the payroll was deposited in the First Cattleman's Bank under each man's name. We have to go to the bank to draw our money out. And the damn bank's closed now, so we'll have to wait till tomorrow mornin' to get our money." His statement was met with a chorus of groans and complaints. Every man was eager to have money in his pocket tonight. It had not been a particularly long drive. But every drive was hard work, pushing ornery cows across a dusty prairie, driving them all day, watching them all night. The pay was forty dollars a month, so a drive this short wouldn't put much money in their pockets. It had only taken a couple of days longer than two months. But it was enough time for them to want to "see the elephant" and ride home broke but happy after a night in Abilene.

Eli got up from his blanket and walked over to talk to Casey. "Why the hell didn't he just hold the payroll and pay us tonight? They've always paid us before," he said to him. "All the years before this, when John Whitmore was running things, we got our money the same time he got his."

"Well, this year, thanks to the way Mr. Dorsey handles it, we'll rest up tonight so we can light up Abilene tomorrow, good and proper. You still got grub to cook on that wagon, don't you, Smiley?"

"I sure do," Smiley said, "and I'm supposed to get some money to feed us on the way back home."

"There you go, boys," Eli declared. "You'll have a good meal in your belly on top of a good night's rest when you attack Abilene tomorrow." He looked then at Davey Springer, youngest of the crew at the age of fifteen — and this, his first cattle drive. "This way, you'll be able to brag about it when you get back home. You can tell 'em you didn't spend all the little bit of money you made until the second night you were in Abilene." Still looking directly at Davey, he said, "You'd best be careful if you fancy one of those little gals that makes her livin' gazin' at the ceilin'. You reach in your pocket and her hand will already be in there, countin' your change."

"You talk like you ain't gonna go into town with the rest of us, Eli," Sam Dunn, an experienced drover at the age of eighteen, remarked.

"Oh, I'll be goin' in with you," Eli said. "Both Me and Casey, I expect. But when you young bucks head for the saloons and the dancehalls, we'll most likely find us a good supper and a drink of likker afterward. Right, Casey?" Casey nodded in reply. "You see, I've left too many a little dancehall gal with a broken heart when I had to tell her I couldn't stay with her. I don't fancy breakin' any more hearts."

His remarks received the mocking he expected. "Maybe when you and Casey finish your supper, you can look for a dancehall where the old ladies are all rollin' around in their wheelchairs," Sam suggested.

"That's a right interestin' proposition," Casey commented. "I like the sound of that."

The jawing back and forth continued right through supper, and for a while afterward, because there was nothing else to do. Dorsey sold the remuda, as well as the cattle, so there were no horses to take care of except the one you kept to ride back home.

There was no reason to roll out of their blankets early the next morning. The bank didn't open until nine o'clock, which to a cowhand seemed more like noon. Smiley was up early as usual, however, to fix breakfast. They were all standing by the front door of the bank when one of the tellers came to open it. He hesitated when he saw the nine cowhands waiting there. Evidently surmising that they could break the door down, he proceeded to open it. They filed in and lined up at the teller's window.

"Good morning," the teller greeted Casey, who was the first in his line. "What can I help you with?"

"You can help me with my lack of spendin' money," Casey said cheerfully. He gestured with his hand at the men standing behind him. "The nine of us work for the Whitmore Brothers Cattle Company. We brought a herd of cows up here that were sold yesterday. And Mr. Ronald Dorsey deposited the payroll for us in your bank so each one of us could pick up our money this mornin'. My name's Casey Tubbs." He stood there waiting for the teller to do whatever he was going to do to give him his money.

The teller could only respond with an expression of complete puzzlement. He had no knowledge of any payroll the bank was holding. "I'm sorry, Mr. Tubbs, I'll have to get Mr. Skidmore to help you. I'm afraid I don't know anything about your payroll." When he saw Casey's immediate reaction, he said, "I'll be right back. Mr. Skidmore will know about it, I'm sure." He left the cage and hurried back to the bank president's office.

In a few minutes, the teller returned with the president following. Casey didn't like the expression on the president's face. It was one of concern, instead of confidence. "Mr. Tubbs," he said, "I'm Malcolm Skidmore. I'm the president of this bank. There seems to be some confusion about some payroll money?"

"This is the First Cattleman's Bank, ain't it?" Casey asked. When Skidmore acknowledged that, Casey asked, "You did have a Mr. Ronald Dorsey in here yesterday to cash a check for the sale of Whitmore Brothers Cattle Company's herd of two thousand cows, right?"

"Yes, we did," Skidmore said.

"Then there ain't no confusion," Casey declared confidently.

But Skidmore still showed plenty. "The check was honored and the cash was picked up by a special messenger before we opened this morning to be put on the train for Chicago. Those were Mr. Dorsey's instructions."

"But there was most likely a separate sum of money that was the *payroll only,*" Casey stressed. "That was supposed to be left here in the bank for us to pick up this morning."

"I'm afraid there's been some misunderstanding," Skidmore said. "Mr. Dorsey said nothing about any payroll. He wanted the entire amount of the money from the sale put on the train to Chicago." Seeing the instant shock of all nine men, he quickly sought to explain his position. "Please understand, the bank is in no way involved with Mr. Dorsey's decision on how the money was to be paid. He had a legitimate check and we honored it. Then, as is often the case with a large sum of cash, the customer wishes to have it transported in the safety of the mail car on the train. In that case, we are happy to provide a guard to accompany the customer to the train station, as we did this morning with Mr. Dorsey before the bank opened."

"So you're tellin' us that the money we worked for went to Chicago this mornin' with Ronald Dorsey?" Eli asked.

Skidmore turned to answer him. "I'm afraid so," he said. "At least it will. That train isn't scheduled to leave here until nine forty-five."

Eli turned to look at Casey. They were both thinking the same thing. "We ain't got much time to find that double-crossin' lawyer," he said.

"No we ain't," Casey said, "let's get goin'!" They headed straight for the door, and Smiley and the six younger men followed.

Outside, they gathered around the three older men, looking for answers. "Whadda we gonna do, Casey?" Sam Dunn asked, plainly bewildered.

Casey looked at the lot of them, all as bewildered as Sam. He made an instant decision. "Me and Eli will take care of it. Smiley, you boys go on back by the creek where we camped and wait for us there. We'll meet you back there."

Too confused to offer any other suggestions, they dutifully climbed on their horses and went back to the place they had camped the night just passed. Casey and Eli headed for the train station at a gallop.

The train was still sitting in the station and still taking on passengers when they

14

pulled their horses to a stop beside what appeared to be the mail car. The intention was to find Ronald Dorsey, so they climbed on the train and entered the passenger car behind the mail car. Since Casey was the only one who had actually talked to him, he led the way as they hurried down the aisle, looking left and right for Dorsey. Not seeing him in the first car, they went into the next car and looked for him with the same results. The same happened in the third car, where they bumped into the conductor.

"Can I help you gentlemen?"

"No," Eli said. "We're just lookin' for somebody. We'll look in the next car."

"That's the caboose," the conductor said.

"Oh, well, I reckon we'll look again in them other cars," Eli said.

"Can I see your tickets?" The conductor was now concerned with the two desperate-looking men.

"We left 'em with our suitcases up in the first car," Casey said, and started back up the aisle, Eli went right behind him. The conductor just stood there for a moment before deciding he'd better follow them and get a look at their tickets, if they actually had tickets.

They hurried back up the aisles with still no sign of Ronald Dorsey. When they got to the door they had first entered, they stopped to decide what to do. "I'm afraid I'm going to have to ask you gentlemen to get off the train, unless you can show me your tickets."

Ignoring his ultimatum, Casey asked, "What's in that next car?"

"That's the mail car," the conductor said. "You can't go in there." Casey ignored him and went to the door, but found it locked. "You can't go in the mail car," the conductor repeated, now past concern and approaching panic. Still, he tried to maintain his posture of authority. "Now, both of you, off the train, unless you show me a ticket."

"Here's my ticket," Eli said, and pulled his Colt .45 from his holster and jammed it in the conductor's back. "You'd best come up with a key to that door right quick. We ain't got time to argue with you."

"Yes, sir," the conductor said right away, abandoning all pretense of authority. "But it won't open if he's slid the bolt on the other side." He fumbled with his ring of keys until he found one for the mail car. With one hand on the back of the conductor's collar and the other holding the gun against his back, Eli pushed him through the door when it opened.

A startled mail guard looked up from a small desk and asked, "What's goin' on,

John?" A second later, he realized what was happening and he started to bolt upright from his chair, only to flop back down when he saw Casey, also holding a gun. Regaining a portion of his valor, he had to exclaim, "Right here? In the station? You must be out of your mind."

"What's your name?" Casey demanded.

"Wesley Logan," he said, staring at the revolver aimed at him.

"Well, I'm gonna make this real easy for you, Wesley," Casey continued. "All you have to do is follow my orders and we'll soon be gone. First thing is to reach over with your left hand and pull that pistol outta your holster and lay it on the floor. Be real careful, Wesley, I druther not have to shoot you." When Wesley laid the revolver on the floor, Casey said, "Kick it over here." Wesley did so and Eli picked it up. "We're here for one sack of money that belongs to the Whitmore Brothers Cattle Company," Casey continued then. "The sooner you give us that sack, the sooner we'll be out of here."

Wesley looked confused. He glanced down at a ledger on his desk, then back up at Casey. "We don't have any bag for Whitmore Brothers," he said.

"How 'bout one for Ronald Dorsey?" Eli asked.

Wesley checked his ledger again and said, "We've got one for him." So Casey asked how much was in the bag. "Fifty thousand," Wesley said.

"Whaddaya think?" Casey asked Eli. "I ain't tried to figure it up."

"We could take two thousand and that oughta cover it," Eli suggested. They hadn't taken the time to figure out exactly what the total should be for the whole crew.

Casey nodded his agreement. To Wesley then, he said, "Open that bag and count out two thousand dollars."

"I can't open it," Wesley said. "It has a lock on it, and Ronald Dorsey has the key."

"Get the damn bag," Casey ordered, "we're wastin' time here." Wesley jumped to follow his demand. Casey followed him to a cabinet and held his gun on him while he opened it and pulled out a canvas bag. As Wesley had said, it had a lock on it.

Eli didn't wait. He stepped forward and stabbed the bag with his skinning knife, and left the knife sticking in the bag. He told Wesley to cut a hole big enough for him to pull the money out. "Reach in there and count out two thousand" — he paused and looked at Casey and shrugged — "three thousand dollars. Hurry up," he ordered when he felt the train jerk as if about to start. "Put it in one of them bags." He pointed to a stack of empty mail sacks on the floor. Wesley kept pulling money out of the hole in the bag until he had counted out three thousand dollars. He paused then and looked up at Eli to see if he was going to tell him to stop. "Three thousand," Eli said. "That's all we came for. Hand me my knife." Wesley dutifully extended the knife toward him. "Turn it around, handle first, you bloomin' idiot."

"Oops, sorry," Wesley uttered, and turned the knife around.

With their guns still trained on the two railroad men, Eli and Casey backed up to the door. "I wanna thank you fellers for not makin' us have to shoot one of ya." He looked at Eli and said, "Come on, partner, we gotta hit the north road outta here." They backed out the door and jumped off the train just as the wheels started to turn over. In the saddle, they dashed away from the station at a gallop, expecting to hear shouts of alarm at any second, but hearing none.

Back in the mail car, John and Wesley were both amazed to still be standing. It was the first train robbery for both and Wesley was still holding the ripped bag. "There's gonna be hell to pay for this," he said, staring at the bag and the ragged tear in its side.

"They were two desperate-lookin' men," John, the conductor, said. "With all the money in this car, I wonder why they didn't want it all. There's fifty thousand dollars in that one bag, and all they took was three thousand."

"Yeah, don't make sense, does it?" Wesley said, still staring at the bag. "They coulda took more and this fellow, Dorsey, wouldn't know the difference. Makes just as much sense if they had took an even five thousand."

"That's a fact," John said. "I'm glad there was two of us witnesses to the holdup, so we can tell 'im what happened. And I expect we'd better report it right away. That fellow, Dorsey, is riding in the caboose. I let him ride back there because he said he had a fear of riding in open passenger cars. He's gonna be fit to be tied when we tell him what happened."

"Right," Wesley agreed, "we'd best get goin'." He reached in the hole again and pulled out two thousand more and gave John half.

Approaching the south end of town, the two train robbers continued their escape at a fast lope. When it appeared there was no one chasing them, they reined their horses back to a walk and Eli pulled up beside Casey.

"What the hell were you talkin' about when we left back there and you said we gotta hit the north road? What's the north road?"

"There's gotta be some road outta here headin' north," Casey said. "So I said that in case they get up a posse to come after us. Wesley and John can tell 'em we were goin' out the north road."

Eli just looked at him and shook his head slowly. "We need to stop and figure our money out before we get back to the camp." Neither one was good at arithmetic, so they dismounted beside the road, and with the road as a blackboard and a stick as their chalk, they figured the split of the money. They finally resorted to moving off the road and into the trees, so they could divide the money in nine little piles. When they were finished, they returned to their camp and the seven anxious souls awaiting them. They all got up to crowd around the two, excited to see Eli holding a sack.

"Boys," Casey announced, "we're happy to tell you that you will all get your wages for two months' work, as the honorable Ronald Dorsey promised. Plus, you're each gettin' a one-hundred-dollar bonus for the delay in receivin' your wages." That brought forth a cheer from the young cowhands.

"What about the money for my supplies?" Smiley asked.

"You got that, too," Casey said to him, "more than they'll actually cost. We all got what was owed us, plus the bonus."

"You musta found ol' Dorsey," Smiley said. "Where'd you find him?"

"We maybe oughta chip in some of our money to you and Eli," Sam Dunn suggested. "We wouldn'ta got a nickel, if you hadn't gone after Dorsey to get it."

Casey and Eli looked at each other to see who was going to explain the special circumstances around the crew's payday. Finally Eli volunteered. "Boys, there are some special conditions that come along with your payoff. It's best that you head straight back to Texas, and don't go into Abilene tonight to spend your money." He immediately captured everyone's attention. "You see, we never caught up with Ronald Dorsey. We caught up with the money he got for the sale of the cattle we drove up here. It was on a train that just left here for Chicago."

"You robbed a train?" Davey Springer asked.

"I guess you could call it that," Casey said

to him. "But it seems only fair. We just took what was rightfully our money and left the rest in Dorsey's bag. If he had been honest with us, he wouldn't have had that money to take to Chicago in the first place. That was ours, and me and Eli just went to get it back."

"That does seem fair," Smiley remarked, "but the Union Pacific Railroad ain't likely to see it that way. You had to break into the mail car to get the money, didn't you?"

"We had to persuade the conductor to unlock the door, so we could get in the car," Casey said. "But we didn't break down no doors, or destroy no railroad property, did we, Eli?" He paused, then said, "Except for that money sack you had to cut open with your knife."

"That weren't railroad property," Eli reasoned. "That belonged to Ronald Dorsey."

"That don't make no difference," Smiley insisted. He was genuinely worried about the two old cowhands. "How'd you persuade the conductor to let you in the mail car?"

Casey looked toward Eli again, but saw no tendency to answer the question, so he said, "We told him they had something that belonged to us in there."

"And he just unlocked the door for you?" Smiley asked.

"That was pretty much what happened," Casey said. After a pause, he added, " 'Course, when Eli stuck his .44 into the conductor's back, he knew we weren't just wastin' his time."

Smiley shook his head, scarcely able to believe what the two of them were telling him. "I swear, Casey, you're talkin' about armed robbery of the Union Pacific Railroad. It don't matter if it was for that little bit of money. You're gonna have Union Pacific detectives lookin' for you, for sure."

"I hope they take the north road to start lookin'," Eli mumbled to himself. Then he announced, "If any of you don't want your share of the money, we'll be glad to take it back." No one opted to return the tainted money, including Smiley, which was of no surprise to Casey or Eli.

Given the special circumstances that insured their pay, plus bonuses, the rest of the crew were in agreement with Casey and Eli's recommendation to leave Kansas at once and return to Texas. All the younger hands were planning to ride the grub line in hopes of finding permanent employment with some of the bigger ranches. The coming winter would be a little easier on their efforts with the extra money Casey and Eli had procured for them. Each man thanked the two for their sacrifice on their behalf and promised to never tell where they got the money.

Smiley was the only one of them who had a place to go. He had already agreed to go to work for another rancher in North Texas he had worked for before. He was replacing an old cook who was making his last trip to market that year. That left the two train robbers to decide what to do.

CHAPTER 2

"I swear, Eli, I don't know if I'm ready to start out on the grub line again," Casey confessed. "I started out in this business as a wrangler for Sid Williams down in Mason County. I was the same age Davey Springer is, fifteen years old. That was thirty-some years ago, and it seems more like a hundred. Maybe I'll change my mind, but right now, I don't wanna push another herd of half-crazy cows across another storm-swollen river or chase another stampede in the middle of a thunderstorm."

"I reckon I know how you feel," Eli said. "I was a few years older than Davey when I got into this business, but I've been doin' it about the same number of years as you have. If Whitmore hadn't shut down, I expect I woulda signed on again for next year, just because there ain't nothin' else I can do but work cows."

"Right now, I'm gonna set right here on

this creek bank and drink the rest of that pot of coffee Smiley made," Casey declared. "I didn't see a sign of anybody noticin' us when we rode away from that train, so I don't really expect to see any posse makin' up in Abilene to come lookin' for us." He looked at Smiley, a dozen yards away, still packing up his chuck wagon, and yelled, "You ain't ready to throw that coffee out, are you, Smiley?"

"Nope," Smiley yelled back. "I'm fixin' to have myself some apple pie with a cup of this coffee. I've got enough of that pie left to make about three servings, if you're interested." He waited for the reaction he was betting on.

"Hell yeah," Eli yelled. "That was damn good pie." Smiley always brought dried fruit of some kind on every cattle drive. And he had the talent to roll out some dough crust and fry it in lard for a treat once in a while.

Eli and Casey went over to the chuck-wagon, and Smiley filled their cups with the last of the coffee and gave them each a serving of pie. "I didn't say nothin' about this till after the other boys had gone 'cause I didn't have enough to feed everybody. Besides, you two deserve a special treat for goin' after that money. I just hope to hell you don't see your names up on the post office wall."

"I don't think we've got much to worry about," Casey said. "We didn't tell them two what our names were."

"A railroad detective might be asking about men lookin' to find new outfits to ride for," Smiley speculated, "since they do know that Whitmore shut down, and that's who you were ridin' for."

"I thought about that, too," Casey said. "That's another reason not to ride the grub line this winter."

They finished up the pie and coffee, and Eli and Casey cleaned their plates in the creek while Smiley washed out the coffeepot. When he was packed up and ready to go, he asked if they were going to head back to the old Whitmore Brothers Ranch.

"I ain't decided yet," Casey told him, and Eli said he hadn't, either.

"Well, I'll see you when I see you," Smiley said, and shook hands with each of them. "Take care of yourselves. You're the only outlaws I know that I can call friends." They enjoyed a good chuckle over that and wished him well. He climbed up into the wagon seat and started out after the younger hands. He figured he'd catch up to them when they got hungry.

The two friends remained there for a long

while, talking about what they could possibly do to earn a living if they didn't try to find another cattle outfit to sign on with. They found themselves caught in a canyon between too young to stop working and too old to start out fresh on some other occupation. The only thing they could think of where they might make a living was prospecting for gold or silver, which neither of them knew anything about.

"At least we've got a little money to tide us over the winter," Eli said, "thanks to the generosity of Ronald Dorsey."

"I think he would agree that as many years as we worked in cattle, we deserved a decent retirement package," Casey joked. After they paid the men their due wages, plus a hundred-dollar bonus, he and Eli came away with over eight hundred dollars each. It was a sum they were unaccustomed to having in their pockets. " 'Course, now that we don't have Smiley to count on, we're gonna have to buy some supplies, plus pots and pans, a coffeepot, everything we'll need to live. Hell, we're gonna need a packhorse to carry all our possibles, too." He looked at Eli then before suggesting, "It'd be a lot cheaper if we was to partner up. Then we wouldn't have to buy two of everything."

"I was kinda hopin' you'd think of that,"

Eli responded, and extended his hand. Casey shook it and the partnership was formed. "Too bad we can't celebrate our partnership with a good supper and a drink of likker."

"I've been thinkin' about that a little more, too," Casey said. "And I don't see why we don't just ride on into Abilene and have supper at the hotel. The only people who saw us take that money are on the train headin' east right now. There ain't nobody in Abilene that knows who we are, except the bank people, and there's a good chance nobody even knows that robbery happened yet. Hell, we can stay in the hotel tonight and buy all our supplies right here tomorrow mornin'."

"Now that I think about it, I believe you're right. Let's do it."

There was only one hotel in Abilene, and it was not hard to find. Called Drovers Cottage, it towered over everything else in town, standing three stories tall. Lavishly decorated for a hotel in a cattle town, it had a large dining room, a billiard room, and a saloon. Casey and Eli decided there could be no better place to celebrate their partnership, so they walked up to the desk and informed the clerk that they desired a room for the night. They were told there was a room available, since most of the cattle owners and buyers had checked out that day. They considered that another sign that things were happening in their favor, since they decided to partner up. The desk clerk took a close look at the two obvious cowhands and informed them that the room rent would have to be paid in advance. He was quite surprised when there was no objection to the price, and both men readily peeled off a couple of bills from a sizable roll. After they were given a key to a room on the second floor, they put their horses in the hotel's stable and took their saddlebags and rifles up to the room.

Taking advantage of every luxury afforded them, they made use of the hotel's washroom to take a bath and shave. All slicked up and wearing clean underwear, they were ready for supper, so they went into the dining room, where they were met by a young man who called himself the maître d'hôtel and asked how he could help them.

"We're wantin' to eat supper," Eli told him. "Reckon there's somebody here to tell us where we can set down?"

"Sir, that's what I do," the young man said.

"Well, do it then, sonny. We're about to

starve to death," Eli said.

"May I ask you to remove your firearms?" the young man responded.

"Is that what everybody else is doin'?" Casey asked. "Or just folks like us that ain't wearin' no evenin' coat?" The young man said it was asked of everyone, so Casey and Eli unbuckled their gun belts and held the weapons out to him. He backed away as if they might go off at any second. Then he pointed to a table where there were a couple of pistols already deposited.

After they left their weapons, the young man led them through the busy dining room, past several empty tables, to the back corner of the large room and sat them at a small table right by the kitchen door.

"Your waiter will be here shortly," the young man said, then did a rapid about-face.

"Damned if he ain't a fussy one," Eli remarked when the maître d'hôtel walked back to his post in the doorway of the dining room.

"Yeah," Casey agreed, "but he must notta been as fussy as he acts. He gave us the best table in the place, right next to the kitchen door."

They were somewhat relieved when their waiter came to the table. "Howdy, fellows, my name's Carl. What can I get you to drink while you're deciding what you want to eat?" They both said coffee, so he said, "I'll go get your coffee while you decide if you're gonna have pork chops or stewed chicken. I don't expect you want beef."

"You're right about that, Carl," Casey said. "I ain't had nothin' but beef for over two months. I'm goin' with the pork chops."

"Me too," Eli said.

"I'll go tell the cook," Carl responded, "and I'll be right back with your coffee." He popped back into the kitchen.

"Ol' Carl's all right," Eli remarked. "If he'da been as finicky as that first feller, I mighta said let's go find someplace else to eat."

In the kitchen, the cook commented to the waiter, "Got yourself a couple of cowboys right off the trail, ain'tcha, Carl?"

"Yeah, Bruce always sticks me with the trail hands that haven't ever been in a nice dining room before. It's good and it's bad. They don't usually complain about the food, but they ain't ever heard about tipping the waiter."

They enjoyed a fine supper with excellent service by Carl; so much so, they decided to make him a present of a couple of dollars to let him know they appreciated the attention. When they told him they were guests in the hotel, he told them they could pay cash for their dining-room charge, or it could be added to their hotel bill. Casey winked at Eli and said, "Let's just add it to the room bill." They had already paid for their room; they just might decide to skip the bill for the dinner, since it was too much, even if it was good.

"I reckon we're ready for that drink of likker now," Eli announced, so they left the dining room and went into the saloon. They noticed a few men in the saloon wearing guns, so they promptly put theirs back on. One man, in particular, caught their attention. Standing at the end of the bar, a tall, somber-looking man, with long, dark hair down to his shoulders and a mustache that hung down to his chin, was idling over a drink of whiskey on the bar before him. He was well armed, wearing two revolvers high on his hips.

"What'll you have, fellows?" the bartender asked.

"What's that feller down at the other end of the bar drinkin'?" Casey asked.

"Bill?" the bartender responded. "He don't drink nothin' but rye whiskey."

"I'll have the same as he's havin'," Casey said. "He looks like he's all business and he's ready for trouble, wearin' a pair of pistols. Do we need 'em in here? Looks pretty peaceful to me."

The bartender chuckled. "He's the reason it is peaceful in here. He's the town marshal. You mighta heard of him, 'Wild Bill' Hickok." He waited, but didn't get the reaction he expected from the two of them.

"The name sounds familiar, but I don't recall where I heard it," Casey said.

"Where are you fellows from?" the bartender had to ask then.

"Texas," Casey said. "I reckon we oughta get out where the people are once in a while." When the bartender moved down the bar to wait on another customer, Casey chuckled and said, "Here we are havin' a drink with Wild Bill Hickok, and he don't even know he's drinkin' with two desperate train robbers. I'm thinkin' the least we can do is buy the marshal a drink."

"What for?" Eli wanted to know.

"So we can say we done it, in case he's famous sometime," Casey said. "We can afford it, and it might bring us good luck."

"It's your money," Eli commented. They had another drink before deciding to call it quits for the night.

They paid the bartender, and since Hickok was still standing there, staring at half a shot in his glass, Casey said, "Here's something for another drink for Marshal Hickok." He dropped a couple of quarters on the bar.

"Who will I tell him paid for the drink?" the bartender asked.

"Tell him just a couple of tired old cowboys," Casey said, "who want him to keep up the good work."

With full stomachs and heads with enough alcohol buzz to tell them it was time to get to bed, they went back to their room. After a solid night's sleep, they woke up early the following morning ready to get started with the rest of their lives. Since it was too early for the dining room to open for breakfast, they decided to go to the stable and get their horses saddled and ready to go. There was no one in the stable. The fellow who showed them which stalls to put them in the night before was not there. Eli spotted him going to the back door of the kitchen. *Probably gets some breakfast before they open up for business,* he thought. He started to call out to him to tell him they wanted their horses now, but decided not to interfere with the man's breakfast. When he walked back into the stable, he found Casey pulling the cinch tight on his horse's belly, but staring at the little gathering of horses in the corral.

"You know," Casey said when Eli picked

up his saddle, "there's some decent-lookin' horses in that corral yonder, and we're needin' a good packhorse."

"I don't know if they've got any horses for sale," Eli said. "Don't you suppose all those horses belong to the guests or the hotel employees?"

"That would be my guess," Casey agreed, "but I never said anything about buyin' a horse. We keep buyin' things and we're gonna be runnin' outta money. Besides, we're already outlaws, ain't we? Won't hurt to put us down for a little bit more."

"Well, in that case, I expect we'd best decide on which one we want and not waste any more time around this hotel," Eli said. "I like the look of that sorrel with the stripe down his face. Whaddaya think?"

"Suits me. Let's look him over and make sure he's in good shape. We don't wanna cheat ourselves," Casey said. "If we're gonna steal a horse, let's steal a good one. You look him over and I'll take another look in the tack room. There just might be a packsaddle in there. Save us the cost of buyin' one." A few minutes later, he came back out, holding up a packsaddle for Eli to see. "Is that our horse?" he asked, nodding toward the sorrel.

"Looks okay to me," Eli said as he tightened his saddle cinch. "Let's see how he likes that packsaddle." The horse proved to be very gentle and showed no objection to the saddle at all. "Danged if I don't believe this ain't the first one he's seen."

"Might be his," Casey said with a chuckle.

"I expect we'd best get goin'," Eli said. "It's startin' to get light, and we don't know how fast that feller that works in the stable eats."

They climbed up in their saddles and filed out the back door of the stable, with Eli leading the packhorse. Their departure was blocked from view by the stables, so Harry Blanchard wasn't aware of the hotel's loss of a horse belonging to one of their guests. Pausing at the bottom of the kitchen steps, he swallowed hard and released a loud belch of satisfaction before returning to the horses in his care.

The two newly minted outlaws, after discussing the best place to buy the supplies they needed, as well as a place to get some breakfast, decided they were pushing their luck to remain in Abilene. They had heard there was another town close by that was rapidly establishing itself as a trade center and a cattle town to rival Abilene. At this point, that seemed their best choice. Salina was a little town about six miles east of the point where the Saline River joined the Smoky Hill River. It was only a little over half a day's ride from Abilene. Neither man had ever been to Salina, but they knew if they followed the Union Pacific Railroad tracks west, they couldn't miss it. And from the looks of the road running along beside the tracks, there was quite a bit of travel between the two towns.

They arrived in the middle of the morning, too early for dinner and too late for breakfast. Entering the town from the east, they rode past the railroad station before coming to a building that proclaimed itself to be SALINA MERCHANDISE. They decided they might as well take care of their supplies first, so they tied their horses at the rail out front and went inside. "Mornin'," greeted a rather stocky man, with thick gray hair cropped off short. "What can I help you fellows with this mornin'?"

"We'll be needing quite a bit of stuff," Casey said. "We were over in Abilene last night and the shed we put all our possibles in caught fire, burned up everything we had. So I hope you're feelin' like dealin' this mornin'. If not, we'll spend our money somewhere else." He glanced at Eli, who had a hint of a grin on his face. So he turned quickly back to the man behind the counter before he caused Eli to chuckle.

"You fellows ain't been in my store before, and I'm guessin' you ain't ever been to Salina before, either. Otherwise, you'd know there ain't no other place near here where you can get everything you most likely need. My name's Jim Lawrence, and if you ask around, folks will tell you that I always work with the farmers and ranchers around this part of the county as fair and square as I can. That's the reason this store is as big as it is, so why don't you tell me what you need? And I'll give you the best price I can afford. How's that?"

Casey looked at Eli again and laughed. "Can't ask for much more than that, can we? We've also got some tired and thirsty horses, and we're gonna take a little time comin' up with everything we need." He shook his head. "I mean, everything we had to make camp got ruined. We couldn't even stop for breakfast. Didn't have anything to cook and nothing to cook it in. So, why don't we turn our horses out by that creek back of your store and let 'em rest up while we're dealin'?"

"That sounds like a good idea," Jim said. "You boys do that and I'll sharpen up my pencil whenever you're ready."

They took the saddles off their horses and

turned them loose to go to the creek. As a precaution, they hobbled their new pack-horse in case he decided he'd go back to his previous owner. Casey was riding a gray gelding named Smoke, while Eli favored a bay that he called Biscuit. When they were working on a cattle drive, they actually used from ten to twelve different horses. The work was too hard to ride only one horse all day, so they were changed often. But every cowhand had a personal favorite that he counted as his horse. The horse knew he belonged to that cowhand, so it was un-necessary to hobble Smoke or Biscuit. They would naturally stay close to their masters. Knowing that, Casey and Eli left the horses by the creek and returned to the store, where Jim Lawrence was waiting to do busi-ness. There was a cheerful-looking woman standing beside him when they went back inside.

"Gentlemen, this is my wife, Mae. She's wantin' to know if you could use a cup of fresh, hot coffee. I heard you say you couldn't even cook any breakfast this mornin', and she put on a fresh pot while you were out taking care of your horses. It'll give you a chance to taste the coffee we sell, and I expect you'll need a good coffee grinder, too, unless you rather beat 'em to death with a hammer and a sack."

"Why, that would be mighty neighborly of you, Miz Lawrence," Casey said. "A cup of hot coffee would taste mighty good right now, wouldn't it, Eli?"

"It surely would," Eli said.

"It would be my pleasure," Mae said. "How do you take your coffee? Sugar or some milk? We've got some milk cooling in the spring box."

"No, thank you, ma'am," Casey said. "We take it black, just like it comes outta the bean." She went to the kitchen to fetch the coffee, and they started calling out the items they were in need of. They started with a coffeepot and a grinder, since that was the topic of the discussion just ended.

As things came to mind, they called off items at random, things they might need, like a hand ax, a spade, a pot, a frying pan, spoons, cups and plates, cooking utensils. All of these were placed on the counter before even getting to the food items. In the middle of all this ordering, Mae Lawrence came in with three cups of fresh coffee. The three men paused to enjoy the coffee, and it was Casey who commented first. "Ma'am, I've gotta tell you, you sure make a fine cup of coffee. I don't know if I've ever had a better cup, or even one as good as this one."

His comment caused Mae to smile as Jim winked at her. "Thank you, sir," Mae responded. "I'd like to take all the credit, but I think more of it will have to go to the coffee itself."

"We ran a little test on you," her husband explained then. "That coffee is a special roasted coffee called Arbuckles'. Fellow named John Arbuckle roasts the beans, mixed with a couple of secret ingredients that hold the flavor in. So his beans don't go stale after the bag has been open for a while. He packs it in one-pound bags, and I just got a shipment of it from back east on the train this week." He paused to let that sink in before continuing. "Now, there ain't nothin' wrong with the roasted beans I've been sellin' ever since we opened this store here. But I just wanted you to try out the Arbuckles' to see how you liked it. You may be thinkin' it's good, but not worth payin' more, but we're only talkin' about two cents a pound over my regular beans."

Eli had to laugh. "Danged if that ain't a sneaky way to sell coffee." He turned to his partner and asked, "Whaddaya think, Casey? You wanna buy some fancy coffee?"

"Why not?" Casey said. "We're startin' out this winter with everything new. Might as well try some Arbuckles'. This whole season is gonna be our Arbuckle season." He looked at the pile of merchandise stacked on the counter already and was prompted to comment. "I believe we're gonna need another packhorse."

"Maybe not," Eli said, "but Smoke and Biscuit might have to give the sorrel a hand." He grinned at Jim then and remarked, "I expect we'd best settle for what we've got there on the counter."

"Right," Jim said, and grinned back at him, although the grin was forced. For the thought just struck him that the whole transaction seemed to be overly amusing to the two strangers, as if it was a joke. And he suddenly wondered if he was being played for a fool and their form of payment might be in the Colt Single Action Army revolvers each man wore. All the conversation seemed to stop, and both men set their coffee cups on the counter while he added up the cost. When he had totaled it and checked his arithmetic, he was reluctant to announce the figure. "Looks like it comes to ninety-two dollars and sixty cents. We can round it off to ninety dollars."

"Dang," Eli commented, "we might have to find a bank to rob. Does that include the two cups of coffee?"

Jim responded with a sickly smile and

nodded.

Eli looked at Casey then and said, "That's forty-five apiece," and reached in his pocket for the money. When Casey did the same, Jim almost reacted with a sigh of relief, but turned it into a genuine smile of appreciation.

By the time they finished buying a new outfit, it was getting along toward the noon hour. And while they were going about packing their purchases efficiently on their new packhorse, they asked Jim if there was a decent place in town to eat dinner. Jim recommended the saloon. "It's called O'Malley's," he said. "He does a pretty good dinner and supper business. He's got a cook named Katie . . ." He paused then and took a quick peek to make sure Mae was not in earshot before he continued. ". . . who can outcook any woman in the county."

CHAPTER 3

"I swear, it looks like we're late for dinner," Eli commented when he stepped down from the saddle, for there was no room at the hitching rail for their horses. As a result, the two outlaws tied Smoke and Biscuit at the side of the wide front porch at O'Malley's. And the sorrel packhorse was tied to a lead rope attached to Eli's saddle. They walked into the saloon to find a long bar on one side of the large room that appeared to be doing a good business, for there were two bartenders pouring the drinks. They were glad to see that there were a few empty tables, however, so they stepped up to the bar to address the older bartender.

"Howdy, neighbor," Bob O'Malley greeted them. The owner of the saloon, he was helping his bartender, Johnny Boyd, handle the noontime crowd. "What's your pleasure?"

"We need to get some dinner before we start drinkin'," Casey said. "Maybe you can tell us how to go about that."

O'Malley smiled. "Never been in before, huh? I didn't think I recognized ya. You just go set yourself down at an empty table and I'll tell Angel you're wanting to eat, and she'll take care of ya."

"Obliged," Eli responded, and he and Casey walked over to claim an empty table in the middle of the room, while O'Malley went to the kitchen door to tell Angel.

After a few minutes, a young woman appeared in the kitchen doorway, stopped there, and looked over the crowded room until she spotted the two strangers O'Malley said wanted dinner. She hesitated then before she finally hurried over to greet them. "Bob said you want dinner," she said bluntly.

"Why, yes, ma'am, young lady," Casey said to her. "I heard you've got a right fine cook here."

"Why'd you pick this table?" she asked, again rather bluntly.

Casey exchanged a puzzled glance with Eli, then said with a question, "Because it was empty?"

"There's a couple other empty tables in the back that woulda been better," Angel stated.

"We musta confused that feller we talked

to," Casey said. "Bob, did you say his name is? You see, we ain't interested in buyin' a table. We'd just like to eat some dinner on one, if that can be arranged." While he was trying to communicate with the young woman, he noticed that she seemed to be switching her eyes back and forth between him and something behind him. He turned around to see what had caught her attention. At the table closest to theirs sat one man, facedown on the table, who was stirring slightly and muttering to himself. Casey understood then. Back to the girl, he asked, "Him?"

She nodded vigorously and whispered, "Rafe Larson, he's passed out drunk, and we're hoping nothing wakes him up till he's slept it off. He's mean as pure sin when he gets woke up too soon. That's why nobody was sitting at this table."

Both Casey and Eli turned around to take another look at Rafe. " 'Preciate your concern," Casey told her, "but we'll be all right here. We won't bother Rafe none. So, how 'bout bringin' us the special, whatever it is, with some coffee and biscuits. We ain't had nothin' but one cup of coffee since yesterday. All right?"

"You don't know Rafe Larson," Angel insisted. When her plea was met with two patient smiles, she said, "It's your funeral." She turned and went back to the kitchen.

"I sure hope to hell she wasn't referring to the cookin'," Eli remarked. "I believe my belly's fixin' to cave in." He turned to give the sleeping drunk one more look. "It looks to me like he's out for the rest of the day."

Angel did return, and very quickly at that, with two cups of coffee, which she set down on the table very carefully, obviously in an effort to make no noise. It was an amusing display of caution to the two hungry partners.

"We'll try not to slurp it too loud," Casey told her. Then he looked at Eli and shook his head, for the saloon was as noisy as any saloon in the middle of the afternoon. It seemed apparent to him that the noise didn't bother the drunken man in the least.

Angel didn't seem to appreciate Casey's humor, and she made another quick trip to the kitchen to return with two plates of beef stew. She set those down as carefully as she had the coffee cups.

"I was kinda hopin' the special would be something besides beef," Eli remarked. "But Jim Lawrence weren't lyin' when he said Katie was a good cook." Casey was in agreement, so they dived into their dinner with the gusto of starving coyotes. "I don't know what they charge for dinner," Eli declared, "but it's worth every penny of it." He raised his cup in the air, and before he thought to be quiet, he called out, "Angel, we could use some more coffee over here." As soon as it left his mouth, he muttered, "Uh-oh."

"What tha hell?" The words came rumbling out of the awakened drunk like cannonballs dropping on the table. He raised his head and shoulders up off the table and glared stupidly at the two men sitting next to him. "Who the hell are you?" Rafe demanded.

"We're your best friends," Casey said to him. "Go on back to sleep and let us eat our dinner."

"Why, you smart-ass, egg-suckin' dog," Rafe Larson immediately responded. "Here's somethin' you can eat for dinner!" He got to his feet and drew his six-shooter. His drunken rage concentrated on Casey, he failed to take notice of Eli getting up from his chair at the same time. Before Rafe could raise his gun to aim at Casey, Eli grabbed a handful of his hair and slammed his head back down on the table, hard enough to knock him senseless for a few moments. Before Rafe had time to regain any sense of what had happened, Eli pulled the gun from his hand and used it to give him a sharp rap on the side of his head, which put him completely out.

It had all happened so quickly that only a few customers close by could testify to the instant solution to the problem. Eli raised his cup again and called out, "Angel, how 'bout a little more coffee?" They could see her standing near the kitchen door, looking at them, but she was making no signs of coming to them. "She musta seen him startin' to get up," Eli decided.

Finally, when there seemed to be no disturbance at their table, Angel picked up the coffeepot and came to fill their cups. "I thought I saw Rafe raising up from the table," she whispered. "But then he got up," she said, nodding toward Eli, "and I couldn't see Rafe, for him standing there."

"Rafe?" Casey said. "He went back to sleep. Musta had a bad dream or somethin', but he went right back to sleep."

She shook her head as if exasperated with them. "It's a good thing he did. You fellows don't know how lucky you are that he went back to sleep. He shot a man in here, back in the spring."

"I take it you folks don't have a sheriff," Casey said.

"We did for a little while," Angel said. "That was the man Rafe shot."

51

"Oh," Casey responded. "That is a problem, ain't it? Sounds to me like you better get your menfolk to start talkin' about a vigilance committee and take care of your problem with Rafe. If you don't, you ain't gonna have a town. And I believe it'd be good for ol' Rafe to get his neck stretched a little."

"You oughta be talkin' to Bob about that," Angel said, her voice a little above a whisper, since there had been no sign of life from Rafe now. "Him and Jim Lawrence are the only two men in town who even talked about it. How about you two? Are you fixin' to settle around here?"

"No, ma'am," Casey said. "We're just passin' through this way. We're on our way to Wichita. We're just stayin' long enough to find out what kinda pie your cook has."

"She made peach today. Are you gonna try a piece?"

"It wouldn't be polite if we didn't," Eli said. When Angel went to slice a couple of pieces for them, he asked Casey, "When did you decide we was goin' to Wichita?"

"I didn't," Casey said. "It was just the first name that popped into my head when she asked me if we were gonna stay in town."

Eli shrugged and said, "Well, why don't we go there? It mighta popped into your

52

head for a reason." Casey shrugged in return, since he couldn't think of any reason not to go to Wichita. "Wichita's two and a half days from here, so I reckon we oughta get started. You reckon we oughta take the north road outta town?" he joked as Angel placed a slice of pie on the table for each of them.

"I reckon," Casey said. So they ate the pie, then got up from the table and went to the bar. "You got any corn whiskey?" he asked Johnny Boyd, the bartender. Boyd said he did, so Casey said, "Pour him a shot of rye whiskey and pour me one of corn." When Boyd poured them, Casey said, "And we owe you for two dinners, plus two slices of pie." Johnny told them the cost was a dollar each. They paid up and left the saloon, climbed on their horses and started out across the prairie in a southeastern direction. Their intention was to intercept the road they had driven the cattle up to Abilene.

As they rode along, Casey thought of something he had wondered about, so he asked Eli. "Abilene is a hundred miles north of Wichita, both of 'em on the Chisholm Trail. Why did we always drive those cows a hundred miles farther, when we coulda put 'em on the train right there in Wichita?"

Eli considered the question for a few moments before answering, "I don't know. Maybe it's because Whitmore always did his business in Abilene before Wichita got the railroad." He thought some more. "Maybe it's because he had a contract or somethin' with the Union Pacific, and the railroad in Wichita is the Atchison, Topeka, and Santa Fe. I don't know," he repeated. "At forty dollars a month, I wasn't paid to think, just drive the cows wherever the boss said."

"The first time I came up the Chisholm Trail, Wichita wasn't nothin' but a tradin' post on the Arkansas River. There weren't no town," Casey said.

"I remember," Eli said. "Now they call it 'Cowtown' for all the cattle that's shipped outta there. It's bigger than Abilene and it's got more places for a cowhand to spend the money he just earned right across the river in Delano. I'd like to see that side of the river."

They set a leisurely pace as they headed back down the way they had just come a couple of days before. Their intention was to ride about twenty miles before they camped for the night. At a walking pace, they were not worried about overworking Biscuit or Smoke, but they were concerned about the sorrel packhorse. So after a couple of hours, they let the horses rest and take on grass and water. They were satisfied that the sorrel was doing fine after checking him out at their first rest stop.

"Looks like we stole a good one," Eli remarked when they were getting ready to start out again. "So far, we're doin' all right for a couple of tenderfoot horse thieves and train robbers."

At the end of the day, when they figured they had ridden close to twenty miles, they started looking for the next stream or creek to camp by for the night. They settled for the first creek they came to with enough trees along it to offer some firewood. After unloading the horses and releasing them to water and graze, they gathered wood for a fire. Then they were ready to prepare supper, using all their brand-new utensils, pan, and coffeepot, waiting to find out what vital tool they might have forgotten to buy. They started out their partnership with the agreement that they would take turns preparing their meals when they were camping out. Since both of them had ridden for years with chuckwagon cooks like Smiley George, they had a fair knowledge of what was needed to make pan bread and biscuits, the simple frying of bacon and beans, and wild game, when they were fortunate enough to find some. They could even make an edible fried pie, when dried fruit of some kind was available. That was the case on their trip from Salina to Wichita, thanks to the fact that Jim Lawrence had a barrel of dried apples. On the second day of their journey, however, Eli was so critical of Casey's biscuits that he was given the permanent job of making them. He took it on with the pride of a professional baker, even though he accused Casey of purposely faking his ineptness at the chore.

As they had planned, they rode into Wichita two days later at about five o'clock in the afternoon. After riding the length of the main street of the town to get a look at what it offered, they turned around and rode back to the Cattleman's Hotel. They liked the fact that it was not too far from Johnson's Stable, so they would be handy to their horses in the event they might need them in a hurry. "I expect we'd best check in the hotel first," Casey suggested, "before we take the horses to the stable." Eli agreed.

As they walked their horses back toward the hotel, they took a look at the First Bank of Wichita, separated from the Friendly Saloon by a narrow alley on one side, and a vacant lot on the other. "That looks like an easy bank to knock over," Eli remarked casually. "And the way we're spendin' money, we're gonna need some more before very much longer."

"I know what you mean," Casey said. "It might not be too hard to rob at that. Leave your horses in that little alley, walk in, take the cash, walk out, and be gone out the back of the alley before anybody knew the bank was bein' robbed."

"Just for the hell of it," Eli suggested, "why don't we watch what goes on at that bank for a couple of days and figure out how we would rob it?"

"That's what any self-respectin' outlaw would do, ain't it?" Casey responded.

"Good afternoon, gentlemen," Dan Hicks, the hotel manager, greeted them at the front desk. "What can I do for you?"

"Afternoon," Casey returned the greeting. "My partner and I are hopin' you can fix us up with a couple of rooms."

"I sure can," Dan said. "Will you be staying with us long?"

"Well, now, that depends," Casey said. "We're in town to get a good look at how Wichita is developin'. Whether or not it has the potential we're lookin' for to invest in the town's future might take a day, might take a week."

"Oh, I see," Dan responded, obviously surprised. "I feel confident you'll find our town a good place to invest your interest." He hesitated, then confessed, "I hope you won't be offended, but judging by your dress, I thought you were a couple of cattle drivers."

Eli and Casey looked at each other and chuckled as if the manager had told a joke. "No, sir," Casey said, "we're not offended a-tall. Matter of fact, we're gratified that you thought so. I'm sure that I don't have to tell you that there is no shortage of hoodlums and robbers ridin' these cattle trails. So it doesn't pay to look like you might be carryin' a lot of cash money when you're riding up through Indian Territory. We figure there ain't nobody that looks broker than a cowboy after the cattle drives. And since the MKT didn't lay their tracks along the Chisholm Trail, we have to travel on horseback." He looked at Eli again and they both nodded their heads in agreement. Dan Hicks nodded his understanding as well. "You weren't completely off in your assessment of us, however," Casey continued. "In our younger years, both Eli and I spent many long hours looking at the hind end of a cow. So it's never really gone from our memory. Right, Eli?"

"Right," Eli said, "especially when I'm wearin' all the dust and grime from so many days in the saddle. I hope your hotel has a first-rate washroom."

"Oh, yes, sir," Hicks said. "I'm sure you'll find it first-rate." He opened his guest register then, preparing to rent them rooms. "So you've come up from Texas, I suppose, Mr. . . ." He paused.

"Doolin," Eli responded. "Eli Doolin. And he's Casey Tubbs. We're from Fort Worth."

"Mr. Doolin and Mr. Tubbs," Hicks repeated as he wrote the names down. "I might suggest that we have the Governor's Suite, if you're looking for some real relaxation after spending a long time in the saddle. It's a suite of two bedrooms and has several little extras that make your stay a little more enjoyable."

"That sounds inviting," Casey said, "but just two clean rooms with a window will be all we're gonna need. After spending the last couple of months on a horse, that'll be fancy enough. Might as well put us down for a week. We oughta have a pretty good feel for the town by then. I reckon your guests use the stable down the street to take care of their horses."

"That's right, Paul Johnson will take good care of your horses for you, and tell him you're staying in the hotel. He'll give you a cheaper rate. The dining room should be open for supper in about ten minutes. There are other places to eat in town, but I think you'll find they don't stand up to our dining room." He hesitated a moment before he asked for payment, thinking not to insult them, but he didn't want to be suckered by a couple of rent dodgers, either. So he said, "The policy of the hotel is usually to ask for payment of the room rate in advance, but if that is not all right with you, we could make it for just the first night."

"No, no problem," Casey quickly said. "As businessmen, we understand your position. We'll just go ahead and pay you for the week."

"That is most gracious of you," Hicks said. "And to thank you, the hotel will pay for your supper tonight. Just tell your server to charge it to your room number and I'll take care of the bill."

"Why, thank you very much," Eli said. "That's mighty neighborly of you."

They paid for their rooms and went outside to get their saddlebags and rifles. After they put them in their rooms, they took the horses to the stables and left them in the care of Paul Johnson, along with the packs the sorrel was carrying. That done, they decided it a good idea to get cleaned up before they went to the dining room for supper, that being the only thing they could do to try to pull off the masquerade they were attempting. Each of them carried a clean shirt and a change of underwear and socks. They also carried a rain slicker and a heavy winter coat, neither of which would serve to improve their image. Shaves and hot baths contributed a great deal to their appearance, however, and for fifty cents, Ross, the elderly washroom attendant, gave their coats and pants a good brushing. The net result was a considerable improvement in their appearances.

Admiring himself in the full-length mirror inside the washroom door, Casey declared, "Maybe we won't frighten any of the gentlefolk in the dinin' room. Whaddaya think, Ross?"

"Well, I don't think Ted will throw you out and the gals will appreciate that you washed your hands," the old man said.

CHAPTER 4

"Good evenin', gentlemen," Ted Potter greeted them when they entered the dining room. "Mind if I ask you to leave your hardware with me while you're eating? I'll put 'em right on this shelf behind me, and you can pick 'em up on your way out."

They both pulled their weapons out and handed them to Potter. "I sure hope the cookin' ain't so bad that you're worried about folks wantin' to shoot the cook," Casey remarked as he surrendered his Colt .44.

Potter chuckled. "No, it's to guard against our customers getting into a gunfight over who gets the last one of Mamie's biscuits. Just walk on in and sit anywhere you like. One of the ladies will take care of you."

Eli led the way toward a table by one of the windows on the side wall. "That's the second time we've been called 'gentlemen' since we walked into this hotel," he joked as he pulled his chair back. "Reckon we oughta be worryin' about what they're up to?"

As soon as they were settled, they were joined by an attractive young woman ready to take their order. "Evenin', gentlemen, what can I get you to drink?"

"Probably anything you wanted us to," Casey said, and gave her a big smile. "But if you're gonna give us a choice, I expect we'd both like coffee."

She smiled in response to his humor and looked toward Eli to see if he agreed with his friend. "You have your choice of baked ham or beef stew tonight. I'll get your coffee while you're deciding."

"There it is again," Eli said when she walked away.

"There what is again?" Casey asked.

" 'Gentlemen,' " Eli said. "Even she called us 'gentlemen.' You can't fool the folks that run this hotel. Even though we're wearin' these old trail clothes, they can see us for who we really are."

"Hell, if they could do that, they'd most likely throw us outta here," Casey remarked just as she returned with two cups of coffee.

"Here we are, gentlemen," she said as she placed their coffee on the table. "My name's Polly and I'll be your server. What did you fellows decide? Are you gonna have the ham or beef stew?" They both chose the baked ham, and she was off to the kitchen again. When she returned, she was carrying two plates of ham, with all the fixings. She was followed by another woman, who looked a few years older than Polly, and she was carrying two plates containing biscuits, one of which she placed on their table. "Thanks, Marge," Polly said, and Marge took the other plate to another table.

As Dan Hicks had promised, the food was good, and the servings were generous. They took their time to enjoy it and the additional coffee afterward. They were long enough at the table that they had occasion to get to know the two servers a little better. Polly Batson was a lovely young girl, still in her teens, while Marge Joyner, in the twilight of her thirties, was widowed by a man who caught her husband dealing from the bottom of the deck. If they could believe what Marge said, it was no great loss in her life.

They left the dining room for a walk around the town, since there was daylight enough to get a look at the shops and businesses they passed. They were in no particular hurry as they strolled leisurely along the street, stopping occasionally to pass the time of day with a shop owner. It was their intention to let the town folk see them as two men who had no reason to be secretive.

They paused a little longer at the corner of the alley that ran between the bank and the Friendly Saloon. The bank was closed now. They looked at the many horses tied at the rail and remembered that the saloon in Salina, O'Malley's, was that crowded at the hitching rail at noontime. And that was because O'Malley had a good cook.

"Tomorrow we'll see what kind of cook Friendly has," Casey said. The town offered many saloons to choose from, they had counted over a dozen so far, but the Friendly was located next door to the bank. It might be critical in their plan to rob the bank. "Right now, I could use a shot of corn whiskey to settle that supper."

Eli said he was ready for a drink as well, so they went inside.

As indicated by the number of horses outside, the saloon was crowded, all the tables taken, so Eli and Casey moved into a gap at the bar. "Howdy, boys," Jug Trask, the bartender, said. "Whaddalya have?"

Casey pointed to Eli and said, "Shot of rye." Then he indicated himself and said, "Shot of corn."

Jug poured Casey's drink out of a bottle on the bar, then pulled a bottle of rye from a shelf behind him. The he said, "Never seen you two in here before."

"That's a fact," Casey said, "first time. Don't look like you were hurtin' for our business, though. And it's still early in the evenin'."

"You sell any food?" Eli asked, and tapped his empty shot glass on the bar for another shot.

Jug poured his rye. "Yep, we've got a fine cook, but we don't do much supper business. Most of ours is breakfast and dinner. You boys lookin' for a good place for supper?"

"No, not tonight," Eli said. "We ate at the hotel. We was just wonderin' about other places to eat here in Wichita."

"It's hard to beat the hotel for supper," Jug said, "but we do pretty good at noontime. We do a good dinner business 'cause folks in Wichita ain't scared to eat in a saloon."

"Is that a fact?" Casey responded. "Why is that?"

"On account of that feller settin' at that table in the corner," Jug said with a nod of his head in that direction. Casey asked who he was, and Jug said, "That's Michael Meagher. He's the town marshal and he keeps a tight rein on the cowboys and outlaws that pass through Wichita. He don't stand for no wild trouble for the honest folks of the town. And he's got all the help he needs in his deputies, one of 'em especially, fellow named Wyatt Earp. 'Course, if it's the wild life you're lookin' for, all you gotta do is cross the river bridge over to Delano. That's where the wild life is, and they ain't got no law in Delano. They got the dancehalls and the bordellos, where you can find about anything you're cravin', and somethin' to take home to your wife, if you're unlucky."

"I expect we'll just restrict our interests to this side of the river," Casey said. His thoughts were still on the man Jug identified as Michael Meagher, and he had the distinct feeling that the marshal was more than interested in him and Eli. His feeling was confirmed moments later when the marshal raised his hand and signaled Jug to come to his table. Jug went immediately to answer the marshal's summons. "I got a feelin' that marshal has been eyeballin' you and me ever since we walked in here," he said to Eli.

"What for?" Eli asked. "We ain't done nothin' to attract the law's attention."

"I think we're fixin' to find out," Casey said, noticing that Jug had his eyes on them as he hurried back behind the bar.

"Marshal Meagher said to invite you

fellers back to his table," Jug announced. "He wants to buy you a drink."

"What the hell for?" Eli reacted honestly. "Does he do that for all the strangers in town?"

"No, he don't," Jug said. "I don't think he's ever done that in here." He chuckled then and joked, "You fellers ain't wanted anywhere, are you?"

"Not so you'd notice," Casey said.

"Well, he's got a bottle on the table, so just take your glasses with you," Jug said. Then remembering Casey's choice, he added, "He's drinkin' rye whiskey."

"I reckon that suits my taste on this occasion," Casey declared. He told himself that there was very little possibility this town's marshal had been alerted about the train robbery, or the skipping out on their hotel bill, or the stolen packhorse. He looked at Eli, who returned the glance with an uncertain one of his own. "Well, that's mighty neighborly of the sheriff, ain't it? Come on, Eli, grab your glass." They made their way through the crowded barroom to the table in the corner.

Meagher got to his feet to welcome them. "I'm guessin' you two strangers are Mr. Tubbs and Mr. Doolin. 'Preciate you lettin' me buy you a drink. I'm Michael Meagher, the town marshal."

"I'm Tubbs and he's Doolin," Casey responded. "This is mighty friendly of you to offer. Is this why they call this the Friendly Saloon?"

"Maybe so," Meagher said with a chuckle. He poured them a drink of whiskey. "I talked to Dan Hicks at the hotel a little while ago and he told me you two fellows were in town for about a week, lookin' us over for some business possibilities. I'm always interested in new businesses that want to start up in Wichita. Being responsible for law enforcement, I'm naturally concerned about what kinda business they're plannin' on. But I also wanna impress potential newcomers with the kind of protection the marshal's office provides for them. Right now, I've got a staff of four full-time deputies that watch the businesses in Wichita. We have an ordinance against gamblin' and prostitution, and my office enforces those ordinances."

"Well, that sure is impressive," Casey said. "And to tell you the truth, it's one of the main reasons Eli and I came to look Wichita over."

"What line of business are you in, Mr. Tubbs?"

Casey wasn't ready for the question put

to him in such a blunt fashion and realized he should have been better prepared to answer it. Eli's wide blank stare was of no help, either, so he stalled for time, hoping his brain would come up with something that made sense. "Mr. Doolin and I are not really in a business, like you think of bein' in an office or a store. So we're not lookin' to find a place to build anything. We're more interested in the feelin' of the town, the businesses already here, and the folks around here." He glanced at Eli, but had to look away again when he saw the wide-eyed look of disaster on his face. "We are land buyers and developers for folks who are looking for places to build," he continued. "Every job is different. In this case, we represent a religion, a group of about two hundred families that have decided to leave their farms back east and start again out here, where there's room to grow the crops they grow." Glancing at Eli again, he saw that his friend's blank stare was now replaced by one of stark disbelief, so he looked away quickly. "So you can see why we're interested in the land for miles around Wichita. And the town would more than likely grow with the added trading potential two hundred families would bring."

Meagher was openly impressed. "That

would be somethin', all right. What religion are these folks? They ain't Mormons, are they?"

"No, no," Casey quickly said, "not Mormons," thinking the marshal was opposed to them for some reason. "They're Quakers."

"So you and Mr. Doolin are Quakers," Meagher concluded.

"No," Casey said. "We ain't Quakers. If we were, we wouldn't be in here drinkin' likker. Like I said, we're developers. We're just workin' for the Quakers."

"That would be somethin'," Meagher commented. "Have you looked at some of the farms already around Wichita? They're doin' pretty well."

"We've seen enough to know it's worthwhile to take a closer look," Casey said, "and that's why we've decided to stay here awhile. We wanna check out the river in both directions, up to what would amount to a half day's drive in a wagon." He paused, then said, "There's somethin' I need to ask you. We're out scoutin' potential land for months at a time, and we carry a substantial sum of cash money, so we can pay down a first option on any land we're afraid we might lose, if we don't tie it up. We ain't comfortable carryin' that much money while we're ridin' through some wild parts of this territory. Maybe you can tell us somethin' about this bank next door. We'd really like to deposit some of our money in the bank while we're here."

"You don't have to worry about the First Bank of Wichita," the marshal assured him. "There ain't ever been an attempt to rob that bank, and with my police force, anybody would be afraid to try. You go in and talk to John Sinclair. He's the president. He'll take care of you." He paused to chuckle then. "Dan Hicks told me you were dressed like a couple of cowhands, ridin' the grub line, so nobody would think you were carryin' any money." The three of them laughed at that. "That ain't a bad idea," he said, "but puttin' it in the bank's a better one. Go see Sinclair in the mornin'. He'll be glad to take care of your money."

"We'll do that, Marshal," Eli finally spoke up. "And thanks for the drink. I reckon we'll walk on back to the hotel now."

"We still owe the bartender for a couple of drinks," Casey reminded him. "We'd best not try to skip out on that. He wouldn't have to go far to get the marshal after us." All three laughed again.

"Jug most likely wouldn't bother me with it," Meagher joked. "He'd just shoot you with that shotgun he keeps under the bar. Then I'd have to arrest him for another ordinance we've got — against shootin' off firearms in the town." He got up from the table then, picked up his half-empty bottle of whiskey, and followed them to the bar, where he handed the bottle to Jug to put away for him. Then he followed them outside and wished them a good evening when they turned toward the hotel, and he went in the opposite direction, toward the jail.

"For a minute there, I thought he was gonna walk us back to the hotel," Eli remarked when they were out of earshot. "Partner, I damn near fainted when you said we was workin' for a bunch of Quakers. How'd you come up with that story?"

"I don't know, it was just the first thing I could think of. I was stallin' for a few minutes at the start, kinda hopin' you'd jump in there and save me from drownin' in a pool of lies. But you got lockjaw."

"Are you japin' me?" Eli said. "You're the one with the big ideas. By the time you got through, I believed we was really workin' for some Quakers, whoever they are." He shook his head when he thought of something else. "You told that marshal we was carryin' a lot of money, so we could pay a 'first option.' What the hell's a 'first option'?"

"Hell, I don't know," Casey confessed. "It just came to me and I thought it sounded kind of official. I don't reckon the marshal knows what it is, either, 'cause he didn't question it."

"Boy, if you ain't somethin'," Eli declared. "We gonna go to the bank in the mornin' to see what was his name?"

"John Sinclair," Casey said.

"Right," Eli said. "While we're there, maybe we can ask him for a loan."

"If things keep goin' the way they have so far, we might have to make him one," Casey said. "I got two of them cigars left that I bought in Salina. Whaddaya say we set in them rockin' chairs on the front porch and smoke 'em before we turn in."

"Sounds like a good idea to me," Eli said. "It'll save me from smokin' up mine." So, when they got back to the hotel, they sat down in two of the four rocking chairs on the porch and lit up. "You know," he commented after a while, "I don't know why we didn't turn outlaw a long time ago."

They were in no hurry to get up early the next morning, since the bank wouldn't open until nine o'clock. Casey was the first up, but not by much. When he knocked on Eli's door, he found his partner in the process of getting his clothes on. "You know, I've been thinkin' about what we're fixin' to do this mornin', puttin' our money in the bank," Eli said. "What are we gonna do if we decide we ain't gonna rob that bank?"

Casey gave him a look to see if he was joking, and when he saw that he was serious, he said, "We'll withdraw it."

"Oh," Eli responded. "I didn't think it through. Let's go get some breakfast." He pulled his boots on, stomped each boot on the floor to settle his feet in them, then headed for the door.

"Good morning," Dan Hicks called out to them when they came down the steps and headed for the door that led to the dining room. "Did you sleep all right?"

"We sure did," Eli said. "At least I can speak for myself. Slept like a baby."

"He's right," Casey remarked. "I reckon we've had to spend so many nights sleeping on the ground lately that it's hard to remember how soft a good bed feels till you sleep on one again."

"You planning to ride out to look over the country this morning?" Hicks asked.

Casey figured he must have talked to Marshal Meagher before they got up this morning. "No," he said. "We've got some banking business to take care of this mornin', and we're still tryin' to get the feel of the town. We're in no hurry to leave here. Everybody we've met so far seems like the kind of people that make good neighbors."

That seemed to please Hicks. "Enjoy your breakfast," he said.

Casey followed Eli into the dining room, where Ted Potter greeted them cheerfully, since they had chosen to leave their weapons in their rooms. They received another cheery greeting from Marge Joyner when she informed them that she was taking care of them this morning. "What's it gonna be, boys?" Marge asked when she put some coffee down for them. "Pancakes with eggs and bacon? That's what I had."

"That sounds okay to me," Eli said, "as long as there's enough of it."

"How 'bout you, sweetie?"

"I'll take the same," Casey said. When she disappeared through the door to the kitchen, he commented, "No 'gentlemen' today. What happened to our status overnight?"

"At least she called you 'sweetie,' " Eli complained.

" 'Sweetie' and 'honey,' " Casey said, "that's what younger women call old men."

"Hell, we ain't that much older than she

is, even if you was to add our ages together," Eli exaggerated.

"I just came in here to get some breakfast," Casey said. "So, as long as she don't put no gunpowder in the eggs, I ain't complainin'." Polly Batson walked past their table then, smiled at them, and wished them a good morning. "There you go," Casey said to Eli, "you happy now? You must remind her of her granddaddy."

Marge came halfway back to the table then and said, "I forgot to ask you how you wanted your eggs. I guess I'm gettin' feeble-minded."

Casey grinned and said, "Scrambled for both of us." When she turned around and returned to the kitchen, he said to Eli, "I reckon you were right."

"She still looks damn good for her age, though," Eli allowed.

Like supper the night before, the food was good and plentiful, and when they were ready to leave, Marge thanked them for coming in and asked if she would see them for dinner. "Reckon not," Casey said. "We've got some business to attend to at dinnertime in the saloon. But we'll be back for supper tonight."

"Ah, that's too bad," Marge said. "Today's the day I always wait the tables nekkid at dinnertime."

"Reckon just this once, couldn't you do it at suppertime, instead?" Eli asked.

" 'Fraid not," she said. "It starts gettin' a little too chilly by suppertime."

Eli could think of nothing more to come back with, so he just grinned and shook his head as he followed Casey out the door.

Chapter 5

After they left the dining room, they still had plenty of time before the bank opened, so they returned to their rooms long enough to get their money out of their saddlebags, leaving a generous amount to cover their expenses while in town. The number they decided to deposit in the bank was five hundred each for an even one thousand. Leaving the hotel then, still with time to spare, they decided to stop by the stable to see how their horses were getting along.

"Morning," Paul Johnson greeted them when they found him inside the stable, in the process of turning the horses out into the corral. "You gonna need your horses this mornin'?"

"No," Casey said. "We're just killin' some time, waitin' for the bank to open. Thought we'd drop by to see if our horses were still here."

Paul laughed. "Yeah, they're still here. I

tried to sell 'em a couple of times, but I couldn't get my price."

They spent a little time with their horses, long enough for Eli to decide it was time for Biscuit to need new shoes. Casey decided Smoke was close enough to needing them, too. They looked at their new pack-horse and discovered that the sorrel had evidently been shoed recently. So they asked Paul about the blacksmith next door to the stables.

"Sam Godsey," Paul said. "He'll do a good job for you, reasonable price, and I ain't never heard anybody complain about him."

So they put the bridles on the two horses and led them over to the blacksmith shop, where they found Sam Godsey repairing a wagon wheel. He told them he would be happy to shoe their horses right away. They explained that they had some business to attend to that morning and asked if he could take the horses back to Paul Johnson when he was finished. He said he'd be glad to, and when they started to pay him, he said, "Wait to pay me till after you see what kinda job I do."

"Fine by me," Eli said. "Can't be more fair than that." They left the horses, confident they would be well taken care of, and headed for the bank.

When they entered the bank, they took a quick look around before they closed the door behind them. There were no other customers waiting, so they were greeted right away by the one teller they saw. There was a name plaque at his window that informed them that he was: PHILLIP REED. As was usually the case, Eli stepped aside to let Casey do the talking.

"How can I help you gentlemen?" Reed asked.

"We're just in town for a week or so," Casey started out. "And we'd like to leave a small amount of cash with you while we're here. We'll be spending a lot of time ridin' around the unsettled prairie along the Arkansas River, and it's just not a good idea to be carrying all our cash with us. Can we open a temporary account for a short period of time?"

"That is an unusual request," Reed said. "I'd best let you talk to Mr. Sinclair. He's the president of the bank. Wait right here and I'll get him." He left the cage and walked across the lobby to an open door. He stepped inside the door, and a few minutes later, he came back out, followed by John Sinclair.

Sinclair was all smiles as he approached them. "Good morning, gentlemen, I'm John Sinclair. Phillip tells me you want to open an account for a short time."

"Yes, sir," Casey said. "It's just cash that we don't want to carry around on our persons. I suppose we could have opened a regular checkin' account and closed it out when we were ready to move on in about a week. But that didn't seem the right thing to do to the bank, open it up, then turn around and close it."

Sinclair smiled patiently. "That's not a big problem, we can hold some cash for you for a short while. How much are you thinking about?" He looked at the cloth sack that Eli was carrying.

"We're just talkin' about a thousand dollars," Casey said.

His answer caused Sinclair to raise his eyebrows in surprise. "One thousand dollars?" he asked, to be sure he had heard correctly. Casey nodded. "You're wise not to carry that sum around on your person. We can certainly make a short-term deposit for you and keep it in our safe until you're ready to withdraw it." Sinclair looked at Reed and said, "I'll take care of it, Phillip. We won't issue any checks or anything. I'll put it in the safe and they can just come in and get it when they're ready to leave town." He turned back to Eli and Casey. "All right, then, Mr. . . ." He paused and waited.

"Tubbs," Casey said. "Casey Tubbs, and this is Eli Doolin. Or you can just use our business name, Doolin and Tubbs."

"Doolin and Tubbs it is, then," Sinclair said. "We'll go into my office and I'll write you up a deposit that you can sign, and I'll sign, and you won't have to worry about your money. I'll put it in the safe with the bank's money."

"If you don't mind me askin'," Casey inquired, "have you got a pretty good safe? It ain't one that somebody could haul outta here and throw on a wagon, is it?"

The question seemed to amuse Sinclair. "I'll let you see for yourself," he said. "Have you got your money with you?" Eli handed the sack holding the money to him. "Come in my office and I'll draw up the agreement, then we'll go put it in the safe."

They sat down in his office for the few minutes it took for him to write out the bank's agreement to hold their money. Then he signed it and had them both sign it. "When you decide you want your money, just bring this paper with you and ask the teller or myself for your money." It took him longer to count the money than it took to write the contract. "All right, gentlemen," he said when he had counted it twice, "follow me and we'll put it in the safe."

He led them into a room next to his office and stopped to let them see the large combination safe built into the wall. "It would be a real job to haul that out and throw it in a wagon, wouldn't it?" He smiled when he saw their reaction, then went over to the safe, cranked the handle, and opened the door. From where they stood, they could see stacks of paper money in the belly of the big safe. "I'm going to put your money right here on this little shelf, all by itself."

"Don't you have to have the combination to open it?" Eli asked, surprised that it had not been locked.

"Yes, indeed," Sinclair said, "and I'm the only one who knows it." He closed the safe and gave the combination a couple of spins. "It's locked now. I open it in the morning when I come in. But it stays open only long enough for the tellers to get their cash trays out." He glanced up at the clock on the wall. "It's closed by now every morning. And it's not opened again, unless I open it." Casey and Eli both glanced at the clock the same time Sinclair did. "There's one other safety factor for you when you have money in this bank and that's Michael Meagher and his police force. It would take a mighty foolish gang of outlaws to strike this bank." He let them think about that for a moment, then asked, "What else can I do for you fellows?"

"I reckon that'll do it," Casey said. "We 'preciate you goin' to the trouble to help us out. How much do we owe you? We didn't expect you to do it for nothin'."

"Well, now that I've got your money locked up, why don't we say about a hundred dollars a day?" he joked. "We don't have any standard charge for performing a service like that, but I appreciate the fact that you feel you should pay something. Let's set the fee at one dollar a week. All right?"

"That's mighty kind of you, Mr. Sinclair," Casey said. "We're obliged." They shook hands and Sinclair walked them to the door.

Outside the bank, the two outlaws stopped to consider what they had learned while inside. "It don't matter if the saloon has a big dinnertime crowd or not now, since that safe's only open from nine o'clock till about nine-thirty," Eli complained. "You reckon we oughta come back tomorrow and withdraw our money?"

"Maybe," Casey agreed. They were very

much agreed on a plan to rob the bank, but they were not in favor of a typical bank job, with a lot of gunplay, and a noisy exit from town, with bullets flying all around. And that was a certainty in a town like Wichita, where the stores were set close together and everybody in town was armed. First hint of the bank being robbed would bring the whole town out to stop you, because it was their money you were stealing. And if you weren't stopped, their money was gone.

"It was mighty temptin' back there when he opened that safe to just draw your six-shooter and take all that money right then, weren't it?" Eli asked. "Too bad our horses were bein' shod. We'da had to walk pretty fast to beat a posse outta town." He shook his head sadly when it looked as though he and Casey weren't going to try what they considered a brilliant plan to rob the First Bank of Wichita. "We might as well eat dinner at the hotel. I wanna call Marge's bluff on her claim she's gonna wait tables naked, anyway."

"I hate to spoil your dinner for you," Casey joked, "but she ain't really gonna do that."

"Well, lookee here," Marge Joyner sang out when she saw Casey and Eli walk in the dining room a little after noontime. "I thought you said you were gonna eat at the Friendly Saloon today."

"We came back here to call your bluff," Eli said. "When's the show gonna start?"

She didn't get it at first; then, when she remembered, she threw her head back and laughed. "I forgot to clear it with Ted, and he said I'd have to schedule it some other day. We've got some folks from the church havin' dinner here today."

"Yeah, that's what I thought," Eli said. "But as long as we're here, we might as well get somethin' to eat."

"Set down and I'll get you some coffee," she said.

"If you're really wantin' to see some gals runnin' around in their knickers," Casey suggested, "we can go across the river tonight to take a look at Delano." He shook his head and added, "Although, I ain't so sure an old man your age could handle a place like that."

Eli chuckled. "I don't think it would hurt me none, if I didn't do nothin' but watch."

"We gotta go pay that blacksmith for shoein' our horses," Casey reminded him. "He said he'd take 'em back to the stable, but I'd like to take Smoke for a little ride to make sure his shoes fit like they're supposed to. We can ride across the river and just look around, as long as we get the horses back before he closes up the stable."

"All right with me," Eli responded. "I would like to see what there is over there. I reckon I'm as bad as the young hands like Davey Springer. I can't wait to go see the elephant." He grinned and declared, "We might as well do what strikes our fancy, bein' independent businessmen like ourselves. Doolin and Tubbs, that's what you told ol' Sinclair, ain't it? I was surprised you didn't say we was Tubbs and Doolin. How come?"

"It's got a better ring to it," Casey said. "Besides, it's in alphabetical order."

"If you say so," Eli said as Marge brought the coffee.

They enjoyed a dinner of corned beef hash, which prompted Eli to ask Marge, "What is 'corned beef'?"

"I don't know," she confessed. "Folks seem to like it, though. Ted gets it from some fellow who raises cows and hogs on a little farm about three miles from town."

Corned beef, Eli pronounced. "Maybe it's beef raised on corn whiskey. That might be what you're made of, Casey."

Before they left the dining room, Ted Potter came over and made casual conversation for a few minutes. It was evident to them that the hotel manager and the sheriff had probably spread the word about their interest in finding land for two hundred Quakers. It only made it more disappointing that a key element in their plan had been buffaloed by the restrictive timing of the bank safe.

"Doggone it, Eli," Casey suddenly declared, "I wanna rob that damn bank. These folks in Wichita are so smug in the belief that nobody would dare try to rob it, makes me wanna call their bluff."

"You thinkin' about just bustin' in there in the mornin' and robbin' 'em?"

"Hell no," Casey said. "I still don't wanna get shot outta the saddle by the barber or the dentist, or one of them deputies the sheriff's got standin' on every corner. Our original plan is still a good one. We just need to work on it a little bit more. Come on, let's go get our horses and take a look at Delano across the river. We need a heap of things, if we're gonna pull off this robbery." He paused then to ask, "You're still wantin' to do it, right?"

"Beats ridin' the grub line," Eli said.

Their first stop was at the blacksmith's shop, where they found that Sam Godsey had finished shoeing their horses. "I was just fixin' to take your horses back to the stable," Sam said when they walked up. "They're ready to go. Hooves all look in fine shape. Didn't see any problems." He lifted the left front hoof of Casey's gray to show him the new shoe. "You can take a look at all of 'em and see if they suit you."

Casey was looking at the horse's hoof, but he looked as if his mind was somewhere else, so Eli asked, "I expect they'll all look like that one, right?"

"Pretty much," Sam said.

"How much I owe you?" Sam told him and Eli promptly paid him. Then he looked at Casey, who still looked as if he was working something out in his mind that had little to do with the horseshoes. "What do you say, Casey?"

Casey suddenly joined them mentally. "What? Oh, right. Looks like a first-class job. I was just thinkin', we need to ride down south of here and look at that riverside property again." He looked at Sam and smiled. "I get somethin' workin' on my mind and I gotta go take care of it." He paid Sam, then said to Eli, "Let's saddle 'em and ride down there tonight."

"Suits me," Eli said as he took his reins in hand and led his horse after Casey. Before they got to the stable next door, he caught up with Casey and asked, "What the hell are you talkin' about? Ride down where tonight?"

"We need to be outta town till tomorrow when we rob that bank," Casey told him. "You feel like campin' out tonight?"

"Not a whole lot," Eli said, "but I reckon you've got some kind of idea goin' round in your head, and there ain't nothin' goin' round in mine."

"I see you picked up your horses," Paul Johnson remarked when they led them up beside the stable. "Sam woulda brought 'em back here."

"I know," Casey said. "He said he was fixin' to, when we picked 'em up. But we decided we need to make up our minds on some river property south of here while it's still available. So we're gonna take a ride down there this afternoon and come back tomorrow."

"You gonna need your packhorse?" Paul asked.

"No, we'll take our bedrolls and a couple of sacks with the coffeepot and some jerky and hardtack. We ain't gonna be gone but one night. No need to fool with a packhorse for just one night." They saddled up and put the few things they thought they might need for one night on the ground. "We'll see you tomorrow," Casey said as they rode out of the stable and headed toward the river road south. They hadn't gone far when Casey said, "You know, I think it'd be a good idea to stop by the hotel and let 'em know we ain't gonna be here tonight."

"What for?" Eli asked. "We've paid for our rooms for the week. We don't have to tell nobody we ain't usin' 'em tonight."

"You're right about that," Casey remarked, "but it would let 'em know that we're out of town on business."

"Right," Eli responded.

Dan Hicks was nowhere around when they stopped in the hotel, so they told Clell Davis, the desk clerk, that they wouldn't be using their rooms that night. "You're paid up for a week," Clell responded. "Are you saying you want to check out of your rooms?"

"No," Casey quickly said. "We still need our rooms. We just thought we oughta tell you we won't be sleepin' here tonight in case your housekeepers might think we were gone for good."

Clell smiled in reaction to what he perceived as surprising naiveté for such mature businessmen. "Don't worry, gentlemen, we won't rent your rooms out while you're gone, but thanks for letting us know."

Outside on their horses again, Eli had to comment. "Well, I reckon he thinks we're both as dumb as a stump."

"Maybe so, but if the subject comes up, he'll sure as hell remember that we weren't even in town tonight."

Although having long careers driving cattle to market, neither of the two had ever been to the township of Delano. They were amazed to find the town to be a beehive of evil temptations, with a multitude of saloons, dancehalls, and brothels. And, as Marshal Meagher had told them, no law. Just west of the river, they found themselves stopped in front of two saloons, built side by side, which had been the scene of a brutal shooting between the two owners. The altercation left one of the owners wounded and the other one dead. Both establishments were still doing a steady business, and would do so, as long as the cattle were being driven to the railheads. Since they were stopped, but still sitting in the saddle, they were approached by an obvious drunk, down on his luck. He asked if they could spare the price of a drink of whiskey.

"I'll buy you a couple of drinks, if you can

tell me who the undertaker is," Casey told him. When the drunk seemed confused by the question, Casey asked, "Who's the fellow that picks up the body when somebody gets shot?"

"That'ud be Willard Moore," the drunk said.

"Where's his place of business?" Casey asked.

The drunk turned and pointed anxiously. "On that street behind the saloon."

Casey turned and looked in the direction pointed out. "On that street? You ain't lyin' to me, are you? I don't wanna come back lookin' for you."

"Honest to God, mister, I ain't lyin'. I need a drink too bad."

"Willard Moore, huh?"

The drunk nodded his head rapidly. Casey handed him a dollar, then wheeled Smoke around and headed toward the backstreet. Eli followed with no more idea what Casey was up to than the drunk had.

"Yep, I'm Willard Moore, what can I do for you?" He hadn't heard any gunshots, or he would have already been investigating. He didn't like to arrive on the scene too late or the body would have already been picked over by the drunks. He stared at the two cowhands standing in front of his small building, and both seemed stone sober.

"I'm thinkin' you must have a lot of clothes and things you've collected," Casey said. "You don't bury everything with the bodies, do ya?"

Willard looked from one of them to the other, not sure he was comfortable with the question. "Not everything," he said. "Some of the clothes I burn on account they been ruined. Anything that ain't been ruined, I keep to sell."

"That's what I figured," Casey said. "We need some clothes, but we ain't got a lot to spend on new clothes. You wanna show us what you've got?"

Feeling more at ease now, Willard said, "Sure, come on in the back and I'll let you look at what I've got on hand."

"What the hell are you doin'?" Eli whispered to Casey as they followed Willard into the back of his little morgue.

"I'm lookin' for some duds to wear to the bank," Casey whispered back.

Willard led them into a room where piles of clothes of all descriptions were lying on a row of tables. "Help yourself," he said, and stood back to watch. For the next thirty minutes, Casey and Eli picked out coats to try for size and cut, to the amazement of

Willard Moore, for the garments they considered were those of the roughest and most worn out. Some had stains and tears, and all were a little too big.

"Hats?" Casey asked, so Willard pointed to some shelves in the corner where there were hats stacked on top of each other. Just as they had with the coats, the two strangers selected two of the most dilapidated hats there.

"What's in the barrel?" Casey asked then.

"That ain't nothin' you'd be interested in," Willard said. "That's just stuff I'm fixin' to burn, wigs and women's underclothes, and such."

Casey walked over to the barrel and started poking around in it. He pulled out a large gray wig and held it up for Eli to see. Then he looked at Willard and asked, "Do you really find things like this on a body?"

"Mister, you wouldn't believe what you might find on a body," Willard said, then asked a question he was really puzzling over. "What are you fellows gonna do with that stuff?"

He was looking at Eli when he asked, so Eli turned to Casey and said, "Tell him, partner."

Without hesitating, Casey said, "We're goin' to a birthday party for an old friend of ours. The whole crew is gonna surprise him and we're all gonna get dressed up in funny outfits."

"It's gonna be hard to beat ours," Eli remarked. "How much you want for everything?"

Willard hesitated. "I ought not charge you anythin', seein' as how you picked out the most worthless ones I have. Gimme fifty cents apiece for the coats and the hats. I won't charge you nothin' for the wig, 'cause I was just gonna burn it up, anyway."

" 'Preciate it, Willard," Casey said as he handed him his dollar. "The boys are gonna get a kick outta this. I bet we win the prize."

Outside, they stuffed their purchases into their saddlebags, including the hats, and climbed on their horses. "The last two items are liable to be a bit more expensive," Casey said as he wheeled Smoke around and headed for a stable he had noticed at the end of the same street.

There was a man standing at the gate of a corral behind the stables, so they rode around to the back and dismounted to talk. "Are you the owner?" Casey asked.

"Yeah, why?" the man said warily.

"You sell horses and tack?"

"On occasion," he said, thinking maybe the two strangers were trying to track down some stolen horses.

"Well, we're lookin' to buy a couple of horses with saddles that we promised a couple of women when we'd had a little too much to think straight." Casey looked at Eli and gave him a look of disgust. "These ladies ain't likely to ride 'em two miles in a month, so we ain't lookin' to spend much for their horses, or the saddles, either. You got any you'd like to get rid of for a fair price?"

"I think I can fix you up with just what you need," the man said. "My name's Leroy Atkins. You boys just come up from Texas?"

"That's a fact," Casey said, "and we'll be headin' back tomorrow about this time, after we give the ladies their horses."

Leroy propped one foot on the bottom rail of the corral and leaned on the top rail. Then he pointed to a roan in one corner of the corral and a sorrel near the middle. "Yonder's your horses. You can look 'em over and you'll see they're in better shape than they look. I ain't got any lady's saddles, but I've got a couple of cheap ones that oughta fill the bill. Gimme fifty-five dollars apiece and you'll get horse, saddle, blanket, and bridle. Whaddaya say?"

"Let's take a look," Casey said, so Leroy went into the tack room to get a couple of bridles. Eli took one of the bridles and went after the sorrel, while Leroy cornered the roan. While Eli looked over the sorrel, Casey took the roan from Leroy and briefly checked out the horse.

"This one will do," he decided after a short inspection of the horse's teeth and the gray hair around its muzzle. "Just gettin' a little old," he said. "He ain't swayback. What about that one, partner?"

Eli said the sorrel was in about the same shape.

"Let's see the saddles," Casey said then, and Leroy went to get them. He came back, carrying two well-worn single-rigged saddles with an old saddle blanket lying across each one. He placed them on the ground for Eli and Casey to look at. They didn't spend but a moment to make sure the cinch strap wasn't worn to the point of coming apart before they threw the blankets on the horses and saddled them.

"Now, if you'll just open that gate," Eli said to Leroy as he stepped up into the saddle, "we'll take a short ride down to the end of the street and back. Just wanna be sure he ain't got no limp or sore foot."

He was followed by Casey on the roan, and they rode to the end of the street at a lope. Turning around, they started back at a gallop until almost reaching the stable again before reining them back to a slow walk around the outside of the corral, where Smoke and Biscuit were tied.

"You satisfied?" Eli asked as they dismounted, fully aware at last that he was going to have to depend on that horse, maybe for his life.

"Yep," Casey said. "This one will do. "How 'bout the sorrel?"

"He'll do," Eli said, so when Leroy came over to join them, he said, "Reckon we'll take 'em. They seem gentle enough, so's maybe the ladies won't break any bones."

"Thank you kindly, gents," Leroy said when they each came up with fifty-five dollars. "Hope these horses will buy you a little extra pleasure from your lady friends."

CHAPTER 6

Avoiding the bridge that crossed the river, they left Delano and rode south along the west bank of the Arkansas, leading the horses they had just bought. When they reached the spot where they had forded the river earlier that afternoon, they crossed back over. Now they were on the east bank, which put them on the same side of the river as Wichita and about two miles south of it.

"We're gonna have to make our camp back in that thick grove of trees," Casey said, pointing toward a section of the river where the trees had grown right down to the water's edge. "We can set up our camp near the water there, where it ain't likely to be seen by anybody happenin' to ride up the river. Them fancy horses we just bought oughta be able to gallop flat out that far before they give out, don't you think?"

"Yeah, they oughta be good for just about

that far," Eli agreed. He was now getting a pretty clear understanding of the direction Casey's mind was going. "I don't expect it's quite as far as two miles back to town from there. You're thinkin' we'll leave my bay and your gray hid in them woods while we ride those two crow baits in and rob the bank. And you're hopin' our horses will still be there when we get back." He paused and added, "If we get back."

"Right now, we ain't done nothin' against the law with that bank," Casey said. "And if you're thinkin' maybe you don't wanna take a crazy chance like this, you can still back out. 'Course, I'll call you a dirty, low-down, suck-egg coward if you do."

"You know you're a bonified lunatic, don't you? But that plan might be crazy enough to work. Anybody would tell you that nobody is dumb enough to try somethin' like we're fixin' to try, but I'll go along with it."

"I knew you would," Casey said with a grin. "You ain't got any more sense than I have. We're gonna have to get back here, get rid of our disguises, turn those old horses loose, and get outta here before a posse has time to form up and come after us."

"Hell, I ain't worried about that a-tall," Eli commented. "They'll recognize us as soon as we walk in the bank and the whole town will be standin' at the door, waiting for us to come out."

"That's another thing," Casey remembered. "There's a heap of money in that safe, but we don't have to get every last dollar. Just fill a couple of them big bank sacks as fast as we can and get outta there before somebody gets up the nerve to be a hero."

"Right," Eli said. "Let's go find us a spot to make camp. I could use a cup of coffee." They turned back toward the start of the thick patch of trees that bordered the river, leading their extra horses through a maze of bushes and cottonwoods until they decided on the best spot. After they let the horses drink, they left Biscuit and Smoke to graze on the tender shoots of grass along the riverbank. Their new horses were given the same freedom, with the restriction of hobbling them so they wouldn't wander. They built a small fire, using mostly the branches cut from the cottonwood trees, after the bark had been shaved off to be used as horse feed.

Before it became too dark to see in the trees, however, they got down to the business of creating their disguises. They were counting a great deal on the bank personnel being taken somewhat in shock, since they were so convinced that no one would dare to attempt a robbery. John Sinclair, especially, was absolutely confident that no criminal mind was insane enough to walk into Marshal Meagher's stronghold to try an armed robbery. Casey was hoping that the shock of facing the barrel of a pistol in a villain's hand would be all that was needed to discourage any opposition. So they pulled the oversized coats over their clothes and covered their faces with bandanas they used when herding cattle. And the old soiled and misshaped hats were pulled down low on their heads. Then for his final touch, Casey took his hat off again and pulled out the gray wig he had bought. With his skinning knife, he cut the wig up in strips, which he laid across his head. Then he pulled his hat down over them, holding them in place. The effect it created was that of an old man with ringlets of gray hair hanging out from under his hat. Eli was at once amazed and insisted that strips must be cut for him as well. Since they had no mirror, Casey was equally amazed when he witnessed the effect the gray curls had on Eli's appearance.

With renewed confidence in their chances of success, they carefully put their outfits away for the night and prepared their spartan supper of coffee, hardtack, and side meat strips, roasted over the fire. They had neglected to get a frying pan out of their packs at Paul Johnson's stable, so the meat was cooked on a stick. As the night grew older, they talked about the possible problems they might face, especially when it came to the question of early customers at the bank. If they were lucky, maybe there wouldn't be any customers there when the bank first opened. Being there as soon as the bank opened would be to their advantage timewise, when the safe was still open. "We'll just have to wait and see," Casey said. "If it looks like there's too many people for us to handle, we can always call it off."

Another question they had no answer for, how many employees did the bank actually have? They had been in the bank only once, and on that occasion, there was no one there but one teller and John Sinclair. Surely, there was at least one more teller. There were two teller cages.

"I reckon we'll get all our questions answered in the mornin'," Casey concluded, afraid that the more they talked about it, the better the likelihood they might decide against it. "So we might as well get some sleep now. Tomorrow's a workin' day."

"At least the Wichita jail oughta have cots to sleep on, so we're guaranteed to sleep better tomorrow night," Eli offered. "We could save a little time, if we just walk into that bank in the mornin' with our hands up."

Both men slept well during the night, as men who wasted little time worrying about what the future held for them usually did. They were awake with plenty of time before the bank opened, so they restarted their fire and made some coffee. "I figure we oughta be gettin' back to Wichita in time to eat dinner at the hotel," Casey speculated.

"Too bad we won't get back to town in time to ride with the posse," Eli remarked. "I always like to do my civic duty."

"There's one more thing I wanna do before we leave here," Casey said. "I wanna dig a little hole to bury those clothes in. If a posse finds this camp, and I think they might, I want them to think they're still chasin' two old men. And I'm lookin' at a good spot to dig it." He pointed to a large cottonwood on the bank that was leaning toward the water. "I didn't think about bringin' a shovel to dig a hole. But I oughta be able to dig the dirt out from between those large roots with my knife and my hands. And it'll be easy to cover that up so's you wouldn't notice it."

"What about those cheap saddles?" Eli

wondered. "Reckon we oughta try to hide them, too? And let those horses run free?"

"I think we'd just leave the horses saddled, like the outlaws likely would, to save time switchin' horses. Those two horses are gonna be wore slap out, but there won't be any weight besides the saddle. They ain't likely to wander far from here for a long spell, anyway. Shoot, we're saddlin' our horses, so we won't have to take the time to do that when we come back here."

So they drank their coffee and ate a little bit of hardtack, but didn't bother with cooking the side meat. Casey took out his knife and, with that as his pickax, dug a hole between the roots of the cottonwood, large enough to bury their outfits when they returned. He didn't dig very far before he found the dirt moist and sticky. When he felt his forehead itch when a gnat landed on it, he reached up to shoo it away. In the process, he left a dirty smear from the damp dirt on his fingers. He swore and started to rub it off, but Eli stopped him. "Hold it," Eli said. "Let me get that." Eli rubbed the muddy smear gently, then reached down and got a little more on his fingers and dabbed that on Casey's forehead.

"What the heck is wrong with you?" Casey blurted.

"Just hold still," Eli told him. "I'm gettin' you ready to start your actin' career." After he rubbed a small amount of the moist dirt on Casey's forehead, and a dab or two around his temples, he stepped back to admire his work. "I wish I had a mirror."

Casey said nothing but got up from the roots and walked around the tree, then walked along the edge of the water until he found a hole where the water was deeper. He knelt then and held his head out over the water. He saw just enough of a reflection to give him a hint of what Eli saw. "Well, I'll be . . ."

He immediately went back to the tree roots to try the same treatment on Eli's face. Grinning like a couple of mischievous schoolboys, they spent the next twenty minutes touching up each other's faces. Careful not to overdo the makeup, they found that a light touch of the wet soil left a subtle aging appearance when it dried completely.

"Let's remember who it was that came up with this idea when we're settin' around braggin' about it," Eli crowed.

"Oh, I'll remember, all right," Casey said. "It was a gnat." He pulled out his watch and said, "I reckon we'd best get into our bank-robbin' outfits and saddle up. It's near 'bout time to ride."

They saddled all four horses, and it was not without some concern that they tied Smoke and Biscuit to a tree, even though with enough rope to permit them to get to the water. Without saying so, both men intended to make sure they told somebody where to find the horses in the event the bank holdup failed. With plenty of time before the bank opened, they held their new horses to a leisurely pace on their way to town. When the buildings of the town came into view, Casey checked his watch again. It was still half an hour before the nine o'clock opening time, so they continued on until they were close enough to pick out a spot by the river to stop and wait for the time to strike. They took the opportunity to give each other a final inspection. Then, at nine o'clock, they got back on their horses and walked them behind the buildings on the main street until reaching the alley between the bank and the Friendly Saloon. Into the alley, they guided the horses up to the front of the bank, where they dismounted and tied them loosely on a corner post of the bank's front porch.

After a quick look up and down the street at the few people on the boardwalk in front of the stores, they exchanged a brief look between them. Eli grinned and winked as they pulled their bandanas up to just below their eyes. Casey nodded, and they walked in the door. Eli closed the door behind him and turned the OPEN sign to CLOSED. There were no customers inside. The teller they had seen when they were in before, Phillip Reed, was in his cage, but was not aware anyone had come in the door until he turned around to find himself facing a dirty-looking old man with a Colt .44 aimed right at his face. Motioning with his pistol, Eli directed Reed toward the door to the room where the safe was. Terrified, Reed had to force his legs to carry him toward the door, where another old man stood waiting, his gun aimed at him, too.

Having gone directly to John Sinclair's office when Eli went to the teller's cage, Casey found Sinclair's office empty. He was hoping that was because he was in the back room opening the safe. When Reed got to the door, Casey motioned him through it with his six-shooter. Then he and Eli went in right behind him, and Eli guided him toward the open door of the safe room with the barrel of his pistol in his back.

They met Sinclair coming out of the room. He started to ask Reed something, but stopped when he saw the two old men behind his teller. In his mind, their pistols looked the size of cannons. "What?!" he exclaimed, horrified. Then he turned to another man behind him in the room and blurted, "Close the safe!"

Instead of reacting instantly, the young man, the bank's other teller, was almost paralyzed with fear at the sight of the two older bank robbers. When he hesitated, Casey stepped from behind Sinclair, his pistol pointed at the young man's head. "You close that safe and you're a dead man," he said, doing his best to sound like an old man might. "Now, all three of ya, set down up against that wall." They did as he said, sitting down on the floor, their backs against the wall. "Now, Oscar, you wanna grab a couple of them bags beside that safe and make our withdrawal?"

Eli did not react at once, but quickly realized Casey was talking to him. "Sorry, Elmer, you know my hearin' ain't been too good lately. I'll get the money."

With his fear gradually being overtaken by his sheer astonishment at the bizarre happening in his bank, John Sinclair worked up the courage to say, "You're making a terrible mistake, old man. The marshal of this town is Michael Meagher and he has four deputies. You won't get out of town with that money."

"We come in here to steal money," Casey said. "We didn't come to do no killin', but if you don't set there and keep your mouth shut, I'm willin' to make an exception in your case. Lord knows, one more ain't gonna make much difference in my case." He brought his pistol to bear directly on Sinclair's face. "How you comin' in there, Oscar?"

"I'm 'bout ready," Eli called back.

"Close enough," Casey declared. "These boys are anxious to get in there." Back to Sinclair and his tellers, he said, "Get on your feet!" He waited for Eli to leave the small safe room, carrying two bags of cash. "Get in there," he directed Sinclair and his two tellers. When they went in, he closed the door behind them, then pulled a chair over and propped it under the knob. Looking at Eli, he said, "I shoulda told Sinclair to give me the dern key, but we'd best not linger." He took one of the bags from Eli, holstered his Colt, and pulled his bandana down as they hurried toward the door.

Through the glass in the door, they could see several people waiting for the bank to open. Three of them were men, and all were looking anxiously through the glass. When he got to the door, Casey reached over and turned the sign around to OPEN. When he and Eli walked out, he said, "Sorry you folks had to wait. You can go on in now, they oughta open any minute. We got all the snakes." He nodded toward the sack he was carrying.

The people filed in the door and one of the women commented, "Snakes! I surely hope they got all of 'em."

Outside, Casey and Eli tied the sacks to their saddle horns and climbed up into the saddle when they heard a shout from inside the bank. "We've just been robbed!" There was no need for discussion, both men pushed their horses to reach a full gallop up the narrow alley by the time they reached the back of the bank. Down along the river, they galloped, the horses already tiring after only about one mile. Finally Eli pulled his horse to a stop, causing Casey to pull up, too.

"What's the matter?" Casey asked. "We're almost there."

"This dang horse is about finished," Eli said. "If I didn't let up, he was goin' down." He turned around in the saddle to look behind them. "There ain't no sign of anybody tailin' us. I don't think anybody knows which way we went." He nudged the sorrel and the horse started walking slowly.

Casey walked his horse along beside Eli's. "I expect you might be right," he said. "I doubt they've got over the bank that couldn't be robbed, gettin' robbed. I reckon there ain't no use to kill the horses. We'll walk 'em on in." He didn't say anything else for a few moments while he thought about what they had just pulled off. Then he grinned and said, "Sinclair looked straight at us — both of us — and never recognized either one of us. Ain't that right, Oscar?"

Eli chuckled. "You almost messed me up back there when you said that. You shoulda told me before we went in there that you were gonna call me that." He chuckled again. "But I got it, and I already forgot what I called you."

"Elmer," Casey said, and they chuckled.

Both were starting to feel a little giddy after having successfully robbed a bank. "If we were smart, we'd just forget about goin' back to town. We'd just take our money and head to parts unknown."

"I reckon there's a lotta truth to that," Eli allowed. "But I think we oughta stick to the plan and see it on through to the end. Like you said, Sinclair didn't recognize us. But if we don't go back there again, it would be the natural thing for somebody to think that was kind of a strange coincidence. We have a room paid up for a week and we disappear right after the bank gets robbed. Besides, I'd kinda like to hear all about the bank robbery."

When they got back to their camp, they were relieved to see that no one had stumbled upon their horses. And even though they felt they had plenty of time, they hurried to make their final escape. They stripped off their disguises, bundled them up, and pushed them back under the cottonwood roots, then covered the hole so it would be very difficult to discover. Then as a reward to their two temporary horses for their part in the robbery, they decided to set them free. As for their bridles and saddles, they threw them in the river. They scattered ashes and traces of their small campfire as a final chore before climbing on their horses and riding down the river in the shallow water for about a quarter of a mile before crossing over to leave the water on the west bank. A little farther down, they repeated the maneuver. After a half mile on that side, they crossed back again and rode straight east for several miles until they struck a road to Wichita. Then they started back toward Wichita, figuring they were no more than an hour's ride from there, and, consequently, with plenty of time to eat dinner at the hotel.

It was at that point when they realized they had a problem they hadn't dealt with yet. They had more money than they knew what to do with. Eli had crammed every bit of money he could into the two bags. They would be mighty conspicuous to come riding into town with them. There was only so much they could pack in their saddlebags. And they had no place to hide the rest. They figured the best solution to the problem would be to bury it somewhere. Again, they had no shovel. Getting closer to town now, they passed a couple of farms with houses they could see from the road. When they came even with the second house, they suddenly heard the sound of the woman of the house banging away on a triangle, announcing that dinner was ready. A few yards farther up the road, they came to a creek. About a hundred yards from the road, they could see a barn or building of some kind and it was only halfway finished.

Casey pulled Smoke to a sudden stop. "They're buildin' a barn!" he exclaimed.

"Yeah, looks like it," Eli responded. "What about it?"

"We need a shovel. Might be one there. And they've gone to dinner."

"You gonna steal a shovel?" Eli asked.

"You don't even know if they've got a shovel there."

"Sure, they got a shovel. You always need a shovel. I ain't gonna steal it. I'm gonna buy it. You just wait here and hold the horses." He slid off Smoke and started running up the creek toward the barn. When he reached the barn, there was no one there, as he had figured. There were various tools lying around, their owners gone to dinner, but no shovel. He decided to chance a quick look inside the half-finished structure, so he made a dash from the creek to the back door. Propped up against the inside wall of the barn, he found his shovel. There was a nail driven only halfway in next to the shovel, so he reached in his pocket and got a five-dollar bill and hung it on the nail.

"Well, I'll swear," Eli muttered when Casey appeared again, carrying a shovel. "You'll rob a bank, but you won't steal a shovel?"

CHAPTER 7

It took a little longer to ride the short distance into Wichita than it normally would have, but they still made it in time to eat dinner at the hotel dining room. Their delay had been caused by the time it had taken to bury the greater part of the bank money in the back side of a ridge a couple of miles west of the town. This was followed by a somewhat shorter delay when they stopped to hide the shovel in a rocky gully at the end of the ridge. They could think of no believable reason for bringing a shovel back to the hotel or the stable, and they would definitely need it to retrieve their buried treasure.

When they walked into the dining room, there was no one at the desk, but they dutifully took their gun belts off and placed them on the shelf where Ted Potter always put them. They turned around to be met by Marge Joyner, who asked, "Have you heard the news?"

"What news is that?" Casey asked casually.

"The news," Marge repeated, emphasizing the words and waiting for some response.

"I reckon not," Casey said, "and it looks like I never will, if you ain't gonna tell me. We just got back in town and came straight to your dinin' room before you closed."

"They robbed the bank!" Polly exclaimed, having heard Marge talking from the kitchen.

"Who robbed the bank?" Eli responded, he and Casey pretending alarm.

"Two old men," Marge answered his question.

" 'Two old men'?" Casey repeated. He looked from one of the women to the other, then asked, "What's the joke?"

"It ain't no joke," Marge insisted. "If you don't believe me, go in the kitchen and ask Mamie. She doesn't joke about anything."

"When did they rob the bank?" Eli asked.

"This morning, right after John Sinclair opened up," Marge said. "Two gray-headed old men walked in with their guns drawn and cleaned the safe out and shut Mr. Sinclair and both his tellers up in the back room. Sam Godsey said he was standin' outside the front door when the two old men came out the door and turned the Closed sign around. Sam said one of 'em told 'em to go right on in. Said they was each carrying a bag full of money and they climbed on a couple of horses they had tied up at the corner of the porch. Sam said he was inside the door when Mr. Sinclair and the other two came running out of the back, yelling that they'd been robbed. Sam said he and another fellow ran back outside, but the two bank robbers were already ridin' out the end of the alley."

It was time for Casey and Eli to perform the reaction they had rehearsed on their ride into town. "Did you say they 'cleaned the safe out'?" Casey asked Marge, his face a mask of alarm.

"That's what Sam said," Polly said for her. "He said both of the old men were totin' a big sack. The old men told 'em they were full of snakes."

Halfway to a table by then, both of them stopped and Casey grabbed Polly by her shoulders and demanded, "Are you sure about the money?" Immediately frightened by his tone, she nodded frantically. He released her and moaned, "We've got a thousand dollars in that bank."

"We *had* a thousand dollars in that bank,"

Eli corrected him, "if what they're sayin' is true."

"God's honest truth," Marge said to them. "We hate to be the ones to give you the news, but it hit a lotta folks hard, although they might notta lost as much as you and Casey."

"Is anybody doin' anything about it?" Casey asked.

"Marshal Meagher and his deputies rounded up some volunteers for a posse and sent them after 'em. Ted went with 'em, and Sam and a few of the younger men who happened to be in town this morning," Marge told him.

"One of the marshal's deputies, Stoney Lewis, is an expert tracker," Polly volunteered. "If anybody can get on their trail, I'll bet it would be Stoney. He used to live with the Sioux when he was younger."

Casey risked a wry look in Eli's direction upon hearing that. Back to the women, he said, "I reckon all we can do is hope he's still got a sharp eye. All that money, gone, I don't know if we coulda been any help if we'd been here this mornin'. Makes me feel kinda helpless right now." He looked at Eli then. "I had second thoughts about puttin' that money in the bank. I shoulda paid attention to 'em."

"Ain't nothin' we can do about it now, but hope the posse has some good luck," Eli said. "We worked hard for that money. We'll just have to work a little harder now to make up for the loss." He was getting tired of the drama and was ready to eat, so he was tickled to hear Marge's urging.

"The best thing you can do right now is set yourselves down and have something to eat," she advised. "Let us girls wait on you and get you a good cup of hot coffee."

"She's right, Casey. We gotta eat whether they run those outlaws to ground or not. We can't just lay down and quit."

"I reckon you're right," Casey responded. "At least we ain't dead broke. We can still pay for our dinner."

They lingered in the dining room a while longer than they normally would have. There were fewer customers than usual, attributed to the big bank robbery possibly, so Marge and Polly filled the plates to overflowing. When they left the dining room, they carried their saddlebags up to their rooms, trusting they would be safe for the short time they would be gone. After locking their doors, they took their horses to the stable, where they rehashed the whole bank robbery with Paul Johnson. They, of course, let him know that they had lost a princely sum in the robbery, too. He offered to slash their bill, or even to simply forgive the debt. But they assured him that they had kept enough expense money to pay their debts. He was very appreciative of their sense of fairness.

It was their intent to be seen around town by as many people as possible in an effort to impress upon the town the fact that they were absent from the town when the bank robbers struck, but very much in town while the robbers were being chased. So, when they left the stable, they went to the Friendly Saloon for a drink.

"Howdy, gents," Jug Trask greeted them when they walked up to the bar. "A shot of corn and a shot of rye," he remembered, "but I don't remember which went to who."

"You do the pourin' and we'll sort it out," Casey said. "If you really care about which one of us gets which likker, all you have to remember is 'Casey' starts with a *C* and so does 'corn.' " Jug poured the drinks, and since he made no mention of the bank robbery, Casey brought it up. "Me and Eli were out of town last night. We just rode back into town a couple of hours ago to hear about the bank gettin' hit by bandits. That wasn't very good news to come back to."

"You missed all the excitement then," Jug remarked. "There's been a lot of drinkin' goin' on this afternoon. I swear, you can tell who had money in the bank, 'cause they're the ones doin' most of the heavy drinkin'. Most of them are merchants and business-men. They're hurt, but they can make it back. My boss got hurt. He had money in the bank, but you know we'll make it back for him. You know who I feel sorry for? I feel sorry for some of these farmers who've come out here and put a little money in the bank. There's one of 'em settin' right over there. He settled on a little piece of land on one side of a deep creek. He musta known Wichita was gonna get a railroad one day and he planned to raise some cattle to ship east. He's been raisin' corn and wheat on a hundred and sixty acres of land and savin' every penny he can get his hands on for the last two years to buy two hundred and twenty-five acres of land on the other side of the creek. He can get it for a dollar an acre, and he came into town about an hour ago with five dollars in his pocket to put with the two hundred and twenty dollars he had in the bank."

"That's a mighty hard piece of luck to choke down," Casey said.

"That's him settin' over there against the

wall by himself," Jug said, "spendin' his five dollars on whiskey."

"Yes, sir," Eli remarked, wishing to change the subject, "that's a doggone shame, all right." But Jug wasn't finished with his story.

"You know what's kinda weird about that fellow? And I don't know if I believe him, but here's the story he told me. Him and his boys are tryin' to build a barn out at his place. And he said today when his wife called 'em in for dinner, they went in to eat. But when they got back to the barn, his good shovel was gone and there was a five-dollar bill stuck on a nail where he had left his shovel." He paused, pleased by the look of disbelief he saw on the faces of the two men, before continuing. "He said it was a sign from the Lord that he had worked hard enough. It was time for him to go get that piece of land. So he jumped on his horse and came into town to find out that the Devil decided to help out a couple of bank robbers." Jug opened his cash drawer, pulled out a five-dollar bill, and laid it on the bar. It had a hole in the center of it. He smacked his hand down on top of it. "How's that for a story?"

Neither Casey nor Eli had much to say, both still astonished by such a coincidence.

Finally Casey said, "That's quite a story, all right."

"I can see you boys ain't buyin' his story, either," Jug said. "You hear all kinds of stories in a saloon. Not many of 'em are straight." Ready to change the subject then, he commented, "You fellers are lucky you're just passin' through town, and you ain't got no account with the bank."

"I wish that was true," Casey said. "The fact of the matter is, we were carrying a large sum of money, so we put it in the bank for safekeepin'. Turned out it wasn't a good idea, after all."

"Well, I'll swear," Jug drew back in surprise. "Here I am, runnin' on about that poor feller." He hesitated, not knowing what more to say. "You sure are takin' it pretty calmly."

"Maybe not as calm as you think," Eli said. "But we decided there wasn't a dog-gone thing we could do about it now. We made a mistake, but it didn't seem like a dumb thing to do at the time. We've still got a tiny little chance that posse will show up back here with those two outlaws tonight."

"I'll drink to that," Casey said. "Pour us another one, Jug." While Jug poured, Casey asked, "Who's leadin' the posse? Marshal Meagher?"

"No," Jug said. "The marshal don't ride on any posse. He's got deputies for that. He says his place is always to stay in Wichita to make sure the town stays peaceful. Wyatt Earp and Stoney Lewis are leadin' the posse. You can't get much better than that. You gonna hang around to see if the posse gets back tonight?"

"I expect we'll go on back to the hotel to wait," Casey said. "Then, if they ain't come back by suppertime, we'll most likely see you after supper." They paid for the drinks and walked out the door.

Approaching the bank next door, they stopped to look at the alley where they had left the horses. It looked even more narrow than it had that morning. If Sinclair and his tellers had forced that chair aside ten seconds sooner, somebody might have gotten out in that alley soon enough to throw a couple of shots after them. And in that narrow passage, it would have been hard to miss.

"I wonder if we've got enough to retire on," Casey declared. At this point, they didn't even know how much they had. They hadn't counted the money they had crammed into their saddlebags, and there was more buried in the side of the ridge, which they couldn't count, unless they dug it up. And they didn't want to do that until they were leaving Wichita for good. "Standin' here now, I wish we'da had bigger bags, so we coulda got every last dollar, since word is the robbers did. But when we were in that bank, I felt like it was takin' forever to fill the bags we had, and I didn't wanna be greedy."

They looked at the bank now. The CLOSED sign was turned out and all the shades were pulled down in the windows. It was little wonder that John Sinclair was not in the mood to receive visitors. They decided to go on back to the hotel, sit on the porch, and decide what the future of Doolin and Tubbs should be. After checking to make sure there had been no tampering with their saddlebags, they went to the porch to talk and smoke the cigars that Eli brought from his room.

After some celebrating over the successful robbery they had pulled off, in what could be considered classic style, they confessed to some remorse for the tremendous effect their action had on innocent people. Still, they could not deny the obvious natural talent they seemed to possess for that particular line of work. By the time the dining room opened for supper, they had fairly decided that outlaws were what they were, but they would try to concentrate their talents on crimes that didn't impact the common people so directly. There were plenty of trains, stagecoach lines, and large corporations to provide a livelihood for two enterprising men like themselves.

Suppertime came with still no sign of the posse returning, so Casey and Eli went to the dining room to sample Mamie's beef roast. The conversational buzz in the room was all about the robbery that morning and the speculation on the possibility of success by the posse. "Don't you think they musta got on those two old men's trail?" Marge asked Casey. "If they hadn't, they woulda been back long ago, don't you think?"

"I expect you're right," he said to her. "Most of the time, when you get a bunch of town folk to volunteer to go with a posse, they lose their enthusiasm for the chase after a mile or two, if there ain't plenty of signs. And that's when they turn around and go home. But like you say, nobody's showed up back here yet, so they musta found something. Paul Johnson told me they didn't take any provisions for a long hunt, so something must be strong enough to keep 'em at it."

Eli nodded in agreement with Casey.

After supper with no sounds of welcoming from outside the hotel, the two bank robbers left the dining room and went to the saloon to join the crowd gathered there awaiting news. At Paul Johnson's invitation, they pulled up a couple of empty chairs and sat down at his table.

"Might as well set and wait with the rest of us to see if we're gonna get our money back," he said. "Right now, the only ones makin' any money offa this bank robbery are the two old men who robbed it and Jay Donavan." He laughed as he held a shot of whiskey up toward a lamp and looked at it. "Jay's selllin' it at half price tonight on account of the robbery, but I ain't sure it ain't watered down to half strength."

It was twenty-five minutes after eleven when someone shouted from the front door, "They're back!" The saloon emptied at once as they all crowded out the door to meet the posse slowly walking their horses up the center of the street. Weary men dismounted from their tired horses as the crowd of spectators crowded around, all searching to see if the bank robbers were with them. There was a general groan of disappointment when it was plain to see they had no prisoners and many quiet expressions of profanity when Wyatt Earp confirmed to Marshal Meagher that they had eventually lost the culprits. Meagher had walked over from his office at the jail to accept Earp and Stoney Lewis's report.

"We lost 'em," Earp said when the marshal walked through the spectators to face him. "Stoney picked up the trail where they left town and fled down the river. We found the place where they camped this mornin'. Found the horses they rode into town on. Looked like they had left a couple of fresh horses there by the river and they switched. They took the saddles and bridles off the horses they rode in on and turned 'em loose. Then they took off on their fresh horses. We followed their trail down the river a good ways before they took to the water. And we found where they came out again. They went from one side of the river to the other, tryin' to lose us, till they finally did." He paused a moment before saying, "To make a long story short, we never did find where they came outta the water the last time. The posse was willin', so we kept ridin' down the river, just on the chance we'd cut sign. But we never did. We didn't take any provisions to stay out overnight, so when it started gettin' too dark to see any sign, we turned back. I'm pretty sure those two are headed to Oklahoma Indian Territory."

"I expect you're right," Meagher said,

then addressed the posse volunteers. "Sorry you couldn't find the men who struck the bank, but I wanna personally thank every one of you who volunteered to try. For all of you who got hurt by the robbery, I'll wire the U.S. Marshal in Fort Smith, Arkansas, to alert his deputies that the two outlaws are headin' their way."

"That'll help one helluva lot," Casey heard someone say sarcastically and rather softly, as if talking only to himself. He glanced over to see who had said it and recognized the man Jug had pointed out as the farmer who had told him the story about the missing shovel and the five-dollar bill. He was standing only a few feet away, holding his horse's reins.

Casey was tempted to say something to him, but decided that would be a big mistake. So he stepped back to keep the horse between him and the man. He was sure the man hadn't seen him near his barn that morning, but why chance it? He was glad when the farmer stepped up on the horse and started back home to deliver the heartsickening news to his wife about the loss of their money.

"Reckon we oughta go back in the saloon with the rest of the victims and drink a little more likker?" Eli posed the question.

"Probably so," Casey said. "We don't wanna look like we ain't bothered by losin' our money." So they went back inside with a large part of the crowd that had assembled when the posse was sighted coming home.

The marshal went into the saloon with them, instead of returning to his office. "Mind if I join you?" he asked when they sat down at a table close to the bar. They, of course, welcomed him. "Jug," he called out, "bring my bottle, will you? And some glasses," he added.

" 'Preciate your kindness, Marshal," Casey said. "But as I recollect, me and Eli owe you a drink. We lost money today, too, but we ain't broke. Badly bent, but we ain't broke. Ain't that right, Eli?"

"That's a fact," Eli responded. "We'd be honored to see you to a snort."

"That's mighty sportin' of you fellows," Meagher said. "But it'll really be Donavan buyin' you a drink. You see, that's one of the benefits of my job."

"In that case, I'll have rye," Casey said, remembering that was the marshal's drink.

"John Sinclair told me you fellows deposited a large sum of money in the bank. I'm sorry as I can be that you had to lose it like this. I was talking to John about you two before. I had my doubts that you were in the business you claimed. When he told me how much you trusted the bank with, I figured you really were ridin' around dressed up like a couple of cowhands to keep from attractin' outlaws. Mormons you're workin' for, is it?"

"Quakers," Casey corrected him, wondering if Meagher was still testing them.

"Right, Quakers," he quickly repeated. "How long are you gonna be here in Wichita?"

Casey waited while Jug set the bottle and glasses on the table, then said, "We're paid up for the week, so we figured we might as well stay that long. We were thinkin' about lookin' around farther west, but our expense money suddenly got reduced overnight. In spite of the bank holdup, we still favor the Wichita area. A bank can get held up anywhere. So unless you run us outta town, we'll probably hang around a few more days."

"We're glad to have you," Meagher said, "and I think this would be good country for the Quakers."

They sat and talked and drank with the marshal for over an hour before both of them were having trouble staying alert. So they said good night to Meagher and a couple of other citizens of Wichita, who had pulled chairs up to join them, and retired for the night.

About two miles east of the town, another soul had just reached his home. Heartsick and depressed, Robert Blunt did not want to give his wife and boys the news he had learned in Wichita. He felt weary and defeated when he rode his horse straight up to the house and got down from the saddle. His eldest son, Thomas, heard him and went out to meet him. "Did you get it, Pa?"

"No, I did not," his father stated emphatically. "Put my horse away, will you, son?" He went into the house to give his wife the tragic news. She was as devastated as he had been when she heard the two hundred and twenty dollars her husband had worked so hard to save up had been stolen. She sought to console him, but was interrupted by her son.

"You forgot your money, Pa," Thomas interrupted when he came back in the room.

"No, son, I didn't forget it," Robert said. "It's gone, lost for good."

"No, it ain't, Pa. I found it. You musta forgot you put it in your saddlebag." He held a roll of money out to him.

Stunned, Robert's hands were shaking so much he couldn't hold it. "Take it, Mama," he finally said to his wife. "Is it real money?"

She took the roll of bills and looked at it. "Yes, it's real money. Robert," she demanded, thinking he was playing a cruel joke on them, "what's wrong with you?"

"Count it," he said.

She unrolled the money and started counting. "Two hundred and twenty-five dollars," she said. Her face lit up with excitement then. "You had me worried there. You were acting so strange. Shame on you."

"Margaret," he told her solemnly. "The First Wichita Bank was robbed this mornin'. All the cash money was stolen, and the robbers got away. Everybody lost every cent they had in the bank, including us. When I left town to come home, I didn't have a cent left. How did that money get in my saddlebag? I think I need to sit down." He sank down on a chair, his eyes still wide in shock.

His mysterious statement left his wife speechless as she continued to feel the money, expecting it to dissolve in her fingers. When it did not, she told her husband, "For whatever reason, we've been blessed by an angel. We must just accept it and be thankful for it. And we don't need to tell anybody about it." She nodded her head emphatically one time, then added, "And we should go to church this Sunday."

CHAPTER 8

Bank robberies were not that common in this day and age. Most of the common people hid their money under the mattress. Or if they had a great deal of money, they buried it in secret hiding places. It had taken John Sinclair two years to instill confidence in the people and businesses in Wichita to entrust him and his giant iron safe with their savings. The bank building was in the center of town. Any bandits attempting to rob it in broad daylight would have to run through a virtual shooting gallery to get out of town safely. The construction of the bank was of double reinforced walls on the back and entrance from the front only. A break-in at night was not likely. Even if they managed to break through the back wall, or escape detection while breaking in the front, there was the problem of the iron safe, too heavy to carry away and too difficult to blow open. And yet, two elderly men calmly walked into the bank when the safe was open and took a large amount of the money, then walked out the door without being challenged.

The next couple of days that followed the bank robbery saw a town that had lost its spark of life. It was like that of a town trying to recover after a smallpox epidemic. There was a loss of confidence in Michael Meagher and his deputies to protect the town, even though it was through no lack of diligence on the marshal's part. A band of gun-toting outlaws riding into town to assault the bank would, without doubt, have met with a different reception. But two harmless-looking old men who quietly walked in and out of the bank, without firing a shot, seemed to rob the bank with no one noticing until well after the fact.

Casey and Eli couldn't even enjoy the irony of the dining room staff's tendency to give them special treatment when they came in to eat. In fact, they felt a measure of compassion for the town's loss.

"We'd better get the hell outta here before we start givin' it all back," Eli complained.

"I'm ready to move on," Casey said. "We've got a couple more days' room rent paid for. You wanna stay till then? Or take off in the mornin'?"

Eli was about to answer, but hesitated

when he saw John Sinclair walk in the dining room.

Casey's back was to the front door, so he asked again, "Which do you want to do?"

"Sinclair just walked in," Eli said, "and it looks like he's comin' this way." They had not seen the bank president since the day of the robbery. In fact, very few people had. "Yep, he's comin' this way," Eli confirmed.

Casey turned his chair to face him when he approached their table. "Mr. Sinclair," he greeted him politely.

"Mr. Tubbs, Mr. Doolin," Sinclair returned. "I'm sorry I haven't come to talk to you before now. I know it does little good to apologize for your loss in the bank holdup, but I wanted to let you know how devastated I am because of it. I would have sought you out sooner, but I have to confess that I was unable to pull myself together right away. There are people who lost more than you that I had to talk to first. But there weren't many. I don't know what I can tell you, other than I am extremely sorry to have failed you. I have some investors who financed my building of this bank, and I am going to talk with them about possible loans to try to repay my customers, at least in part." He elected not to tell them that he had to decide who lost all their money and who did not. Since they were likely to be only passing through, he decided they would be among the unfortunate ones who were wiped out.

"Why don't you sit down, Mr. Sinclair?" Casey invited. "Have a cup of coffee with us. You want some coffee?"

"Yes, I think I would like some," Sinclair said. Eli reached over and pulled a chair out for him, and Sinclair sat down heavily as if carrying a load.

Casey signaled Marge for a cup of coffee and she brought it at once. "Let me set you straight on one thing," Casey said as Sinclair sipped his coffee. "Eli and I don't have any hard feelin's toward you because of that holdup. Matter of fact, we feel sorry for you, more than anybody else that had money in your bank. You lost a helluva lot more than any of us. Now, if you were in cahoots with those two fellows who robbed the bank, then it'd be a different story."

"Oh, no, no," Sinclair insisted at once. "I was certainly not involved in robbing my own bank."

"We didn't think so," Casey said. "It was just bad luck. Hell, we've lost a thousand dollars in a poker game. Ain't we, Eli?"

"You have, I ain't," Eli said, and they both chuckled.

"We wish you luck in gettin' some backin' from your investors," Casey told him. "But if you run short, don't worry about payin' us our money until you're back in business again."

Sinclair's eyes became a little red, almost to the point of shedding a tear. "I can't begin to tell you how much I appreciate your kindness," he said. "I appreciate your attitude. I've found that not many of my customers have been as gracious as you two gentlemen. It's men like you and Mr. Doolin who make this country great." He got to his feet. "I thank you for the coffee and wish you good luck in placing your religious community." He turned and hurried out of the dining room, clearly struggling with his emotions.

"I ain't sure I know what to say about that," Eli commented. "It's hard for me to get it around my brain that he don't recognize me and you. He must notta seen anything but the muzzle of our guns."

"I reckon, while we're ahead, we oughta saddle up and go make some other part of this country great," Casey said. "First thing you know, ol' Sinclair might start thinkin' those two old men wore boots just like Doolin and Tubbs wear, and their trousers were identical to the ones we've got on." He waited for Eli to give his opinion and when he didn't, he asked, "Whaddaya think?"

"I expect you're right," Eli said. "I ain't got no idea where we oughta go. I wanna go back to Texas, but I don't wanna run into the other boys. It'd be pretty hard to explain how we suddenly got rich."

"I favor goin' back to Texas, too," Casey said. "But we don't have to go back to that part of Texas. We can afford to go anywhere we want to, and I've kinda got a hankerin' to see what the eastern part of Texas looks like. You ever seen that part of Texas?"

"Not since I was about nine years old," Eli said.

That was a surprise to Casey. "You went to that part of Texas when you were nine?"

"Nope. I went there nine years before that, in my mama's belly. I was born there, in Nacogdoches."

"I swear, you never told me that."

"You never asked me where I was born."

"I didn't care where you was born. What did you call that town?"

"Nacogdoches," Eli repeated. "Oldest town in Texas."

"Who says that?"

"I don't know. My pa told me. I don't know who told him," Eli said.

"Let's go back there and see if it's changed

any since you left," Casey suggested.

"Fine by me," Eli declared, and so their plans were settled. They decided to leave the following morning, make a stop at the ridge east of town to make another withdrawal, and then ride the Chisholm Trail back down through Oklahoma. Then another thought occurred to Eli. "You reckon that's really a smart plan, since Meagher said he was gonna wire the U.S. Marshal in Fort Smith and tell him there was two bank robbers headin' down their way with two sacks full of money?"

"Hmmm . . . that is somethin' to think about, ain't it?" Casey had already decided he liked the sound of Nacogdoches. "But, hell, they'd be lookin' for two gray-headed old men, not two cowhands comin' back from Abilene, dead broke."

They sat for a while longer and talked it over some more. The idea of going to Nacogdoches was possibly the furthest thing in Eli's mind before he mentioned it as his birthplace. Now he found he had a real hankering to visit the little town as a man of means. "If there are any deputy marshals in Oklahoma on the lookout for two bank robbers, they'll most likely look for them to come straight down from here on the Chisholm Trail into Oklahoma. I don't think they'd expect us to head straight east from Wichita till we strike the MKT railroad, then follow that south through Oklahoma. Where we're headin' in Texas, it won't make much difference in distance, 'cause if we went straight south from here, we'd have to ride east to strike the MKT after we got to Texas." He waited for Casey's thoughts on that.

Casey shrugged. "I don't really care one way or the other. I ain't familiar with Kansas east of here, so I couldn't say for sure. Seems to me, we oughta be able to ride a little southeast from here, instead of straight east, and maybe cut some of the distance down to hit the railroad." He shrugged again and said, "We'd just follow the railroad south wherever we strike it. From what you tell me, it's gonna take us about seven or eight days to get to Nacog-doches, whatever way we go. So we'd better see what we've got in the line of supplies."

"We oughta be in good shape," Eli said. "We ain't stayed out overnight but a few times since we bought supplies from Jim Lawrence."

"What are you two talkin' about?" Marge Joyner interrupted. "Looks like it's some-thing important."

"We were just talkin' about how disap-

145

pointed you're gonna be when we leave here tomorrow mornin', right after breakfast." He paused to ask Casey. "After breakfast, right?" Casey nodded his agreement. "Right after breakfast," Eli went on. "And it ain't no tellin' when you'll see two fine gentlemen like us again."

"You're leaving?" Marge responded. "You're checking out of the hotel? Where are you going?"

"We are checkin' out," Eli said. "And we don't know where we're goin' yet. We're just gonna follow the river north to see where it leads us." He told her north, because he was thinking it a good idea not to leave town heading east. He glanced at Casey, who nodded in response. They didn't want to risk leading someone to the ridge where their money was deposited. "So you've got the rest of this day and tomorrow's breakfast to do your best to make us want to come back."

"Y'all come back now, you hear?" she drawled deadpan. "How's that? It make you wanna come back?"

"Be still, my beatin' heart," he said sarcastically. "We might leave before breakfast in the mornin'."

"You want some more coffee?" she asked.

"Or is a gallon enough for you this morning?"

"I reckon we'd better drag ourselves outta here while we can still walk," Casey said. "Was there any charge for that breakfast?"

"Ha!" she reacted to his joke. "I oughta charge you double to pay for all that coffee you two drank." She walked with them to the front desk, where they stopped to pay Ted Potter with cash. She remained there after they walked out. "They said they're leavin' tomorrow," she told Ted. "I'm gonna miss seein' them come in."

"Did they say where they were going?" Ted asked.

"Just said they were gonna follow the river north of here," she said.

"I don't think they want to admit it," Ted told her, "but I think they're just running outta money. They got hit pretty hard on that bank holdup. I don't think I'll charge them for breakfast in the morning."

When they left the dining room, the two outlaws walked to the stable to check on their horses and make sure they had all the supplies they needed. When they walked in, they found Paul Johnson in a conversation with the deputy Wyatt Earp. They all exchanged good-morning greetings, and Paul

147

and Earp halted their conversation while Paul paused to see what Casey and Eli wanted.

"Don't let us interrupt you," Casey said. "We'll be leavin' in the mornin' and we just wanted to make sure our horses wanted to go with us."

"Oh," Paul said. "Well, I hope you fellows will be back this way again before too long."

"Thank you," Casey said. "We appreciate the way you took care of our horses. You can be sure we'll stop in if we're out this way again."

Earp spoke up then. "I never got a chance to talk to you gentlemen," he offered. "I'm sorry you had the misfortune you did when you visited our town. I'm sorry we had to come back empty-handed. I still don't understand how those two old buzzards gave us the slip."

Casey looked him in the eye. A big man, Wyatt Earp stood fully six feet tall, and from all reports, he could handle himself in a fist-fight or gunfight. "We'll tell you what we told Marshal Meagher. We don't lay any blame on you for that bank holdup. The circumstances were just not in our favor. It was bad luck, that's all." Casey smiled and said, "Sometimes those old buzzards come up with new tricks, I reckon."

"I have to admire your attitude," Earp said. "Like Paul said, come back to see us." Casey nodded, and he and Eli went to see about their horses.

They looked through their packs and determined that they had supplies enough to camp for five or six days if they bought some bacon. They spent a little time with the horses before determining that everything was ready to go. Then they told Paul they weren't leaving until after breakfast, so he needn't worry about an early departure. They shook hands with Wyatt Earp and headed back to the hotel. They told Dan Hicks that they would be checking out after breakfast in the morning and suffered through another display of compassion for their loss in the bank holdup. He did not offer to refund any of the room rent they had paid in advance when they had first checked in. They figured the hotel must have had money in the bank.

"It's too bad we paid for a week in advance," Eli remarked after they left Dan, and went upstairs to their rooms. "He might not have charged us for our rooms."

"At least he gave us the weekly rate," Casey allowed.

The rest of the day went by pretty slowly, and by suppertime, they were questioning their decision to wait until the next morning before leaving. "We coulda been a helluva long way down the road by now," Eli bemoaned. After supper, they went to the Friendly Saloon for a drink and conversation with Jay Donavan, who complained that his business was the only one in town that would not prosper if they located their Quaker colony near Wichita.

"I wouldn't be so sure of that," Casey told him. "Those Quakers are real thrifty folks. They're liable to drive the merchants in town so crazy, they'll all be drinkin' more likker."

The next morning, they were at the dining room when Ted opened the door. Since they were the only customers to arrive that early, they were waited on by both Marge and Polly, causing Eli to comment, "Well, now, this is the kind of service I expected to have every time we came in here. It's more like what me and Casey are used to."

"We're just in a hurry to get you two outta here as soon as we can," Marge said, in true form. It was followed by a sweet explanation from Polly that Marge didn't really mean that. Ted allowed them to park their rifles and saddlebags behind his desk, since they had already checked out of their rooms, and they hadn't picked up their horses yet. The saddlebags were carrying a total of six thousand dollars, divided equally between them, that being the amount they had taken out of the bank sacks before burying them.

They did not linger long over their breakfast and insisted on paying for it when Ted offered it free of charge. Then Eli counted out nine dollars and divided it into three piles, one for each of the girls, and one for Mamie, the cook.

"Now I'll say it," Marge said, impressed by his generosity. "Y'all come back, you hear?"

When they arrived at the stable, they found that Paul had saddled their horses. "You'd best check your cinches to see if they're like you like 'em," he said. "And I left your packhorse for you to load."

" 'Preciate it, Paul," Casey said. "We'll be out of your way in a minute or two. How much do we owe you?"

"Nary a cent," Paul said. "Didn't they tell you when you checked into the hotel that it wouldn't cost you anything to keep your horses here?"

"They told us, you'd give us a reduced rate, and that the hotel would pay part of our bill, not all of it," Eli said. Paul started to protest, but Eli cut him off. "We're good for it. We didn't put every penny of ours in the bank. Next time we're in town, we'll have somethin' to talk about, when we see how you folks came back from that robbery." He looked over at Casey then and said, "We'd best get started, Elmer. If we wait around much longer, we might be makin' our first night's camp in the city limits of Wichita."

Casey stared at him, but didn't answer for a moment. Then he said, "I reckon we better," and offered his hand to Paul, who shook it, then offered his to Eli. "We'll take the north road out of town," Casey said as he climbed up into the saddle and led the packhorse out, a faint smile on his face when he thought about their escape after robbing the mail car on the train in Abilene. After he was away from the stable, he reined Smoke back a little to let Eli catch up with him. "This time, we really are takin' the north road outta town," he said when Eli came up beside him.

"I caught that," Eli said. "I knew you was japin' about the train job."

"Yeah, I knew you were sharp enough to catch it. I oughta tell you, though, my name ain't Elmer."

Eli looked at him, totally puzzled by the comment. "Well, who said it was?" he responded before it suddenly struck him. "Oh, Lordy! I didn't call you . . ." He hesitated as he tried to think back. "I did call you that!" He automatically turned in the saddle to look behind them, expecting to see someone chasing them. "I swear, that slipped outta my mouth without me even knowin' it. Why would I do that?"

"I don't know," Casey said. "Sounds like a good reason to keep your mouth shut, though. Don't it?"

"You reckon Paul caught it?" Eli worried.

"I don't know, maybe not, but we ain't outta rifle range yet," Casey said. "Maybe he's like you, and he don't turn his brain on all the time. Either that, or maybe John Sinclair ain't told everybody about Oscar and Elmer."

"That's gotta be it," Eli said. "He was so scared, he most likely didn't remember what we called each other."

Behind them, Paul stood at the corner of the corral, watching them until they disappeared on the road that led north out of town. *Two pretty fine fellows,* he thought. *Wonder what he called him? Sounded like Elmer or something similar to that.* "My hearin' is gettin' where it ain't worth a nickel."

CHAPTER 9

When they felt sure they were well out of sight from anyone in town, they left the road and rode in an eastern direction, planning to take a wide circle around Wichita. Riding across mostly wild prairie, they knew, they would eventually strike the road that approached the town from the east. They knew they were near it when they saw the long ridge that ran parallel to the road. So, instead of continuing on to strike the road, they pointed their horses toward the point where the ridge first began to rise up. It was still there in the narrow rocky gully where he had left it. Casey dismounted and picked the shovel up out of the gully. "Well, it'll really be good if what we buried with this five-dollar shovel is still where we left it." Since he was now carrying the shovel, he handed the packhorse's reins to Eli, and they rode around the foot of the ridge to its back side. Since there were no trees on the low ridge, they had both taken a picture in their minds of the way the ridge sloped to form a small depression halfway to the top. They pulled the horses up short of the ridge and scanned it; after that, they compared their conclusions.

"Where do you think it is?" Eli asked.

Casey pointed to a spot on the side of the slope and said, "I think it's right yonder about halfway down where there's a shadow on that little dip. Where do you think it is?"

"I'm lookin' at the same spot," Eli said. "I hope that money is still all right, bein' buried in those canvas bags like they are."

"I don't know why it wouldn't be," Casey said. "We ain't had no rain. It's dry as can be, and it ain't been buried that long, anyway."

They climbed up to the spot they had both identified and were happy to find that the ground had not been disturbed. Casey went to work with his shovel and soon emptied out half of the dirt filling the hole. A little more digging found the first of the canvas bags, and Eli grabbed it and hauled it out, while Casey continued digging. In a few more seconds, he was pulling out the second bag. Then they opened them to find the stacks of bills in fine shape.

"I wonder how much we've got," Eli said.

"It sure looks like a lot, don't it? You wanna count it now, or wait till we make our first camp?"

"Let's wait," Casey said. "I'd rather be camped somewhere that ain't out in the open prairie, like this spot."

"You're probably right," Eli said. "We'll count it later. Let's get goin'."

"Gimme a couple of minutes," Casey said, and started shoveling the dirt back into the hole. "The least we can do is put it back the way we found it, since the ridge was kind enough to hide it for us."

"What the hell? Are you an Injun or somethin'? It's a pile of dirt!" Eli exclaimed. "We've fooled around so much already that's it's gonna be dark before you know it."

"I don't know. It just seems like the thing you oughta do is thank somebody or something for keepin' an eye on it. Besides, you ain't the one usin' the shovel, anyway."

"Whaddaya gonna do next, return the shovel to the fellow you stole it from?" Eli asked.

"I hadn't thought about that," Casey said, "but it would be the right thing to do, even though I bought it from him. I didn't steal it. It's a damn good shovel. It don't make no sense to just throw it away when there's a fellow who could use it."

"I swear, Casey," Eli said, shaking his head perplexed. "You sure ain't cut out to be an outlaw. You oughta be doin' missionary work somewhere." He paused while he thought about it, then added, "Maybe with the Quakers."

Casey finished filling the hole and smoothed the dirt out, and then they returned to the horses, each man carrying a sack of money, and Casey still carrying his shovel. When they wheeled the horses back toward the road, Casey turned in the saddle and yelled, "Thanks, Mr. Ridge!" It was just to aggravate Eli, and it worked.

A short distance down the road brought them to the creek where they had stopped before. Without asking or explaining, Eli pulled his horse to a stop. "Hurry up," he said, "and don't get caught."

Grinning like a naughty schoolboy, Casey slid down from the saddle and ran up the creek bank toward the half-finished barn. Luck was with him because there was no one working on the barn that afternoon. Had there been, he had planned to simply leave the shovel on the creek bank, somewhere it would be easily seen. But since there was no one to see him, he ran in the back door of the barn and returned the shovel to the exact location where he had found it. He left it leaning against the wall, next to the nail half-driven into it. Sitting on Biscuit, waiting for his truant outlaw partner, Eli continuously looked ahead and behind him, in case he had to ride the horses up into the trees. Finally, after what seemed a long time, he heard Casey running through the bushes beside the creek. As a precaution, Eli drew his .45 from his holster, then reminded himself, *I'm not breaking any laws.* So he put the gun away. Then he thought, *But I'm sitting here holding two sacks full of money stolen from the bank.* He drew his pistol again. Casey emerged from the bushes at that moment, chuckling to himself as though he had just gotten away with something big.

"Anybody chasin' you?" Eli questioned. When Casey said there was not, Eli said, "Get on your horse and let's get our butts away from here."

Although it was a late start, they were under way at last. It was already well into the afternoon, but they had ridden only about six miles from Robert Blunt's farm. So they rode on, still following the wagon road, since it continued to lead in the general direction they wanted to go. All three horses seemed in good shape, so they moved on until late afternoon, when they at last came to a wide creek.

"I'm glad to see that," Casey declared when they spotted the long straight line of trees that signaled a watercourse of some kind. "I was about to think we were gonna have to get off the horses and walk."

"I am, too," Eli remarked. "My belly thinks my throat's been cut." When they reached the creek, they found it to be a popular place to camp, as evidenced by the numerous old campfire ashes. They walked the horses downstream until they found a spot with grass and trees that had not been stripped of lower limbs by campers too lazy to walk far in search of dead branches. After unloading the horses, they turned them loose to water and graze while they gathered wood for a fire. "You wanna fix somethin' to eat first, or count the money first?" Eli asked, holding the coffeepot.

"I don't know," Casey said with a shrug. "We've waited this long. I reckon we could wait a little longer. Go ahead and fill the coffeepot. We might as well have some coffee while we're countin'." He changed his mind then and said, "If it don't make no difference to you, let's go ahead and fry up some bacon and hardtack first. I'm kinda hungry."

"Makes no difference to me," Eli said, and went to the creek to fill the coffeepot, while Casey took some bacon out of their packs to slice up and put in the pan. It proved to be a good decision, for the bacon was barely done when company arrived. The horses warned them first, so Eli got up from the fire and walked back along the creek until he could see the road. After a minute or so, he came back to the fire. "Two riders comin' up the road from the east," he said quietly. "Maybe they'll just cross the creek and keep on goin', but we'd best be ready for visitors."

"What did they look like to you?" Casey asked.

"Like every drifter you meet on the trail, I reckon, maybe cowhands, I don't know."

"We probably built too big a fire," Casey said. "But this close to dark, I didn't think anybody would notice. Maybe they won't. I expect we'd best get ready for 'em, though." He pulled the frying pan out of the flames and set it on a couple of limbs by the fire. Then he moved back away from the fire. "Throw that bag beside your saddle, like it was a pillow." He demonstrated with the other bag, folding the mouth under and propping it up against his saddle. Then he pulled his rifle out of the saddle and laid it beside him on the ground. Eli did the same, and they sat down to wait and listen.

They didn't wait long before they heard their horses acknowledging the strange horses and those horses answering. In a few seconds, they saw the two riders, walking their horses cautiously along the bank toward them. When they reached the small clearing where Casey and Eli had built their fire, they pulled up, looking right to left, from the horses by the creek to the two men sitting on the other side of the fire, watching them.

"How do?" one of the strangers asked, obviously the older of the two. "Name's Deke Dawson. This here's my boy, Lem. We was headin' to Wichita and seen smoke risin' back here. Thought we'd best make sure it weren't no wildfire fixin' to rear up."

"Howdy," Casey said. "Nope, no wildfire. Just a little fire to cook some bacon and hardtack, and to rest the horses. If you're hungry, we could spare some bacon. We ain't got much more'n that to offer. We drove a herd up from Texas and we didn't go back with the rest of the boys 'cause we wanted to celebrate a little. Made the mistake of visitin' Delano, across the river from Wichita. So, if you're headin' to Wichita, I'd advise you to stay on this side of the river."

"Thank you kindly for the offer," Deke said, "but me and Lem ain't hungry. We et some supper 'bout an hour ago. Where you boys headin'?" When Eli said they were going to Texas, Deke said, "You're goin' on a kinda roundabout way of gettin' there, ain'tcha?"

"Not really," Casey said. "We're goin' to East Texas, down near Nacogdoches."

"What's in them sacks you're a-layin' on?" Lem spoke up for the first time.

"What? Them?" Casey said as if he'd forgotten he was leaning on one. He was totally surprised that the rather dull-looking man guessed they were sacks right away. So he had to come up with some explanation. "That's where we carry clothes that need washin' and old clothes and old sheets and stuff like that you can use for bandages. They make a good pillow." He studied their faces and decided they didn't buy it. He glanced over at Eli and saw what the two strangers saw. Eli did not look very comfortable, lying back against the canvas sack that looked as if whatever was inside it was not soft or yielding. The thought ran through his mind that it might have been more believable had he said the sack was full of dry firewood.

"I reckon it ain't none of our business what's in them sacks, son," Deke said. "You fellers will have to excuse Lem. His ma died before she got a chance to teach him any manners. We'll be gittin' on our way, since there ain't no danger of a wildfire. Come on, Lem." He wheeled his horse and started back toward the road. Lem gave them one final look before following his father.

"I'm mighty glad we weren't in the middle of counting our money when they showed up," Eli commented when they left.

"We ain't through with that pair," Casey said, "not by a long shot. I wish we coulda hid those sacks, but we didn't have time before they got here. I can't believe either one of 'em has ever seen a bank sack like that before, so I don't think they'd even know what they were used for."

"But I think they know there's something in 'em that we didn't want 'em to see," Eli said. He picked up his rifle and ran up the creek bank after them to make sure they didn't circle around behind them.

Casey grabbed his rifle and picked out a spot at the edge of the clearing where he could fire from cover in case Eli suddenly came running back with Deke and son on his tail. After a while, he saw Eli walking back through the trees and brush. "When they got to the road, they turned west toward Wichita," Eli said as soon as he saw Casey. "I watched 'em till they rode outta sight."

Casey walked out to meet him. "We ain't done with those two," he repeated. "What we need to do is pack up and get outta here, but our horses ain't rested near enough. We're kinda in a tough spot. You could read it in their eyes when they were starin' at those bank sacks. We shoulda put that money in our packs when we dug it out of that ridge."

"Whaddaya think we oughta do?" Eli asked. "I don't know how tired their horses are, but ours ain't gonna go very far if we start out now, especially that packhorse."

Casey weighed the possibilities in his mind, then came up with the only suggestion he could think of. "One thing, for sure," he began, "this clearin' right here is too wide open. They can come at us from any direction. So we gotta move from here as quick as we can."

"What about our horses?" Eli objected. "They're just not ready to travel."

"I'm not talkin' about gettin' back on the road and startin' again," Casey explained. "I mean we oughta move our camp farther down this creek and set up a dummy camp to see how serious they are about seein' what's in those sacks. We're gonna have to do it fast before they decide to come back."

So, with Casey directing the action, they quickly saddled the horses, put out the fire, and packed up the frying pan and the coffeepot. Moving as fast as they could, they emptied the money out of the bank sacks and packed it on the sorrel. Then they led the horses downstream another fifty yards or so to another likely-looking camping spot. While Eli quickly built another fire, Casey collected enough dead branches to wrap a blanket around so that it was about the size of a body. He placed his dummies near the edge of the bushes that surrounded the camp. Eli took a look at Casey's handiwork and had to comment about them. "They ain't gonna fool nobody, even in the dark."

"They ain't supposed to," Casey said. "Come on, we ain't done yet." Taking Smoke by the reins, he led the way farther down the creek to yet another possible camping site. "This is the one that's gonna decide the issue," he said. "This will tell us if they want those sacks bad enough to kill for them." They repeated the camp setup the same as the one before, with Casey's fake bodies wrapped in their rain slickers substituting for their blankets. They finished just as the sun dropped below the horizon and darkness swept across the prairie. "Now we've got to find us a place to wait," Casey said.

About a mile up the road to Wichita, Deke and his son watched the sinking sun disappear as it dropped beneath the dusty road far ahead of them. "Let's go see what's in them bags," Lem said, but his father told him to wait to give the two men time to settle down for the night. Lem understood, but it was hard for him to be patient, he was so anxious to see what was in the sacks.

When Deke said it was time, they climbed on their horses and started back to the creek. Once they reached it, they dismounted, and Deke got down on his hands and knees where the two strangers would normally ride out of their camp to strike the road again. He struck a match and used it to search the ground for hoofprints that would tell him they had decided to move on down the road, and there were none. "They're still here," he said to Lem. So they led their horses into the dark stand of trees that lined the creek.

When they reached the clearing where

they had first found Casey and Eli, Lem exclaimed, disappointed, "They're gone! They lit out!"

"Keep your voice down!" Deke scolded. "They just moved their camp. Their horses are tired out. We'da seen tracks out by the road if they'd lit out. That's just what they want us to think. But all it tells me is that they're carryin' somethin' they're scared they're gonna lose. We'll leave our horses here. I don't want our horses talkin' to their horses, like they did before."

With their rifles in hand, father and son sneaked cautiously down the creek bank until they approached another small clearing. When they got close enough to see into the clearing through the bushes, they could see a fire dying out. Beyond it, closer to the trees on the other side of the clearing, they saw two forms on the ground that looked like bodies. Lem raised his rifle and cocked it.

"No!" his father commanded. "Don't pull that trigger! That ain't their camp!" He recognized the setup. "That's just what they want you to do. That's an old trick. You fire that rifle and it'ud rout them outta their blankets in a hurry." He looked all around him then and decided the stand of trees beside the creek was not wide enough to hide them. So he figured they were still farther down the creek. But now, it was a question of whether or not they might be lying in wait for him and Lem to come after them. "We ain't as dumb as they think we are," Deke said. "You keep that rifle cocked. We're gonna slip around that camp, real quietlike, you on one side, me on the other. If we're lucky, we might catch 'em layin' up in the bushes, sightin' in on that clearing. If we go all the way around it and don't find 'em, we'll meet on the other side and keep goin' till we do find 'em."

So they parted and moved cautiously around the clearing, like they would if stalking a deer. When they met on the other side of the campfire, Deke asked, "What'd I tell you? It was a setup. They was hopin' we'd shoot them dummies they left there and rout 'em outta wherever they're hidin', so they could shoot us." He looked at his son and smiled. "Now let's go wake 'em up." He pushed on through the bushes for another forty yards before stopping again and waiting for Lem to catch up. He motioned for him to be quiet, then pointed to a larger fire and two objects lying almost hidden at the edge of the bushes. "That's what you wanna shoot," he whispered. He squinted his eyes trying to focus on the two figures. "They're layin' on them canvas sacks."

"Can we shoot 'em now?" Lem asked anxiously.

"You take the one on the right," Deke said. "I'll take the other'n. Take dead aim and make sure you kill him. We'll both shoot at the same time. I'll count to three, all right?"

"Yes, sir, on three," Lem said excitedly, and aimed his rifle.

"One, two, three!" Deke counted, his voice lost in the eruption of rifle fire that ensued as he and Lem fired, cranked in another and another until the two unsuspecting objects were torn to shreds and left two ragged lumps.

"Hot damn!" Lem whooped as he ran across the clearing toward the fire, his pa right behind him. He was the first to stagger awkwardly when Casey's bullet struck his chest, and he collapsed, his momentum causing him to land in the fire. Deke tried to stop when Lem went down, but he did not avoid Eli's rifle shot.

"I swear," Casey uttered regretfully, after he took hold of Lem's boot and dragged the young man off the fire. "He don't look much older than Davey Springer."

"At least he never knew what hit him," Eli

said. "Before you start feelin' so dang sorrowful for shootin' that piece of dung, maybe you oughta remember how he tore that bundle of sticks up, thinkin' it was you."

"Yeah, I reckon you're right," Casey said. "It's just a waste of a young life, though. How 'bout his pa? Is he dead?"

"He's on the way," Eli said. "I hit him in the chest, but it wasn't in the heart like your shot."

Casey came over to take a look. There was no doubt, the man was dying, but his eyes flickered open and he tried to ask a question. Casey assumed he was asking about his son, so he leaned over closer to try to hear him. He could just barely make out his words. "It was worth a lot of money, weren't it?" Deke forced out painfully. "Them sacks, they was worth a lot, right?"

To give him some bit of satisfaction, Casey said, "They were bank bags. We robbed the bank in Wichita and stole two sacks full of money."

"I knew it," Deke gasped, coughing as he tried unsuccessfully to keep from choking on the blood that filled his throat. "I told Lem there was somethin' in those bags worth killin' for." He relaxed then, as if he had found justification for what he had attempted to do. He continued to stare lifelessly up at Casey for a long time till Casey realized he was dead.

"I reckon you're sorry now that you gave that shovel back," Eli joked. "We could ride back to that fellow's farm and ask to borrow it just one more time."

"I ain't inclined to bury either one of 'em," Casey declared. "Most likely, this might be the only chance those two have to do somethin' useful in their lives. They can feed the buzzards and the coyotes."

"Well, let's drag 'em back on the other side of the trees, away from the water," Eli said. "Then I reckon we'd best go see if we can find their horses. After that, I'm countin' that money before I go to sleep tonight."

After stripping them of weapons and ammunition, they ended up carrying them on their shoulders, since the bodies proved to be prone to snagging on every root and bush they passed. They weren't carrying them very far, so it wasn't worth the trouble to take some rope and hitch them up to a horse to drag them away from the camp. After the bodies were dumped beside a rotting tree that looked to have been struck by lightning, they walked back toward the road until they came to two horses tied to a tree. They led them back and took the saddles off, then turned them loose to join their horses. All the little chores done, Eli declared that before he went to bed that night, he was going to find out how much money they had stolen.

Casey revived the dying fire, while Eli got all the money out of the packs. They spread the bullet-riddled bank sacks on the ground beside the fire to count the money on. "Not too close," Eli warned. "After what we went through to get this money, I'd hate to see a little breeze kick up and blow some of it in the fire."

It took a little time because there were stacks of bills in different denominations. There were a lot of ones and fives, so they sorted them all out for counting. When it was all finished, they counted it again to make sure. The total came to $31,022, and when the $6,000 they carried in their saddlebags was added to that, it gave them a total of $37,022.

"That ain't a bad profit for a couple of days' work," Eli allowed.

"It ain't all profit," Casey said. "A thousand dollars of that was our money that we lost in that holdup. And we had to buy extra horses, and clothes."

"Right," Eli responded, and stared at Casey as if he was crazy. "We barely scraped by with a profit."

CHAPTER 10

Preparing to leave early the next morning, they talked about the two horses they had gained the night before. They were both sorrels in decent condition, too good to abandon. The topic of their discussion was not the horses, but rather the saddles. "I don't know if it's a good idea to trail those horses with saddles on 'em, when it's pretty dang obvious there ain't no fannies settin' in 'em," Eli said. "I don't know if there's any towns between here and the MKT railroad, or not. I doubt if there is, but with the amount of money we're carryin', I wouldn't want somebody to get to wonderin' what happened to the previous owners. I think maybe we should keep the horses, but leave the saddles here. They're in pretty sorry shape, anyway. Whaddaya think?"

"You're right about that," Casey agreed. "They're cheap saddles, to start with. We could use 'em to take some of the load off our packhorse, though. We ain't got nothin' to rig up packsaddles to put on 'em and he's carryin' a pretty good load. He could sure use some help."

"We could rotate 'em," Eli suggested. "Let those two spell our packhorse. Use all three. Tote the packs half a day, then get the rest of the day off to rest up. Whaddaya think? If we hit a town, maybe we can buy a packsaddle, or two packsaddles."

"That'll work," Casey said. "Let's leave the saddles here. Two empty saddles are liable to make folks wanna ask questions." So that's what they settled on and set out for Oklahoma Indian Territory and the MKT, not sure how far it would be, and relying on their natural sense of direction to stay on course. After their first stop to rest the horses, they tried the packsaddle on one of their newly confiscated horses. It was obvious the sorrel gelding was not comfortable with the strange contraption, but it did not buck or try to avoid it, even when the packs were loaded. From the way the horse acted, Casey guessed its former owner had been a cruel master, quick to punish if not obeyed. He gave the horse a few minutes of gentle affection before tying it on a lead rope.

They started out again, traveling only about four or five miles before coming to a rolling, hilly terrain of tall grass with scarcely a tree in sight. Ahead on the path they chose to follow were high, rolling hills of grass higher than their knees. It was not at all like the western part of Kansas they knew as cattle drovers. There was concern at first glance for the availability of water for the horses. But while the soil seemed rocky and unsuitable for farming, the grass was green and lush on the hills for as far as they could see. Keep going, they decided, for the grass was getting water from somewhere. To reassure them, a couple of little streams crossed their path as they followed a narrow canyon that led in the direction they favored.

After another half day found them leaving the high grass hills and still holding to the east-southeast course they had chosen, they came to a well-traveled road. It was heading in a more east-west direction and showed tracks of horses and wagon wheels.

"Damned if I wasn't convinced that me and you were the only livin' people this side of Wichita," Eli felt inspired to comment. "I wonder where this road goes."

"I wonder if it leads to someplace where a woman cooks food," Casey said. "I've about satisfied my needs for bacon and hardtack. I was wishin' we'd talked Smiley into comin' with us."

"Whaddaya say we follow this road and see where it goes?" Eli suggested. "We sure as hell ain't on no time schedule, and we're probably lost, anyway. Maybe we can at least find out where we are."

"That suits me just fine," Casey responded, so they turned back toward the east and followed the road.

They were more than three hours on the road before they saw a small settlement near the bank of a river.

"I was beginnin' to wonder if this blame road led anywhere," Eli stated. "We might as well walk these horses right on down by that river." Not waiting for Casey's usual agreement, he pointed Biscuit in that direction and the bay needed no further encouragement. They relieved the horses of their saddles and packs and turned them loose on the grassy bank of the river.

Casey and Eli were both flat on their bellies drinking the river water between Biscuit and Smoke when they heard the voice behind them.

"You fellers look like you're mighty glad to see this river."

They both lifted their faces out of the water and turned to see who had spoken. When they saw a squarely built man with a bald head and a long drooping mustache, they both got to their feet. Both were relieved to see his only weapon was a fishing pole.

"You got that right, neighbor," Casey said cheerfully. "I declare, we didn't see you when we came down to the river. Did we mess up your fishin'?"

The fisherman laughed. "No, not at all. I was done fishin'." He turned and pointed to a big rock a dozen yards away. "I was settin' on that rock yonder when I heard your horses comin' down the bank. Sounded like you was needin' some water."

"Indeed, we were," Casey said. "We didn't find much west of here. What is the name of this river?"

"This is the Verdigris River," he said. "You boys just come through the Flint Hills?"

"Why, I don't know. We must have. Are they a big bunch of rollin' tall grass hills? We rode through some like that. We didn't find much water there."

"There's plenty of water up there, you just have to know where to look for it. Back, a long time ago, there used to be a lot of buffalo in the Flint Hills. They're gone now, but there's still a lot of elk and prairie chickens up there."

"Well, we didn't see any of either one," Eli commented. "Does this little town have

178

a name?"

The fisherman smiled. "This is Coffey-ville, Kansas," he proclaimed good-naturedly.

"I like the sound of that. I could use a cup of coffee. How far are we from Indian Territory?" Casey asked.

"One mile," he said, "thataway." And he pointed south. Casey thought he detected a slight tightening of the man's eyes, as if suddenly suspicious. "You fellers in a hurry to get to Injun Territory?"

Casey smiled. "We ain't in no particular hurry to get to Indian Territory, but we know we gotta go through it to get to Texas. And we are anxious to get back to Texas. My name's Casey Tubbs," he said. "And this is my partner, Eli Doolin. We drove a herd of cattle up to Wichita and we decided we'd ride across the eastern part of Kansas, since we're headed to the eastern part of Texas. Neither one of us has ever been to this part of Kansas, or East Oklahoma, either."

"Well, welcome to Coffeyville," he said. "My name's Tom Appleby. I've got a forge here, if you're needin' a blacksmith."

"Can't think of anything," Casey said. "We just got new shoes on the two we're ridin'. Come to think of it, though, it wouldn't be a bad idea to take a look at the two extra horses we kept when the rest of the remuda was sold in Wichita." Neither he nor Eli had looked to see what kind of shape their hooves were in.

"Let's take a look," Eli said. "We're gonna be here for the night, anyway." They walked over to the three sorrels at the edge of the river and Eli indicated the two they were concerned about. He wasn't surprised when they discovered Deke and Lem's horses both needed shoeing.

"If you boys are campin' here tonight, I can shoe those two horses for you before dark. There's a good place to camp behind my forge, if you want to. Nothin' but a wide pasture between my shop and the river. I've got a big pile of firewood back there and you can just help yourself to wood for a fire."

"That sounds to my likin'," Eli said. "Whaddaya say, Casey?"

"Fine by me," Casey said. He smiled at Appleby then and asked a question. " 'Coffeeville,' how'd they happen to name the town that? Do they grow coffee beans around here?"

"Nah," Appleby said with a chuckle. "Fellow by the name of Colonel James A. Coffey built a tradin' post for the Injuns here on the river. That's where the name came from. And that's all there was here till a few settlers came round, but it didn't really get to be a town till the railroad ran tracks through here. They needed to name it somethin', so Coffeyville seemed like the thing to call it."

"Speaking of coffee," Casey asked, "is there someplace here to get a cup of coffee with a good supper?"

"There sure is," Appleby responded. He turned and pointed toward the small cluster of buildings. "See that saloon there in the middle of the street? That's the Riverboat Saloon. It's the best place in town to eat. Wink Martin owns it and his wife, Betty, is the cook, and you can get a drink of likker afterward, if you want one. That's where I eat most of the time." He paused to watch them as they looked at each other to decide. "And if you make your camp behind my shop, you can see it from the Riverboat in case somebody starts nosin' around it. 'Course, you oughtn't not have to worry about that, since I'll be at the shop shoeing your horses while you're eatin' supper."

"Anyplace will be better than what we can cook for ourselves," Eli said. "Might as well try the Riverboat."

Casey was in agreement, so they moved the horses into town and made their camp behind the blacksmith shop. Appleby led the two extra horses into his shop, and since they were in town, Casey and Eli hobbled the other three, so they wouldn't wander from the riverbank. Of major concern were the two large flour sacks on their packsaddle, since there was only a little over a pound of flour covering a bag containing eighteen thousand dollars in large bills in the bottom of each sack. It was the reason they ate hardtack with their bacon, instead of biscuits. The balance of their fortune was stuffed into their saddlebags and their pockets. It was not the ideal way to transport that much money, but they had little choice. Consequently, when they arranged their saddles and packs on the ground, they were careful to lay them so that Appleby's shop would not block their view of the camp from the saloon. "It's kinda funny now, ain't it?" Eli asked.

"What is?" Casey asked.

"That tale we was tellin' those folks in Wichita about how we dressed up like cowhands to keep outlaws from thinkin' we might be carryin' a lot of money. Now we really do have to worry about it."

"We're probably worryin' about nothin'," Casey said. "As long as the blacksmith is right there in the shop, it ain't likely anybody would go pokin' around our camp."

"I expect you're right," Eli agreed, "but it's still kinda hard to forget about it."

"Hell," Casey concluded. "If somebody steals it, we ain't lost nothin'. It wasn't ever ours in the first place. Let's go get some supper." With a yell to Tom Appleby when they walked past his shop, Casey announced they were going across the street to eat.

"Howdy, gents," Wink Martin greeted them when they walked into the Riverboat Saloon. "Whaddaya gonna have?"

There were not many people in the saloon, but they saw a couple of men with supper plates before them on the table. "We're lookin' to get some supper before anything else," Casey told him. "The blacksmith across the street said this was the best place in town to eat."

"Yes, sir," Wink said. "I believe Tom Appleby is the best advertisement we've got. And we can sure fix you up with some supper. Set yourself down wherever you want and I'll tell my wife she's got a couple of hungry cowboys out here. You want some coffee with that?" They said that they did, so he went into the kitchen to tell his wife and came right back with the coffee. "Won't be but a minute," he said, and went back to tend the bar. It was the ever-popular beef stew, and it was brought by a young girl of perhaps ten or eleven years of age. She said she would be back with some biscuits.

"You reckon that's his wife that does the cookin'?" Eli asked when the girl left. When she returned with the biscuits, Eli said, "This stew tastes mighty good. Did you cook it?"

"No, sir," she said. "Mama does the cookin'."

"Well, you tell your ma a couple of hungry old men said it was mighty fine stew," Eli told her. She said she would tell her ma that and went back to the kitchen. "I'm glad we got that straightened out," he told Casey. "I didn't wanna think poorly of ol' Wink."

In a few minutes, the little girl came back into the saloon, carrying the coffeepot. She came directly to their table and filled their cups. Then she said, "Mama said, 'Thank you very much.' "

"Tell her she's welcome the same amount," Eli responded, and she gave him a smile.

"Hey, bring some of that coffee over here," a gruff voice called out from a table behind theirs. She immediately went to serve the two men who were eating supper when Eli and Casey came in the saloon.

"You're a smart-lookin' little girl," they could hear the man saying. "What's your name?"

The little girl spoke too softly for Casey and Eli to hear, but they heard the man when he repeated it. "Evelyn, huh? Well, Evelyn, like I said, you're a smart-lookin' little girl, but I bet you there's a lotta things your mama ain't told you about men. Set down here in my lap and I'll tell you a secret."

Again, Evelyn talked too softly for Eli and Casey to hear her response. But they could guess what it was when they heard the man say, "Your mama didn't mean that for every man. Come on, set down in my lap and I'll tell you a secret."

When they finally heard Evelyn, it was too much for Eli to ignore any longer.

"Let go my arm!" she cried out, clearly frightened.

Eli got up from his chair and walked back to the table to find the rough-looking man grinning maliciously at the terrified little girl as she struggled to pull her wrist from his hand. The other man at the table grinned as well, seeming to enjoy the girl's fright. When Eli stopped to stand over him, the bully growled up at him, "What the hell do you want?"

"I wanna sit in your lap," Eli said, and promptly sat down on him. "Now tell me a secret."

Stunned, the bully released Evelyn's hand and she immediately ran to her mother. With Eli sitting in his lap, the bully fought to get his hands on Eli's neck, while Eli continued a series of short jabs to the bully's nose. The struggle between them resulted in the chair going over backward onto the floor, with Eli on the bully's chest, hammering him with left-and-right-hand punches. Quick to come to his friend's rescue, the bully's companion stepped up behind Eli, holding a full bottle of whiskey. When he drew back to deliver the blow, however, his wrist was caught in Casey's steel-like grip and his arm was forced back until he screamed in pain when his shoulder went out of joint. That was as far as the brawl went before it was halted by the report of Wink Martin's shotgun into the ceiling.

"Now, by God, take your brawlin' outta my saloon, the lot of ya!" Wink railed, his blood boiling with rage. The bully started to protest, but Wink yelled at him, "Take your filthy mouth out in the street, or so help me, I'll blow your head off." When they were slow about moving, he cocked the other barrel of the shotgun. "Out!" he bellowed, and motioned toward the door with the shotgun.

Eli got up off the bully and Wink motioned with the shotgun again. "Out!" When it was obvious that he meant all four of them, Casey took Eli's arm and pulled him toward the door. The bully was in no condition to jump right up. Half-unconscious, he struggled to get to his feet. Blood was flowing freely from his nose and his jaw sagged unhinged. His companion tried to help him with his one good arm, while still grimacing with the pain from his dislocated shoulder. They were in no condition to continue the fight and they ignored Casey and Eli, who were standing ready in the street in case they needed to defend themselves.

When the two men managed to get on their horses and promptly rode out the far end of the street to the north, there were two sighs of relief from Casey and Eli. "I wish that coulda waited until I had a little bit more of that stew," Casey lamented, "or at least finished one cup of coffee."

"Yeah, me too," Eli said. "I'm sorry, partner. That was just too much for me when that slimy dog got hold of that little girl."

"Oh, don't apologize for what you did.

That was what needed to be done. I just ain't lookin' forward to eatin' bacon and hardtack after I got a taste of that stew."

"Me neither," Eli said with a chuckle. "I think I bruised my knuckles up good, too. I know you stepped in when that other one started to do somethin'. But I couldn't see what he had in mind. I was busy at the moment."

"He was gettin' ready to serve you a drink of likker without takin' it outta the bottle," Casey said. "At least ol' Wink didn't ask us to pay for the supper."

They walked back across the street to the blacksmith's shop to find Tom Appleby standing in front, looking toward the saloon. "I heard a shotgun," he said when they approached. "Who got shot?"

"I'm afraid we got into a tussle with a couple of fellows in there and it got a little outta hand," Casey said. "So Wink had to use his shotgun to get our attention."

"I saw them two fellers walk out after you did," Appleby said. "They looked like they got the worst part of the tussle." Neither Casey nor Eli seemed inclined to elaborate, so he informed them, "I got your two horses ready to go. You need to take a look at 'em while it's still light enough to see."

They followed him through the shop to

the woodpile out back where he had the two sorrels tied. They then inspected his work and expressed their complete satisfaction with the job and paid him for it.

"Good," he said, "I appreciate the business. I went fishin' this afternoon. Didn't catch any fish, but I caught a couple of horses to shoe." He chuckled at his humor, then said, "Now I'd best get across the street before Betty throws the scraps to the hogs. You fellows help yourself to the firewood."

They took the two sorrels over to graze with their other horses, then went back for firewood. "My belly is gonna think I'm playin' some awful tricks on it," Eli remarked, "teasin' it with some of that good beef stew, then fillin' it with old salty bacon." By the time they got their fire going strong, the darkness started settling in. "Tomorrow mornin', we'll head into the Nations, Indian Territory. Five and a half or six days, we oughta be in Texas."

"We got company," Casey interrupted, and they both became alert with hands on their weapons as two forms appeared out of the darkness.

"Don't shoot. It's me, Wink Martin, and my daughter, Evelyn."

They walked into the firelight then and

Casey and Eli could see that Wink was carrying a large tray, covered with a cloth, and Evelyn was carrying a plate in one hand, also covered with a cloth. In the other hand, she was carrying a coffeepot.

"Well, I'll be . . ." Casey started when he realized what they were doing. "Is that what I hope it is?"

"We brought you some supper 'cause yours was interrupted," Wink said. "I feel so bad about what happened back there. I wasn't payin' enough attention to what was goin' on, and when the fight started, I just flew off the handle. After I ran you-all out, Evelyn and her mama came and told me what started it. And I swear, I wish I had shot that fellow that grabbed my daughter. Then Tom Appleby came in to eat supper and said you two were fine fellows and didn't seem the type to start a fight. But anyway, Evelyn says you're her hero." He paused to ask her, "Which one, honey?" She pointed to Eli, and Wink continued. "She says you came and saved her, and I wanna thank you, sir, for that. I figured the least I can do is bring you the supper you didn't even get a chance to get started on."

Eli was speechless, so Casey stepped in. "That's just Eli doin' what he's best at, steppin' up to protect beautiful young ladies, Evelyn. His name's Eli Doolin, or 'Saint Eli,' if you druther." He looked back at Wink then and declared, "You can't imagine what a great reward this supper is. We were just fixin' to fry some ol' salty bacon. My name's Casey Tubbs and we thank you and your wife, and especially Evelyn. We'll certainly need to pay you for the two suppers."

"I wouldn't hear of it," Wink said. "We'd best get back now. We left Betty to mind the bar till I get back."

"Well, thank you again," Casey said. "We'll bring the dishes back after we eat and maybe have a drink to go to sleep on." He watched until they disappeared into the night, then turned and said, "Put that coffeepot on the fire."

"I like it," Eli said. "Saint Eli, it suits me."

CHAPTER 11

They left Coffeyville early the next morning, following the Verdigris River down into the Nations to strike the MKT railroad somewhere, hopefully near Muscogee, then proceed along the railroad to Texas. When they left, they felt they had made some friends in Coffeyville, should they ever return. When they had returned the Riverboat Saloon's dishes, they had received the thanks of Evelyn's mother and she had sent them back to their camp with a sack of biscuits for their breakfast in the morning. A couple of drinks before they retired to their campfire capped off the evening.

Choosing not to push their horses too hard, especially the sorrel whose turn it was to carry their packs, it took them almost three days to reach Muscogee, a distance of only about ninety miles. The biscuits that Betty Martin gave them were consumed on the first stop to rest the horses after leaving

Coffeyville. They inspired Eli to skim off a little of the flour they had put on top of their stolen money, in an effort to make something more edible than hardtack. The problem was, it wouldn't take but a couple more times before the edges of the bags holding the money could be seen, if you looked closely. It wasn't bad luck that caused the time it took to reach Muscogee, however. It was actually good fortune, for they saw their first wild game since leaving Wichita, after one day's travel down the Verdigris River. When they picked a spot to rest the horses after a half day's travel, they had startled four deer crossing the river. Equally as startled as the deer, both men grabbed their rifles and fired. Both aimed at the same deer, a young doe, who was a little behind the others. The doe was hit with only one bullet, a perfect shot, a lung shot, right behind her front leg. It was enough to create a debate as to whose bullet had actually killed the deer, with neither man willing to admit to a complete miss. The rest of that day was spent skinning and butchering it while fresh venison roasted over a fire. They ate their fill and wrapped some in the hide to roast the next day. The biggest part of the meat was staked out to smoke-cure to eat later.

The next morning, they wrapped their supply of smoked venison up in the deer hide and tied it on one of their sorrels, after a breakfast of fresh deer meat. Feeling like two fat ticks, they resumed their trip through the Cherokee Nation. They reached the little town of Muscogee late in the afternoon of the third day. Having never been there before, they were glad to see there was a large general merchandise store among the smaller shops. That was their first stop. They were greeted by an elderly white man who wore his hair Indian style with a headband.

"Evenin'," he said. "Somethin' I can help you fellows with?"

Casey was craning his neck to see what was in the store, and he said, "It looks like you've got some harnessin' and stuff back there. We're in need of a packsaddle. We're carryin' a pretty good load for one horse, and we're gonna need some more supplies."

"Yes, sir, I've got some packsaddles. I'll let you take a look at 'em, see if it's what you're lookin' for." He led them toward the back of the store.

As they started through the open doorway to his back room, Eli asked, "What's in the barrels?"

"That first one right there is dried apples,"

the store owner said. "The other two are molasses."

"I'm gonna need some of that," Eli said at once, "the dried apples, anyway."

Casey laughed. "I reckon so." They had reached their fill of hardtack and bacon.

"First time in Muscogee?" the owner asked when he handed Eli an army-style packsaddle, with two large metal hooks to hang things on.

"First time," Eli said, took one look at it, and then said, "This'll do." The one pack-saddle they already had was a crossbuck style, but either one would do the job.

"I've got some heavy bags made to hang on the packsaddles, too, if you need any of those. Where you boys headed?" He suspected they might be headed for a hideout somewhere west of there, maybe the Arbuckle Mountains or somewhere as remote.

"We're on our way back home to Texas," Casey said. "Started back from Wichita after we drove a herd of cattle up from Texas and we ain't ever come back this way before. So to keep from gettin' lost, we're gonna follow the MKT railroad right down to Texas."

The owner laughed. "I reckon that's a sensible idea. My name's Wayne Freeman. I 'preciate your business."

"Casey Tubbs," he returned, "and that's

195

my partner, Eli Doolin. We're gonna need some flour and some lard and some salt and sugar. What kinda horse feed you got?"

"I've got plain oats and I've got some mixed grain," Freeman said.

"How's it come?" Casey asked.

"Fifty-pound bags, but I'll weigh out however many pounds you want."

"I think we'll take one hundred pounds of the mixed grains," Casey decided. "We've got five horses that ain't had no grain in a while. And we'll need a couple of those bags that hang on the packsaddle." He looked at Eli then and asked, "Two packhorses and one spare, that oughta take care of us, don't you think?"

Eli nodded and said, "That, and ten pounds of them apples."

With their supplies taken care of, they moved back into the front part of the store, where they each bought a rain slicker. "We both lost ours in a thunderstorm up in Kansas," Casey said in explanation. "Oh, I almost forgot, a bucket, like that little one over there on the shelf."

When that seemed to be the final item, Freeman added up the bill and watched with interest as the two men figured out what half of it would be, then promptly pulled a roll of bills from their pockets and laid that much money down. "Thank you very much, gentlemen. Are you gonna be in town for a spell, or are you ridin' right through?"

"I reckon we'll just be passin' through," Casey said. "We'd think about buyin' some supper somewhere, but we've got some deer meat out there that'll likely start to turn if we don't cook it pretty soon."

"Thanks again," Freeman said, and picked up a couple of the items just purchased and carried them out to the horses. "That horse is loaded down pretty good," he said. "You weren't lyin' about that."

They were not especially careful about loading their purchases because they planned to set up camp as soon as they found a suitable place. He stood there in front of his store and watched them as they rode out of town, following the road beside the railroad.

"Good order," he muttered to himself, and turned to go back inside. When he went in the door, he found his wife waiting for him.

"Who were those men?" Lark, his Cherokee wife, asked. "I never see them here before."

"Just a couple more outlaws runnin' to the Nations to hide out," he said. They were friendly enough, he allowed. "But they didn't care how much anything costs. They had plenty of money to pay for what they bought." He chuckled then when he remembered. "They bought a hundred pounds of grain for their horses. They'll be lucky if the horses don't blow up."

The two outlaws rode only as far as the first good-sized creek they came to after they left the town. They turned off the road and followed the creek until well out of sight of the road. When they found a spot they liked, they unloaded the horses and let them go to the water. Then they cut open both sacks of grain, and while Eli gathered wood for a fire, Casey used the new bucket to feed each horse a portion of grain. When that was done, he opened the flour bags and dumped the flour that was covering their money on the ground, making no attempt to salvage any of it. Once his fire was going strong, Eli came to help empty the fifty-pound bags of grain onto their new rain slickers spread on the ground. They left a bed of grain in the bottom of each bag for the money sack to rest on. Then they filled all around the sack when they poured the rest of the grain back in. Once the bags were filled, Casey tested them by plunging his hand down into the grain. They repeated the test several times and were satisfied when they couldn't reach the top flap of the sack holding the money. To save a little time in the morning, they brought one of the sorrels up to fit the new packsaddle on him. They decided the grain bags and their smoked deer meat was enough load for one horse. With their grain bags the guardians of their wealth, looking innocent and uninteresting, they turned their attention to the feeding of themselves. And to celebrate their successful finding of the MKT at Muscogee, just as they had planned, Eli opened some of the new flour and tried his hand at some fried apple pies. Casey made the coffee, a chore he felt he had a much better chance of success with than Eli had with the pies.

Always alert when they went to their blankets at night — since they became wealthy men — they slept peacefully all night, with nothing to disturb them but the noises of the creek and the insects that dwelled there. They awoke early the next morning and saddled their horses. Then they selected the sorrel for the honor of carrying their money on this first day with two packsaddles. All packed up, they put out their fire and returned to the road to follow the railroad south.

They reached the town of McAlester at noon the next day, knowing the town only by its reputation. Neither Casey nor Eli had ever been to McAlester, but they had heard of it by its original name of Perryville. It was called that because it had started out as a trading post owned by a fellow named Perry. During the Civil War, Perryville was the site of a Confederate munitions depot that was destroyed by Union forces. And after the soldiers destroyed the depot, they burned down the whole town to discourage the rebuilding of it. Afterward, a fellow by the name of J. J. McAlester built another store close to the railroad and that's where the name of the new town came from.

The two outlaws were surprised to see the town thriving so well. They decided they were due a nice dinner at a decent restaurant and figured their best bet was the hotel. And there was one right next to the railroad station.

"That looks like a suitable place for gentlemen such as ourselves to dine," Eli declared. They tied their horses to the long hitching rail out front and went inside.

The outside entrance took them to a hallway, and another door on the right had a sign over it, identifying it as DINING ROOM. A long hallway led off in the other direction to the hotel. They went in the dining-room door, where a man dressed like a preacher confronted them. He took a hard look at the two dusty trail riders, each one wearing a pistol and holding a rifle, before he spoke. "Good evening, gentlemen," he said after a pause. "I assume this is your first visit with us. Otherwise, you would know you are not permitted to carry your weapons into the dining room."

"We figured that might be the rule," Casey couldn't help responding. "So you don't have to worry. I'm holdin' his rifle and his pistol, and he's holdin' mine."

The man was not amused and said with a tired smile for Casey's humor, "I think it would be even better if I put your weapons on the table behind me, and you can pick them up when you leave. I might also suggest there's a washroom right down that hallway, if you would like to freshen up a little before dining."

They were both unbuckling their gun belts when he made the suggestion. Eli immediately started to make a countersuggestion, but Casey interrupted. "I think that's a fine idea. I would like to wash a little trail dust offa me. Wouldn't you, Eli?" He handed the man his weapons. "Right down this hall, right?"

"That's right," he said, relieved when Casey prevented what might have been an ugly scene. "Your firearms will be safe here, and I'll ready a table for you when you get back."

"If you hadn't cut me off, I was fixin' to tell that slick smart aleck where to put his suggestions," Eli remarked as they walked down the hallway.

Casey laughed. "I know you were, but I wanna eat in this fancy dinin' room. Besides, my face and hands could use a little washin'."

Both of them took advantage of the soap and water provided in the washroom and both admitted feeling a little less grimy when they returned to find the man at the door waiting for them.

"Right this way, gentlemen," he said, and led them past a half-empty dining room, through a door to a small room, where there was one long table set with knives, forks, and spoons for two places. "Have a seat and Patsy will be right with you." He turned and left immediately before there was time for any objections.

Casey and Eli didn't say anything for a long moment. They just looked at each other, then both of them suddenly roared with laughter. "You can't get no more special treatment than this," Casey said after another moment, "our own private dinin' room."

"I'm surprised there ain't no trough to feed us," Eli said.

They sat down on the benches on either side of the table, and in a few minutes, a woman came in the room. She was a husky woman with long blond hair, pulled back into a ponytail, hard to tell how old she was, but she wasn't young, and she wasn't old.

"I reckon you're Patsy," Casey said. "Do you take care of all the folks not fit for the dinin' room, or is this just your unlucky night?"

"Why, hell no," Patsy said. "As soon as I saw you two come in the door, I said, 'Let me have those two.' Now whatcha wanna drink with your supper?"

"Coffee," they said simultaneously.

"Don't you cowboys ever drink anything but coffee?"

"I didn't know there was anything else," Eli said.

"Two coffees," Patsy said. "Did you look at the menu board when you walked through the big room? It tells you what you can order tonight." When they said they hadn't seen it, and didn't know to look for one, she said, "That's all right. I'll call 'em off." She started reciting then, "Roast beef, pork chops —"

"Stop right there," Casey interrupted. "I'd like some pork chops."

"Me too," Eli said. "We don't get a chance for pork chops very often."

"Do you wanna know what comes with it?" Patsy asked.

"I don't care," Eli said. "Long as it's hot and ain't wiggling around on the plate, I'll eat it."

She couldn't suppress a grin. "All right, I'll get you your coffee." She left and was back in a few seconds with two steaming hot cups. "Here you go," she said, "cowboy coffee. I stirred it with a branding iron, so it oughta be good."

"Depends on the brand," Casey said, picked up his cup, and took a sip. "Pretty good, could be a little stronger, but it ain't had a chance to grow up yet. Maybe by the second cup, it'll age a little bit." She shook her head and chuckled as she left the room.

It wasn't long before she returned with two heaping plates to place before them on the table. "That smells good enough to eat," Eli said as he attacked one of the two chops on his plate with his knife and fork. He looked up at her and grinned. "You thought I was gonna eat it with my hands, didn't you?"

She laughed outright. "I wouldn't have been surprised," she said. "I hope you enjoy it. I'll go get you some more coffee."

The food was good, and when they cleaned their plates, Patsy insisted that they should try a piece of real apple pie. They swore there was no room left inside for even a bite, but they finished it off with no problem.

"That was a helluva big slice of pie," Eli said. "You ain't gonna make much profit if you serve slices that big."

"Tell you the truth," she confessed, "I cut those slices when nobody in the kitchen was watchin'. I didn't want you boys to go away from here hungry."

"Well, you did the job," Casey told her. While she and Eli had been joking around with each other, he had been looking around the room while he sat finishing the last of his coffee. It occurred to him that this room was where the hired hands ate their meals. He chuckled to himself, thinking he'd best not tell Eli until after they left the hotel. When they were finally finished, he asked, "Do we pay you?"

"No," she said. "You pay Harold on your way out, if you want your guns back." She chuckled and said, "It was a pleasure servin' you boys."

When they got up from the table, Casey reached in his pocket and pulled out a roll of bills. He peeled off a ten-dollar bill and laid it on the table in front of her.

"No," she said, "you pay Harold out front."

"We will," Casey said. "That's for you, for takin' such good care of us."

She was shocked. "Ten dollars!" she exclaimed, hardly believing it was real.

"Me and Casey are partners," Eli said. "We split everything fifty-fifty. Here's the rest of it." He placed a ten-dollar bill on top of the one Casey put down. Unable to believe her good fortune, she sat down hard on the bench, for once in her life speechless.

The two outlaws walked through the dining room, and when they reached the front desk, Eli asked, "How much will it cost us to buy our guns back, Harold?"

Obviously displeased to have Eli call him by his name, Harold asked, "Did you have dessert?"

"We had pie," Eli said.

"Then three dollars and fifty cents each," Harold said, and turned to retrieve their weapons. When he turned back around, he saw seven dollars on his desk. He handed them the guns, one by one, as if afraid one might go off unexpectedly.

"Eatin's kind of expensive here," Casey commented. "But the food was good, and that Patsy is the best server I've ever had waitin' on me."

He and Eli walked out the door, just moments before Patsy recovered enough to come out into the dining room, holding her money in the air so the other servers and the customers could see it.

"I didn't even think to thank them," she exclaimed to Grace, the server closest to her.

"My stars!" Grace blurted. "Those two cowboys gave you two dollars? What did you do in that room?"

"Two dollars, hell," Patsy came back, and stuck the two bills up in front of Grace's face.

"Twenty dollars!" Grace shrieked. "Are they stayin' in the hotel?"

Outside the hotel, both partners were groaning over the amount of food they had just consumed. "I can't believe I got that slice of pie down," Eli said. "I ain't gonna need to eat for two days." He chuckled then and commented, "That ol' gal was tickled to get that money, weren't she? That's pretty doggone foolish to hand out money like that, ain't it?"

"Where's the fun of havin' a lot of money if you don't spend it like a fool sometimes?" Casey asked. "It was worth twenty dollars to see the expression on her face."

"Yeah, it was," Eli agreed as he stepped up on Biscuit. "Now I reckon these horses would appreciate it if we take 'em somewhere and take the load off of 'em."

Chapter 12

When they left their camp just outside of McAlester, they figured it was no more than two days to Denison, Texas, which was just across the Red River. There was another town about halfway to Denison, called Atoka. They decided it made sense to camp overnight in Atoka, depending on how early they got there. It was an uneventful ride, boring in fact, for they were simply following the railroad in a straight line into the Choctaw Nation. They ate smoked venison for breakfast and dinner; so when suppertime rolled around and they were approaching the town limits of Atoka, they were inclined again to look for a likely place to get a good meal. But this time, the hankering for a real fancy supper was no longer appealing. When they rode the length of the main street, they saw only one place that looked a likely winner, a small business next to a boardinghouse. It was called Lottie's Kitchen. Just as they had done in Mc-Alester, they tied their horses outside, planning to eat first, then make their camp for the night.

"Good evening, gentlemen," Lottie Mabre greeted them at the door. "Are you looking for some supper?"

"Yes, ma'am," Casey said, "if you don't mind feedin' old stray saddle tramps like us."

She smiled and said, "We'd be happy to feed you, and since you're new here, I'll ask you to please leave your firearms on the table over there. You'll be more comfortable without them, and so will everybody else in the dining room."

"Since you asked so nicely, we'd be glad to," Casey said, and he and Eli unbuckled their gun belts and walked over to deposit them on the table. "I see the sign on the table now. I'm sorry I didn't notice it before."

"Thank you, sir," Lottie said. "Just sit at any table you like, and Lou-Bell will be taking care of you. I hope you'll enjoy your supper."

There was one long community table in the center of the room, but they sat down at a small table by the window, where they could keep an eye on their horses. "That's more like it, ain't it?" Eli commented. "She's a little more friendly than ol' Harold was, back at the Railroad Hotel."

Casey was about to answer, but was interrupted when the waitress appeared.

"Blue Bell," Eli said. "With a name like that, I was expectin' to see an Indian gal."

She laughed, then corrected him. "It's Lou-Bell, my name is Louise Bellone, but my friends call me Lou-Bell. You fellows want coffee?"

"We do," Eli said quickly. "Is it all right if we call you Lou-Bell?"

"We'll have to see if you behave yourself while you're in here," she teased.

"Fair enough. We'll be on our best behavior. Right, Casey?"

Casey grinned and nodded.

"What's for supper?" Eli asked then.

"Beef stew, or sliced ham, you get your choice," Lou-Bell said. They both said they'd try the stew. "I'll be back in a minute," she said. She was as good as her word, for she returned right away with their coffee, went back in the kitchen, then returned with two plates of stew and some hot biscuits. "I'll check on you after you've had a chance to try it," she said, then left to check on another table.

"This is more to my likin'," Eli remarked

as he loaded a fork with stew. When Casey didn't respond, he looked up to see that something outside had captured his partner's attention. "Somethin' catch your eye out there?"

Casey continued to look out the window when he said, "Couple of fellows seem mighty interested in our horses."

That caught Eli's interest at once. He stared out the window as well, prepared to get to his feet if it was necessary. But the two men turned away from their horses and came toward the dining-room door. Eli turned his chair slightly at an angle, so he could better watch the door. "Just a couple of curious fellows, I reckon," Casey said.

In a few seconds' time, the two men came in the door and paused just inside to look the room over. There weren't that many customers in the dining room at that time, so it didn't take long for the two men to focus on them. They seemed to capture their gaze immediately, for they said a few words hurriedly, then took off their gun belts before Lottie came to greet them. That action was encouraging to Casey and Eli. After Lottie greeted them, they chose to seat themselves at the end of the long table in the middle of the room.

"No, thank you, ma'am," Casey declined

when Lou-Bell asked if he wanted more biscuits or more coffee. "I can't hold another thing," he pleaded. "Eli's gonna have to help me get on my horse, already. I didn't know I could eat that much." He forced himself out of the chair, knowing the horses had to be taken care of and a camp set up.

Lottie came over to join them as they were preparing to leave. "Ladies," Casey pronounced grandly as he pulled some money out to pay Lottie, "you get my vote as the best dinin' room in the entire Indian Territory."

"Amen," Eli added, "and the service was outstandin'."

"Are you gonna be here for a while?" Lottie asked.

"No, ma'am," Casey said. "We're on our way back to Texas. We'll be movin' on at first light in the mornin'."

"That's too bad," Lou-Bell said. "We enjoyed havin' you. Well, don't forget to stop in, if you're back this way again." With that, she turned her attention to the other customers she was serving.

They rode out the south end of the street, continuing to follow the railroad tracks, which would ultimately lead them to the Red River and Texas. Their ride on this night, however, would be no longer than it took to come to the first decent place to camp. And that came less than a mile out of town, where the railroad tracks crossed over a wide creek with no name. The creek seemed to be heavily wooded in spots as it snaked away from the road.

"It's as good as any," Eli judged, and Casey agreed. So they guided their horses under the narrow bridge, and followed the creek away from the road for about a quarter of a mile before finding the spot that suited them. Without a word between them, they went through a routine that was second nature to them now and required no questions or suggestions. First responsibility was always the horses. After that, they saw to their own comfort. On this night, however, after the horses were watered and fed, there was more to talk about.

"Whaddaya think about those two fellows back at the dinin' room?" Casey asked. "Did you get the feelin' they were more interested in us than they oughta been?"

"Yeah, I got that feelin'," Eli said, "and I hope I'm wrong, but I wouldn't be surprised if they were the type that likes to make late calls on folks."

"You think we oughta get a couple of camps set up again, like we did with those two maniacs back in Kansas?" Casey asked.

"I don't know," Eli said, "and go buy another new rain slicker? Damned if I ain't tired of that already. I'd just as soon lose a little sleep tonight, set up and wait for them to find us, and shoot 'em down when they first come sneakin' around our camp. Be done with it, then sleep some in the mornin' if we've a mind to."

That seemed a little fierce coming from Eli, but Casey had to agree that, no matter how they went about defending themselves, it was going to end up with somebody getting killed. They had to assume that if someone planned to surprise them in the middle of the night, they had no intention of leaving them alive to possibly come after them. "I reckon you're right," he finally agreed. "And we might as well get ready for 'em this time. Take care of business when we're ready, instead of waitin' for them to take the first shots."

At approximately the same time Casey and Eli were thinking about defensive positions from which to protect their camp, the men who had aroused their suspicions were finishing a leisurely supper at Lottie's Kitchen.

"Looks like they do a nice little business here," Jake Queen remarked to his partner,

Butch Peters. "And I can see why. That was damn good stew."

"It sure was," Butch said with a chuckle. "And we almost passed it up." They both chuckled then.

"You was the one who got spooked when we saw them horses tied out front," Jake reminded him. "Hell, I hadn't even thought about it till you started up about 'em." That was true, but Jake had to admit that it struck home with him as soon as Butch had questioned it. It was well known in Indian Territory that a fine horse, wearing a good saddle, was often the sign of a U.S. deputy marshal. And the two horses wearing the saddles in that gang of five sure looked to fit the bill. They weren't sure they weren't about to go in the dining room to dine with two deputy marshals. They were happy now that they had decided to go on inside and eat supper. Once they were seated at the table, they could see no sign of badges on the two men sitting at a table by the window. As further encouragement, the men had left their guns at the table, knowing that rule usually didn't apply to law enforcement. They almost laughed outright when the two men they had been watching so carefully got up and left the dining room, got on their horses and rode away.

"I reckon I'm about ready to go, too," Butch declared. "Are you done?"

"Yeah, I reckon," Jake said. "I thought about maybe one more cup of that coffee, but I'm liable to bust if I do."

They got up and walked to the front of the dining room to retrieve their weapons from the table. Lottie saw them and went to the desk to meet them. "How was your supper, gentlemen?" she inquired.

"It was the best supper we've had tonight," Jake said, and chuckled in appreciation of his clever remark.

"I'm glad you enjoyed it," Lottie said as she opened her cash drawer. "That'll be seventy-five cents each."

Jake buckled his gun belt on and pulled off a cloth sack that had been wrapped around the belt. Holding the sack out toward her, he drew his pistol, cocked it, and aimed it at her face. "Now, little missy, you just empty that cash drawer into the bag, and don't be shy about them dollar bills in the corner there."

Butch pulled out a cloth sack as well and drew his weapon.

Speaking loudly to the shocked patrons in the room, Jake said, "My partner will pass among you now to accept your donations. Nothin' to worry about. It'll be just like you

217

do in church, only tonight you'll give everything you've got on you. If you don't, your sin will be punished much quicker than you want."

Back to the stunned Lottie, he said, "Lady, if you don't empty that drawer right now, I'll shoot you down and empty it myself." Frightened enough to move then, Lottie emptied the money into the bag. "You're showin' some sense now," Jake said. "Now we're gonna go in the back room there and open that safe." He wasn't sure there was one, but he felt sure she kept her money somewhere in the building.

"I don't have a safe," she responded fearfully.

He gave her a sharp rap on the side of her face with the barrel of his pistol. "You're pushin' your luck, woman. I don't care what you call it. You've got a strongbox with a lock on it, and if you don't open it right now, I'm gonna put a bullet right between your eyes."

"All right, all right," she gasped desperately. "It's in the kitchen!"

"We're goin' in the kitchen to get the cash box, partner," Jake called out to Butch. Then, with one hand on the back of Lottie's neck, he guided her toward the kitchen, using her body as a shield, in case someone in the kitchen might be waiting to ambush him.

"All right, partner," Butch responded. "I'll finish takin' up the collection. If you hear us singin' a hymn, you'll know I'm ready to go."

"You slimy dog," Lou-Bell spat. "I knew there was something rotten about you two."

Butch laughed at her. "Won't do you no good to try to flatter me, darlin'. I want that money you got hid down in your bodice somewhere."

Inside the kitchen, Jake and Lottie were met with one terrified cook and one elderly man, who was the dishwasher. Neither offered any resistance. Jake gave Lottie a hard shove, almost knocking her to the floor. "Get the cash box!" he ordered, only then hearing the back door open. He turned to see Eli standing in the doorway, his six-shooter aimed in his direction. Jake wheeled around to fire, but was struck in the chest before he could pull the trigger.

In the dining room, when he heard the shot, Butch stopped dead still. His first thought was that Jake had shot someone, but then he questioned it. He knew the sound of Jake's Remington. He had heard it many times. And this shot sounded different. There was a chance Jake had run into trouble. He had to decide in that moment, so he decided to run. He ran out the front door, right into the butt of Casey's Henry rifle, to be laid out flat on his back. Casey pinned Butch's wrist to the floor, long enough to pull the pistol out of his hand, then stood watching the stunned man and yelled, "Eli! You all right?"

Eli came from the kitchen, supporting Lottie, who was still trying to recover. Behind them, the cook and Fred, the dishwasher, followed. Casey picked up the sack of money Butch had dropped and dumped the contents in the middle of one of the clean tables. "Reckon you folks are gonna be on the honor system to claim what's yours." He went back to stand over Butch again when he started showing signs of moving.

"I'm gonna need some rope," he said to Lou-Bell. "Is there any rope here anywhere?"

She shook her head, then remembered, "There's some clothesline."

"Just as good," Casey said. She turned at once and went to the kitchen to get it. He could guess, but he asked Eli, anyway. "The other one dead?"

"Yep," Eli said. "It was his choice."

"Are you all right, ma'am?" Casey asked

Lottie as he accepted the clothesline Lou-Bell handed him.

"I am now, thanks to you two," she said. "How did you know? Are you deputy marshals?"

Both men laughed. "No, ma'am," Casey said. "We just had a funny feelin' about these two fellows when we were here earlier." He gave her a smile. "Then Eli said he had a good idea about how we might get us a free breakfast in the mornin'."

They all laughed at that, and then Lottie said, "I think you can count on that." Already recovering from the rough handling she just suffered, she permitted Lou-Bell's insistence to examine the cut on the side of her face.

Casey tied Butch's hands behind his back, then tied his feet together, and tied them to his hands. When he was securely bound, he dragged him over against the wall. Then he asked, "Is there a marshal or a sheriff in town?"

"You're forgetting you're in Indian Territory," Lou-Bell said. "For white-man law, you have to wire Fort Smith to send a U.S. deputy marshal to arrest someone. Then they have to send a jail wagon to take him to Fort Smith for trial."

"Doggone," Casey said. "I shoulda shot him."

"There's a Choctaw policeman who lives here, and sometimes a deputy marshal will keep a prisoner in the Choctaw Jail until they can transport him," Lottie said. "The prisoner doesn't like it very much, because it's really an old smokehouse they're using for a jail."

"So the Choctaw policeman can't arrest him, but he'll keep him in the smokehouse?" Eli asked. "Are you tellin' me we have to let him go, then hope a deputy marshal can find him and arrest him?" He looked at Casey and said, "You shoulda shot him."

"There's a way around it," Lottie said. "My husband's the mayor. We have a town council that works with the Choctaw. The council can take an outlaw in custody and put him in the Choctaw Jail. We feed him and the marshal service pays us for the food, and the Choctaw policeman takes care of his jail. Stanley Coons owns the stable. He'll take care of their horses. The Choctaw policeman usually checks by here every night before he goes home. When he does, we'll load that fellow up, and Fred, here, can lead him down to the jail. The Choctaw will take it from there."

As it turned out, Jim Little Eagle checked

the dining room before Casey and Eli left, so they carried Butch down to the jail. Before leaving Lottie's Kitchen, however, they promised to return for breakfast in the morning. Then they returned to their camp as fast as possible, thinking about their other three horses and their grain sacks worth about thirty-seven thousand dollars. It had been a hell of a foolish thing to do, but they were glad they did it when they returned and found their camp had not been disturbed.

They would have usually left earlier the next day, but Lottie didn't open for breakfast until six o'clock. They were only one day's ride from Denison, Texas, so it wouldn't make that much difference and they were looking forward to the breakfast. So they were loaded up and back at the dining room a few minutes before six, waiting for the OPEN sign to appear. Once it did, both Lottie and Lou-Bell met them at the door and showed them to a table. Fresh, hot coffee was served immediately, and it was followed shortly by eggs, bacon, grits, and griddle cakes in quantities that caused them to question their horses' ability to tote them.

"This is what we call our 'Hero's Breakfast,' " Lou-Bell told them. "So far, ain't nobody had it but you."

Lottie threatened to get emotional when she wanted to tell them how much she appreciated their caring enough to come back to see that they were safe. "Well, you know, me and Casey didn't have anything else planned for last night. So we decided, what the hell?"

When they had eaten all they could hold, they were escorted to the door and invited back whenever they might find themselves in Oklahoma again. When finally on the road toward Durant, they couldn't help but enjoy the irony of the whole occurrence.

"That's the way outlaws should be treated," Eli joked. "Here we are, bonified bank robbers, and they was wonderin' if we were deputies."

It was about thirty-two miles from Atoka to the little town of Durant, so they stopped to rest the horses about twelve miles short of that town when they came upon a nice creek. They were both so stuffed from eating so much breakfast that there was no incentive to even make coffee. They spent the time lying on the creek bank complaining about the size of their bellies. It would have been a good time to talk about what they planned to do with their money, whether to use it to buy land for farming or ranching, neither of which they wanted to do.

"Maybe we could start us up a little business in Nacogdoches," Eli suggested.

"Doin' what?" Casey wanted to know. "The only thing we've ever done is tendin' cows and horses. But it looks like we're pretty good at robbin' trains and banks. Maybe we oughta stick to what we know, but I kinda like havin' more money than I need." They pondered that thought over for a spell. Then suddenly Casey sat up and declared, "I got it. I know what kinda business we can open."

"Yeah, what's that?" Eli responded, not really interested.

"Cattle inspectors," Casey said. "Cattle inspectors for the government."

"Shoot," Eli said, "I ain't never heard of cattle inspectors."

"I ain't, either," Casey declared. "And I don't expect anybody else has. That's the good part about it. We can open us up a little office in any town and go and come when we please. Tell folks we have to travel a lot, go where the government tells us to go. When our money starts to get low, we'll just go on a little trip and take somebody else's money."

"How 'bout when our likeness shows up

on the post office wall?" Eli asked.

"I thought about that," Casey said, "and I'm thinkin' we shouldn'ta buried our disguises between the roots of that tree. But we know where we can get more disguises. We'll let the law chase after those two old men that robbed the bank in Wichita. Me and you will be legitimate businessmen workin' for the government, way down in Texas." He waited a moment for Eli's response before he pressed, "How 'bout it? Whaddaya think?"

"I think you're crazy, is what I think," Eli said. "And I think I'd be crazy to go along with you. I don't know, Casey, we might be better off just layin' low. Besides, we're already outlaws, a couple more jobs ain't gonna make much difference." He chuckled and declared, "Doolin and Tubbs, back in business again, representing the U.S. government." He paused to think that over again. "You know, we're gonna have to buy some new clothes. We can't go around lookin' like two cowhands if we're gonna be proper businessmen." He decided to let it lie for a while and maybe a better idea would strike them.

CHAPTER 13

When they felt the horses had rested enough, they got back on the road. In a little over a couple of hours, they came to Durant, a little town that started out as a trading post owned by a French-Choctaw man named Dixon Durant. Now, thanks to the railroad, it offered a hotel in addition to Durant's general merchandise and various shops, a post office, as well as a doctor's office. It was after twelve o'clock when they reached Durant, but they were both still feeling the effects of their big breakfast. So they decided to ride on through town and fix something to eat when they struck the Red River in about two hours, at around two in the afternoon. Since they could afford it, they took the ferry across the river to Texas. "Comin' home in style," Eli pronounced it, instead of swimming the horses across.

Their newly acquired wealth presented its

problems, however. And that was due to the awkward fact that their entire fortune was buried in two sacks of horse feed. They could not afford to leave it out of their sight, and to repeat the incident when they left it unguarded in Atoka would definitely not be allowed to happen again. They could afford to stay in a hotel, but if they did, they would have to leave their five horses in a stable. It might be hard to explain to the stable owner what they dug out of the two sacks of grain. It might also be awkward carrying the two bags of money into the hotel. If the hotel had a safe, it was a rather large amount to put in the hotel's hands for safekeeping. It was bound to arouse suspicion. Then there would be the question of whether or not it was safe to leave the money in the room when they went to the dining room or stepped out to a saloon for a drink before bedtime.

"I never thought about how big a pain in the neck it is to be rich," Casey remarked when he pulled Smoke's saddle off the horse. "We need to get this money in the ground somewhere, so we can enjoy havin' it."

"Just as soon as we find a place we're gonna stay at for a while," Eli said. "Right now, though, let's find a better spot than this to cook some dinner."

There was not much in the way of firewood by the river. So they lingered there for only long enough to let the horses drink all they wanted. Then they followed a stream away from the river until they found a suitable stopping place. After the horses were unloaded and left to graze on the grass, the two partners prepared to roast some more of their smoked deer meat and make a pot of coffee.

"You know, Sherman ain't but about ten or eleven miles from here," Eli said. "It won't be much after four o'clock when we get there. And if we take the trail to Nacogdoches from there, ain't much of anything on that road till we get to Nacogdoches. And that'll be about three days' travel. You wanna camp at Sherman tonight, eat supper there, maybe get a drink of likker, before we move on to Nacogdoches?"

"Suits me, if that's what you wanna do," Casey said. "We ain't in no particular hurry to get anywhere. Maybe they've got a place fancy enough to feed a couple of wealthy gentlemen like us."

When approaching the town of Sherman, they passed a large grove of trees where a wide creek crossed the road. It appeared to be a favorite place to camp, judging by the many ashes of old campfires dotting the ground here and there. "Hope there's a place as good as this on the other end of town," Casey said. "If there ain't, we can come back and camp here tonight."

They slow-walked their horses up the main street, past several saloons and stores, as well as a jail and a post office. "Nice-lookin' bank right in the middle of town," Eli remarked.

At the far end of the street, they came to the Sherman Hotel and noted that there was an outside entrance to the hotel dining room. And with the row of windows across the front, it looked like it would be possible to keep an eye on their horses. Agreed on the hotel for supper, they turned back down the street and decided on Archer's Saloon for a drink of whiskey before supper. They dismounted and tied the horses to the rail.

"Howdy, gents," bartender Billy Sage greeted them. "Whatcha gonna have?"

"Have you got a real good rye whiskey?" Casey asked.

"I sure do," Billy said. "I've got some one-hundred-proof Tennessee rye."

"Good," Casey said. "Give my partner a shot of that and I'll take a shot of the cheapest corn likker you've got."

Billy laughed and reached under the bar for a bottle to pour Eli's drink. Then he poured one for Casey from the bottle sitting on the bar. "You boys ain't been in before, have you? You passin' through or stayin' awhile?"

"Just passin' through," Casey said. "Right now, we're on our way to Nacogdoches."

"Just came down from Injun Territory, did you?" Billy inquired.

"That's a fact," Casey said. Deciding to try out their assumed identities then, he added, "We've been up in Kansas, workin' for the government."

"Is that so?" Billy asked. "What kinda work do you do for the government? Are you deputies?"

"No, we're cattle inspectors," Casey said.

" 'Cattle inspectors'?" Billy repeated. "I ain't never heard of a cattle inspector." Casey looked at Eli and winked. "Whaddaya inspect 'em for?" Billy asked.

Casey had to pause a moment to think. "You know, for disease and ticks, stuff such as that."

"Well, I never . . ." Billy started. "Whaddaya do if you inspect the cows and find out they got somethin' like that? Do you have to kill 'em?"

"No," Casey said, wishing now he had

231

never opened his mouth. "We don't let 'em drive their herd to the railroad."

Billy thought about that for a moment while he poured them another shot. "What are you fellers doin' over here in East Texas? There ain't no cattle ranches to amount to much in these parts. Looks like you'd wanna be over in cow country. You said you was on your way to Nacogdoches, and I know there ain't no cattle ranches over that way."

"We have to check to make sure," Casey suggested. He looked at Eli for help, but received nothing but an amused grin in return. Then hoping to change the subject, he said, "Maybe you can help us. Is there a road outta town here that leads to Nacogdoches?"

"You mighta seen a road that heads off from the square and goes between the bank and the feed store. That's the road to Tyler. If you stay on that road after you get to Tyler, it'll take you all the way to Nacogdoches."

"Much obliged," Casey said. " 'Preciate your help. Been nice talkin' to ya." He put some money on the bar and said, "Come on, partner, we need to get movin'."

"Right," Eli responded. "We need to get movin'." He tossed his drink back and headed for the door after him.

Outside, Casey said, "Don't say a word. The cattle inspector story won't work. This ain't cattle country. It might work if we were back in San Antonio, but it ain't gonna work in East Texas."

"Whatever you say, partner," Eli responded, making no attempt to hide his amusement. "We might as well go on up to the hotel and see if the dinin' room is open yet."

"Evenin'," Casey said when he opened the door and stuck his head inside.

The two women standing near the kitchen door stopped talking when they heard him call out.

When they both turned to see who called, he said, "We was wonderin' if you were open yet. There weren't no sign on the door that said one way or the other."

"We were just about to," one of the women said, and she held up a piece of cardboard she was holding that had OPEN printed on it. "You and your friend come on in and we'll get you seated."

"Thank you, ma'am," Casey said, and he and Eli walked inside. "You want us to take our guns off?"

"We would appreciate that very much,"

she said. "You can leave them right over there on that table." She pointed to a small table in a corner. They dutifully went over and left their weapons. "Thank you," she said then. "That makes it fair for everyone. If you don't like something we serve you and run for your guns, that gives us a chance to run for ours." She seemed so sincere when saying it, Casey and Eli weren't sure she was joking until she chortled and asked, "This is your first time eating with us, isn't it?"

"Yes, ma'am," Eli said to her.

"Well, we're always glad to see new faces," she said. "I hope you find the food good enough to make you want to come back. My name is Blanche Roberts, and this young lady is Sally Bowen. We're going to do our best to help you enjoy your supper. You're both big boys. Do you want to sit at the big table in the middle of the room?"

"No, ma'am," Casey said. "If you don't mind, we'd rather sit at one of those little tables by the front window there." He pointed to one in the middle.

"Whatever you wish," Blanche said; then considering the way they were dressed, she said, "I'm gonna guess you want coffee." When they both nodded right away, she said, "Good. Sally is going to be taking care of you. She'll bring you some coffee and tell you what's on the menu tonight."

"Thank you, ma'am," they said together, and went over to the table that gave them the best view of their possessions. She walked back to the door and placed the OPEN sign on a hook on the outside, then went to the kitchen, where Sally Bowen was already filling two coffee cups.

"I swear," Eli said, "that's the politest woman I ever met in one of these places."

"I expect it's because she recognizes real gentlemen when she sees 'em," Casey said.

The dining room was featuring pork chops that night, served with beans and rice, which suited the two outlaws' fancy. They were figuring on about two and a half days to ride from Sherman to Tyler, and as far as they knew, there was nothing in between. The smoked venison would give out by the end of the first day's ride, and it would be back to bacon. Since their recent status as men of wealth, they were rapidly becoming addicted to full-course dinners and suppers.

When Sally brought them a plate with hot biscuits, right out of the oven, and a little bowl of butter, Eli had to comment on it. "I swear, I'm gonna have to learn to eat all over again. My belly's gettin' to where it starts swellin' every time we ride into a town."

They took their time eating their supper, enjoying the feeling of not being in a hurry to get anywhere. Sally stopped by the table often to see if there was anything they needed, even after the room started filling with more diners. When they were finishing up the last of their coffee, Eli dropped a casual remark that caused them both to think.

"I wonder how the rest of the boys are makin' out," he said.

"Well, they ain't had much time to hook on with anybody yet," Casey allowed. They were mostly young boys, except Smiley, and he had a place to go. "I expect they'll be ridin' the grub line all winter, tryin' to find a job with one of the ranches around San Antonio, maybe the Rockin'-T, or the Double-D."

"Maybe Smiley coulda helped one or two of 'em hook on with that ranch he's gonna cook for," Eli suggested. "I swear, I don't know if he ever said the name of the ranch or not. Just said it was in North Texas."

They didn't say anything more about the fate of the young crew for a long moment, and then they both started to speak at the same time. Casey held his tongue and let Eli talk.

"I hate to say it, but we've got the money to buy a small herd of cattle. We could put those boys to work raisin' our own herd."

"Ha!" Casey blurted in response.

" 'Ha,' yourself," Eli came back. "It ain't a crazy idea. Hell, it's all we know, and those are some good, hardworkin' boys."

"I didn't say they weren't," Casey insisted. "I said 'Ha' because I was just fixin' to say the same thing you said. I'm thinkin' we could set those boys up to raise cattle for us. And we, bein' the businessmen we are, don't have to nursemaid the cows. We'll handle the financin' and the managin'."

"I swear, I can't believe we're talkin' this kinda talk," Eli said, "as sick of workin' cows as we are."

"Yeah, but it wouldn't be the same this time around," Casey was quick to say. "We worked a lot of years for Whitmore Brothers Cattle Company, and we never saw either one of the Whitmores workin' with the cattle. It could be the same way with me and you."

"So you're sayin' you're ready to give up this outlawin' business and go back to raisin' cattle?" Eli asked.

"Hell no!" Casey responded. "I'm sayin' our legitimate business could be raisin' cattle, but we need our outlawin' business to finance the cattle business. All you got to do is dig down in those feed bags out there on that packhorse and that'll tell you what business we're most successful at."

"It is a helluva lot easier way to make a livin' than what we were doin', ain't it?" Eli said. "You ready to go find us a place to camp?"

They got up from the table and walked over to the small table where they had left their guns. Blanche met them there to ask if everything had been to their satisfaction. They both said that it had been, and they regretted the fact they were just passing through. They paid her and walked outside to find a large, bulky man standing in front of the hitching rail, obviously looking at their horses. He turned to face them when he heard them approaching.

"Evenin'," he said. "You belong to these horses?"

"Evenin'," Casey returned. "Yes, sir. At least they belong to us. Same thing, I reckon."

"My name's Walter Ross," he said, and opened his coat to show his badge. "I'm the sheriff here. I like to get a chance to meet strangers comin' through town. You fellows in town for a while, or just passin' through?"

"We're just passin' through," Casey said.

"Just had a mighty fine supper in the dinin' room. Sorry we ain't gonna be here to try out some more of their cookin'."

"Blanche will be tickled to hear that," Ross said. "Which way you headin'?"

"Well, we thought we'd camp here tonight and head toward Tyler in the mornin'," Casey said.

The sheriff watched the two of them closely while they talked and decided they were of no concern to him. So he said, "I got a telegram this mornin' to look out for two fellows that tried to rob the bank in Tyler. They didn't get away with any money, but they shot a teller, and they were most likely headed for Indian Territory."

Casey grinned and said, "You figure me and Eli look like a couple of bank robbers?" He chuckled and remarked, "I can understand that, lookin' at Eli, though. He's got that kinda shifty look about him. Did the bank teller die?" The sheriff shook his head. "Well, that's one good thing, ain't it?"

"I reckon so," Ross said, but his mind was elsewhere as he continued to stare at the horses. "If you don't mind me askin', what are you boys carryin' on those packhorses?"

Casey acted surprised by the question. "Why, what everybody carries when they're travelin' on horseback, I reckon, just whatever we think we need before we get to where we're goin'."

"That one horse is carryin' what looks like two fifty-pound bags of grain or flour or somethin'," the sheriff observed.

"Right the first time," Casey said. "He's carryin' two fifty-pound sacks of grain. But it ain't no ordinary grain. It's a special mix of two or three different grains, and we're gonna see if we can grow the same grains over near Nacogdoches. We hauled that grain all the way from Kansas."

"What's so special about it?" Ross wanted to know.

"It'll make your horse stronger and quicken his step, too," Casey claimed. "You wanna try some on your horse?"

Ross hesitated, then said, "My horse is in the stable. Most likely already fed tonight." He hesitated further, then confessed, "I wouldn't mind feedin' some of it to my horse. Lemme take a look at it." He followed Casey over to the pack horse and Casey untied the top of one of the sacks. Thinking his partner had lost his mind, Eli positioned himself behind the sheriff, his hand resting on the handle of his Colt, and praying Casey knew what he was doing. He had no desire to shoot an officer of the law.

Casey reached in and came up with a

handful of grain and held it up for Ross to see. "Hold your hands together," Casey said, and when Ross did so, Casey dumped the handful of grain into the sheriff's cupped hands.

The sheriff stared at it for a few moments before saying, "It looks just like regular ol' grain."

"It does, don't it?" Casey said. "That's the same thing I thought when we bought it from this fellow in Kansas. I'm sorry I ain't got a little sack or somethin' to put some of this in for you. Maybe you could carry a couple of handfuls in your bandana, only you ain't wearin' one." He looked at Eli. "You got a little sack or somethin'?" Eli just shook his head.

"Never mind," Sheriff Ross said. "I don't think I wanna try it, anyway. I ain't gonna go to Kansas to get it, and you boys better keep all you've got. I'm gonna go in the dinin' room and get my supper now. Come back to see us if you're over this way again." He held his cupped hands over the feed sack and dumped the grain back inside. He nodded to Casey, then to Eli. Back to Casey then, he asked, "Does he ever talk?"

"Only when he's hungry," Casey said. "Then he can make the awfulest racket you ever heard. But he's been fed."

241

Casey tied the grain sack again, they stepped up into their saddles, and headed for the road to Tyler. The horses needed to be fed and rested, so they planned to stop at the first likely-looking place for a camp. They didn't have to go far before crossing a creek that offered what they were looking for. As was their usual practice, they left the road and followed the creek back upstream, until they were well away from any passing traffic on the road. When the horses were taken care of and the bedrolls were spread before a small fire, they talked about their chance meeting with the sheriff.

"I gotta give you credit, partner," Eli confessed. "Damned if you ain't the slickest-talkin' outlaw in the territory. I believe that ol' boy really thought we had some magic grain there for a while."

"Well, I thought I gave you a lot of chances to jump in with the story," Casey said. "But you just left me to choke on whatever story I could make up."

"You were doin' so good, I didn't wanna mess up your timin'."

About a mile and a half behind them in the hotel dining room, Sheriff Walter Ross was laughing with Blanche and Sally about the two drifters who had just left there.

"They seemed like nice enough fellows," Blanche remarked, "so nice and polite."

"You're probably right," the sheriff said, "but dumb as a stump. Somebody got ahold of 'em up in Kansas somewhere and sold 'em some magic grain for their horses. And now, they're totin' two big fifty-pound sacks of it all the way back to Nacogdoches. I didn't have the heart to tell 'em they'd been japed." He shook his head and laughed. "Ain't no tellin' how much they paid for that grain. They tried to give me some of it. I took a look at it, and it's the same grain you get from the feed store right here in Sherman."

"That's too bad," Sally said. "They were such nice men. And they didn't seem stupid to me."

CHAPTER 14

They left Sherman at sunup the next morning, following the road to Tyler. They had talked for quite a while before climbing into their blankets, trying to decide the best course of action for the two of them. Still undecided when morning came, they started out with Nacogdoches as their destination, simply because they preferred not to remain in Sherman. The only agreement they arrived at was to decide for certain when they reached Tyler whether to continue to the southeast to Nacogdoches, or southwest toward the Whitmore Brothers Ranch. The only thing they were definitely decided upon was to finance whatever they settled on with other people's money. They were still discussing the pros and cons of remaining in the cattle business when they came upon a good place to rest the horses after a ride of about twenty miles.

When the horses were free of their saddles

and packs, Casey got a fire going, and before long, he and Eli were chewing on the last strips of smoked deer meat as they enjoyed their first cup of coffee for the day. By the time the horses were ready to go again, they had pretty much decided there was nothing they could do in Nacogdoches, so they might as well turn west when they left Tyler and head toward Waco. So they set out again on the road to Tyler.

After riding for only about fifteen miles, they were surprised to come upon the buildings of another small town. It was definitely a farm town, from the look of it, with several wagons tied in front of the stores and the one saloon they saw. "Sleepy" would be the word they would have picked to describe the town. The road they traveled went straight through the middle of town, and when they met a man driving a wagon on his way out of town, Eli called out to him, "Howdy, neighbor, what town is this?"

The man looked at him as if he was amazed Eli had to ask, but he said politely, "Greenville, this is Greenville."

"Much obliged," Eli said. He turned to Casey then and asked, "You wanna stop and get a drink of likker? I didn't expect to find a town between Sherman and Tyler."

"I wouldn't mind stoppin'," Casey said.

"But I druther have something to eat, instead of a drink of likker. That little strip of deer meat didn't take up much room in my belly."

"You might be right," Eli reconsidered. "My belly's kinda empty, too. Maybe we need to eat a little somethin', and then have a drink of likker."

Agreed then, they rode the length of the street, looking for someplace to buy some dinner. When they found no hotel and no dining room of any kind, they pulled up next to the boardwalk and asked a man standing in front of the general store if there was someplace to get something to eat.

"Sure is," he said, looking their string of horses over. "Reckon it is hard for a stranger. You can get you a good meal at Grainger's Saloon. Leon Grainger owns the saloon, but he built a kitchen and a dinin' room on the back of it, separate from the saloon. Connie Grainger operates the dinin' room. She's Leon's sister and she's a good cook. If a good dinner is all you're lookin' for, you don't even have to go in the saloon. You can go around back and there's a door back you can use. You'd best hurry, though, 'cause she'll be shuttin' dinner off pretty soon."

"Much obliged," Casey said, then looked

over at Eli, who nodded yes, before Casey asked him the question. So they turned their horses around and hurried back down the street. When they came to the saloon again, they rode around behind it and discovered a wagon and a couple of saddled horses tied at a long rail. After tying their horses, they went in the door with a sign over it that read simply: DINING ROOM.

Inside, they found a long table in the middle of the room that had about a dozen place settings. Against one wall, were three small tables that seated two only. On the opposite wall, there was one table with four chairs. A man, his wife, and two youngsters were occupying that table, and that was a good sign to Casey and Eli. If a man brought his family, the food must be all right. There were two men seated at one end of the long table. Casey and Eli sat down at the opposite end of the table. Beyond it, there was a door with a sign over it that said PLEASE USE FRONT ENTRANCE TO SALOON.

Recognizing them as strangers, the diners didn't try to disguise their curiosity and ogled the two openly. After a minute of the unabashed staring, especially from the woman at the table for four, Casey was about to ask if he and Eli were the first strangers they had ever seen, when it occurred to him. He turned to look back at the door, and sure enough, there it was, the little table with two gun belts on it. He got up from the bench and said to Eli, "Gimme your gun belt before that lady sics her young'uns on us."

He walked over and placed their weapons on the table, then paused at the four-chair table. "Sorry if we offended you, ma'am. We didn't notice the gun table when we came in."

She relaxed her frown, smiled sweetly, and said, "Thank you, sir." Her husband nodded as well.

"What did the food look like?" Eli asked him when he sat back down at the table, knowing he probably looked at the plates when he stopped to apologize to the woman.

"I don't know," Casey said. "It's some kind of stew, maybe chicken or pork, I ain't sure, but it smelled good. I reckon we'll find out," he said when a little round woman, with her gray hair pulled back into a ball behind her head, popped through the kitchen door.

"Well, good afternoon, gentlemen," Connie Grainger exclaimed, sounding as if she was genuinely pleased to see them. "I was taking a pan of biscuits out of the oven, and I didn't hear you come in. I believe you boys are new to my dining room."

"That's a fact, ma'am," Eli said. "What are you servin' today?"

"Rabbit stew," she said excitedly. "It's one of the favorites of my regular customers. Pinto beans and hot biscuits go with it. What do you want to drink?" They both said coffee, so she spun around and went back to the kitchen, speaking to one of the two men at the other end of the table as she went by. "Biscuits just out of the oven, Robert, I won't be but a minute."

"I swear," Eli said, "she didn't ask if we wanted rabbit stew or not."

Overhearing his comment, one of the men at their table said. "She wasn't lyin' when she said it was a favorite. Most folks like it a lot. She raises the rabbits herself. Got a hutch out back. She raises chickens, too. Come back Sunday for some good fried chicken."

"Has she got a cook back there?" Casey asked.

"Nope," the man said. "She does the whole thing all by herself, cooks it, waits on the customers, and cleans up afterward."

"Plus raisin' the rabbits," Casey added. "I'm really wantin' to try that rabbit stew now." Connie reappeared at that moment carrying a large tray with three plates of biscuits and two cups of coffee. Both he and Eli immediately grabbed a biscuit and took a bite with a sip of the coffee. "I declare," Casey commented, "I don't even know what she charges, but the coffee and biscuits are worth whatever the price is. I don't know, Eli, maybe we oughta settle down right here." Everyone in the little dining room laughed at that remark. "I'm surprised she ain't got more business than this," he had to wonder.

"She does," the lady at the other table volunteered. "We just all got here too late. Connie opens early and she almost always has a crowd as soon as she opens the door. We couldn't get here any sooner, but she baked up a whole new batch of biscuits, so we could all have fresh ones."

The other man at the long table, who had not spoken before, commented then. "I was talkin' to Leon about Connie's business. And he said he wanted to build her a better place, bigger so she could handle the folks that come here to eat. But he don't have the money it would take to do the whole thing like it oughta be done. He said they had figured the cost and it would run around nine or ten thousand dollars to do it, and he ain't got that kind of money."

"Who has?" Casey said. "These days, it's

all you can do just to get by. But if she stays as busy as you folks say she is, maybe she'll save up enough to build her bigger place."

"I doubt that," the lady said. "Not Connie, she don't charge enough for her cookin', to start with. And if they don't have the money to pay for a meal, she don't turn anybody away." She stopped talking when Connie came back in the dining room with two plates of food for Casey and Eli.

The two men at the long table and the woman and her husband, everyone but the two small children, stopped eating and watched the two strangers as they tested their dinner. In a few short moments, they all smiled when Eli commented, "Doggone, this stew is mighty tasty." He looked up from his plate at Casey. "Whaddaya think, partner?"

Casey swallowed a big mouthful of rabbit stew, then said, "I think these folks weren't lyin'. I ain't ever et no rabbit that tastes this good."

"I told you," the man Connie had called Robert said, "the best cook in Texas."

"You'll get no argument from me," Casey said as he continued to attack the generous serving of rabbit stew.

The spontaneous discussion that had developed over the high quality of Connie

Grainger's cooking now settled into friendly conversation. "You fellows are new in town. Are you just passin' through?" The question was asked by the lady's husband.

"Of course, they are," his wife immediately said to him. "Nobody comes to Greenville on purpose."

"She's right when she says we're just passin' though," Eli said. "We're on our way to Tyler. Never been on this road before."

Robert spoke up again. "When we rode up, there was another stranger goin' in the saloon, but he tied his horse up at the front. You fellows came in the back door. Was he ridin' with you? 'Cause if he's thinkin' about eatin', he's gonna be too late."

"No, he ain't with us," Casey said. "It's just Eli and me. Came down through Indian Territory on our way to —" He didn't finish his statement when it was interrupted by the report of a gunshot, accompanied by a hole in the top panel of the door to the saloon. Everyone automatically dived down behind the tables. Casey looked at the man trying to shelter his wife and children. "You'd best get them out of here."

"I ain't paid for our dinner," the man said.

"Don't worry about that," Casey shot back. "I'll pay for you. Get your family outta here." He ran to the back door and held it open while they scrambled up from the floor and ran outside. Then he grabbed his gun belt and tossed Eli's to him. When he saw Connie in the kitchen doorway, her eyes wide with fright, he barked, "Get back in that kitchen and get behind something, like the stove or something!"

The two men who had been at the end of the table decided the man and his family had done the smart thing, so they bolted for the back door, snatching up their weapons as they passed the corner table.

"Looks like it's just you and me, partner," Eli commented as he buckled his gun belt on. "Wanna leave Connie some money for them that left, and take off, too? Or you wanna see what the trouble is in the saloon?" They could hear a loud voice on the other side of the door that had the sound of threats; then another shot was fired, which put a second hole through the door panel.

Casey had taken a glass off the table by then and was holding it up against the wall with his ear pressed against it. He was able to understand a word now and then, enough to get the picture. "It's a holdup," he said to Eli. "He's robbin' the saloon!" He paused a moment to figure out the reason the door was the target for the two bullets. "The bar must be backed up to this wall, and he's got his gun on the bartender." He pointed to the sign over the door. "That's the reason for the sign. You go through that door, and you come out behind the bar." He gave Eli one determined shake of his head. "These folks can't afford a holdup. I'm goin' in." He picked up a heavy wooden box holding extra silverware and started for the door, then stopped and looked at Eli. "What was her brother's name?"

"Leon," Eli said. "I'm right behind you. I hope that door ain't locked."

It wasn't. Casey opened it and went in, startling Leon and the gunman on the other side of the bar in the process. "I brought the rest of the money out, Leon." He held the silverware box up to show him. "Ain't no sense in anybody gettin' shot over a few hundred dollars."

Leaving Leon to gape in total confusion at a couple of men he had never seen before, Casey walked around the end of the bar and approached the smirking gunman. "Here you go. Here's all the cash we've got in the place."

The confused gunman reached out to take the box with his free hand, only to find it too heavy to hold with one. So, with his gun still in hand, he reached under the box with that hand, too, unaware that Casey's Colt

.45 was under the box as well. The metallic click of the two weapons bumping each other under the box only served to confuse him further as he took possession of the box. He was not ready for the barrel of Casey's pistol laid squarely across his nose with all the force Casey could summon, however. He dropped like a rock, and Eli pulled the gun from his hand as soon as he hit the floor.

"Got any rope?" Casey asked the astonished owner.

When Leon found his voice and said that he didn't have any rope, one of the spectators to the robbery attempt, who had all backed up to the far corner of the barroom, said that he did, and ran outside to fetch it.

He was gone for only a few seconds before returning with a coil of rope, which he handed to Eli, and Eli quickly demonstrated how to tie up a wild steer. "Have you got a sheriff or a jail?" Eli asked Leon.

"No," Leon said, still confused. "I mean, yeah, we got a jail, but we only have a part-time sheriff . . . deputy really. Who are you?" he then inserted.

"Just two fellows tryin' to enjoy a peaceful dinner at your sister's dinin' room, before your customer started shootin' through the door at us," Eli said. "That's a dangerous situation you've got there, with that dinin' room backed up to your saloon. It's a wonder ain't nobody been killed in there. Your sister, maybe? You oughta build her a separate place. Her customers would sure as hell appreciate it."

"I wanna do that — build her, her own place," Leon said, gathering his wits about him finally. "But I ain't able to, right now."

"Anybody know where that sheriff or deputy is?" Casey asked the few spectators, who were crowding around the fallen gunman tied up on the floor.

"He's in the jail," one of the onlookers said. "I'll go get him." He ran out the door.

"I'da thought he would already be here, if he heard those two shots," Eli remarked.

"Why not, Leon?" Casey asked.

"Why not what?" Leon said.

"Why ain't you able to build a separate place for Connie and her dinin' room?"

"Money," Leon said, getting exasperated again. "I ain't got that kind of money. Who the hell are you, anyway?"

"I told you, Leon, we're just two dinin' room customers who don't like bein' shot at when we're eatin'. You'd best pick that silverware up off the floor before Connie sees it." He looked down when he heard the trussed-up gunman making groaning noises.

"You're welcome for that."

"Right," Leon blurted, realizing he had expressed no words of appreciation to Casey and Eli for taking the gunman down. "I reckon I owe you for savin' my bacon, sure enough."

"That reminds me," Casey thought just then, "I need to go talk to your sister about the bill and let her know you're all right. I expect she might be worried about that." He hurried back behind the bar and went through the door to the dining room. He didn't see her in the dining room, so he went into the kitchen. He found her, sitting on the floor behind the stove, holding a revolver in her hand. "Good for you," he said. "But you won't need that now. Your brother is all right. There was a fellow tryin' to rob him, but he's trussed and waiting for the sheriff or deputy to pick him up and take him to jail."

He offered his hand and helped her up off the floor. "I came back to settle up with you. I need to pay you for Eli and my dinner, plus that family of four, plus those two fellows who were settin' at the big table with us. With the shots fired, they thought it would be a good idea to get out before somebody got hit."

"Oh, no," she said, "that's not fair for you

to have to pay for their dinner."

"It's all right," he assured her. "They didn't run out on you. I told 'em I'd take care of it. So add it all up." He put his hand in his pocket and felt the money. "I'll be right back. I need to get a little more outta my saddlebag."

"All right, if you insist," she said, and went to get a piece of paper to add all the dinners together. "It's uncommonly kind of you," she said as he went out the back door.

When he came back inside, she showed him the total, which amounted to three dollars and fifty cents. "I'll tell you the truth, Miss Grainger, that rabbit stew was mighty fine eatin'. I've got a five-dollar bill here. Why don't you just take that and we'll call it even?" She started to protest, but he put it in her hand and closed her fingers over it. "I'm gonna go back to the saloon and get your box of silverware now. I sorta borrowed it, so I'll put it right back where I found it."

"You're about the sweetest man I've ever met." She beamed at him. "I hope you come back this way again sometime."

"You never know," he said. "That's the thing about Eli and me. I'll go get your knives and forks." He went back into the saloon.

"Where you been?" Eli asked. "We had us a young deputy sheriff come in here and haul that gunman away. He weren't too happy with the job you did on his nose, the gunman, not the deputy. He gave me a message to pass on to you. You listen to this now. He said his name is Johnny Mack Jenkins, and the next time he sees you, he's gonna shoot you down and hang your guts on a fence post."

"I don't reckon he had any message for you, did he?"

"No, he didn't have one for me. I think you musta really impressed him with your gun barrel."

"Well, I expect we'd best get on our way before he breaks outta jail," Casey said. "We've got horses standin' out back loaded down. We need to get them rested up before we start 'em out again this afternoon."

"Listen," Leon said, "I owe you boys for what you did. There ain't no tellin' how that mighta ended, if you two hadn't stepped in when you did." Fully aware now of how close he had come to certain disaster, and the risk they had taken to help him, he said, "I feel I should repay you somehow."

"Well, that would be right sportin' of you, Leon," Eli said. "Whaddaya think, Casey? Say one shot of whiskey on the house oughta take care of it."

"Sounds about right," Casey said.

"I swear," Leon responded. "Thank the Lord you boys dropped in." He put two shot glasses on the bar and poured one corn whiskey and one rye, as they requested.

"Where's the silverware box?" Casey asked. "I told Connie I'd put it back where I found it."

Leon told him not to worry about it, he'd return it.

But Casey said, "We're goin' right out the back door, anyway." He picked up the box. "Ain't no forks or nothin' missin', is there?" He was assured they had picked up every utensil, so they shook hands with Leon and went back through the door to the dining room. Casey paused briefly to make sure the box was exactly in the spot he had found it in. Then he followed Eli out the back door.

Hearing the door close, Connie came from the kitchen, too late to catch them going through, but she opened the door and called out to them, "You boys be careful, and thank you again."

They waved as they rode out of the back-yard of the saloon and headed back on the road to Tyler. They planned only to get out of town a little ways, then rest the horses. It was still early in the afternoon, so they would continue on before camping for the night.

Behind them, Connie was left with a bigger job of cleanup than she usually had after the midday meal. Due to the frantic exodus of her customers when two shots ripped through the door to the saloon, she had overturned tables and chairs to put back in place. There were dishes and scraps of food scattered on the floor as well. "At least none of my customers were hurt," she muttered to herself as she wiped up a spattering of beans from the floor. She intended to go into the saloon to see how Leon was doing, after the robbery attempt, but she wanted to clean up her dining room first.

On the other side of the door with the two bullet holes, her brother had a little mess to clean up as well. Tables and chairs had been toppled when his customers backed away at the sudden appearance of the drawn gun. He was a mean-looking stranger, big in the chest and shoulders, but he didn't say more than two words while he drank a couple of shots of whiskey. When he had moved down the bar to confront him, Leon thought he was going to pay for his whiskey. Instead, his hand came up with a gun in it. Leon was caught completely by surprise. He kept a double-barrel shotgun under the bar for such occasions, but he was too far from it when the gunman drew on him.

Thinking about that now, he blamed himself for not watching the stranger more closely. But he had never before been confronted by a holdup man. Again he gave silent thanks to the two strangers who made it their business to save his life. He was thinking about that when he heard Connie scream.

At once alarmed, for it sounded like a terrified scream, he remembered to snatch his shotgun from under the bar and bolted through the door to the dining room. She was bending over the box that held her silverware, her back to him.

"Connie!" he blurted frantically. She slowly turned around to face him, both hands holding banded packs of money. "What the . . . ? Where did . . . ?"

Equally speechless, she just stood there, gaping at him, her eyes like saucers, her mouth open, but no sound coming forth. He dropped his shotgun on the floor and went to her, staring at the money in her hands. Finding his voice at last, he asked, "Is it real?"

She nodded her head rapidly. Then, when her voice finally returned, she gushed rapid-fire. "I think it is! There's more in the box!" With her wits about her again, she exclaimed, "I was cleaning up the room, and I knew I was going to have to wash all that silverware that got dropped on the floor in the bar. I looked in the box and there it was! I almost fouled my bloomers. Let's count it!"

They started counting. It took a little while, and when they finished, there was a total of ten thousand dollars. "There's my new dining room!" Connie squealed, and sat down, exhausted.

"Ten thousand dollars!" Leon exclaimed, hardly able to believe he wasn't having a dream, and afraid he might wake up and turn it into a nightmare. "The Lord sure does move in mysterious ways," he felt inspired to say.

"I know now what angels look like," Connie said, picturing the two rather rugged-looking cowhands. She thought of how polite they were, but far from angelic.

CHAPTER 15

The rabbit stew dinner was still too recent for Casey or Eli to even think about something to eat as they sat beside a small creek while resting their horses. They did build a small fire and made a pot of coffee, however. The conversation was casual, mostly about the look on the face of Johnny Mack Jenkins, seconds before the barrel of Casey's six-shooter put a permanent dent in his nose.

When they tired of that topic and there was a sizable gap created in their banter, Eli broached a new subject. "When are you gonna tell me about why one of them grain sacks was opened and tied up again?"

"I expect I would have gotten around to it sometime," Casey said. "I didn't know you were watchin' 'em so close, especially since it was my sack of grain that had been opened."

"Shoot," Eli reacted, "I always keep an eye on those sacks, mine and yours. That's some mighty expensive grain. I don't want to lose any of that grain." He waited for Casey to explain, and when he didn't, Eli asked a question. "You went back in there and left those folks some money for that new dinin' room they wanna build, didn't you?"

"Well, hell, that's a bad situation they've got there," Casey said. "Dangerous too. We saw that firsthand. And that little woman is the doggoned best cook I ever saw, so I decided to see that she stays in business."

"How much did you give her?" Eli asked.

"Well, you heard 'em when they were talkin' about it in the dinin' room. They figured the cost of it would be about ten thousand dollars."

"Did you give 'em the whole amount?" Eli asked, appalled.

"I figured I might as well give 'em enough to get the whole job done. You give 'em just part of the cost, who's gonna give 'em the rest?"

"I thought we was partners," Eli said.

"We are," Casey insisted, "but I couldn'ta asked you to go in on that deal. That weren't no investment. That was a plain, damn-fool gift."

"I thought I was a soft touch," Eli declared. "But danged if you ain't a complete puddin' head." He looked at him and shook his head slowly, then said, "I'll give you five thousand outta my sack of grain. Don't even start," he told him when Casey was about to object. "We're partners — only from now on, let's talk about it before we give away a fortune. All right?"

"All right, partner," Casey responded with a big grin. "But you also owe me a dollar seventy-five for half of the dinner bill."

"We've got a losing streak started here," Eli said. "We're in a stampede to get from rich businessmen to broke cowhands. We might have to get another loan from the bank sooner than we expected."

"Well, that was our plan right from the start, weren't it?" Casey said. "We was just hopin' to make withdrawals a little less often." He cocked his head to one side and stroked his chin. "You know," he started again, "I've been thinkin' about our chosen line of business. I'm thinkin' it would be a good idea to do some shoppin' before we leave this part of Texas."

"Shoppin' for what? What the hell are you talkin' about?"

"Clothes," Casey said. "I'm convinced that one of the reasons that bank job we pulled went so smooth was because we looked like two gray-headed old coots. Nobody expected we was bank robbers till it was too late. So I think we oughta get those two old men back in business, and let the law go after them, instead of chasing two upstandin' businessmen like us. I ain't sure how big a town Tyler is, but maybe it's big enough to have a good undertaker, and that's the best place to find the clothes we're lookin' for." He paused then. "Whaddaya think? You got any opinion on that?"

"I think I agree with what you're sayin'. I like the thought of that, throwin' those two old boys back into action," Eli said. "Besides, I ain't got no better idea." So they agreed on that plan of action, and when the horses were rested, they started out for Tyler.

It would take them a day and a half before they reached the town. Tyler was the county seat of Smith County, and it proved to be a fairly busy little town. They walked their horses past the brick courthouse shortly before noon and headed for a cluster of stores and shops they saw beyond. Judging by the number of wagons they saw, they figured Tyler, like the town they had just left, appeared to be a farming community. But during the War Between the States, Tyler had been the site of a large Confederacy munitions plant. Always a first priority, they had to take care of their horses, so they rode out the other end of town until coming to a stream big enough to water the five horses. They were not alone at the site, for there were a couple of wagons farther up the stream, both with women and children. Evidently, it was a common site to park in when the family came to town.

"Today must be Saturday," Eli remarked, and looked to Casey for verification. But Casey shrugged his shoulders in response.

While they watched the horses drink from the stream, they were surprised by a visitor. She looked to be around four years old, and she suddenly appeared behind them as they sat there talking. "Whatcha doin'?" she asked, startling both of them.

They both laughed, to have been given a start by the youngster. "Why, we're just sittin' here watchin' the horses," Casey said to her. "What you doin'?"

"Nothin'," the child said.

"Well, you're doin' a good job of it. Ain't she, Eli?"

Casey was about to ask her where her mama was when they heard someone calling her name. "Bonnie!"

The little girl didn't answer.

"Bonnie," Casey asked her, "is that your name?" The youngster nodded her head, so Casey stood up and called out, "She's down here. Bonnie's down here." Then, to keep the child occupied until her mother found them, he continued to talk to her. "I bet that's your mama lookin' for you. Is that right?" Bonnie nodded her head again. Casey looked over toward Eli and said, "That's mean ol' Uncle Eli. You were smart comin' to me." Eli made a scary face in reply. "Over here, ma'am," Casey called to the woman when she came out of the trees. Seeing them, she hurried over to collect her child.

"Bonnie," she scolded when she approached. "What are you doin', botherin' these men? I told you to play around the wagon." Looking at the two rugged-looking men, she said, "I'm sorry she was botherin' you fellows."

"She weren't no bother, ma'am," Eli said. "She was just sayin' howdy." Bonnie dutifully went over to her mother and took her hand. "Lotta folks in town today," Eli said. "Is today Saturday? Me and Casey have been on the road for a while, and I lost track of the day of the week."

"Well, it is Saturday," the woman said. "But there does seem to be a lot more folks in town than usual. I expect a good many of them came into town to go to the show this evening."

"What show is that?" Casey asked.

"Freeman and Hardy," she said, and when her answer was met with two blank expressions, she explained. "James Freeman and Willard Hardy, they're two actors from the stage in New Orleans. They travel all over East Texas, giving performances of famous debates and different works of Shakespeare and other famous authors. I hear they're very good actors."

"Sounds interestin'," Eli remarked politely.

The woman laughed at the tone of his remark. "You sound about as interested as my husband. But if you change your mind, the show starts at seven o'clock and it's in the community house, behind the courthouse."

"Will you and your family be there?" Casey asked.

"No, indeed," the woman said. "My husband's hitchin' up the mules right now. We're fixin' to leave for home." She reached down and playfully tweaked Bonnie's nose. "Whether we found this little urchin or not."

"We're just passin' through town," Casey said. "Any good place to get some dinner?"

"Weldon's boardin'house," she said at once. "You don't have to be roomin' there to buy dinner or supper. It's good country cookin'. I don't know what time it is now,

270

but they're open for dinner till one o'clock. There's a creek right behind the house. If you're worried about your horses and things, you could just take them over there behind Weldon's."

Casey looked quickly at Eli and they both nodded, so he said, "Well, thank you very kindly for the information. I think we've got time to get there."

She hurriedly told him how to find the boardinghouse and how to recognize it, while Eli went to fetch the horses. "Ed Weldon owns the house, but Cora Findley runs it and handles the dinin' room. She's got a cook named Biddy, who knows what to do in the kitchen. I hope you enjoy the food," she said, and took Bonnie by the hand and headed back to her wagon.

Thanks to the woman's directions, they made it to the boardinghouse with time to spare. When they pulled their horses up front, Ed Weldon was sitting on the porch. He got up from his rocker and stood at the edge of the front porch. "Can I help you fellows?"

"Yes, sir, I hope so," Casey said to him. "We're just passin' through your town and a nice lady told us that this was the place to get the best dinner in Tyler. So we got here as quick as we could. As you can see, we've got some horses we need to take care of. Any chance we could give 'em a rest behind your place while we buy some dinner?"

"Don't see any reason why not," Weldon said. "There's plenty of grass all the way back to the creek. Just take 'em on back there by the barn. I'll tell Cora she's got two more for dinner. After you take care of your horses, you can just come in the back door if you want."

"Much obliged," Casey said, and he and Eli took the horses down by Weldon's barn and pulled their saddles and packs off. When the horses were taken care of, he and Eli went in the back door of the house and walked up the hall to the dining room. They were warmly welcomed by Cora Findley, and the friendly faces of eight boarders seated around the table.

"Come in, gentlemen. My name's Cora Findley. Ed said you're just passing through our town. We're glad to have you join us for dinner. Most everybody has already finished, but don't let that bother you. Everybody's still drinking coffee. One of you can sit on that side of the table" — she pointed to an empty chair — "and the other one can sit on this side."

No sooner were they seated than the cook brought two heaping plates of food for them. "Thank you, Biddy," Cora said. "I assume you want coffee." They said they did. The food was good, but Casey would not rate it on par with Connie Grainger's. Eli might argue that it was, but Casey had committed too much of their money to admit that anyone could cook as well as Connie.

After a few minutes of questions from the other guests about where they had come from and where they were going, Weldon asked a question. He had come in to see how they were doing. "If you don't mind me askin', what's that you're carryin' on that one horse?"

They knew, of course, which horse he was referring to. "That's grain in those sacks, special mix they're raisin' up in Kansas. We're tryin' to see if it's somethin' we wanna raise in Waco, Texas." It was obvious that Weldon would have been interested to hear more about it, but he was kind enough to let them concentrate on their food. Pretty soon, the conversation returned to the subject being discussed before the two strangers arrived.

"So, what about it, Marvin?" one of the guests asked the man seated next to Casey. "Are you gonna go see Freeman and Hardy tonight?"

"I hadn't planned to," Marvin said. "Why?

Are you goin'?"

"I don't know. Folks that have been to their shows say they're pretty good. They're regular stage actors, you know. They don't just talk it. They get dressed up in the costumes, whether it's Roman emperors or Thomas Jefferson, with makeup and wigs. They say it's just like you were there when the real men debated."

"Maybe you oughta go, if you're interested in that sorta history stuff," Marvin said. "But I reckon I wouldn't have been interested, if I'da been there at the time their play really happened. I saw 'em when they pulled into town. I was at Riker's store when they drove by. Two mules pullin' what looked like a little circus wagon, decorated all up with their names painted all over it. I reckon they sleep in the wagon."

"I think they do," another guest spoke up then. "It's parked behind the community house. I reckon it's their dressin' room for the shows."

The conversation continued for a while, and the two late arrivals to the table did not participate, but Casey, in particular, found it quite interesting. When they had finished, they complimented Cora on the quality of the food, and promptly paid her.

Cora was pleased by their praise for

Biddy's cooking and said she would pass their comments along to the cook. "I just realized how rude I was," she confessed. "I forgot to ask your names. I didn't introduce you to the others at the table." They both identified themselves and assured her that they had not been offended. "Well, Mr. Tubbs and Mr. Doolin, I hope you'll take supper with us tonight, if you're still in town."

"Well, now, that's mighty temptin'," Casey said. "Since Mr. Weldon has been so kind to let our horses graze behind your house, I think we might take you up on that invitation." He hoped she hadn't noticed the sudden look of surprise on Eli's face as he continued speaking. "Eli and I thought we'd like to see a little bit more of the town, so we'll be back for supper."

"Wonderful," Cora exclaimed, taking it as another compliment. "Five o'clock, we'll look forward to having you back." She walked with them to the back door, and they headed back to their horses.

As soon as they were out of earshot from the house, Eli released it. "What in the Sam Hill are you talkin' about? We weren't plannin' to hang around here any longer."

"I wanna get a look at that fancy circus wagon they were talkin' about at the table,"

Casey told him. "They said they use it as a dressin' room."

"Well, I sure as hell ain't gonna set through a lotta actin' by a couple of fancy dandies for a couple of hours," Eli declared.

"I ain't, either," Casey said. "But I wouldn't mind takin' a look inside that wagon they're drivin'. There must be all kinds of wigs and whiskers, and everything you'd need to look like somebody you ain't. Better'n the undertaker, I'd bet."

"That's just what I was fixin' to say," Eli lied. "Might find everything we need for our actin' business. But we gotta wait till they're givin' the performance tonight," he stated, answering the next question he was about to ask. "But we get to eat another fine supper. What are we gonna do till then?"

"Look around the town a little bit, I reckon," Casey said. "I'll tell you, though, I'm beginnin' to think we need to just put our money in the packs and get rid of those damn grain sacks. Everywhere we go, somebody wants to know what's in those sacks. They just don't look right. And nobody ever wants to know what we've got in the regular packs. Might as well put the money there and take a chance on nobody gettin' ahold of 'em. Whaddaya think?"

"That's what I thought all along," Eli

claimed. "Let's dig the money outta them sacks."

"Good idea," Casey said sarcastically, but Eli didn't recognize it as sarcasm. They decided it would be the proper thing to make sure Ed Weldon was okay with them leaving their goods by his barn, and letting their horses graze there until they left after supper. So they walked back around the house to see if he had returned to the front porch. They found him in the same rocker he had previously occupied. "We don't wanna take advantage of a friendly offer," Casey started. "We've decided we're gonna hang around a little longer today, so we can eat supper here again tonight. But we thought you might expect a little something for lettin' our horses graze all afternoon."

"I wouldn't think of it," Weldon said. "I don't expect your horses will graze it all bare in one afternoon," he added with a chuckle.

"That's mighty neighborly of you, so I'll tell you what we'll do. We'll leave you a couple of buckets of that grain you were askin' about, and you can see how your horses do on it."

"Say, now," Weldon responded. "I would be interested in trying some of that feed. You goin' down there now?" They said that they thought they would, so he said, "I'll go down to the barn with you and get you a couple of buckets to put it in." He came down the porch steps immediately to join them, and they started toward the barn. "Don't worry about your possibles, if you're thinkin' about goin' into town for a drink or something. Ain't nobody gonna bother 'em here."

"That's what we were thinkin'," Eli said. "If you've got somethin' we could use as a scoop, that'ud be handy, too."

They walked down to the barn and Weldon went inside while Casey and Eli went to their packs and saddles, which they had left in a half circle close up against the side of the barn. They each stood by one of the sacks, to be sure the grain was emptied without exposing the bank bags buried within. In a few minutes, Weldon came back, carrying two buckets with a scoop in one of them. "I woulda told you to put your stuff inside the barn if I knew you were gonna be here awhile. We can still tote it inside."

"It won't hurt it to stay right where it is," Casey told him. "We're gonna be packin' it up to move on out, just as soon as we finish supper."

"Why don't you just camp right here

tonight and start out in the mornin'?" Weldon asked, thinking it made no sense to start out at night.

Every bit aware as Weldon was that their plans to leave after supper didn't make sense, Casey attempted to try to make it sound reasonable at least. "We're afraid we might be tempted to hang around longer in the mornin' just so we could eat breakfast with you," he joked with a chuckle. "We keep this up and we might not ever leave this town." Then he put on a serious face. "We'll load up and ride outta here after supper, and we'll make camp before it gets hard dark. And tomorrow mornin', we'll start out at first light and ride till the horses need a rest. Then we'll cook some breakfast." He took the buckets from Weldon and gave one of them to Eli.

When Casey untied his sack, Weldon walked over to look at the grain inside. "Looks like any other grain," he commented.

"That's what we said," Casey said. "That's why we're tryin' to see if it makes any difference in the way our horses work. The horses like it all right. We'll just have to wait and see."

While Weldon was staring into the sack of grain, Eli hurriedly filled his bucket and retied the sack. He tossed the scoop to Casey and handed the bucket to Weldon, who immediately dug his hand into it, so he could take a closer look at the grains. While he examined it, Casey filled his bucket and retied his sack. "Here," he said. "Here's another bucket. That oughta be enough to let you see some results."

"I declare, that's mighty generous of you boys to share your grain with me," Weldon said. "You sure you wanna give this much away?"

"Yep, the cookin' was worth it," Casey said.

"I'll put these buckets in the barn," Weldon said, and proceeded to do so.

"I swear," Eli said. "I felt the top of that money bag with the last pass I made with that scoop. It's a good thing that bucket was full. Ol' Ed woulda sure loved to have a scoop of what's in that bag."

Weldon talked awhile after he came back out of the barn, but finally announced that he felt a calling from his lower regions and thought he'd best answer it. So he finally left them to walk back up to the outhouse right behind the house. They went to work right away, repacking their possessions and supplies, while keeping an eye on the outhouse. They were happy to see that when he did come out of the privy, Weldon went back into the house. They took more care then to hide the cash money throughout the packs on both horses. When they were satisfied they had done the best they could to hide their wealth, they decided they could take the risk of leaving it for a couple of hours. So they saddled Biscuit and Smoke and rode leisurely out of the side yard toward the courthouse square and the main street of the town.

As they had been told, the community house was easy to find, even though there was no sign of any kind on it, or near it, to identify it as such. It was sitting on a backstreet that ran behind the courthouse. They walked their horses along the backstreet, past the community house, and discovered what they were looking for. Like the boardinghouse guest named Marvin had said, it was painted in multiple colors like a circus wagon.

"That's a sizable wagon" was Casey's first comment upon seeing the odd-looking vehicle, enclosed with a roof and windows along the sides. It was like a little house on wheels. "It oughta hold a lotta doodads and such."

"Don't look like there's anybody home right now," Eli commented, noticing the padlock on the door. "Wonder if they keep that padlock on the door when they're doin' one of their shows? We might better borrow a crowbar from Ed if we can find one in the barn."

CHAPTER 16

They rode back to the main street and stopped at a saloon to have a couple of drinks of whiskey while they discussed their plans for the Freeman and Hardy show that night. They decided it might be a better idea to buy a tool to work on that padlock. Weldon would most likely find that his was missing. And even though that might be after they were long gone, there was no sense in leaving him with the suspicion that they were the culprits. When in the process of hiding their money in their packs, they discovered they needed to buy coffee and lard, too. So, after they left the saloon, they went to a general merchandise store called Riker's to pick up the articles they needed. They were disappointed to find that Riker had never heard of Arbuckles' special blend of coffee, for they had developed a special liking for it. But it was a long ride back to Jim Lawrence's store in Salina, Kansas, just to buy some coffee.

When they returned to Weldon's boarding-house, they went back to the creek to check on their three packhorses and their packs. They were gratified to see that their packs had not been disturbed while they were away. They had not really expected Ed Weldon to snoop around their possessions, but they could not say the same for any of the guests at the house. At any rate, it was reassuring to find all the little telltale pieces of thread and horsehair, which Eli had so carefully placed on the flaps of the packs, were still in place.

When the tiny ring of Cora's dinner bell reached them, they figured it must be five o'clock and supper was evidently ready to be served. Casey checked his watch to make sure that it was suppertime, and they walked up to the house when he verified it. Weldon's regular guests welcomed Casey and Eli once again. "You say you boys are fixin' to head out to Waco after supper?" Marvin asked. "How long you figure that'll take you?"

" 'Bout two and a half days," Casey said. "We mighta been halfway there by now if Cora didn't set such a good table." His comment brought a laugh from the boarders and obviously pleased Cora, although she gave the credit to Biddy. They enjoyed another pleasant meal with the guests, and when they took their leave, they were invited back whenever they were anywhere close to that part of the county.

"Well, we stretched that supper out about as far as we could, I reckon," Eli commented when they walked back down to the barn. To take a long time with supper had been part of their plan in an effort to kill time. The performance in the community house didn't start until seven o'clock, and this time of year, it was just getting dark around that time. It was now about six, so they would take their time loading the packhorses and preparing to leave. Originally they had thought to head out of town and find a spot to camp for the night. Then they were going to leave the packhorses there, while they rode back to town and broke into the actors' wagon. But the more they thought about leaving their horses and packs unguarded while they were a mile or more away, the more they decided they couldn't afford the risk. So their alternate plan was to keep the packhorses with them. There was a stand of oak trees on the street behind the community house, and they decided to tie them in those trees while they searched the wagon.

When the horses were ready to go, they rode out the side yard again, and gave Ed Weldon a wave of the hand when they passed by the front porch. He watched them as they rode toward the road to Waco. It never occurred to him that one of the packhorses was no longer carrying two large grain sacks. Carrying that much grain was a little inconvenient. But it was good grain and they kept half of it to feed their horses. They left the rest of it in Weldon's barn, thinking it should give him something to ponder.

Out of sight of the house, they slowed the horses to a walk as they rode through town to take another look at the stand of trees where they planned to leave the horses. They rode silently past the wagon to see a light through the two windows from a lamp inside. The actors were no doubt getting in costume and applying makeup for the performance set to start in less than half an hour. They continued on until reaching the road to Waco, pointed out to them that afternoon by the young man who sold them the crowbar in Riker's. As soon as they were well away from the town, they started scouting for a spot to camp that night, one they could find in the dark, hopefully. The light was already failing rapidly when they came to a creek that looked to be what they needed. They pulled their horses up into the trees that lined the creek and took a look around.

"Looks all right to me," Eli said. Casey agreed, and there would be no trouble finding it, even in a hard dark.

While there was still a little time, and a little light as well, they gathered some wood for a fire, so they wouldn't be searching around in the dark for it later. When Eli's watch showed it was after seven, they stepped up into the saddle again and led their packhorses back to town. The lamps were lit in the community house when they rode down the backstreet behind it. As they approached the trees where they were going to tie the horses, the lamps in the community house went down, except for those in the end of the house where the stage evidently was located.

"Must be startin' the show," Casey said.

They rode into the oak trees and dismounted, then quickly tied the horses. It was fully dark now and there was no concern about being seen running across the lane behind the place. Once across, they stopped to listen and looked around them for a sign of anyone seeing them. They realized right away that they were alone back there. Any activity was on the street that ran in front of the community house.

"All right," Eli said, repeating their decision, "you're goin' in and I'm standin' lookout."

"That's right," Casey said, and started for the front of the wagon, only to stop at once. "There's a light in the wagon. They're still in there."

"What the hell are they doin'?" Eli whispered. "I thought the show already started."

"So did I."

"What are we gonna do?" Eli asked.

"Nothin' we can do but wait till they go in to do their actin'," Casey said. So they waited. Still, no one came out of the wagon. "Maybe one of 'em is in there by himself, 'cause it ain't time for his part yet."

Eli crept around to the front of the wagon. "Come on," he suddenly called to Casey, no longer whispering. When Casey came to him, Eli pointed to the padlock on the door. "They just left a light on in there, so you wouldn't have no trouble findin' what we need," Eli said, then went to work on the steel plate that held the hasp, knowing he would have a hard time forcing the padlock open. In just a few minutes' time, he separated the hasp from the door frame and opened the door.

"Don't take all night," he told Casey when he stepped up into the dressing room on wheels.

Once inside, Casey found himself in a packed jumble of props, costumes, makeup, wigs, beards, and mustaches. Unsure of how much time he might have before one or both of the actors came back to change characters or clothes, he was pleased to quickly find a cabinet that held hair. These were items that he knew would be hard to find, even at the undertaker. He realized at once that he had discovered a gold mine. For there were long gray wigs of all sorts, made from real hair, apparently. Seeing a cloth bag hanging on a rack, he took it and stuffed several wigs into it, as well as beards and mustaches. He ignored the clothes because they were mostly too stylish and of an earlier time period. He saw eyeglasses and took a couple pairs. There were several different jars of creams, and he took those to experiment with to see what they were for. Satisfied that he had all that could be useful to Eli and him, he prepared to leave, but stopped when he heard voices outside. He drew his six-shooter and listened.

"Who are you?" It came from a strange voice.

"I'm the man who makes sure nobody

bothers this wagon." Casey recognized Eli's voice.

"I just want an autograph from one of the actors," the strange voice said. "One of 'em is inside the wagon. I can see somebody movin' around. Which one is it?"

"It's Mr. Freeman," Eli said, "and he ain't got but a minute to get back on the stage. What's your name? I'll tell him to give you one when the show's over. He'll look for you."

"James," the voice said, "the same as his. Tell him James Gordon. I'll be right outside the door when it's over."

"I'll tell him. Now get outta here. He's got to get ready." He waited to make sure the man didn't linger to get a glimpse of his idol. When he saw him disappear around the front of the community house, he opened the door and said, "Let's get the hell outta here."

Casey couldn't help laughing at him. "Maybe you oughta be in there on the stage with the other actors. I don't feel right about stealin' from these fellows. I'm gonna leave some money to pay for what we took. How much you think I oughta leave?"

"Hell, I don't know. I don't know what you took," Eli responded. "You decide, but do it now, and let's go."

Casey peeled off two hundred dollars and left it under a hand mirror on the table. Since there was no sign of any other visitors to the wagon, Eli put the hasp back in place on the doorjamb and tried to drive the nails back in. His crowbar wasn't very effective as a hammer, so he had to settle for a pitiful attempt to secure the door before he gave up and ran after Casey, who was already crossing the road where they had left the horses. It was their desire to escape town this second time without witnesses. And it appeared that was to be the case as they rode out of the trees and followed the back road out to the end, before cutting over to strike the road to Waco again.

They rode until they came to the creek again, then carefully guided their horses back up the creek away from the road, until reaching the spot they had picked for their camp. After the horses were taken care of and their bedrolls situated, they built a small fire, mostly for the light it would provide. Eli was eager to see what Casey had found for them to use.

"It's mostly hair," Casey said. "But look at it. It looks like real hair to me, and it's white as snow, most of it, anyway. You wanna wear a beard? I got just the one for you, and I'm hopin' there's something in one of these little jars they stick 'em on with." Like two kids, they tried on the different wigs and whiskers, showing off to each other, until they tired of it. They decided it had been a good decision not to have looked for an undertaker, thinking it not a smart idea to do all their shopping in one place for their disguises. "We'll find something in Waco," Casey predicted, "if we don't come across something before then."

The two old outlaws passed a peaceful night and were on their way to Waco at first light, the next morning, following a well-traveled road. Had they known of the mystery they had left behind them in Tyler, it would have tickled them both. It seemed the performance by the talented team of Freeman and Hardy was interrupted when someone broke into their dressing room and stole some of their props. Young James Gordon told the sheriff that he had talked to the guard at the dual thespians' dressing-room wagon and was told that Mr. Freeman would meet with him after the show. Mr. Freeman, of course, had no knowledge of it, and, in fact, had been on the stage at that particular time. The actors had been most gracious about the incident, since there had been no great loss of their inventory. They had not felt the necessity to report the discovery of two hundred dollars under a hand mirror.

The end of their second day of travel from Tyler found them approaching a small town on the Navasota River, about forty miles east of Waco. After two days of eating their own cooking, they were in the mood for supper cooked by a woman. The road in took them by the railroad station to the main street beyond. They pressed their horses to a trot to get over the tracks when they heard the train whistle as it began braking for a stop in the town.

Casey looked up at the name of the town over the platform and pronounced it. "Mexia," he said. "Didn't know there was such a town."

"Well, it must be a good'un," Eli said, "or the train wouldn't stop here."

"Then they oughta have a decent place to eat," Casey said. "Let's go find it."

"That looks like it might be a good prospect right yonder," Eli said, and pointed to a small building jammed between a general merchandise store and a saloon. It had a simple sign that proclaimed it to be BERTHA'S. "It don't say Bertha's what," Eli remarked, "but it looks like it might be

Bertha's kitchen or dinin' room. And I don't see no place else that looks likely."

"Looks that way," Casey agreed, so they started their horses toward it. Neither man noticed the name of the saloon next to Bertha's until they were a little closer. The word "saloon" was prominent in large letters, but the name of the saloon was written in smaller letters that identified it as HENRY'S. "Henry's and Bertha's," Casey declared. "You reckon they might be married?"

They tied their horses out front and walked into Bertha's to find a narrow dining room furnished with nothing more than a long table, which was half-filled by six customers. All six stopped eating to gape at the two strangers.

A large woman, who could only be Bertha, was slowly circling the table, dishing beans out, one big spoonful for each person. "Where you settin'?" That was her only welcome, so they picked an empty spot, sat down on the bench, and turned the plates right-side-up in time to get a serving of beans.

"Meat's on the platter," Bertha said. "I'll bring more," she said before they had a chance to complain that there were only a couple of small scraps on the platter in the center of the table. "Taters and gravy on the way," she announced as she went to the small kitchen at the end of the dining room. She was back right away with a bowl in the crook of her arm and a plate of biscuits in her hand.

Sensing it to be an eating competition, Casey and Eli got set to attack as soon as she placed the biscuits on the table. But out of a sense of fairness, she served them before she put the plate on the table.

"I'll bring you some coffee," she said then.

" 'Preciate it," Eli said. "How 'bout some meat?"

"Soon as it's done," she said, and went to get their coffee.

"Don't worry. She'll make sure you get all the food you pay for," the young man sitting next to Eli said. Evidently, one of the early eaters at the competition, he had satisfied his hunger and was just nursing a cup of coffee along. "Nobody goes away hungry from Bertha's." He paused to finish off the coffee in his cup. "You fellers are strangers to Mexia, ain'tcha? Just passin' through?"

"That's right," Eli said. "We've never been here before. We're headin' back toward Lampasas County. I expect we'll camp here tonight." He had to ask, "Any chance Henry's next door is owned by Bertha's husband?"

The man laughed. "That's a fact. They are married. Nobody knows for sure, but the story most folks believe is that they had a big fallin'-out when they built these two places. And when it came to pickin' names for 'em, they just wanted to let folks know who owned what."

"Well, it's a nice-lookin' little town," Casey spoke up then. "We'll take a look around while we're here. Do you live here in town?"

"Yes, sir. I'm Jack Myers. I'm the blacksmith."

"You don't say?" Casey said. "You interested in shoein' a couple of horses tonight? Or are you finished for the day? Me and Eli was just talkin' about that this mornin'."

"No, sir, I ain't quit for the day," Jack quickly assured him. "I just get here early for supper to make sure I don't miss out on the best chops. My wife's out of town, gone to visit her folks for a week or so. That's why I'm eatin' at Bertha's. I'd be glad to take care of your horses soon as you finish your supper. With my wife gone, I ain't in no hurry to get home. And since you're figurin' on campin' here tonight, there's a dandy spot right behind my shop by the creek. Grass and water right there for you."

"That sounds like we found the right place

to stop. Just like the setup we had back in Kansas, behind the blacksmith," Casey said to Eli. "We're leadin' three packhorses," he went on to say to Myers, "but their hooves look all right. It's the two horses we're ridin' that need shoes. We were talkin' about havin' it done in Waco, but if you can do it tonight, we'll do it right here." He looked at Eli. "That all right with you, partner?"

"Yep," Eli responded. "Fine by me." He was somewhat surprised by Casey's sudden decision to have Biscuit and Smoke shoed, but they had talked about that this morning. Even though it was not critical that they get it done immediately, he suspected Casey had other reasons for suggesting it that he would no doubt inform him of later.

Just as Jack had predicted, Casey and Eli did not walk away from Bertha's hungry. The meal was filling and good tasting, well worth the modest price she charged. Jack waited with them until they had finished eating, then they led the horses down to his shop near the creek. They let the horses drink after they removed their saddles and packs, then led Biscuit and Smoke up to Jack's shop. When they walked back to the creek to set up their camp, Eli said, "At any time, now, you ready to tell me why you suddenly decided to let this fellow shoe our horses?"

"It's this town," Casey responded. "Nice peaceful little town, and the Houston and Texas Central Railroad stops here. Sooner or later, we're gonna be plannin' our next job, and this looks like a good place for two old men to wander into town and grab some cash."

"Maybe so," Eli said, not convinced. "But look around, I don't even see a bank. I ain't sure they've got one."

"I ain't talkin' about a bank," Casey said. "I'm talkin' about the train. I'm thinkin' how easy it was up in Abilene when we just walked away from that train settin' in the station. It oughta be easier'n that in this little town. We needed new shoes on our horses, so I thought it'd be worthwhile to go back up to his shop and chew the fat with the blacksmith while he's workin'. We oughta be able to find out if that train stops here at this time every day, and maybe what other times it stops."

"And if it stops every day, or just some-times," Eli said.

"Right. We need to know when it goes south and when it comes back. That train still settin' there is headed north, so it came from Houston. Wonder which way it carries the most money? Maybe we need to go over to the station and find out more about their schedule."

"Are you thinkin' about robbin' that train now?" Eli asked. "Because if you are, it ain't gonna be a very good time to do it when our horses are gettin' new shoes."

"No, I ain't thinkin' about doin' it now," Casey said. "But I got a feelin' it won't be as long as we thought before we'll be doin' the next job. And to rob the mail car on that train, while it's parked in the station, might be the best idea for two old fellows like us."

"Maybe so," Eli agreed. "I wonder if they've got a peace officer."

"I don't see anything that looks like a jail, and I'd bet it would be hard to get up a posse to go after the railroad's money."

"I weren't talkin' about the town," Eli said. "I was talkin' about the train. Don't know about this railroad, but the Union Pacific has guards that ride some of their trains. Maybe this railroad does, too. Let's go up to the shop and talk to Jack, and maybe we can get a better idea if the town folks would get up a posse if somebody robbed the train."

It was a good idea, for Jack Myers liked to talk when he was in a good mood. And he was in a good mood because he picked up a couple of horses to shoe when he went to supper, and he had a couple of drinks bought for him at Henry's afterward. By the time their horses were finished, Casey and Eli knew enough about the town to feel safe in leaving their camp while they went to the saloon for a drink. At one time, the town had had a sheriff, Jack told them, but he moved on to a better-paying job in Waco. The town had noticed no increase in crime since he had gone, so there was never any rush to replace him. By the time they said good night to their good friend Jack, they had decided to delay their departure the next morning for a visit to the stationmaster at the railroad office to get a schedule of the comings and goings of the train.

They packed up their camp the next morning before Jack came to open his shop for the day. Not wishing to explain the lateness of their start to Waco, they rode the horses past the railroad station and waited in an oak grove for some signs of life in the stationmaster's office. He arrived a few minutes after five-thirty, and Eli and Casey rode back to the station a minute or two after.

"Good mornin'," Casey called out cheerfully. "We were headin' out to Waco and noticed you openin' up your office, so we thought we'd stop and ask you a few questions, if you don't mind."

"What kind of questions?" he asked, standing by his stove, just before starting his fire for his morning coffee.

"We work for a shippin' company in Fort Worth," Casey said. "Maybe you've heard of it, Doolin and Tubbs." The stationmaster shook his head slowly. "Well, anyway," Casey continued, "the company's been shippin' goods and money outta Waco, but they sent us to scout out better shippin' points. And one of the towns they're considerin' is Mexia. I was wonderin' if you could tell us how often the trains come and go here."

Apparently relieved, the stationmaster said, "I can give you a schedule of the times of every train that passes through Mexia, and the direction they're goin' in." He threw the few pieces of firewood he had been holding into the stove and went to his desk to fetch a copy of the train schedule. "That's up to date, and it'll tell you everything you need to know."

"Much obliged," Casey said as he glanced at the schedule. "This oughta please our boss. What is your name, sir? I wanna tell him how helpful you've been."

"My name's David Gage. I'm glad to help any way I can," he said.

"Thanks again, Mr. Gage," Casey said as they headed toward the door. He paused then, before going out the door. "Once in a while, we have to ship money up from Houston. Is there a guard ridin' in the mail car?"

"Sometimes," Gage said, "but not all the time. If there's an extra big shipment of money, there's usually a guard ridin' the train. So if you're sendin' an extra big shipment, you can talk to the stationmaster down there."

Casey looked over the schedule as they walked back to their horses. "This ain't just for Mexia," he said to Eli. "It tells the times the train hits every town on this line. This was worth gettin' a late start this mornin'."

"It ain't but forty miles to Waco, so we'll still be there tonight," Eli said. "But if we're still thinkin' about goin' back to Lampasas County, back to the Whitmore Brothers Ranch, that's gonna be two more long days, unless we make two and a half days out of it." He looked over and gave Casey a concerned stare. "I ain't sure we're doin' the right thing, talkin' about roundin' up the boys again. How the hell are we gonna explain where we suddenly found a place where we can get money to buy cattle? They're gonna know there ain't but one way we could come by that kind of money, and that's to steal it."

"We'll tell 'em I've got a rich old grandpa and he's left me with all his money," Casey said. "They ain't gonna believe it, but if we stick to that story, they'll just have to accept it, whether they believe it or not. 'Cause if I'm right, we're gonna find those boys layin' around with no place to go. I expect they've contacted every ranch around that valley and they ain't had no luck a-tall. They'll ride for us because they want to eat, and there ain't no other offer."

He watched Eli chew on that in his mind for a while, then Casey said, "They're gonna be treated better than any other cowhands in the valley. We're gonna take care of 'em. And remember, it'll just be you and me on the wrong side of the law. If the law catches up with us, they'll be left with whatever we've built and a range full of cattle."

Eli pushed his hat back so he could scratch his head, then shrugged and said, "When you put it that way . . ."

CHAPTER 17

They reached the bridge over the Brazos River at noontime on the second day after leaving Mexia, having decided to make the trip a little easier on their horses. They decided they were in no particular hurry to get to Waco, anyway. It was no ordinary bridge. It was a suspension bridge that measured four hundred and seventy-five feet, which the people of Waco had raised the money to build, and it had opened the town up to settlers coming from the east. Casey and Eli were not sure that was a good thing because they figured it would ultimately lead to all the grazing land west of the Brazos going under the farmer's plow. But they were both duly impressed by the structure. At any rate, it made for an easy crossing of the Brazos.

Although they had talked about remaining in the business of raising cattle ever since they left Sherman, there was still a cloud of uncertainty about that decision. This was after agreeing that taking the risks involved with their recent choice of professions seemed senseless unless they enjoyed the rewards that resulted. With that in mind, they checked into the McClellan House Hotel on the corner of Fourth Street and Austin Avenue. Although they could afford separate rooms, they settled for one room with two beds. The desk clerk informed them that the dining room would be open for another hour.

So, after they carried their saddlebags and several other bags from their packhorses to the room, they took the horses to a stable several blocks from the hotel. Leaving only the packhorses, they paid for all five, but said they'd bring their riding horses back later. Horace Temple, the owner of the stable, let them pile their packs in the corner of the stall at no extra charge.

They rode back to the hotel dining room with plenty of time to spare, where they were politely asked by Thelma Townsend if they were guests at the hotel.

"We're stayin' in the hotel," Eli said to her, "but we ain't guests. We're payin' to stay here."

She ignored his attempted humor, and with an expression of boredom on her face, she asked them to remove their weapons and leave them in a small coat closet near the door.

"What if we need to shoot somebody?" Eli asked, just to see if she had a sense of humor.

With no change of expression, Thelma said, "Come to me and I'll get it for you." She turned her head in the direction of a young woman carrying a couple of plates to a table nearby. "Frances will be happy to take care of you," she said, and seated them next to a table where two men were eating. They were obviously businessmen and they seemed to be in deep discussion about something important.

Looking around them, Casey and Eli realized they stood out by virtue of their trail clothes and broad-brimmed hats. "Maybe we'd best be real quiet, so we don't disturb none of these folks," Eli whispered to Casey. "We don't want 'em chokin' on their chuck."

"Maybe you're right," Casey said with a chuckle. "We'll probably get good service, though, 'cause they'll most likely wanna get us outta here as quick as they can." He saw the server coming toward them, so he warned Eli, "Look out, here comes Frances."

"Okay, cowboys, what's it gonna be?" Frances said cheerfully, much to their surprise. "Coffee, tea, or water?" They both said coffee. "Shepherd's pie, or pork loin?"

"Pork," Casey said.

"I'd try the pie, if I knew it came from a tender shepherd," Eli couldn't resist saying.

"You win the golden biscuit for being the first clown to come up with that one today," Frances said, but couldn't help smiling. "Our cook is Irish and every so often she'll bake a shepherd's pie, but she's using beef, instead of lamb, because we don't have any lamb. You wanna try it? It's good. You can take my word for it." Eli said he'd try it, and Casey changed his order, too, after hearing what a shepherd's pie was.

They found the shepherd's pie to be as good as Frances said it would be, good enough, in fact, to quell their conversation for a long period while they concentrated on their plates. It was during this lull that Casey heard one of the businessmen at the table next to theirs make a remark that captured his attention. He stopped chewing and listened to the other man's response, and he had to interrupt.

"Excuse me, gentlemen," Casey said. "I couldn't help hearing what you just said." They both became tense and stopped talking immediately. "If you don't mind me askin', I was wonderin' why you said the cattle business was dead."

Then, seeing no threat in Casey's tone, the man who had made that statement said to him, "It had to happen. The country's industrial capacity got so good following the war that it caused a decrease in the value of products. Cattle is one of those products that isn't worth what had been paid for it. The big cattle outfits are going into bankruptcy, the small ranches can't pay for their loans. Right now, if you drove a herd up to Wichita or Abilene, they wouldn't give you a dollar per cow. If you are in the cattle business, I expect you already know this."

"For a fact, I didn't," Casey said. He looked at the other man. "Is that the way you see it?"

"I'm afraid so," he said. "All the government's money is going to the railroads. And the railroads can go any damn place they please. No matter if you own a small farm or a large ranch, if the railroad wants to lay tracks across your land, they do it with the government's backing. I hope you're not raising a big herd right now that you'll be trying to sell."

"No, sir. We just sold our last big herd, so I reckon we're some of the lucky ones.

Thank you for the information." He looked back to see the look of woe on Eli's face, then asked one final question. "Do you think the price of cattle will ever come back?"

"Oh, hell yes," the man said. "The country has to have meat. It's just a question of when it will recover."

The discussion caused a drop in the conversation at both tables as Casey and Eli finished their shepherd's pie. Eli wanted to leave a little something extra for Frances, which he did, much to her surprise. They paid the stern-faced Thelma for their dinner and collected their weapons and departed.

Outside, Casey said, "Let's go to the Reservation just to look around." He had heard about that brothel section of Waco, but he had never been there.

Eli was still thinking about the comments made by the two men in the dining room. "I reckon that kinda kills our plans to get in the cattle business."

"Hell no," Casey responded. "That means we're gonna buy us a startup herd dirt cheap. Like the man said, the country has to have meat. If there was ever a time to buy cattle, it's right now, and I'm thinkin' we're gonna need some more money quicker than we thought. So this afternoon we'd best find some clothes to work in. And I think to find the kinda clothes we're lookin' for, we need to find us an undertaker in the Reservation."

So they rode over to the section known as the Reservation and walked their horses slowly along the street of saloons, dancehalls, and houses of prostitution, but no sign that advertised an undertaker's services.

"You know there's gotta be somebody who picks up the dead drunks and the gunfight losers," Casey said. "I reckon we'll have to go to a saloon to find him."

"How 'bout the Dead Dog Saloon?" Eli suggested. It was next door to a house bearing a sign that identified it as THE PLEASURE HOUSE. "Wonder what they do in there?" Eli joked.

"You've got enough money to go in there and find out," Casey joked as they dismounted and tied up in front of the saloon.

"That's a fact," Eli came back, "but I ain't so sure I've got enough to get cured of whatever I'd pick up in there."

They walked into the Dead Dog and found it with only a few customers, since it was early afternoon. There was a three-handed card game at a table near the front and a couple of men standing at the bar, talking to the bartender. Otherwise, it was dead. Casey and Eli walked up to the bar. The bartender, a short, bald man with a bushy red mustache, came down the bar to serve them. "Howdy, boys, whaddaya drinkin'?"

"What's that you're pourin' shots from on the bar?" Eli asked, and pointed to the bottle.

"Corn whiskey," Ned, the bartender, said.

"How much you charge for that?"

"Quarter a shot, just like every other saloon on the street," Ned said.

"Whaddaya charge for the good stuff, that stuff that's under the counter?" Eli asked.

"Fifty cents," Ned said. When Eli asked why, Red said, " 'Cause it's ninety-proof rye whiskey."

"Gimme me a shot of that," Eli said.

Ned reached under the bar and pulled out another bottle. He poured a shot for Eli, then held the bottle over an empty glass and looked at Casey.

"No, thanks," Casey said, "I'll take the cheap stuff. One of us needs to stay sober enough to find our way back to the hotel." They tossed the shots down and had Ned pour another. Then Casey asked, "Who's the fellow who picks up the bodies around here?" When the bartender cocked his head to the side, but didn't answer, Casey said, "You know, the undertaker, who does that job here in the Reservation?"

"Oh," Ned said. "You talkin' about Carl Pope? He takes care of any corpse that ain't been claimed by nobody."

"Right, Carl Pope. What does he do with 'em when he picks 'em up?"

"Hell, I don't know," Ned said. "I ain't never thought about it. He just picks 'em up and hauls 'em away. He might butcher 'em and eat 'em, for all I know."

Casey and Eli exchanged looks of disgust at that, then Casey asked, "Where's Carl's place of business?"

Ned was stumped for a moment before answering. "Carl ain't got no place of business. He just comes a-runnin' when he hears shootin'. Or the sheriff or somebody goes to get him when we find a dead drunk layin' in the street."

"Where do they go to get Carl?" Casey asked.

"He's got a little barn buildin' on the street behind the saloon, two or three blocks that way," he said, and pointed north.

"Much obliged," Casey said. "You want another shot?" he asked Eli, but Eli said he'd had enough, so they paid Ned and started to leave.

"You goin' to look for Carl?" Ned asked.

"Yeah, we thought we would," Casey said. "We've got a little business to talk to him about."

Ned shook his head. "He ain't there."

"How do you know that?" Casey asked.

" 'Cause he's settin' right over there with them other two fellers, playin' cards," Ned said.

"Well, damn," Eli swore, thinking Ned was an idiot, but he didn't tell him so. Instead, he and Casey walked directly over to the table to confront the three men, who were now staring at them. "Carl Pope?" Eli asked.

Pope didn't respond, but he didn't have to. The two men he was playing cards with both turned to stare at him. "Mr. Pope," Casey said, "we need to have a word with you."

Pope was obviously reluctant to talk with them. They were dressed like all the other cowhands who passed through Waco. And he couldn't help thinking the only business they might have with him could be a grudge because he buried one of their friends or kin. And maybe that person had some possession they wanted back. His mind was racing backward, trying to think if there had been any such item. He could think of nothing.

"Mr. Pope," Casey said, "the governor has authorized us to pay you ten dollars just to take a look through any clothing you may still have that might give us a clue that the person we're lookin' for might have been killed in this town."

"You ain't thinkin' I mighta had anythin' to do with killin' whoever you're lookin' for, are ya?" Pope asked.

"Not a-tall," Casey said to him. "We just wanna see if you mighta buried him. We're pretty sure we can recognize any clothing of his that you might still have. That is, if you don't always bury your bodies with everything they had on. Do you, Mr. Pope?"

"No, sir," he said at once. "When there ain't no funeral, it don't make sense to throw good clothin' in the ground where nobody can use 'em."

"We figured you would have the right attitude. We hate to interrupt your card game, but the governor is anxious to get this business cleared up, and we need to get back to Austin."

"And get back into some comfortable clothes, ourselves," Eli remarked, "instead of wearin' these cowboy duds." Casey gave him a look that said that wasn't necessary.

Pope got up from his chair. "Ten dollars just to look at 'em, ain't that what you said?"

"That's what I said, ten dollars," Casey said. "We won't keep you long, then you can get back here and lose it to these two fellows."

They walked out the front door, untied their horses, and led them up the street while they walked back with Carl Pope. When they got to the corner, they turned down a side street to end up on the back-street where Pope had built a barn to prepare the bodies for burial. He lived in a small portion of it, walled off from his mortuary. When they walked in, they saw the body of an old man lying on the table. It was clothed only in his underwear.

"Who is that?" Eli asked.

"That's an old drunk that's been hangin' around the Dead Dog for about a week, beggin' for money to buy whiskey. Ned found him this mornin' outside the door, deader'n hell. Looks like somebody knocked him in the head. I'll bury him tonight before he starts gettin' ripe. He's one like we was talkin' about. Don't nobody know who he is, there won't be no funeral, so it ain't no use buryin' his clothes on him. His clothes was in pretty bad shape, but he musta had a decent pair of shoes, 'cause he was barefoot when Ned found him." He shrugged indifferently. "If you knew what kind of shoes he wore, I expect you might could find who hit him in the head." As an afterthought, he asked, "He ain't the man you fellers are lookin' for, is he?"

"Nope," Casey said, "he ain't our man. Where do you keep all the clothes, hats, and such?" Pope gave them a wave of his hand to follow him and led them to the back end of his workshop.

"This is my storeroom," he said, and opened the door to a small room that was half-filled with garments for men and women. "I sell 'em to folks who ain't got a lot of money to spend on new outfits and ain't too proud to wear secondhand clothes from dead people." Quick to defend his actions, he said, "The city pays me two dollars to go get a body and bury it. They know I can't hardly make it on that, so they let me sell the clothin'."

"Ain't nothin' wrong with that," Eli told him. "You're doin' the city a service. We'll look through your cheaper stuff to see if we can find what we're lookin' for. Here's your ten dollars the governor owes you for lookin' at 'em."

"What are your prices for these coats and trousers?" Casey asked.

"That side of the room where you're standin', everything on hooks or shelves, I get a dollar for. The other side is where I put the poorer quality items and they're just fifty cents apiece."

"We'll make this as quick as we can," Casey said to Pope, "so you just go about your business, if you've got something else to do."

"Right," he said, but he didn't have anything he needed to do, so he just stood around and watched the two strangers go through his wares. He couldn't help thinking they resembled men shopping for a new suit more than a couple of investigators looking for a particular piece of clothing. Occasionally one of them would even hold a coat or jacket up in front of himself for the other one to look at. And most of their looking was in the section of poorer-quality clothing. *I reckon they know what they're doing,* he decided.

"Sorry," Casey finally said. "Looks like it took longer than we said it would. To try to make it up to you, we bought some items to take with us. We know some folks who are havin' some hard times and they could use these clothes. Plus, I want this shabby old hat. It looks like one my grandpa wore when I was a boy. So add all this up and we'll pay you for it. Then we'll get outta your way.

I'm sorry we didn't find the piece of clothin' that would tell us our man was here, but we did some shoppin' for two old buzzards who will appreciate it."

"Always glad to help the governor," Pope told them. He was, in fact, truly appreciative of their surprise visit. With the articles of clothing they bought added to the ten dollars from the governor, he was showing a profit of nineteen dollars and fifty cents. He didn't even mind having to bury the corpse on his table that night. He walked outside with them, while they secured their purchases behind their saddles, then watched them ride away. There was still a little time before supper, so he walked back down to the Dead Dog Saloon.

Horace Temple met Casey and Eli at the corral when they returned to the stable to leave Biscuit and Smoke. They told him they might get their horses the next day or wait another day. They hadn't decided yet. With what they had learned at dinner that day about the immediate fate of the cattle business, they knew they had a lot to talk over. And if they took the course of action that Casey favored at the present, they might be planning a rendezvous with the Houston and Texas Central Railroad. If that was the case, they would be retracing the forty miles back to the little town of Mexia. They might have considered pulling the planned holdup at one of the other small towns on the line, but Mexia was the only one they had seen.

"What are you boys talking so seriously about tonight?" Frances asked when she brought them their coffee. "You've had your heads together like you're discussing the future of the world."

"Tryin' to decide if it's best to have a steak or a pork chop," Eli said to her. "We ain't used to havin' to make a choice when it's time to eat."

"Well, that's a relief," Frances said. "I'll have to tell Thelma. She was convinced that you were probably thinking about robbing the place. I told her, if that was what you two were talking so hard about, you woulda probably wore your guns again."

"We did talk about that," Eli went along with her nonsensical banter. "We forgot we left 'em in the room. And we was tryin' to decide if one of us could hold you up long enough with a fork till the other'n got back with our guns." He gave her a big grin. "But we decided to eat first, and then go get our guns. And what we're tryin' to decide now is if we might feel too full to rob the place and we'll just take a little nap, instead."

Frances threw her head back and laughed. She had no comeback for that, so she asked, "Steak or chop? Those chops were cooked up in a heavy gravy. You might like them."

"You sold me," Eli said, and Casey nodded his agreement. Frances went to the kitchen to fill their plates, and the two outlaws resumed their discussion on whether or not to hold up the train. They were both still bothered to some extent about the bank robbery in Wichita and the fact that so many hardworking folks had lost their savings. Based on what they had been told earlier by the two businessmen in the dining room, they felt less conscience stricken when they thought they were taking money from the railroad. And the railroad could spare it.

After supper, they went up to their room in the hotel to try on the clothes they had selected from Carl Pope's storeroom, as well as experiment with the various jars of makeup they had taken from Freeman and Hardy's wagon. They found one jar in particular that gave their faces an almost sun-baked look, making them seem older. They found that one of the jars held a sticky salve that worked well to hold whiskers and mustaches in place. They selected the wigs that went best with the beards and mustaches.

"Those maids are gonna wonder what in the hell we were doin' tonight, when they clean up this basin of water," Casey commented. "Maybe we'd best carry it down to the washroom tonight and empty it and fill up our pitcher again."

Satisfied they could apply their makeup to fool close friends about their age and identity, they turned their attention to their wardrobes. That part was much simpler, for while they selected them at Carl Pope's barn, they were careful to judge if they were close to the right size. The clothes they bought were of the simplest fashion and well-worn, with morning coats long enough to cover their sidearms. When picking them out, they tried to find clothes that looked a little bit large to contribute to a dumpy-looking effect. They judged each other, and when they both had put together outfits that both of them approved, they bundled them carefully to be put in their packs. Now they were ready to face the critical part, the planning of the robbery. It was not going to be as easy as the time they walked away with a bag of money from the train in the Abilene station. And they didn't have a couple of old worn-out horses to willingly abandon, like the two they rode into the bank in Wichita. The planning would continue on into the night before they decided they had a general plan that, hopefully, they could refine on their way back to Mexia.

CHAPTER 18

They did not check out of the hotel the next morning, thinking it a good idea to be registered there in Waco when the train was robbed in Mexia. Knowing they would need at least one of their packhorses, they left two of their five horses in the stable, with a great proportion of their packs. They told Horace Temple that they were going to be away for a night or two while they looked over some land for sale up the Brazos River. Temple assured them he would take good care of their horses. And Eli told him he could feed their horses grain outta the one burlap sack beside their packs and save his own.

Temple exclaimed, "Oh, is that what's in that sack?"

Like he didn't know, Eli thought.

Since it was only about forty miles to Mexia, they decided to eat breakfast before they left Waco. That would eliminate one meal they had to carry. The bulk of the light load on the packhorse was made up of their money and enough supplies for a few spartan meals. They figured they would eat when they got back to Waco. Their haste did not go unnoticed by Frances or Thelma.

"You two are mighty quiet this morning," Frances commented. "You musta gone hunting on the Reservation last night."

Casey laughed. "Nope, it's been a few years back since we thought we had to go see the elephant. We've just got to get started on a little trip up the Brazos this mornin' and we're kinda sad we ain't gonna be here to eat with you at dinnertime."

"That's a fact," Eli said. "We'll be eatin' nothin' but salty ol' bacon and hardtack."

"Well, that just ruins my day," Frances joked, and refilled their coffee cups. They didn't linger, finishing off their breakfast in workmanlike manner, then headed out the door.

They rode a little farther than halfway before they found a spot that suited them to rest the horses. It was a fairly deep creek, bordered by a belt of oak trees with small randomly spaced grassy plots for convenient grazing. After the horses were relieved of their burdens, Casey and Eli gathered wood for a fire. Traveling light, they had only brought coffee, bacon, hardtack, the coffeepot, and a frying pan. To supplement their first meal on the trail, however, they had brought a couple of biscuits from the hotel dining room. Frances had wrapped them in a napkin for them on their way out. While they ate, they went over their plan once more — if there was no guard riding in the mail car and if there was a guard.

"The five-fifteen train to Dallas," Casey declared once again. "Today is Thursday, right?" Eli said that it was. Casey pulled out his schedule and checked it again. "Thursday," he read. "Mexia, five-fifteen tonight." He looked at Eli. "And it is a passenger train."

When the horses were rested, they continued on. The next site they picked would serve as their base close to town, where they would change into their disguises and get ready to ride into town as soon as the train pulled in. There was one risk they had considered, but decided it was not a likely one. The blacksmith in Mexia, Jack Myers, could identify Biscuit and Smoke, if there was any chance he might be anywhere near them. But they figured that chance was so small, it would hardly be likely.

"I swear," Eli declared, "if we don't pull

this one off, I hope whoever ends up with ol' Biscuit treats him right."

"If they do catch us," Casey said, "ain't they gonna be surprised to find the money we're carryin' in our packs and saddlebags?" He switched to his impression of an old man's voice and said, "Maybe we'll have to try to tell 'em we weren't gonna rob 'em, we were tryin' to give some money back."

It was approaching four-thirty when they reached the creek outside of Mexia where they had spent the night after leaving the town before. There was no time to spare, so they rode up the creek, into the thicker cover of trees and bushes, before they stopped to let the horses drink. Leaving Biscuit and Smoke saddled, they took the packs off the packhorse and covered them with branches from the trees, hoping they wouldn't be noticed if someone stumbled upon the horse. They immediately started stripping off their clothes to get into the worn-looking outfits they had selected for this adventure. With the one hand mirror Casey borrowed from the hotel room, they began applying the olive-colored makeup that made their skin appear to be darker and craggy. The gray wigs, beards, and mustaches were the last touches. To test the firmness of his wig's fit, Eli put on his dilapidated old hat, took it off, and put it back on several times to make sure his dirty gray hair stayed in place. Casey put his battered old hat through the same test.

Conscious of the time now, they took a final inspection of each other. "I can't see nothin' else we could do," Eli commented. "I believe we're ready to go. Hell, I think I even feel older, and you sure as hell look old enough to be my daddy. I expect my daddy woulda been a better-lookin' man, though."

They tied the packhorse to a tree, using a long enough rope to let him get to the water, if he wanted to. They each carried a large canvas bag they hooked on their saddle horns. One of these carried a coil of rope. The final test for their disguises came when Eli's bay gelding shied away when Eli approached him.

"Well, I'll be . . ." Eli started. "He don't know it's me." He took hold of the horse's ears and pulled his head down against his chest to let him get a smell of him. "He still ain't sure," Eli said. "It's the smell in these old clothes." Biscuit jerked his head up as soon as Eli let go of his ears. "Ain't that somethin'?"

"Look out he don't buck you off, old man," Casey joked. He climbed up into the saddle. "Smoke knows who's ridin' him."

"Shoot, Smoke'll let anybody get on him," Eli mocked. "He ain't never been particular." He climbed up on Biscuit then and the big bay gelding settled down at once, evidently feeling the familiar weight on his back. They made their way back through the trees to the road and proceeded toward the railroad station. Just as they pulled their horses up to the end of the platform, they heard the whistle of the approaching train, so they dismounted and tied them there. Then, feeling as if everybody in town was staring at them, they tried to walk up on the platform as casually as they could. The few people who were on the platform paid them no mind, concerned more about getting on the train, or meeting someone getting off. Everyone turned toward the track as the train pulled into the station.

"Yonder's the mail car," Casey said. He recognized the station master when he walked back to it and waited with a bag of mail for the mail clerk inside the car to open the door. Carrying their canvas sacks, Casey and Eli walked quickly over behind the stationmaster, who was exchanging neighborly greetings with the mail clerk. The clerk took the mailbag offered him and gave the stationmaster one in exchange. He wished the clerk a safe journey and turned to take the bag to the mail room right away, totally unaware of the two old men behind him.

The clerk started to bring the door down to lock it, when Casey commanded, "Whoa, young feller! Ain'tcha gonna take the rest of it?" He and Eli quickly stepped off the platform and into the mail car. "We got more mail here."

"What the . . . ?" the clerk blurted. "You can't come in here!" He stepped back, startled and tripped on the mailbag the stationmaster had just given him, landing flat on his back. Eli reached up and pulled the door down and locked it. The clerk started to scramble to his feet, but was stopped cold by the sight of Casey's Colt Single Action Army .44 pointed right at his face.

"I think it'll be better for you if you don't try to get up from there," Casey told him. "Me and Oscar was kinda hopin' we wouldn't have to kill nobody this time, like we did last time. Oscar, see if you can find that money."

"There's a safe over there with the door open, Elmer," Eli said. "But that can't be that big payroll that's supposed to be on here. I'm tellin' you, I'm too old to come on another one of these jobs and the money ain't there when it's supposed to be. You know that's the only reason I shot that Union Pacific mail clerk."

"Are you crazy?!" the clerk exclaimed. "You two old coots are facin' a federal offense! You can't be in this car!"

"Who you callin' an 'old coot'?" Eli reacted at once, pulling out his six-shooter and aiming it at the terrified mail clerk. "If you don't tell us where that payroll is, I'm gonna put some air-holes in your head."

"Better check them doors, Oscar," Casey said, referring to the doors at each end of the mail car. "We don't want nobody walkin' in here till we get what we came for."

Eli went at once to make sure the doors were locked. He found that both were locked with a key, but there were also bolt locks that were not locked, so he locked them.

Casey kept his gun on the bewildered mail clerk. "I'm gonna give it to you straight, young feller. I ain't got nothin' to lose if I blow a hole in your head, but if you wanna get any older than you are right now, you'd best give me what I came for. We was told there's a big payroll on this train and you'd better tell me where you put it, 'cause you're runnin' outta time."

"I swear to God, there ain't no big payroll

on this train," the frightened clerk pleaded. "The only money on the train is in those two bags in the safe and they both belong to the railroad. One of 'em's got fifteen thousand in it, and the other one has twelve. They go to two different banks."

"See if he's lyin', Oscar," Casey said. " 'Cause if he is, so help me . . ." He cocked the hammer back on his Colt, causing the clerk to flinch in panic.

"Yep," Eli said after a few moments. "There's two bags in here with money in 'em. There's also some cash that ain't in no bag. Throw me your sack." Casey took the rope out of the bag he had carried and the napkin he had put in there with it, then tossed it to Eli.

"Albert, unlock the door." The call came from the front of the car.

"Who's that?" Casey asked the mail clerk.

"The conductor," Albert said, his eyes wide with fear of the desperate old man holding the gun in his face.

"Tell him you'll be a minute," Casey ordered. The mail clerk hesitated, so Casey asked, "Is it worth your life?"

"I'll be a minute," the clerk called out timidly.

"I was just gonna tell you we're gettin' ready to roll," the conductor called back.

"I'll check with you later." They heard the sounds of the conductor closing the doors between the cars.

Aware of how little time they had to get off the train, Eli stuffed the money into the two bags, while Casey gave the clerk an ultimatum. "You wanna live, Albert?" The clerk nodded his head rapidly. "Roll over on your belly and put your hands behind you." Albert did so, and Casey quickly tied his hands to his feet. Then using the napkin the biscuits had been wrapped in, he fashioned a gag to tie in Albert's mouth. Finished, he said, "Don't swallow, Albert." And he joined Eli, who had already unlocked the door.

With guns still drawn, just in case, Eli opened the door and they stepped out on the platform between the mail car and a passenger car. They quickly holstered their guns, and Eli opened the door to the steps.

There were still quite a few people moving about on the platform, so Eli took a quick look to make sure he saw no railroad people before he stepped off the train. Casey followed, but the train lurched into motion just as he was stepping off, causing him to lurch forward, almost falling. He would had fallen, for sure, had he not been caught by a young man standing with his wife, who had just arrived on the train.

"Sorry," Casey mumbled.

"Think nothin' of it," the young man said. "Looks like they coulda waited till everybody got off, don't it?"

Casey looked up to meet the smiling face of Jack Myers, the blacksmith. It almost stunned him, but Jack gave no indication that he recognized him. "Thank you, young man," Casey muttered, and turned to join Eli, who seemed stunned as well. They walked away, forcing themselves to emphasize the slowness of their pace. When they looked back, they were relieved to see that Jack was not staring after them but helping his wife into a buggy, instead. Encouraged at that point, they hooked the canvas bags over their saddle horns and stepped up into the saddle.

As the train disappeared to the north, they leisurely turned in the other direction toward their camp setup on the creek. Once they got there and checked to see that nothing had been disturbed, they decided there was no need to worry about anyone chasing them. They had pulled it off, even though Casey had done his best to expose them by almost knocking Jack Myers down. Now they could laugh about it. Instead of getting on their horses and putting some territory between them and the site of the robbery, they decided it best to get out of their disguises and camp right there for the night. They even considered riding back into Mexia to get a real supper at Bertha's. But more sensible thought told them not to push their luck, and it was not a good idea to place themselves in the same town where the robbery took place. So they built a nice fire. Then they stripped down and jumped in the creek and took a bath, ridding themselves of all the olive makeup and the sticky paste that held their mustaches in place.

After they were dried off enough, they climbed back into their regular clothes and made a pot of coffee to help them down the thick slices of bacon in the frying pan and the hardtack that soaked up the grease.

They started back to Waco early the next morning, their packhorse carrying a load that consisted almost entirely of cash. They had counted the cash they had just stolen from the train, and it was, as Albert had said, a total of twenty-seven thousand dollars. There were also some small bills that added up to three hundred dollars. This was in addition to the money they already carried in their packs, so their biggest concern was to keep an eye on their packhorse. In light of this, it became necessary to convert most of that money to cattle right away, if the cattle business was as bad as they had been led to believe. Consequently, they didn't plan to stay long in Waco. They had definitely decided that it was best in the long run for them to invest in the raising and selling of cattle, since that was the only working experience either of them could lay claim to. Their plan was simple. They needed land to raise their cattle, and they were counting on claiming the Whitmore Brothers Ranch, knowing it had been abandoned. They both felt strongly that it would be the place where they would find the crew they had worked with. Once the land was secured, they would buy the cattle. They had enough money to start with a herd of two or three thousand cows with money left to operate the ranch, including cow hands' salaries. Whenever necessary, they would rob a train or a bank to pay their expenses. If things worked out the way they hoped, maybe one day they might reach the point where they could operate honestly.

They started out for Waco early enough to make sure they made it there in plenty of time for supper in the hotel dining room, a decent meal having moved to the top of their priority list. With one stop a little over halfway, they crossed the suspension bridge and rode into Waco around four o'clock, plenty of time to unload the large portion of their packs and put them in their hotel room. They took what was left on the packhorse down to the stable to be piled in the corner of a stall with their saddles and other packs. They told Horace Temple they were planning to leave early in the morning, depending upon how early he opened up. He told them he was usually there around five o'clock, so they said they would be there shortly thereafter.

"What's over that way?" Temple asked.

"Country we're familiar with," Casey said to him. "We're plannin' on takin' over a ranch we worked for, for a lotta years. Fellow we used to work for called it quits after we drove his last herd up to Kansas."

"Word's goin' around now that they ain't payin' nothin' for cattle anymore," Temple said. "They're sayin' the cattle market's dead. I hope you fellers know what you're doin'."

"You gonna give up eatin' beef?" Casey asked him. "Just gonna eat pork and lamb?"

"Nope," Temple said. "I ain't gonna quit eatin' beef. I'll raise my own, if I have to."

"That's right," Casey said. "But all those folks back east who want beef are gonna have to pay for it. They can't raise their own. The cattle market will recover," Casey insisted, "and when it does, we'll have the cows."

"Well, you sold me," Eli joked. "Let's go get somethin' to eat before they close the door. We'll see you first thing in the mornin', Horace." They walked out to the street and heard Temple yell after them.

"Lemme know if they serve you any beef." He punctuated it with a chuckle.

"Uh-oh," Thelma Townsend commented when they walked into the outside entrance. "You forgot to leave your guns in your room again."

"We couldn't take a chance of being late for supper," Eli responded.

"You know what to do," Thelma told him, her stoic expression never changing as she watched the two of them get rid of their sidearms.

"You know, Miss Townsend, I'm gonna miss your smilin' face when we leave here in the mornin'," Eli said. She looked at him as if he smelled bad and said, "Frances is waiting to serve you."

"Anybody ever tell you that you've got a way with women?" Casey wisecracked as they headed for an empty table.

"So you did come back," Frances greeted them with a smile. "We missed you boys yesterday."

"I see you did," Eli said. "Thelma's still pinin' over it."

"I expect she'll get over it," Frances said. "I'll go get you some coffee while you're deciding what you're gonna have. You have two choices, what we cooked . . . or nothing. Be making up your minds." She spun on her heel and headed for the coffeepot.

When she returned with two cups of coffee, Casey asked, "That meat that you cooked tonight, is it beef?"

"No," she said, "it's a pork roast. Are you getting picky on me?"

"I was hopin' you had some kinda beef tonight," Casey said.

Puzzled, because he was never particular before, she looked from him to Eli, who had a silly grin on his face. "If you wanted beef, you shoulda been here last night. We had beef."

"We choose the pork roast," Eli said with a chuckle. She figured it was an inside joke, so she wasn't going to ask, but Eli volunteered, anyway. "Casey's worried about the reports about the cattle market goin' to hell, and us headin' out in the mornin' to start up a new cattle ranch in Lampasas County."

"You really leaving here in the morning?" Frances asked.

"That's a fact, darlin'," Eli said. "Me and Casey are gonna start stockin' a cattle ranch that's gonna be the biggest thing in these parts."

She glanced at Casey, who was looking at Eli with a raised eyebrow, as if it was news to him. Back to Eli then, she remarked, "You mean you and Casey are going to work for a new outfit tomorrow. Well, we're gonna miss you here in the dining room."

"I mean me and Casey are gonna build the ranch," Eli said, "and hire the hands to do the work."

"Is that a fact?" Frances responded. "And I've been treating you two like a couple of ol' cowpunchers."

"I expect that's just what we are," Casey said then. "Sometimes Eli doesn't remember that."

Eli gave Frances a smile and declared, "We are leavin' early in the mornin', and we're gonna miss visitin' with you and Thelma."

"We'll miss having you come in," Frances said. "Thelma too. She just has a hard time showing it."

When Frances went to the kitchen to fix their plates, Casey looked at Eli and asked,

"What was that all about? Missin' them? Them missin' us? They'll miss us just like you miss a nail after it's pulled out of your foot."

"Don't never hurt to let folks know you appreciate 'em," Eli said. "Besides, Frances had a need to know we appreciate her tryin' to make us feel welcome here."

"If you say so," Casey said. "I don't know if I'da told her about how we was fixin' to build a big cattle ranch. I like it better makin' 'em think we'll most likely be dead broke when we leave here."

"Yeah, I know, but who the hell is she gonna tell? And we'll be gone from here in the mornin', anyway."

Casey gave him a long, hard look before finally remarking, "You know you're just wastin' your time, don't you? She knows a broken-down cowhand when she sees one."

"Hell, I know that," Eli insisted, "but they still like to have you admirin' them."

Casey shook his head. "And here I've been ridin' with you for how many years? And I never even knew you were such an expert when it came to handlin' the women."

"You coulda learned a little somethin', if you'd been smart enough to know that a long time ago," Eli said as Frances brought their supper to the table.

"Did you say you weren't gonna be here for breakfast in the morning?" Frances asked as she set their plates down.

"That's right, darlin'," Eli said. "We'll be eatin' a pitiful little breakfast about twenty miles from here with our horses beside the Leon River." She looked at Casey for confirmation. He shrugged and nodded.

"Well, if you ever hit Waco again, be sure to stop in and see us," she said, and left to serve another table.

"Looks to me like she's eatin' her heart out over you leavin'," Casey said sarcastically.

"You saw that, too?" Eli said, and dived into his plateful of food. "Let's get finished here and get back to check out of the hotel."

CHAPTER 19

Something awakened him from a sound sleep. It was pitch-black in the hotel room with no light coming in the window. He rolled over on the narrow bed to see if Eli had been awakened, too. There was just enough light for him to see Eli's covers pulled back and the bed was empty. With a small fortune in the packs stacked between the two beds, he was at once concerned.

"Eli," he called out.

"What?" came the whispered reply.

"What are you doin'?" Casey whispered back. "Where are you?"

"I'm over here by the door. I've gotta go out to the outhouse. It's early. Go on back to sleep."

"The outhouse?" Casey asked. "Ain't you got a thunder mug under the bed?"

"Yeah, but I need more'n that. Go on back to sleep," he repeated.

"Got your key?" Casey asked. Eli said he

did. "Lock the door when you go out."

"Right," Eli said, and went out the door. Casey lay propped up on his elbow until he heard the sound of the key in the lock. Then he turned over and went back to sleep.

He woke again. It was still dark in the room, but he felt like he had slept well. It might be time to get up, so he rolled over to see if Eli was awake. He was already up. At least he was not in his bed. "Eli," he called. There was no answer. He swung his feet over onto the floor and fumbled for his matches on the bedside table. When he found them, he struck one and held it up to see his watch. It was four-thirty, almost time to get up. There was enough light from the one match so he could see that Eli was not in the room. The match sputtered and went out. He struck another one and lit the lamp with it. He took another look at Eli's bed and decided it was just as he had left it earlier in the evening when he went out to the out-house. His gun belt was on the chair on the other side of his bed. *He hasn't come back!*

Greatly concerned now, Casey hurriedly got into his clothes, fearing that Eli had met with foul play. He strapped his gun belt on and checked his six-shooter to make sure the cylinder was loaded. Should he unlock the door and walk out and take the chance that someone would be waiting to ambush him? Or should he stay there in the room and make them come through the door? He didn't know if Eli was all right. He might even be dead! *Damn it, Eli,* he thought, *why couldn't you just use the chamber pot?*

Moving as quietly as he could manage, he went to the door, pressed his ear tightly against it, and listened. He could hear no sounds from the other side, so he decided to risk going out. He had to find Eli. He inserted his key in the lock as quietly as he could, then slowly turned it to unlock the door. He drew his pistol again and turned the knob, prepared for a sudden charge against the door. But there was none, so he eased it open gradually, until he could see the empty hall outside his room. Someone had lit the lamps at each end of the hallway, and he started toward the front of the building and the stairs that led down to the front desk. Then he changed his mind and went back the other way, to the steps that led to the back of the hotel, where the washroom and the staff's rooms were located. Eli would have gone this way to get to the outhouse behind the hotel.

Casey hurried past a door that led to the kitchen, thinking he would check outside first, for it was most likely that whatever Eli had run into would have been outside the building. Having never ventured into this part of the hotel before, Casey went to what appeared to be the door to the outside. When he went through it, however, he found himself in a short hallway with four doors, all closed, before a large, heavy door at the end, which was obviously the outside door. He started toward that door, but stopped right away when one of the side doors opened, and Eli walked out into the hall. Both men froze, not sure at first in the dim light of the hallway.

A long moment later, Frances stepped out behind Eli, and she froze for another moment before speaking. "I reckon this belongs to you," she said, holding Eli by the back of his collar. "I think he got lost."

"Mornin', partner," Eli spoke up cheerfully. "I was just comin' to wake you up."

"Oh, you were, were you?" Casey said. "Damn you, you got me searchin' all over this hotel, fixin' to shoot somebody."

"Whatever he tells you, I'm calling him a liar," Frances said. "I don't wanna see either one of you in the dining room again. Now get out of here. I've got to go to work."

"What the hell did I do?" Casey asked.

"You brought him to this hotel," she said.

"If you come back to Waco, find some other hotel. Now . . . git!"

Eli turned to her and said, "I'll never forget you, darlin'."

"Git!" she responded.

All smiles then, he walked past Casey, who stood dumbfounded until Eli said, "Come on, partner, we'd best get those horses loaded and get on our way. I don't think she wants us around no more."

All three walked back up the short hall. Frances went in the door to the kitchen, while Casey and Eli retraced their way back to the room.

When they got back to their room, Eli strapped on his gun belt and asked, "Ain't you even gonna ask me what happened?"

"I'm just tryin' to decide whether I oughta shoot you or not," Casey said to him. "I wake up in the middle of the night and you're gone who knows where. I have to go to the trouble of searchin' for you. Thought somethin' terrible musta happened to ya."

Eli grinned sheepishly. "Somethin' happened to me, all right, but I wouldn't call it 'terrible.'"

"Shoot!" Casey spat. "With Frances? I don't know if I'd believe that or not."

"Well, I don't want you to think bad things about Frances," Eli said. "She's a fine, upstandin' woman. But I expect there's a lot of upstandin' women who'll be a whore just one time for a hundred bucks."

"A hundred bucks! I shoulda known," Casey said. "Tell you the truth, though, I'da thought she'da wanted five hundred." He shook his head in exasperation. "You made an impression on her. I gotta give you that."

"You know, in a real partnership, you'd ante up fifty bucks, since it was for the good of your partner's disposition," Eli suggested.

"Mornin', fellers," Horace Temple sang out when he saw them come into the stable carrying their saddlebags over their shoulders, and large packs in each hand. "Lemme give you a hand," he said, and took a sack from each one of them. "You boys are loaded down, ain'tcha? You coulda just left them packs here with the rest of your stuff."

"Reckon we coulda," Casey said. "But it's just a lot of maps and papers, and such. We like to work on 'em at night, so we have to carry 'em back and forth."

Horace nodded as if he understood. He helped them saddle Biscuit and Smoke and stood by while they tied their packs so they would ride properly. When they were ready, they paid him what they owed and started for the road to Lampasas County. There were a couple of trails leading out west and southwest from Waco. Temple stood by the corner of his corral watching to see which road they took.

"Maps and such," he mumbled under his breath. "I wonder what them boys are really carryin' in them packs."

It had been quite some time since Casey and Eli had ridden the old Comanche Trail between the Whitmore Brothers Ranch and Waco. They were trying to decide exactly how long as they left Waco behind them and headed west. They finally agreed on the week after branding, year before last.

"We sure as hell didn't stay in the Mc-Clellan House that time, did we?" Eli chuckled, then they both laughed when they thought about that time.

"Two years ago," Casey remarked. "I swear, it feels like ten."

"It is a little different this time, though," Eli said. "When we rode back that time, we was dead broke. If I remember right, I don't think we had anything to eat all the way back."

"We ain't a helluva lot better off this time when it comes to chuck," Casey reminded him. "A little bit of bacon and some coffee."

"That oughta be enough. When we get to

the ranch, there'll be some strays hangin' around, so we'll butcher a cow." They rode along in good spirits, planning to make it to the Leon River before they rested the horses.

Meanwhile, in Waco, Horace Temple heard a familiar voice behind him. "Whatcha say, Horace?" He turned to see his wife's brother coming in the stable door.

"Marty," Horace said. "How long you been in town? Anybody after you?"

"Good to see you, too," Marty responded sarcastically. "We just got here, and there ain't nobody chasin' us."

"Who's 'we'?" Horace asked. "Who's with you?"

"Riley Black," Marty said. "You don't know him. He ain't never been here before. He'll be in, in a minute. He had to take a leak."

"Did you go by the house to see your sister?" Horace asked, knowing the answer before he asked the question. Marty never gave a cuss about his sister, but Sarah was always concerned about him, afraid the law was finally going to corner him, and he'd spend the rest of his life in prison. She was always pressing Horace to take Marty into business with him at the stable, hoping Marty would forsake his lawless ways.

Horace never told her that he was already in business with her brother, but that business was selling stolen horses.

"I told you, we just got here," Marty said. "We've got some horses we need to sell. We're runnin' a little short of cash and I need to get more for 'em than you got for the last six I brought here."

"Those horses you brought in here last time wasn't nothin' but skin and bones," Horace complained. "You're lucky I got anything for 'em. If you're gonna steal horses, you've got to let 'em eat and drink water. You can't run 'em to death and expect me to get top dollar for 'em." He walked over to the stable door and looked out to see eight horses, tied on lead ropes of four each. "Where'd you get 'em? Am I gonna have somebody from a nearby ranch come in here lookin' for his horses?"

"No, we picked these horses up off a little ranch on the Bosque River, forty miles from here. And he ain't gonna come lookin' for 'em. Matter of fact, he ain't goin' nowhere, 'cause he was unlucky enough to interrupt us when we was invitin' them horses to come to Waco with us."

"You killed the man who owns 'em?" Horace charged.

"I didn't," Marty said. "Riley did. It was

the old fool's fault. He come ridin' at us, yellin' and hollerin' like a lunatic, so Riley shot him. I was ready. I was gonna shoot him if Riley missed, but Riley's a pretty fair shot. Anyway, you ain't gotta worry about anybody knowin' they're stole."

"I'll take a look at 'em and then we'll talk about how much I can get for 'em." They walked out back of the corral, where the stolen horses were tied. A sullen-looking young man, wearing a dirty derby hat, was leaning against the corner post. Horace ignored him, accustomed to the brainless young men that Marty partnered up with. He walked around and inspected the horses, which he found to be in excellent condition and not too old. "Well, they could be a lot better stock. They ain't been took very good care of. But I'll try to sell 'em for ya, and take my usual commission."

"You take too much for your piece of it," Marty complained.

"Well, you can take 'em somewhere else and see what you can get for 'em. I'm the one holdin' the bag here. If the law comes claimin' they're stolen horses, I'm the one they'll put in jail. You and your friend here will be long gone." He watched for Marty's reaction for a few seconds, then he remembered something else. "You oughta been here early this mornin'. For the past few days, I've been takin' care of five horses for a couple of fellows. They were usin' three packhorses and they was loaded down with somethin' they didn't want anybody to see. They left their saddles and packsaddles in the stable, but they took whatever it is they're carryin' out of the packs and took it up to their hotel room every night."

"You ain't got no idea what they was carryin'?" Marty asked.

"No, I ain't, and I'd give a pretty penny to know what they had that was so precious they couldn't just leave it here in the stable with the rest of their goods. They left early this mornin', and when they came to load up, they was carryin' all their sacks and stuff. I offered to help and you shoulda seen how they watched me when I toted two of their packs into the stable. I ain't got a doubt in my mind that whatever those two are carryin' is mighty damn valuable. I just wish I coulda got a look in those packs."

"You say they left this mornin'?" Marty asked. "How long ago?"

"Hour and a half, two hours at best," Horace said.

"Hell, we can make that up," Marty said. "I'd kinda like to see what they've got in their packs, too. Ain't that what you say, Riley?"

"Damn right," Riley said, his only two words to that point.

Back to Horace then, Marty asked, "You have any idea what direction they went?"

"I know exactly which way they went," Horace assured him. "They rode outta here on the old Comanche Trail to the west. They was talkin' about stoppin' to rest their horses on the Leon River, and they're headin' for a ranch on the Lampasas River." He could see the light of opportunity shining in Marty's eyes, excited by the prospect of stealing something of more value than a horse. "I get the same deal on whatever you find, just like the horses," Horace reminded him.

"Oh, don't worry, brother-in-law, I'll see you get your share. I gotta take care of sis's husband." He winked at Riley.

"Damn right," Riley said.

"We're gonna need two fresh horses," Marty said. "Ours need a good rest. Let's see what you've got in the corral. We need somethin' to eat, too. We et up everythin' we was carryin'."

"You gonna take a packhorse?" Horace asked.

"Nah, we ain't gonna take no packhorse,"

Marty said. "We don't wanna mess with no packhorse if we're tryin' to catch up with those two fellows. When we catch up with 'em, we'll eat whatever they've got to eat. Right, Riley?"

"Damn right," Riley responded.

"But we need somethin' to eat to hold us till we catch up with 'em," Marty continued. "Ain't you got nothin' to eat here at the stable?" Horace told him he had some jerky and a couple of biscuits Sarah had wrapped in a napkin for him to eat later. "That'll do just fine," Marty said. "Any coffee in that pot?"

"It's still about half full, but it's been settin' on the edge of the stove ever since I got here this mornin'."

"That don't make no difference. That's the way we like it. Ain't that right, Riley?"

"Damn right," Riley said.

They picked out a couple of horses from the small bunch that Horace owned, although they saw several they preferred that had other owners. They saddled up, finished off the jerky and biscuits that Horace had planned to eat later, and were soon on their way.

"We'll be back tonight or in the mornin'," Marty told Horace, "and you'll get to see what was in those packs. Right, Riley?"

"Damn right," Riley said.

Horace stood in the doorway of his stable, watching the two ride away. He remained there until he saw them turn onto the old Comanche Trail just short of the hotel. "There goes the curse that came with the marrying of Sarah Flynn," he muttered.

When it came to horses stolen from people he didn't know, people with no names, it didn't seem so bad to take them off Sarah's sick brother's hands. But now that he had done it, he felt kind of bad for setting those two on Casey and Eli's trail. As far as he could tell, they were two decent men, and he didn't know why he had done it. All he could think to blame it on now was his insane curiosity to see what was in those packs, plus an opportunity to send Sarah's brother and his talking dummy off somewhere away from Waco.

Damn right, he thought, and shook his head. *I reckon I'm going to hell, anyway. I might as well get on the top floor.*

"This looks like the trail, all right," Marty said as he stared down at the dusty track ahead of the horses. "Them tracks is recent, and they look just right for five horses. They're makin' it easy for us, long as they stay on this road." He gave his horse a kick to increase his gait to a trot for a little while, before pulling him back to a walk again. By alternating the pace, he hoped to gain on Casey and Eli, counting on them to hold their horses to the steady walking pace their tracks seemed to indicate. "They ain't in no particular hurry, it don't look like. We're bound to be gainin' on 'em. We might not catch up with 'em when they stop to rest their horses, but we won't be far behind. And we'll catch 'em for sure when they stop for the night."

"Damn right," Riley said.

A couple of hours ahead, Casey and Eli saw the line of trees and shrubs that indicated the Leon River a quarter of a mile ahead.

"There it is," Eli said. "Looks like he's still here." A mile or so back, they had begun speculating on whether or not the store was still standing on the bank of the river. It had been there ever since Casey or Eli had signed on to work cattle for the Whitmore Brothers Cattle Company. It had started out long before that as a trading post and was now operated by an old man nicknamed "Pappy."

Pappy had been a small child when his father, Alexander Travis, built the trading post. It had survived the years and was still in business, supported by the small ranchers and farmers who went to Pappy's to buy coffee, sugar, flour, dried beans, rice, and other basic items. Casey and Eli were happy to see the store was apparently still open, for they needed basic supplies.

"Reckon the old man is still here?" Eli wondered as they walked their horses down toward the old building on the riverbank. "He must be about two hundred years old."

Casey chuckled. "Well, there's somebody sittin' in that rockin' chair on the porch with a lot of snow on his head. He looks like Pappy. Wonder if he's still got his memory?" He remembered that the old man had a good memory.

"Afternoon," Casey called out as he pulled Smoke to a stop and dismounted. "Pappy?"

"Yes, sir," the old man said. "Come in." He remained seated in the rocking chair as he watched them tie their horses. "I expect it's been two years since you boys was in here."

"That's a fact," Eli said. "I'm surprised you remember that." He looked at Casey and saw that he wasn't surprised at all.

Pappy frowned like he was trying to remember something. Then he said, "Casey and Eli. I don't remember your last names. Don't know if you said 'em or not. You worked for the Rocking-W, the Whitmore Brothers Ranch. You boys were broke that night, though, just back from a trip to Waco."

"Yes, sir," Casey said, "that's exactly right." His memory of that trip had slipped his mind, but it was coming back upon seeing Pappy. He glanced at Eli to see if he remembered, and he could see by his expression that he did. They were sure enough broke, and hungry, too. Pappy and Miss Atha had fed them and told them not to worry about the cost.

Casey felt ashamed that he had never taken a ride back over there to repay the old couple. It was a day and a half's ride to the ranch, and they were pretty busy at the ranch getting all the stock ready to be sold. Still, he could have found some time to ride over there and pay them for the food. He decided then. "Yes, sir, we've been held up by one thing and another, but we've come back this afternoon to pay what we owe you and Miss Atha for takin' care of two hungry cowpokes."

"That's right," Eli said at once. "We're here to pay our bill, plus interest."

Pappy threw his head back and cackled. "I told you boys you didn't owe us nothin'."

"And we're needin' to buy some supplies,

too," Casey said. "You're still in business, ain'tcha?"

"Yes, sir," Pappy said. "We've got the baby with us now, and he's helpin' run the store. You boys come on in the store and we'll see what we can do for you."

"Before we do that," Casey said, "we need to take care of our horses. We'll take 'em a little way upriver and let 'em water and graze. Then we'll be right back."

"Always best to take care of the horses first," Pappy said. "I'll tell Alex and Miss Atha you'll be comin' in."

They unloaded the horses and let them go to water close enough to the store, so they could keep an eye on their packs. While they unsaddled Biscuit and Smoke, they discussed the amount they should give Pappy and Miss Atha.

"Are we talkin' about givin' 'em a fair price for supper, plus a little extra? Or are you thinkin' about layin' out a hundred dollars, like you laid on Frances?" Casey asked.

"I don't know. It might be worth a hundred bucks to see that old lady's face light up," Eli said.

"Maybe you could offer it to her for the same kinda deal you made with Frances," Casey joked.

"Maybe so," Eli came back, "but since this

is an equal partnership, I believe it would be your turn."

The horseplay between them continued all the way back to the store before it stopped when Pappy opened the door and invited them in. Miss Atha, Pappy's wife, greeted them cordially. Gray and fragile, she looked to be nearly as old as Pappy, even though she was fifteen years younger. Standing behind the counter was "the baby," as Pappy referred to him. Alex Travis, named for his grandfather, was a giant of a man and fifty years old.

"We're so happy to see you boys are still around," Miss Atha said. "We didn't have our son with us the last time you were here. This is my youngest, Alex."

Eli couldn't contain it. He looked up at the huge man, then looked back at his frail little mother. "How in the world could a woman as tiny as you have a son that big?"

"He weren't that big when I had him," she said.

They called off a list of basic supplies that they knew they would ordinarily need, even though they only planned to be on the trail for another day. Uncertain what they would find when they reached the ranch, they thought it a good idea to at least have food to cook. Seeing Pappy and Miss Atha reminded them of Miguel and Juanita Garcia, and they wondered if they had stayed on at the ranch house after Whitmore deserted it. It was their hope that they had. They also hoped that the cowhands had gone back there, too. Tomorrow, at this time, they would find out.

"I reckon that's about all we need," Casey finally said. "Add it up, Alex, and we'll pay you. Then we'll say good-bye till next time. We're gonna build a little fire over where our horses are and heat up a little coffee to go with some of this bacon we just bought. And when the horses are rested up, we'll be on our way." He looked at Eli and winked. "Oh, I almost forgot. One of the reasons we stopped by was to pay what we owed you for that supper two years ago. We figured it all up, what with the interest on the loan and all, and came up with this total." He walked over to Miss Atha. "I expect we oughta pay you, since you're the one that did the work." He placed two fifty-dollar bills in her palm. "Thank you, ma'am." He and Eli turned at once and walked out the door.

She stared at the two bills in her hand for a moment before she realized they were not one-dollar bills. "A hundred bucks!" she exclaimed. Casey and Eli heard her at the foot of the steps as they hurried away, loaded down with the supplies they had just bought.

CHAPTER 20

After a meal of bacon roasted over the fire and a pot of coffee, Casey and Eli talked about the visit with Pappy and his wife and son. It felt good to give that frail little woman a gift, one that to her was so great, but to them had become so small.

"I'm afraid we're gonna have to change our ways," Casey declared, "or we're gonna give away everything we've got."

"Pretty soon, we'll get to buyin' cows and horses and stuff we need to build that ranch back up. We won't have any money to give away," Eli stated. He got up from the stump he had been sitting on and poured the last of his coffee on the fire. "I expect we'd best get on our way."

They saddled up and loaded the pack-horses and were about to step up into the saddle when they heard a shout behind them. They both turned at once and saw big Alex Travis running toward them carrying something. "Uh-oh, what did we forget?" They waited until he came panting up to them.

"Here," he said. "Mama was afraid she couldn't get it baked before you fellers left, so she cooked it in the fryin' pan." He handed each of them a cake of corn bread wrapped in a rag. "She said she was sorry she didn't get it done in time to go with your bacon and coffee."

"Well, bless her heart," Eli said. "That sure is gonna make my belly happy. You tell her she's an angel."

"That's what she said you fellers were," Alex said.

"Boy, that sure is good," Casey said after a big bite. "Don't she want these cloths back?"

"Nah," Alex said. "She said she can afford to buy some new rags with a hundred bucks." He laughed and then he got serious. "God bless you fellers." He turned and walked back toward the store then.

"Ain't that somethin'?" Eli said. "I don't recollect ever bein' blessed before. I've been cursed a time or two, but never blessed."

They crossed over the river and picked up the Comanche Trail on the other side, still eating corn bread, since the river was not very high. If they chose to push the horses hard, they could make the ranch by that night, but they were not inclined to tire their horses unnecessarily. Consequently, when they had traveled what they estimated to be around twenty miles, they started looking for a good place to camp for the night, even though it was not yet approaching darkness. The place they finally came to was a creek winding its way across a grassy plain before pushing through a stand of trees and thick bushes. They left the road and followed the creek into a grove of trees until they came to a spot big enough to have grown a little grass.

"Most likely as good as we're gonna find," Eli remarked. "All right with you?"

"Suits me just fine," Casey said.

So they dismounted and started stripping the horses of their saddles and packs. When the horses were taken care of, they decided to build their fire in a pocket in the creek bank. It would make it handy to get to the water and they could stack their packs around the sides of the pocket, with room to spread their bedrolls between the fire and their packs.

"Perfect," Casey declared. "I like to sleep by a warm fire with my money wrapped around me."

"What are we gonna do about our money when we get back to the ranch?" Eli suddenly asked. It had been worrying his mind for the last couple of hours. And even if they found things as they hoped to find them when they got back, there was still the question that needed an answer. So he voiced it. "Are we gonna tell the boys about all this money we've got? Not only that, but how we came by it?"

"You been thinkin' about that, too," Casey said. "I wish I knew what's best, but I'm thinkin' we can't let 'em know how much we've got. I don't think that would be a good idea a-tall. And I ain't interested in startin' up a gang of outlaws. We gotta tell 'em we came by some money somehow, enough to buy some cattle at a cheap price, and enough to pay their wages for a few months. We've got till tomorrow to think of exactly where we got the money. Maybe we'll think of something by then. If not, we'll use the rich grandpa story."

"What if they don't believe it?" Eli asked.

"If they don't accept it, we'll ask 'em if they'd like to work for a couple of outlaws." They talked about it for quite a while after they ate their supper of fried bacon and johnnycakes Eli made with some of the flour, lard, and sugar they bought from

Pappy Travis. When the light finally began to fade toward darkness, they still had no tale to tell to explain their luck to the crew of the Rocking-W. But all the discussion about it caused them to think it might be best to stay awake all night to make sure nothing happened to their money, now that they were so close to home with it. The final decision was for one of them to stand guard half the night, while the other one slept, then switch over for the rest of the night. Eli volunteered to take the first watch, since he wasn't sleepy after all the talk about their plans. So Casey crawled into his bedroll and tried to get to sleep. Like Eli, he found that he was not so inclined.

"That old fool knew more than he let on," Marty Flynn declared, referring to Pappy Travis. "He acted like he didn't even know those two fellows were at his store, and their tracks led right up to the front door."

"Damn right," Riley Black said.

"I was fixin' to put that old polecat outta his misery till that giant came outside," Marty claimed. "I ain't sure my .45 would put that ox down. You might need a good buffalo rifle to stop him. At least he said they was there, but I don't think they was gone as long ago as he said. I might wanna pay him another visit on the way back."

"Damn right," Riley responded.

"Wait a minute! Hold up!" Marty exclaimed as they approached a creek. He reined his horse back. "I saw sparks comin' up outta them trees yonder." He pointed to a grove of trees. "Like somebody threw a piece of wood on the fire. You see 'em?" They both stared at the trees Marty had pointed to, and in a few minutes, a faint trail of smoke snaked up out of the branches of the trees. "By Ned, we caught 'em! They've gone into camp!" He looked frantically around him. "Trouble is, we're out here in the open on this road. If they're watchin' the road, they've already seen us. What we need to do is keep on ridin', cross on over the creek, and keep a-goin', like we don't know they're in them trees. We'll just ride on up this road till we're outta sight. Then we'll wait till dark and come back to see 'em. Then we'll see what's in them packs they're guardin' so hard."

"Damn right," Riley muttered.

They started up again, walking their horses toward the creek. And when they reached the crossing, Marty reined up again at the edge of the water. "Let 'em drink before we cross over, like we ain't got nothin' on our minds. That oughta be easy for you." If Riley heard the insult, he made no indication of it. He stopped and let his horse drink, then pushed on through the water and followed Marty up the road.

"Whaddaya think?" Eli asked.

"I don't know," Casey said. "Maybe they belong to a ranch around here somewhere. They ain't got a packhorse, so it don't look like they're goin' very far. Why would they be followin' us, anyway? We ain't gave nobody any reason to follow us. Whaddaya think?"

"I think we both better stay awake tonight," Eli said. "I don't like the looks of those two."

"I think you're right. I ain't sleepy, anyway."

They had no way of knowing if the two riders knew of their presence there in the trees. When they stopped to let their horses drink, they didn't look down the creek as if they had a clue. "They mighta seen some smoke from our fire," Eli speculated. "They might be back when it really gets dark. I think it'd be a good idea for me and you to crawl outta this hole we're camped in and find a better spot to watch our camp. You on one side and me on the other."

"Sounds like a good idea to me," Casey

said. "It'd be a real shame to lose all this money when we're just about home. Hell, we'll sleep tomorrow night."

Since they couldn't know if they were dealing with someone simply intent upon stealing their horses, or someone who somehow was after what they had in their packs, they didn't know how desperate they might be. But they had to prepare for the worst. They decided to pick their spots to lie in wait so that both of them knew where the other was hiding, so they might not shoot at each other, if it came to that. In case the two riders might be thinking about running the horses up or down the creek, they picked positions to prevent that, no matter which way the riders stampeded them. When they were settled on their plans, Casey and Eli took their rifles with them to their ambush spots, hoping they would find in the morning that they had gone to a lot of unnecessary trouble.

They left the road a hundred yards short of the creek and rode directly where Marty had guessed the camp to be. They were no longer afraid of being spotted riding across the open prairie, now that darkness had fallen. When they reached the trees lining the creek, they rode into their dark cover and dismounted. They left their horses there and proceeded on foot, moving as quietly as possible along the creek bank until they spotted the camp on the other side.

"Yonder it is," Marty whispered. "They got 'em a nice little camp set up in that bank, with their packs lining the hole. Only thing is, they ain't got no protection from this side of the creek. They don't think anybody will come across the creek at 'em, 'cause they'd have to get in the water. But they don't know me and you."

"Damn right," Riley whispered.

"We ain't wantin' anybody over there alive when we leave here," Marty reminded him. "Dead men tell no tales, right?"

"Damn right," Riley whispered.

"All right, then, let's go. Hold your fire till I shoot. Then fill them two bedrolls full of lead. Try not to hit the packs. We don't know what's in 'em." Marty stepped down off the bank into the water. Having crossed it at the road when they had ridden across earlier, they knew how deep the water was. So they held their gun belts up above their waists until starting up the opposite bank, where they quickly buckled them back on. They sneaked up the bank until they were level with the fire and the bedrolls beyond it. "Say howdy to the Devil for us, boys!"

Marty yelled, and opened fire. Riley cut loose with his six-shooter right behind him. In a matter of seconds, they put twelve shots into the empty bedrolls, then quickly reloaded.

While they were in the process, Eli, fifteen yards upstream, steadied his Winchester '66 against the tree he had been hiding behind. He took careful aim and squeezed the trigger, sending a bullet that struck Marty in the center of his chest. Marty dropped on the creek bank. Startled, Riley flattened himself on the ground beside him, just as a bullet from Casey's rifle clipped a limb off a bush over his head.

"It's a trap!" a desperate and dying Marty Flynn gasped painfully. "I'm shot! We got to get outta here. I need help."

Riley, afraid to raise his head, tried to look left and right, but realized the only escape was to back into the water. So he started to slide back away from the edge of the bank to the sounds of rifle slugs zipping over them from two different directions.

Marty tried desperately to crawl with him, but could not do it. "Riley, are you leavin' me?"

"Damn right," Riley said, and slid down to the bottom of the bank before turning to enter the water. Marty rolled over on his side, raised his six-shooter, and put a bullet between Riley's shoulder blades. Riley collapsed in the waist-deep water and drifted slowly downstream.

There were no more shots fired for a short time, with both Eli and Casey unsure about the second man. Eli had a clear view of Marty, so he called out. "Casey, one of 'em is done for, I'm pretty sure about him. It's the other'n I ain't sure about, but I think he escaped back in the creek."

"I think you're right," Casey called out. "I saw just enough of him to take a shot, but he slid back down the bank. I don't think I hit him. I'm comin' out."

They both moved very cautiously through the bushes to meet at Marty's body. They found him dead, all right. The strange part about it was the fact that he was lying partway over on his side, his right arm pointed straight back toward the water, his pistol in his hand. "Ain't no doubt about him," Eli said. "I had a clear shot at him. But I need to know about his pal. Did he run, or is he sneakin' around here someplace? It's hard to see in these blame trees."

"We need to find their horses," Casey decided. "That'll at least tell us if he took off, or if he's still here."

It was just a guess at this point, because

their own horses got stirred up when all the shooting started. So, with all their noise, it was impossible to determine if they heard the sound of the other man riding away. Without hesitation, they both went into the water, holding their rifles high, and crossed over to the other side. Deciding to stay together to reduce the possibility of shooting each other, they searched upstream first, back toward the road. They walked no more than about twenty yards before they found the two horses tied in the trees.

"He's still here somewhere, and, I swear, I don't know if I hit him or not," Casey said. "We better find him."

"I saw him slide back down that bank," Eli said, "but I couldn't see him anymore after he dropped below the rim of it. That other fellow back there, layin' on his side, pointin' his gun toward the water, you reckon he mighta shot him 'cause he was runnin' out on him?"

"That's a possibility," Casey said, "but we ain't gonna know for sure unless we find him."

They untied the two horses and led them back where their horses were, then they began a search for the missing assailant. After more than an hour searching along both sides of the creek, they were ready to say he was gone. Whether he had walked away, floated down the creek, or was hiding in a hole somewhere, they couldn't say, but they were not ready to assume he was gone and no longer a threat. So they did the only thing they could do, put a pot of coffee on the fire and sat up watching their horses to make sure none were stolen during the night.

Even though the two weary outlaws believed the long night would never end, the sun finally made an appearance, gradually bringing light filtering through the leaves of the trees and calming the chirping of the crickets. Casey got up from his position, sitting with his back against a tree. Convinced they had never been in danger of a counterattack by the missing assailant, he cursed him for the long night just passed, then picked up the empty coffeepot and walked to the creek to fill it with water. Squatting beside the creek, he rinsed the pot a couple of times before letting it fill. Out of the corner of his eye, he detected a slight movement of a large rock or stump rising slightly above the water. His attention was captured at once. Unaware that his coffeepot was filled with water, he stared at the strange object as the sun's rays began to clear away the mist on the creek.

"Eli!" he called out when he realized he was looking at the doubled-over body of a man, his back protruding above the surface of the water. A black hole was clearly visible between his shoulder blades. "Eli!" he called again. "I found him."

CHAPTER 21

After a couple of tries, Eli was able to throw a rope over the bulk of Riley's body and, with a few tugs, pull him loose from the root that the toe of his boot had snagged on. "I swear," Eli marveled, "he was right in front of us all night long." They pulled the body to the bank and carried it back away from the creek to drop it in an old stump hole. They dragged Marty's body up from the creek and tossed it on top of Riley's. A search of both bodies had produced nothing of value, except a weapon and ammunition. They figured Riley's gun was lying on the bottom of the creek.

"He learned somethin' last night I already knew," Casey said.

"What's that?" Eli asked, suspecting a joke was going to follow.

"Don't never turn your back on a feller that says he's your friend. He's liable to shoot you in the back."

"Damn right," Eli said.

Once they felt the threat to their lives and their fortune no longer existed, they decided to catch up on the sleep they had missed. So they built up the fire and stripped off all their wet clothing and propped them up on some tree limbs to dry. Wrapped in blankets then, they caught a couple of hours sleep. In no hurry, since they were no more than three hours from the ranch now, they cooked some bacon and hardtack before they started out again.

"Well, I'll be. . . . Sam!" Davey Springer yelled at the top of his lungs. When there was no immediate response, he yelled again. "Sam!"

"What the hell is wrong with you?" Sam Dunn called out from the barn door.

"Look!" Davey exclaimed. "They came back! It's Casey and Eli!"

"Where?" Sam demanded, squinting his eyes in an effort to see better. When he followed the direction of Davey's forefinger, he saw the two riders leading a string of five horses. They sure looked like Casey and Eli. He ran out to join Davey near the front porch of the house. "I'll be doggoned. I never thought we'd ever see them back here again. They musta found out the same thing we did. Ain't nobody hirin' cowhands."

"It's good they got here today," Davey said. When Sam asked why, Davey said, " 'Cause they'll get to see Miguel and Juanita before they leave in the mornin'."

"Yeah, that's right," Sam said. "Miguel's in the barn. That's what I was doin' in there, helpin' him fix up that old wagon so he can haul their stuff in it." He watched the two riders as they approached the gate to the ranch headquarters. "Looks like me and you are gonna have to ride out toward the river and pick up a couple more strays to butcher. I swear, I hate to tell 'em how bad things have got."

Sam drew his pistol from his holster and fired three shots up in the air. It produced the effect he intended, for four of the boys came hustling out of the bunkhouse to see what was going on. Miguel came out of the barn, and a moment later, Monroe Kelly came out of the outhouse.

It was Monroe, one of the older men at twenty-one, who yelled, "What's all the shootin'?"

"It's Casey and Eli," Sam shouted back, and pointed toward the two riding through the front gate.

"Well, I'll be . . ." Monroe ran to join Sam and Davey in the front yard. "I hope they ain't comin' back here lookin' for work, 'cause they're gonna be mighty disappointed."

"Howdy, boys," Casey sang out when he and Eli pulled up in front of the house. "What's everybody doin', hangin' around the ranch. Ain'tcha got work to do?"

"Doggone it, Casey," Monroe shot back. "If you two ain't been on the moon since we left you in Abilene, you know dang well ain't no cowhands workin' in Texas."

"I swear," Eli said. "Me and Casey knew you boys would just be layin' around the bunkhouse doin' nothin'. So we figured we had to come back and get you workin' again."

"Them wages and the bonus money you and Casey stole off that train was supposed to hold us over till the ranches started hirin' again," Corey Johnson spoke up. "But it's already used up just to keep this place up."

"That's right," Monroe said. "There ain't no money to buy cows to take care of, even if you could drive 'em to market, 'cause there ain't no market."

"Maybe you and Casey oughta rob another train to pay our wages," Corey suggested.

Casey smiled and calmly said, "I expect we're gonna do better than that. Me and Eli

380

are plannin' on buildin' a cattle ranch. And we're gonna need a crew to work it for us."

The whole gang gathered there turned speechless for a long moment before Monroe blurted, "What are you talkin' about, Casey?"

"I know what you've heard," Casey said to him, "the market's dead. There ain't gonna be no more drivin' cattle to the railroads. The market won't pay the price for cows anymore. I'm sayin' use your good sense. People ain't gonna stop wantin' beef to eat. The market will be big again, we just have to wait a little while and it'll be back."

"Yeah, but we need a job right now," Monroe said. "We can't wait for the market to come back."

"All right, we're hirin' cowhands right now, forty dollars a month, just like you got from Whitmore. Your first month will be paid in advance. Anybody interested?"

"You're japin' us, and right now it ain't very funny," Corey remarked.

"It's your choice, Corey, we ain't gonna beg you to work for us," Eli told him. "It ain't gonna be any trouble findin' a crew. We just felt like we'd give our old friends first crack at a steady job."

"I'll work for you," Davey spoke up then.

"Me too," Sam followed.

"Where will you get the money to pay all of us forty dollars a month?" Monroe asked.

"What difference does it make where we get the money to pay you?" Casey asked him. "Did you ask Whitmore Brothers where they got the money to pay you?"

Monroe just shrugged.

"Well, me and Eli just rode all the way from Waco, so we need to get settled." Seeing the cook's husband standing there, Casey asked, "Miguel, are you and Juanita still staying in the ranch house?"

"*Sí*, Senor Casey, but we are leaving tomorrow."

"Leavin'?" Casey said. "Why? Don't you like it here?"

"*Sí*, we like, but there is no money."

"Well, there is now." Casey said. "You stay and you'll get the same wages you got from the Whitmores. All right?"

Miguel nodded rapidly and grinned from ear to ear.

"You go tell Juanita you're stayin' and that she'll be cookin' for Eli and me. Is anybody else in the house?"

Miguel shook his head.

"Good. Eli and I will each use a room."

"Who's gonna cook for us?" Sam asked. "Juanita has been cookin' for us in the bunkhouse since Smiley left."

"She can keep cookin' for all of us till we get a cook to replace Smiley," Eli said. "Hell, maybe we can get Smiley," he said, looking directly at Casey. "He's most likely lookin' for work, like everybody else."

"Anybody know where he is?" Casey asked.

"I know," Monroe said. "He's at the Corbett Ranch."

"First chance we get, we'll see if he's interested in comin' back to work with us," Casey said. "That's another thing. Either tomorrow or the next day, we're gonna need to take a wagon into town and pick up the supplies Juanita needs to cook with."

"That's gonna be a problem," Corey said. "There ain't much of a town there anymore. Frank Carter's talkin' about closin' his store and movin' out. He said all the ranches he was doin' business with dried up and he can't make it without their business. The small farmers weren't too happy about it, either, 'cause he was the closest store around."

His statement made Casey pause to think for a moment, then he continued to speak. "So we'd best drive into town in the mornin' to get our supplies and let Frank know we intend to be in business," Casey remarked. "Maybe he'll stick around a little bit longer."

It was obvious that the crew of the new ranch was still in a minor state of shock and were not totally sure they could believe things were going to be as Casey and Eli promised. There were many questions asked and not all of them were said. Finally Eli told them that they had to stop and take care of their horses, promising to explain where they got the extra ones.

"We need to unpack these horses and move this stuff into the house. I expect Juanita can use the cookin' supplies we just picked up. Maybe there's enough for her to fix a couple of meals before we get more for her." Eli looked over at the front porch, where Juanita was now standing after Miguel gave her the news. She nodded excitedly to him. Addressing the men again, he said, "So everybody get your gear ready to work, and me and Casey will get set up in the house. 'Cause today's payday for anybody who signs up to ride for the D and T Ranch."

His little speech brought a cheer from the group of men standing by the porch, as well as the man and wife on the porch. Everyone volunteered to help carry the packs inside the house and take care of the horses. There was a new sense of confidence floating in the air, for there had not been time yet for the doubt that was bound to follow. After all, the two who had come to build a ranch were still the same Casey and Eli they had worked cattle with before and stayed as broke as the rest of them.

When they went into the house with Juanita and Miguel, Casey and Eli chose a room for themselves. They were the bedrooms used by the two Whitmores, and the rooms were just as they had left them when they walked out on their last day. It seemed odd to Casey and Eli because either room was far and away nicer than the small room the housekeeping couple shared. Juanita's first assignment was to make a list of what she needed to feed everybody. When he saw it, Casey told her he was going in the morning, for sure, and asked if she had anything to cook for supper and breakfast in the morning.

"Beef," she said. "That's all I cook for the last week. The men find strays and butcher them. Not much else to cook."

"I thought Miguel raised some pigs," Casey said. "What happened to them?"

"I cook them week before last," she said. "I tell Miguel to hide the chickens, or we don't have no eggs."

"That's the only cattle work going on here, boss," Miguel offered, already addressing Casey and Eli as "boss," for it was obvious to him that the two former cowhands had taken over the running of the ranch. "The men ride out to round up any stray cows they can find. They drive them back here and they eat them."

"Maybe Miguel and I better take a couple of packhorses with the wagon over to Carter's store tomorrow mornin'," Casey said to Eli.

"Maybe I go with you," Juanita said. "Then you don't forget everything I need."

Once they were settled in the ranch house, they called their six-man crew of cowhands together for a meeting in the bunkhouse. "You boys have worked long enough with me and Eli to know we ain't never give anybody the short rope when it came to chores. And we're gonna try to run this ranch as good as we can for all of us. The first thing we're gonna do is pay you for last month's work. After that, it'll be on the first of every month." He produced a half-used ledger he found in one of the Whitmores' rooms. "I wrote each one of your names down in the book, and when you sign your name beside the one I wrote, Eli will give you forty dollars. If you can't write, just make your mark."

"Whadda we gotta do that for?" Tom Tuttle asked.

" 'Cause when you come back after spendin' all your money on whiskey, sayin' we ain't paid you," Eli said to him, "we can say the hell we didn't. And show you your mark."

"I don't understand, Casey," Sam Dunn spoke up. "You're payin' us forty dollars a month to work cattle and we ain't got no cattle."

"We're gonna buy some cattle," Casey told him. "There's some small ranches around here that got stuck with cattle they were figurin' on sellin' at next year's market. Now they ain't worth nothin', so we'll buy 'em for almost nothin'."

"He means like Nicholson's ranch on the west side of the Lampasas," Corey Johnson said. "He's got a thousand head of cattle grazin' on his range and he can't sell 'em for a dollar a head. At least that's what his daughter said. Shut up!" Corey said when he got several catcalls about the daughter. "That ain't the worst part," he continued. "He borrowed two thousand dollars from the bank in Waco to buy the cattle and build a new barn. And he can't pay the bank for the loan. They're talkin' about losin' their ranch."

"I reckon we'll be goin' over to talk to Joe Nicholson first thing," Casey said. "But I told Miguel I'd take him and Juanita into town in the mornin' to build her supplies back up. If we get back here early enough, Eli and I will ride over the river and see if we can catch Nicholson at home." The Nicholson Ranch headquarters was close to the river, so there should be time to call on him, unless he was riding the western boundary of his range. If the financial situation was as bad as Corey said, then it was ideal for his and Eli's plans. Not only that, but it would be a short cattle drive to move them to the D&T, as Casey and Eli were already referring to the new establishment.

There was a definite air of excitement in the bunkhouse. It appeared that the pair of older cowhands had come to rescue them again, although not one of the men being rescued had any notion how it could be possible. One by one, they filed by to sign or make a mark by their name in Casey's ledger, then examine the four ten-dollar bills they received from Eli. When they determined the bills were, in fact, genuine government-issued currency, they finally accepted everything Casey and Eli had been telling them as the truth.

After everyone was paid, the new bosses

set the crew to work cleaning up the bunk-house and the barn. As far as the two of them, they had other problems to solve and that was where to store their money. With their combination of bank and train robberies, they had to find some way to hide something in the neighborhood of fifty-four thousand dollars. And that was after the payroll just paid the crew and Miguel and Juanita.

The obvious place to keep money was in the large safe in one of the bedrooms they had moved their few possessions into. It was in the room Eli selected and the safe was bolted to the floor in a corner, standing there with the door open. Whoever had emptied it didn't bother to close it and lock it. Eli took a look at it, but had no idea how to set a new combination, so the safe was of no use to them, unless they could figure out how to change the old combination to a new one. The only article left in the safe was a small envelope with instructions on how to open the safe, but no combination or how to set one.

"Wait a minute," Casey said. "Somebody wrote somethin' on the back of this envelope." He showed it to Eli. Someone had written a series of numbers with a pencil and each number was followed by either an

R or an *L.* "That's the combination, I bet. We can just use the old combination. Nobody else but the Whitmores would know that combination, and they ain't likely to be comin' back."

"What if that ain't the combination?" Eli asked. "Then we'd have to dynamite the dang safe to get to our money."

"Try it with the door open," Casey said. "Lock it."

Eli locked the open door. Casey called out the numbers and Eli dialed them in. "Now try the handle." The lock released. Still reluctant to risk their fortune, Eli closed the door on the empty safe and spun the dial. Then he tried the handle to confirm it had locked.

Casey read the numbers out again, and the door unlocked. Even so, they tried it one more time to be absolutely sure. This time, Eli placed a five-dollar bill inside, as if to test the safe's evil intentions. But it opened again. They looked at each other and shrugged, then filled it with stacks of cash money.

Casey copied the combination down on another piece of paper and gave it to Eli. "Be awful careful where you keep this," he said.

"You don't have to tell me that," Eli said,

then asked, "You reckon Juanita knows the combination to that safe?"

"I'd be mighty surprised if she did," Casey said. "Lock it up." Eli locked the safe, now filled with cash. Casey opened the bedroom door and called out, "Juanita!"

She hurried out of the kitchen. "Senor Casey?"

"Juanita, just call me Casey," he said. "Come here." She paused, looking a bit uncertain, but came to the bedroom door where he was standing. He pointed to the safe. "That thing's locked. Do you know how to open it?"

"*Sí,*" she said. "Open with secret numbers. Only Senor Whitmore knows secret numbers. He keep important papers in there."

"I just wondered," Casey said. "I thought if you knew how to open it, we'd just look in it and see if there's anything inside."

"He don't let nobody watch him when he open it," she said.

"It's not important. We'll just let it stay locked."

Juanita turned around and returned to the kitchen. When she had gone, Casey knelt down and tried the combination one more time, just for good measure, and grinned up at Eli when the safe opened.

CHAPTER 22

After breakfast the next morning, Miguel hitched the horses up to the wagon while Casey saddled Smoke for the four-mile ride into town. When they were ready to go, Juanita came out of the house and climbed up on the wagon seat beside her husband. Since the trip was simply to buy supplies for Juanita's pantry, Eli decided to remain at the ranch. He was fully confident of Casey's ability to convince Frank Carter he might be passing up an opportunity to do quite a lot more business if he closed his store and left the little town.

There was also a little bit of concern on leaving the house empty at this early stage of their new management — especially with his and Casey's money in the house. Having worked with this group of cowhands for so long, he felt guilty about any doubts regarding their honesty. He guessed it was one reason rich men seemed to distrust everybody.

When they pulled into the small settlement of Little Bow, Casey saw at once that the men had not exaggerated the fact that the town was dying. He saw several vacant buildings where shops had been and were now vacant. The saloon was still open. The Texas Rose. He wondered who still had enough money to buy a drink of whiskey. Riding beside the wagon, he passed the stable and the blacksmith, but saw no sign of Dub Swinson or Jake Turner. *Probably waiting for Monroe and the boys to spend the last of the bonus Eli and I gave them in Abilene,* he thought. *Dub and Jake will move out.* Casey continued on to Carter's Merchandise, where he stepped down and tied Smoke's reins loosely around the hitching rail. He stepped over to the wagon and helped Juanita down from the seat.

"I declare, Casey Tubbs!" Frank Carter sang out. "Those boys told me you'd checked out of here for good. When did you come back?"

"Howdy, Frank. I got back yesterday, and it's a good thing I did. Juanita, here, has run out of about everything. She's made up a list and I wanna go ahead and get a two-month supply at least."

Frank's smile froze on his face as he suddenly felt uncomfortable. He glanced at the list Juanita handed him and hesitated for a few moments before he responded. "That's a mighty big order. You know, Casey, you and me was always good friends. But I ain't sellin' anything on credit these days, especially an order this size. I can't afford to. You probably ain't noticed it yet, but the folks in this town have either left or are fixin' to leave. I'm loaded down with a helluva lot of inventory, and the only reason I ain't left yet is because I'm hopin' to sell a little more of my stock so I don't have to haul out so much. Believe me, I appreciate the business I've done with the Whitmores, but I can't afford to carry you on the books anymore." He looked directly into Casey's eyes and shook his head sorrowfully. "And it hurts me to tell you that."

Casey, waiting patiently for him to pause, finally responded. "Would it hurt you to sell me everything on that list, if I was to pay you cash?"

Frank was struck dumb. "You're japin' with me now. I don't blame you for bein' a little bit sore, after all the business we've done over the years. But it's just the way things are right now."

"I swear, Frank, I didn't remember you bein' so hard of hearin' the last time I talked to you. I said I'd give you cash, so let's get started on that list. You start addin' it up and Miguel and I will start hauling it out to the wagon. I've got some other business I need to take care of this afternoon."

Frank was still not totally comfortable with the situation, even though it was an order he dearly needed. He always liked Casey, but Casey was anything but predictable, and these were especially hard times for everyone. He couldn't really be sure, but what if times had gotten so desperate for the folks at the old Whitmore Brothers Ranch, that Casey might be bluffing his way to a wagonload of supplies? However, he couldn't bring himself to demand to see the money.

Finally he threw all caution to the wind and yelled, "John! Come in here!" In a few seconds, Frank's sixteen-year-old son came in from the back of the store. "I need you to pull some stock. I'll call out each item and how much of it to pull."

"Yes, sir," John said, showing no excitement for the chore.

While they were bringing out the items to be placed on the counter, Juanita shopped around the main store, since Casey had given her permission to pick up anything else she may have forgotten to put on the list. As each item was placed on the counter, Frank wrote it down and priced it. Casey and Miguel carried it out to the wagon as soon as Frank priced it.

When the last item on Juanita's list was carried out to a wagon packed as full as one could be packed, Frank found himself in an unusual position. He had gambled and now it was time to find out if he had won or lost. He realized that he was not in a hurry to find out.

"I make it two hundred and thirty-five dollars," he said, and turned the paper around, so Casey could see. "When I talked to some of the boys from the ranch, they said you and Eli Doolin had took off for parts unknown and were gone from here for good. What made you come back?"

Casey pulled a roll of cash out of his vest pocket and counted out the total price on the counter. Then he said, "Because these hard times are goin' to pass pretty soon, and this ranch and this town is too good a place to abandon. Eli and I will be runnin' the ranch and we'll be raisin' cattle, just like we were before the Whitmores decided to get out of the business and shut it down. Cattle will sell again. The eastern markets will be back. People want beef to eat and we plan to raise it for 'em. I was sorry to hear you're thinkin' about leavin' Little Bow, 'cause you're so much closer to us for all our supplies. We can get supplies somewhere else, but we'd have to go all the way to the Leon River. We'd rather deal with you."

"I'll tell you one thing," Frank declared. "After dealin' with you today, I can afford to hold on a little bit longer. I'd kinda like to see if you're gonna build that ranch back to where it once was." He put his hand out. "Thank you for your business."

Casey shook his hand, then went outside to help Miguel tie a canvas cover over their load to help stabilize it. When that was secured, they started back for home. It was still fairly early in the morning, but Juanita was eager to get back to the ranch. Casey was surprised to see how excited the normally calm and reserved woman was. Miguel told him she was anxious to fix a good dinner, now that she had everything she needed. When they pulled up into the yard at the ranch, Casey was amused to see his young cowhands as excited as she when they ran from the barn to help carry in all the new supplies for her pantry.

"What about Carter?" Eli asked Casey.

"I think he's gonna stay for a while longer just to see if you and I are gonna whip this ranch into a payin' proposition," Casey told him. "I was thinkin' about gettin' over to see Nicholson right now, but after seein' how excited Juanita is over havin' somethin' to cook, I think I'll wait till after dinner."

"That sounds like some smart thinkin' to me," Eli declared. "I hope Nicholson has got as many cows as Corey said he has. We're gonna have to build up our remuda, too. We ain't got anywhere near enough horses to work even one thousand cows. Half the boys ain't even got one extra horse. If we make a deal with Nicholson, I hope we can bring his remuda."

"I reckon we'll find out this afternoon," Casey said, "after dinner."

The dinner was every bit as good as everybody had hoped it would be, with hot baked biscuits for a change. Juanita even made an apple cake. It was like a celebration for Casey and Eli coming home to save the ranch. After a final cup of coffee, the two outlaws saddled their horses and climbed aboard, both complaining of a stomach stretched beyond its designed capacity. They rode out to the west, until they came to the river. When they crossed over, they were on Nicholson's range, but only a couple of miles from the headquarters.

"Two riders comin', Pa," fourteen-year-old Joe Jr. called out from the hayloft, where he had been throwing down some fresh hay for the milk cow.

"Who is it?" Joe Nicholson called back. "Can you tell?" He wasn't in the mood to receive strangers. The latest visitors were sent by the Waco Cattleman's Bank to notify him that he had thirty days to repay his mortgage or face eviction from the ranch he had built and worked for the last ten years.

Called "Buck" by his family, the teen said, "I don't know. Just looks like two ranch hands."

"All right," Nicholson said, "most likely ridin' across our range and saw some cows, and they're thinkin' we still might be workin' cattle. When they find out we ain't hirin' nobody, then they'll settle for somethin' to eat. They don't look like them last two from the bank, do they?" he asked to be sure.

"No, sir," Buck said, "they ain't the same two."

"I'll see what they want." He walked out of the barn and headed out to meet them. "Afternoon," he called out after taking a good look at them. He thought maybe he had seen them before. "Somethin' I can help you fellows with?"

"Afternoon," Casey returned. "We're from

the old Whitmore Brothers Ranch across the river."

"I thought I had seen you before," Nicholson said, "one or two times at roundup, I reckon."

"Most likely," Casey agreed. "We noticed you still got some cattle scattered around."

"Yes, I have, but I wish I didn't," Nicholson was quick to reply. "You mighta also noticed that there weren't nobody roundin' up those strays you saw. I'm sorry, boys, if you're lookin' for work, I can't help you. There ain't nobody left workin' here, but me and my son. And we're gonna have to leave in thirty days. I can't pay nobody to work the cattle I've got, and I can't sell 'em for enough to pay the bank for my loan. So they'll be takin' over my house and my land." He thought he might as well lay all his cards on the table and save a lot of time.

"Well, sir, that's the reason me and Eli rode over here to see if we couldn't talk some business that might help us all out. Mind if we step down?"

"No, I reckon not," Nicholson said reluctantly, thinking, *This is the part where they ask if I can at least spare some grub.*

They dismounted. "Joe Nicholson, right?" Casey asked. Nicholson said that he was. "I just wanted to be sure I was talkin' to the right man," Casey continued. "My name's Casey Tubbs and this is my partner, Eli Doolin. How many cows do you think you have?"

"About fifty or sixty more than a thousand is what I *know* I've got," he said. "That's the count them fellows from the bank came up with. You used to get four dollars a head here in Texas and forty dollars when you drove 'em to Abilene or Wichita. Now it's hard to sell 'em for a dollar in Texas, and they don't want 'em at all in Abilene." He paused to shake his head. "I don't know why I'm tellin' you all this. Unless you've been on the moon for the last month, you know what I'm talkin' about." He paused again to let himself simmer down. "Excuse my manners, boys. If you're hungry, I've got some beef jerky you're welcome to."

"That's mighty neighborly of you, but we just had a pretty big dinner before we rode out here," Casey said. "If you don't mind me askin', how much is the loan you have to pay off?"

"I don't mind you knowin'," Nicholson shrugged. "I owe the bank two thousand and fifty-nine dollars. I don't care who knows it. The fact of the matter is, I ain't got that much money, not even half that much. So, even if I could sell my cattle for a dollar a head, I'd still be short of the loan."

"Well, Eli and me, we're lookin' to buy some cattle to get our herd started. A thousand cattle would be a good start. We've still got enough hands to handle that many. Lemme talk to my partner a second." He turned to Eli to see if he was in agreement, then he turned back to ask Nicholson. "Would you be interested in sellin' us your cattle for around two dollars and fifty cents a head?"

"Say what?" Nicholson questioned, not sure he was hearing right.

"We'll give you twenty-six hundred dollars for your cattle, cash money. Are you interested?" Eli made the offer. "We'll just round it off to make it easier. That would pay your bank loan off and leave you with a little extra money."

Feeling suddenly faint, Nicholson took hold of Biscuit's bridle to steady himself. "Twenty-six hundred dollars, pay the bank off, keep my house and my land, free and clear." He wasn't really asking, as much as he was reassuring himself that he had heard right.

"That's right," Casey said. "And you can tell Waco Cattleman's Bank to keep their greedy hands offa your property. If things go like we think they will, the cattle business will be right back where it was. If you decide you wanna give it another try, you can count on us to give you a hand."

Nicholson was almost beside himself, afraid he was being led into some kind of scheme to take anything he had left after the bank claimed his property. "I don't know," he said. "I don't know," he repeated. "Are you fellows on the level?" Then he thought to ask a question he thought he should have asked, to begin with. "You said cash. When do you intend to give me the money? After you drive all my cattle off?"

"How 'bout right now?" Casey asked. "Will that suit you better?" He opened the pocket on his saddlebag and pulled out a sheet of paper that was wrapped around a bundle of bills, all hundreds and fifties. He counted out twenty-six hundred dollars and handed it to him. "You count it, to make sure." He waited until Nicholson finished before he asked, "Can you read?" Nicholson said that he could, so Casey gave it to him to read. "It's nothin' more than a simple agreement between you and Eli and me. It just says you sold one thousand and fifty cattle to us for two thousand and six hundred dollars. We'll write those numbers in where I left it blank. We'll all three sign it and there won't ever be any question about who owns the cattle, or where you got your money. It's best we do it with an ink pen. Have you got one?"

"I sure do," Nicholson said, no longer harboring any doubts. "At least my wife has one. Let's go in the house."

He didn't wait for them to tie their horses, but headed straight for the kitchen door. They dropped their reins on the ground and followed along behind him. They walked in the kitchen to find him excitedly explaining to his astonished wife that the Lord had not forsaken them, after all, and she was not going to have to leave her home.

"Honey, go get your pen and ink, so we can sign this agreement. Then make some coffee for these gentlemen." He looked back at Casey and said, "Somethin' stronger mighta been better, but coffee's all we've got."

"Coffee's fine," Casey said, "but we don't wanna cause you no extra trouble, ma'am."

"No trouble," Nicholson said before his wife had a chance to respond. "This is my wife, Meg. Honey, this is Mr. Casey Doolin and Mr. Eli Tubbs. They're buyin' our cows."

"It's the other way around," Casey said to Meg. "It's Casey Tubbs and Eli Doolin. I'm Casey. I'm pleased to meet you."

"Is that true?" Meg asked. Like her husband, she was thinking there was a catch to it somewhere.

"It's true, Mama," Buck Nicholson said, standing in the open kitchen door. "I heard the whole thing. Pa's already got the money, and they're gonna start roundin' up all the strays tomorrow. I'm gonna help 'em."

"You know, Casey, there's another problem we ain't discussed yet, and we're gonna need 'em right away," Eli reminded him.

"Horses," Casey said at once, remembering then. "We're gonna be needin' horses. When Whitmore Brothers sold all the cattle, they sold the remuda, too. Have you still got all your horses?" he asked Nicholson.

"Yes, sir, I do," Joe said. "And I'll be sellin' most of 'em. Now that I'm keepin' our house and land, I expect I'll go back to farmin', so I don't need thirty horses."

"Well, we'd like to take about twenty or twenty-five of 'em off your hands," Casey said, "if we can work out a good price."

"Well, let's see," Joe scratched his chin whiskers. "The horse market ain't gone down the same road with the cattle. A good price for a decent horse is forty dollars. But since you've paid me twice what I could get for a cow, I reckon I could sell you horses for one half what I could get somewhere else."

Casey went to his saddlebag again and returned with five hundred more for the horses. He scratched a short note on the bottom of the contract to include the horses. The rest of the visit was spent drinking the coffee Meg had made. Tomorrow they would pick out the horses they had just purchased, and the D&T hands would start riding Nicholson's range to round up all the cattle for the short drive to the D&T range.

When they said their good evenings, Meg walked to the door with them and expressed her heartfelt thanks to them for saving their home from the evil folks who owned the Waco Cattleman's Bank. "They're taking advantage of this panic in the cattle market to own all the land in this county," she said. "They don't care about the people they put out in the cold."

When Casey and Eli rode away from the Nicholson spread, Casey said, "The Waco Cattleman's Bank sounds like the kind of place Oscar and Elmer oughta visit next time they need a loan."

"You might be right about that," Eli said. "And I've found out one thing since we became wealthy men, it sure is a lot easier spendin' money than it was makin' it. And the way we're passin' out money, we'd better be thinkin' about our next loan. There ain't no tellin' how long it's gonna be before the cattle market gets right again."

"Once we get the boys back to the work of takin' care of cattle again, we'll be free to take some of those business trips when we think they're necessary," Casey predicted.

CHAPTER 23

On the ride back to the ranch, they talked about the necessity of giving one of the men the job of foreman. There had not been an official one during the last five years of the Whitmore Brothers operation. The reason was simple. Casey and Eli were older and more experienced in the business of raising cattle than the other men on the payroll. And they were generally in agreement when it came to the right and wrong ways to do everything. So it was a natural thing for the Whitmores to tell them what they wanted done. And Casey and Eli told the men how to do it.

Now, since they had promoted themselves into the role of owners, they no longer intended to work the cattle with the men. So they figured they had best designate one of the men to direct the work of the crew. Corey Johnson, at twenty, and Monroe Kelly, at twenty-one, were the oldest, so they naturally thought it would be one of the two. They decided they would make a decision over the next few days while they worked with the men to round up their new herd and drive it across the river.

While the two cowhands, turned outlaws, turned ranch owners, were getting ready to get the first herd of cattle for the D&T Ranch, a conversation that was held in U.S. Marshal Quincy Thomas's office would have been of interest to them. Thomas, located in San Antonio, was in command of the Western District of Texas.

"Marshal Thomas," Earl Dutton asked when he stuck his head inside the door, "you remember that notification from Kansas about two old men robbin' a bank in Wichita?"

"Yeah," Thomas said. "Two old men. I remember. They thought they might be heading for Texas, but they never showed up."

"Well, looks like maybe they did," Earl said. "I don't know why they didn't wire us before this, because it happened several days ago."

"What happened? Did they hit a bank in Texas?"

"No, sir, they held up the train in Mexia,

if it was the same two old men. And from the description given by the mail clerk, it sounds like the same two."

"Mexia?" Thomas responded. "That should be handled out of the court in Waco. Are they asking for help from here?"

"No, sir, they say they're just advising us of their investigation, but they wanted us to be aware of them, in case they do show up down here."

"Huh," Thomas grunted. "From the description they sent us, I'da thought those two old coots would have died of natural causes before now."

"They said they've put one man on assignment to track the old men down." Earl paused to refer to the paper he was holding. "His name's Colton Gray. That's all they said."

"Two old men," Thomas repeated. "I wouldn't think it would take long to run down two old fellows like that. Sounds to me like two old outlaws who are too damn old to cut it anymore, and they've just decided to see how far they can take it until they're stopped for good. Probably figure the worst that can happen to 'em is to sit out the rest of their lives in prison with three meals a day and a cot to sleep on."

"I think you're probably right," Earl said.

"Maybe we'll soon hear if Deputy Marshal Colton Gray is able to catch up with 'em before Father Time does."

U.S. Deputy Marshal Colton Gray rode into the quiet little town of Mexia, Texas, a few minutes after four o'clock in the afternoon. He guided the bay gelding he rode directly toward the railroad depot, dismounted, and tied the bay and his sorrel packhorse to a corner post of the platform. Then he went up the steps and headed for the stationmaster's office.

David Gage looked up when he heard the door open, at once impressed by the tall young man who seemed to fill the doorway. Gage got up from his desk and walked over to the window of the ticket cage to meet the stranger.

"Are you Mr. Gage?" Colton asked.

"I am," Gage said. "What can I do for you?"

"I'm Deputy Marshal Colton Gray," he said, and pulled his coat aside so Gage could see his badge. "I've been assigned to investigate the train robbery that happened here recently. The only information we have on the two men who robbed the mail car is that they were two pretty old fellows, and they match a description of two old men who robbed a bank in Wichita, Kansas. I'm hopin' to find out anything I can about the two. Had you seen them in here before that day?"

"No, sir," Gage said. "I'm afraid I'm not gonna be of any use to you at all. They didn't come in this office. And I've been told they were standing behind me when I took the mailbag out and gave it to the clerk in the mail car. And I didn't even see 'em. They were right behind me, but I never turned around. I wanted to get the mail into the office here to hold for the post office. But there were people here that day that did see 'em. One you need to talk to, for sure, is Jack Myers. He's the blacksmith. He was here to meet his wife who came in on the train. He was standing back by the mail car when those two robbers stepped off the train. One of the old fellows stumbled when the train jerked as it was startin' to roll, and he liked to fell down if Jack hadn't caught him."

" 'Jack Myers,' huh?" Colton repeated the name in an effort to lock it in his memory. "The information I got was that the two old men got inside the mail car."

"That's right," Gage said, "they got inside the car."

"How do you suppose they got inside?"

412

Colton asked.

"I was wonderin' that, myself," Gage said. "Everybody knows you ain't supposed to go into that car."

"Maybe the mail clerk in the car could tell us," Colton suggested. "Accordin' to my information, it was the five-fifteen train. Is that right?"

"Yep, that's right." He glanced at the clock on the wall. "And she oughta be rollin' in here within the next few minutes," he said.

"Is it usually the same mail clerk on that train all the time?" Colton asked.

"It usually is," Gage said. "Albert King is the one who's usually ridin' the mail car." He paused with the first sound of the whistle announcing the train's approaching. "Speak of the Devil. I gotta lock up the office while I take some mail out to the train. You wanna go with me and talk to Albert?"

"Yes, sir, that's what I'd like to do." Colton walked back to the door and waited while Gage locked up his ticket cage and his office. Then they walked out onto the platform and waited for the train to come in.

"It was just like this on that day," Gage said. "Just a few folks standin' around, waitin' for the train. I don't know where those two coulda been. You'da thought I would have seen 'em." He shook his head, as if he'd been careless, and he watched the train slowing as it approached.

"I reckon you had your mind on gettin' your mail on the train," Colton suggested. "You wouldn't likely be thinkin' about the train gettin' robbed."

They walked in pace with the mail car as the train slowly rolled to a stop. And when the door was suddenly raised, Gage said, "Howdy, Albert, this here is Deputy Marshal Colton Gray. He's tryin' to get on the trail of those two old buzzards that robbed you."

"Mr. King, right?" Colton asked, and Albert said that he was. "I don't want to delay the train, so let me just ask you, was there anything about them that was unusual?"

"You mean other than the fact they both looked like they were damn near a hundred years apiece? I couldn't believe they got into this car so quick and slammed the gate down before I could stop 'em."

"I mean, did either of them have any unusual features, or scars, or something that they couldn't hide?" Colton asked. "Maybe one of 'em walked with a limp, or there was something else unusual about them. I don't have much to go on except they're too old to be holdin' people up."

"I swear, Deputy, I wish I could help you. The only thing I remember about 'em was they were too damn old to be doin' what they were doin'. But they stepped right on into this car, wavin' big ol' Colt pistols, and I knew they meant business. It was their attitude. Like it didn't matter to them if they had to shoot me or not." He apologized for not being of more help, but there was not much more he could say about them.

"I appreciate your help," Colton told Albert. He stepped back from the car. "Not much to go on, but I'll not hold you up any longer." There were no passengers getting on or off, so the engineer blew his whistle, and the train was soon in motion again.

Colton thanked Gage. "I'll go see if I can find the blacksmith now. Jack Myers, right?"

"Right," Gage said, "and good luck."

Colton found the blacksmith in his shop doing some repair work on a buggy. "Mr. Myers?" he asked when he pulled the bay gelding up before Jack's shop.

"Yes, sir, Jack Myers," he said. "What can I do for you?"

Colton introduced himself and said that he had been told that Myers was the only person in town who had really had any contact with the two train robbers.

Jack had to chuckle when Colton told

him. "That was a helluva thing, all right. My wife had just got off the train and we was just standin' there talkin', when all of a sudden, a door opened between two cars and these two old fellers stepped down off the train. And the blame train was startin' to move.

"One of 'em got off the step all right, but the other one behind him liked to fell down. I saw what was happenin', so I reached over and caught him by his elbow, kept him from fallin' down, 'cause he was fixin' to go flat. I think he was mighty embarrassed. He begged my pardon and thanked me for catchin' him. Then him and his partner walked off. I didn't look to see where they was headin'. I had to get my wife's suitcases in the buggy." He paused to chuckle again as he thought back on it. "I do remember he was tryin' to hold on to a canvas bag while he was about to trip. Come to find out, it was full of money him and the other old feller just stole from the railroad."

Colton asked him the same questions he had just asked David Gage about any physical features that might help identify the two outlaws. He got the same response — there was nothing unusual about them except they were too old to be robbing trains. He asked one more question, though, that he had not asked Gage. "Mr. Myers, do you think there's any possibility that the two are really younger men dressed up like old men?"

"Tell you the truth, that never occurred to me," Jack said, picturing the two men. "If they are just disguised to look older, they did a mighty good job of it, especially when that one damn near landed on his face."

"You didn't happen to notice how they left the station, did you?" Colton asked. "Horseback or wagon?"

"No, sir, Deputy, I'm sorry I just weren't payin' attention to much of anything but my wife."

"Given the choices, I reckon that's understandable," Colton said. "Thank you for tellin' me what you could. One more question, it's gettin' on toward suppertime, where do I eat?"

Jack laughed. "Bertha's, that's the best in town. You stayin' in Mexia tonight, or are you headin' out for someplace else?"

"I thought I'd hang around for a little while in the mornin', just in case I run into somebody else that mighta talked to those two or seen 'em somewhere. I'll just find me a place to water my horses and lay my bedroll down."

"You ain't got much to go on, have you?"

Jack asked.

Colton shrugged. "Sometimes you just have to be patient and they'll pop up somewhere." But he was actually thinking, *You don't know how right you are.*

"If you're gonna make a camp somewhere for the night, you might as well do it right behind my shop. Plenty of grass for your horses all the way down to the creek. You won't be the first to camp down there. Bertha's is right over yonder, across the street, and won't nobody bother you behind my place."

Colton took a look down toward the river and remarked, "That's damn neighborly of you. I think I'll take you up on that. I'd be pleased to buy your supper, if you'd care to eat at Bertha's with me."

"No, thank you kindly, but I'll be eatin' at home," Jack said. "I'd invite you to come on home and take supper at my house, but to be honest with you, you'll get a better supper at Bertha's. My wife's the sweetest woman ever born, and she learned to cook at her mother's knee. But her mother is the worst cook in the county."

"Much obliged," Colton said.

He climbed back on his horse and rode the short distance to Bertha's, then tied his horses at the rail in front. He felt sure he could have left them behind the blacksmith shop, as Jack suggested, but he didn't want to be that far away, especially in a town he'd never been before. He couldn't help noticing the saloon next door, wearing its sign, HENRY'S. He came to the same conclusion that Casey and Eli had when they first saw it. It brought a trace of a smile to his face as he walked into Bertha's and found one long table that was about half-filled with hungry customers.

The large woman standing near the head of the table seemed to have read his concern, for she welcomed him. "Come on in, stranger. Take any empty seat. There's plenty of food to go around. Tall as you are, you better take that place at the end, give you more knee room." He nodded and sat down where she indicated. When he did, she got a glimpse of the badge he wore. "Are you a Ranger?" Her question caught everyone's attention at the table and all conversation stopped while they awaited his answer.

"No, ma'am, I'm a deputy marshal," Colton said.

"Come to arrest one of our fine citizens or just passin' through town?" Bertha asked. "You want coffee?"

"Yes, ma'am, I'll drink coffee, and I expect I'll just be passin' through, since nobody seems to have any information about those two old men that robbed the train when it stopped here. They didn't come in here to eat, did they?"

"Nope," Bertha said. "I wish they hadda. It'da give my place some free advertisin'." She went to get his coffee.

The conversation at the table for the rest of the meal centered around the blatant holdup on the five-fifteen train. When he had finished eating, he complimented Bertha on her cooking, said a good evening to those still at the table, and took his horses back down by the creek behind the blacksmith shop.

There was still light enough to see where the last campfire had been built, as well as a stack of wood for a good fire. It caused him to wonder who could have camped there last and if they were thoughtful to have left wood for the next fellow. More likely, Jack Myers brought the firewood down there while the deputy was at Bertha's eating supper, because there were not many trees along that stretch of the creek. He would remember to thank him in the morning. After he took care of his horses and made his camp, he built a small fire, saving most of the wood for a better fire in the morning to make his coffee. He drifted off to sleep wondering about the two old men he had been sent to find. It might be a helluva long search.

CHAPTER 24

The days that followed Casey and Eli's visit to the Nicholson Ranch were going to be busy days for the cowhands of the D&T Ranch. And they were going to need a chuckwagon because they would not be coming back to the bunk house at night. They would have a herd to watch. So Casey and Eli would go to the Corbett Ranch and hire Smiley back.

"What if he don't wanna come back?" Eli asked.

"We'll make him an offer he won't be able to say no to," Casey said. "We've got to have a cook."

When Casey and Eli crossed the creek that ran behind the house and the barn, the Double-C Ranch looked to be deserted like so many other farms and ranches.

"Well, I'll be . . ." Smiley George uttered as he got up from the steps of the cook-house, where he had been sitting, drinking a cup of coffee. He ran out to attract their attention as they were heading for the front of the house. "Eli! Casey!" he called out to them, and they turned to meet him. "I swear!" Smiley exclaimed. "What are you boys doin' here? I hope you ain't lookin' for work, 'cause Corbett's laid everybody off, includin' me."

"How's it goin', Smiley?" Eli asked. "You're japin', ain'tcha? 'Cause you always talked about Gary Corbett bein' a friend of yours and wantin' you back."

"He is a friend of mine," Smiley insisted. "He just got hit like everybody else in this business. I'm still here because I ain't got no place else to go. And he ain't got the heart to tell me he can't afford to feed me no more." He paused to shake his head sadly. "But what are you boys doin' here?"

"Lookin' for you," Casey said. "It's time to put you back to work."

"Doin' what?" Smiley responded.

"What you always do," Casey said, "cookin'. Is that chuckwagon of yours ready to roll? 'Cause we've got the boys workin' and they're needin' a cook."

"What the hell are you talkin' about, Casey?" He looked at Eli, who was grinning like a dog eating yellow jackets. "What's he talkin' about, Eli?"

"He's talkin' about a job cookin' for the D &T Ranch," Eli said. "Right now, we're fixin' to move a herd of a thousand cows to that ranch and we need a good cook. Are you interested or not?"

"Where's the D &T Ranch?" Smiley asked, thinking he had heard of every ranch in this part of Texas except that one.

"It's the old Whitmore Brothers Ranch," Casey said. "You've heard of them, ain't you?" he joked. "What about it, you wanna work for seventy-five dollars a month or not?" He got his ledger out of his saddlebag and handed Smiley a pencil. "Sign right there and you'll get seventy-five dollars, cash."

Smiley took the ledger from him and looked at the sheet of names. "This is the old gang," he blurted. It was obvious that he wasn't going to do anything until they told him what was going on. "Where did you get a thousand cows?" Knowing they had robbed a mail car on the train in Abilene to recover their wages, he was concerned about getting into any deal that was against the law.

"We bought 'em from Joe Nicholson and we've got his signature on the sales contract to prove it. And we paid him twice what they were worth. Eli and I were lucky to run up on a big-money politician who wants to buy into the cattle business while it's down, 'cause he knows it'll be back. We'll run the ranch and he'll furnish the money and keep his name out of the newspapers. So you ain't got to worry about where the money comes from. You'll be hirin' on to do an honest job, just like the rest of the men. So, do you want a job or not?"

"I'll sign up," Smiley said, and scribbled his name beside the one Casey had printed on the page. "I need to go tell Gary right now."

"We'll go with you," Casey said, "just to be polite. We don't want him to think we came here to steal his help, even if we did. By the way, this politician who's bankrollin' the ranch don't want anybody to know about it, till he's ready to retire. That's why we're callin' it the D and T Ranch." He counted out seventy-five dollars and handed it to Smiley, who by this time was living up to his name.

They went with Smiley to the front door of the house, where Smiley called Gary Corbett out to meet Casey and Eli. Corbett was visibly delighted to hear that Smiley was leaving to go back to his old position as trail cook. He wished Smiley the best of luck, and in answer to Casey's inquiry, Gary told him that he had no cattle left to sell. He was keeping the few he had to butcher for food. So they helped Smiley pack up his wagon and hitch up his horses, then departed for home, a little over twelve miles away. Since the road went through Little Bow, they stopped there at Frank Carter's store to buy all the supplies Smiley needed for his wagon and the cookhouse at the ranch. The transaction brought a new wave of smiles on the faces of both Smiley and Carter.

The twenty-five horses purchased from Nicholson were not driven over to the D&T right away because the men were rounding up the cattle on Nicholson's range. They found that the majority of the cattle had settled in a big curve of the river, so the men spent their time bringing up the strays to that spot. When Eli and Casey were satisfied that they had found all the cattle that were to be found, they began their cattle drive that was to take two days.

Young Davey Springer was in charge of the remuda, and Corey Johnson was the trail boss. It was obvious to the two outlaws that Corey knew what he was doing and the other men tended to follow his lead. So there was really no tough decision for Eli and Casey to make. Morale was increased considerably when Smiley arrived with his chuckwagon. Everything felt like it was back to normal, except Casey and Eli were no longer working the cattle.

"They're gettin' more like the Whitmores," Sam Dunn commented to Smiley one afternoon after the herd had been driven from Nicholson's range to the D&T. "They don't even sleep in the bunkhouse with the rest of us no more."

"They've took on a lot more responsibility just so all the rest of us could have good-payin' jobs," Smiley told him. "I'll tell you somethin' I just happen to know, if you can keep it to yourself." Sam assured him that he could. "The money behind this operation don't want nobody to know they're bankrollin' it." He went on to tell Sam the story Casey told him about the rich politician. "That's why they've been takin' a couple of trips to Waco lately, meetin' with that man about other cattle to buy." When Sam slowly nodded his head as if he understood, Smiley said, "Now . . . don't breathe a word of this to the other fellows."

There was one speck of fact in Smiley's story. One of the trips Casey and Eli took, soon after the cattle were moved over to their range, was to Waco. The purpose, however, was to scout the Waco Cattleman's Bank. The two outlaws had spent more of their cash supply for repairs and new construction than they had foreseen at the ranch. And while there was still a fair amount of money in their safe, they decided it might be wise to acquire more to insure the future. They decided to check out the Waco Cattleman's Bank because of Joe Nicholson's ranting about the greed of the bank in its efforts to acquire land. That decision was easy, but Casey had to convince Eli that his next idea was necessary.

Just as they had done in Wichita, it was Casey's belief that, if they opened an account in the bank with a deposit of a thousand dollars, it would avail them of an introduction to the manager of the bank. He would be happy to tell them all the bank's safety features to insure their money was safe.

"Why put a thousand dollars in the blame bank again?" Eli wanted to know. "I don't see why we have to put so much in there."

"Because less than that might not get us a meeting with the bigwig," Casey explained. "And he's gonna want to show us everything they do to protect the money."

"I reckon you're right," Eli said when he thought about the attention they were shown at the bank in Wichita. He didn't tell Casey, but he was just naturally reluctant to deposit money in a bank he thought might be easy to rob.

The other trip they took was not actually to Waco. It was a visit to the small town of Groesbeck, about twelve miles south of Mexia, and listed as a stop on the Houston and Texas Central Railroad. When they rode into town, they found that it was a little larger than Mexia. Groesbeck had a town marshal. It also had a bank, a branch of the Waco Cattleman's Bank. To get some feel of the town, they ate dinner at the Groesbeck Kitchen and enjoyed the cooking of a lady of uncertain age named Wilma Rogers. As far as Eli was concerned, that was reason enough to decide on Groesbeck for their next job. They had discussed the possibilities on the long ride home, as well as the risks involved, and the only thing definitely decided was that they should go ahead and do one or the other pretty soon.

Now, two weeks had passed since then. It was time to get it done. So they told Miguel and Juanita, as well as Corey Johnson, that they had to make another business trip to Waco and they weren't sure how long they would be gone. They took a packhorse with them, along with what they needed from

Juanita's pantry, since they would be cooking their own meals until they got to Waco. They left money with Miguel to go into town and replace it. It seemed to Juanita that they packed several bags that she assumed were clothes, but she could not understand why they would need a lot of clothing. Neither man had more than one or two changes of clothes, to begin with. Maybe, she thought, they were the clothes, or whatever, they kept locked in the large trunks at the foot of each of their beds. She was curious about what might be in the trunks, but she dared not ask.

It was two days from the ranch to Waco. They broke camp early on the second morning, so they would have plenty of time to do what they had to do to prepare for the bank visit. When they stopped beside a wide creek to rest the horses that afternoon, they changed into what Eli referred to as their working clothes, put on their makeup and wigs and beards. After they inspected each other to make sure the disguises were perfect, they rode the last mile into town, a little before the bank closed. As they had assumed, no one paid any attention to the two old men riding up the street, and when they were certain no one was watching, they rode up the alley behind the bank. They tied the horses there beside the outhouse and walked around to the bank entrance. It was now only a few minutes before the bank closed, so they went inside.

"You ready to play your part, Oscar?" Casey whispered.

"I'm ready, Elmer," Eli said.

Leonard Crawford commented to the other teller next to him, "Look coming here, right at closing time." He rolled his eyes in the direction of the front door and the two shaggy-looking old men wearing long coats, which looked a couple of sizes too large for them. "Maybe they'll pick you."

"Sorry," John Williams said with a chuckle, "looks like they're coming to you." In fact, it appeared that the two old-timers were confused. One of them seemed to be hanging back, while the other one stepped up to Leonard's window.

"Yes, sir," Leonard greeted Casey, "how can I help you?"

"I know it's gettin' close to quittin' time," Casey said to him, "but we just this minute rode into town and we need to open a bank account. We're carrying a thousand dollars in cash, and I don't like to walk around with that much, so we need to put that in your bank."

431

"I think you're very wise not to carry that much," the teller said, fairly astonished. "Let me introduce you to Mr. Kennedy. He's the bank manager, and I'm sure he will take care of you. Just follow me." He left the cage and motioned for them to follow, leading them to an office across the lobby. He stuck his head in the door and talked to the man behind the desk, while Casey and Eli stood waiting outside.

Kennedy came to the door to greet them and invited them into the office. "Come in, gentlemen," he said. "I'm Thomas Kennedy. Leonard says you want to open an account."

"That's a fact," Casey responded. "I'm Elmer Crouch and this is my brother, Oscar. We need to put our money where it'll be safe. I apologize for gettin' here so close to closin' time, but as your teller probably told you, we're carrying too much cash on us to feel comfortable walkin' around in town."

"Well, I certainly don't blame you," Kennedy said. "A thousand dollars, is that what Leonard said you wanted to open an account with?"

"That's right, sir," Casey said. He reached in a cloth sack he was carrying and pulled out two even stacks of bills and placed them on the desk. "I think I counted out the right amount."

"We always make doubly sure," Kennedy said. "We need to fill out some papers to set you up an account. Then we'll call one of the tellers in and we'll both count it."

While Kennedy was taking down all the information for the account, Eli and Casey were paying attention to what they could see through the open door of Kennedy's office. Of particular interest was what time it was when one of the tellers walked to the front door, locked it, and turned the CLOSED sign around. He stood by the door then and unlocked it when the last customer was ready to leave. Then it was quickly locked again, and the shade pulled down.

"We're awful sorry to get here so late," Casey said. "I reckon you've got a lot to do to close the bank up."

"That's quite all right," Kennedy assured him. "We won't be very long getting you all set up as a customer of our bank. We won't lock up the safe until the tellers finish their count and we'll put your money in there before we lock it for the night. We are one of the few banks in Texas that have the time lock, recently invented by a fellow named James Sargent. Nobody can open our safe until the lock says it's time."

That statement brought a question to the

mind of Eli Doolin. He scratched his chin for a second before asking, "What if that lock don't work one day, and the safe won't open?"

Kennedy smiled as if he'd said the question before. "Well, you see, Mr. Crouch, there are actually three locks inside the door. All of them are set for the same time, and the safe will open if any one of them works. And it's not likely all three locks would fail on the same day. So your money's safe and readily available to you when you need it."

"I declare, Oscar," Casey said, doing his best to make his voice sound as old as his disguise. "Ain't that a wonderment? I never knew they could do that." Playing his part, Eli didn't reply. Instead, he just made a show of anxious nervousness. So Casey said, "Just try to hang on. We'll be through here in a minute."

Puzzled, Kennedy asked, "Is there a problem? Is your brother not well? Would he like a glass of water?"

"No, sir," Casey said. "That's the last thing he needs. My brother has trouble holdin' his water. It don't matter what he wants, when his water bag wants to empty, it's just liable to empty anywhere, and don't give him much notice. He's scared now he's

434

gonna pee in your office."

That was warning enough for Kennedy. "Come on, we'll count your deposit in the back." He led them out of his office and headed for the door to the safe room. "Leonard!" he called out. "Do a count with me on this money. There's a man here who doesn't feel very well, so we need to make this as fast as we can." He turned back to face Casey. "But we'll do it carefully, so there's no worry about the safety of your money." Back to his tellers again, he said, "John, go ahead and put your drawer in the safe." Very softly then, so that no one but the two tellers could hear him, Kennedy stated, "These two old buzzards had to hit us at closing time. I'd tell them they have to come back in the morning, but I want that thousand dollars they're carrying around in that dirty old sack."

Eli released a painful groan then, which prompted Casey to ask anxiously, "You gonna make it?"

"I don't know," Eli groaned painfully. "I'm wantin' to bust loose in my britches."

Kennedy was not at all happy to hear that, but he forced himself to be courteous. "There's an outhouse behind the bank. Can you make it to the outhouse?"

"I don't know," Eli gasped painfully. "I

435

can try." He looked so miserable that Casey felt sorry for him. "Don't you have no chamber pot or a bucket or somethin'?"

"No, sir!" Kennedy said. In fact, he did. He had one in his office, but he was not willing to share it with the bedraggled-looking old man. "Leave your drawer where it is," he barked at Williams then. "Take him out the back door to the outhouse. At least get him outside. Leonard and I will complete the new account and do the money count." Then to Eli, he said, "Don't you worry, Mr. Crouch, we'll take care of everything with your brother."

"Thank you, sir," Eli groaned miserably. "I'm powerful sorry this caught me like this, but I can't help it."

"I know you can't," Kennedy told him. "You have nothing to apologize for. You'll feel a lot better as soon as you get outside in the fresh air." He looked back at Casey then. "I'm really sorry for your brother. I know how much this embarrasses him, but you're a member of our bank family now, and we don't talk about family members."

"I 'preciate it, Mr. Kennedy, and I'm sure Oscar will, too. You reckon I could see where you're gonna keep our money?"

"You certainly can. I was just going to suggest that you might want to see where your money will be sleeping tonight."

"Yes, sir, I would like that," Casey said, and followed Kennedy through the door to the room where he saw a large safe, built into the wall. The door was standing open, and even from the doorway into the room, Casey could see stacks of money inside.

"You through with the count, Leonard?" Kennedy called out.

"Yes, sir," Leonard said, "one thousand dollars exactly."

"Well, bring it on in here and we'll lock it up." Kennedy looked at Casey and grinned.

Casey grinned back at him and stepped aside to give Leonard room to come through the door. When he did, Casey tossed the sack he had brought the money in to Leonard. "Put it in this," he said.

"Oh, that won't be necessary," Kennedy told him. "We'll just stack it in there with the rest of the money."

"Leonard, put that money that's in the safe into the sack with our thousand," Casey calmly instructed the confused young man. As he said it, he reached unhurriedly inside his oversized coat and drew his Colt six-shooter from the holster he wore high on his left hip. Both Leonard and Kennedy were stunned to the point of paralysis, unable to move for long moments while Casey trained his pistol on them.

"Let me tell you where we stand," Casey informed the two stricken souls, who were shocked to find he was wearing a gun inside his ill-fitting coat. "Oscar and I are near the end of our trail. We don't have but a few days left. I'm tellin' you this so there won't be no doubt in your minds. I will shoot you if you don't do as I tell you to. Me and Oscar ain't got nothin' left to lose, and that's a fact. We're after money. If you don't get in our way, you'll live to see the sun come up tomorrow." He paused to listen when he heard the back door open and close. "Is that you, Oscar?"

"Yep, it's me," Eli said. "That other teller decided to sit this one out, so I left him in the outhouse. I brought some rope back with me." He walked into the safe room to find Leonard on his knees before the safe, and Kennedy standing with his back against the wall. Casey was standing beside the safe, holding the safe door open with one hand, while holding his gun on the two frightened employees. "I kinda hated to have to truss him up after he was nice enough to wait while I took a big leak," Eli commented, trying to remain in character. He and Casey agreed about the importance of maintaining their charade as old men.

"Get busy, Leonard." Casey prodded him in the back with the muzzle of his gun. "Fill that bag and we'll be outta here." Eli kept his gun on Kennedy.

Recovering somewhat from the nightmare he was first convinced he was having, Thomas Kennedy tried to discourage the two old men from going through with their insane robbery. "You know you haven't a chance to get away with this, don't you?"

Casey glanced at him long enough to reply, "I don't know. It looks like we're doin' okay so far. Oscar, you might as well go ahead and tie him up."

"There'll be a posse on your trail as soon as you walk out of this bank," Kennedy insisted. "You're not thinking straight. They'll hunt you down and shoot you on sight."

"At least, I'll die a rich man," Casey said. "Ain't that right, Oscar?"

"That's a fact, Elmer, and that's all we ever wanted," Eli said. He turned Kennedy around to face the wall as he pulled his hands behind him and tied them together.

"If you'll come to your senses and stop this insane holdup, I won't have you arrested. I'll have them let you go free and just not come back to town anymore," Kennedy pleaded. "I could do that, if you'll stop right now and free us."

"Thanks for the offer, but I'd rather die a rich man," Casey said. He grabbed Leonard by the back of his collar and pulled him away from the safe. "We ain't wantin' to spend the night here, Leonard. Here's another'n for ya, Oscar." Eli promptly grabbed Leonard's hands and pulled them behind him to be tied together, while Casey started emptying the safe.

"I'm gonna need another sack," Casey said. "This one's gettin' too full." He looked around him and saw some of the bank's bags on a table, so he got one of them. "We need to divide it up into two bags, anyway, since we're splittin' up when we leave here." He thought that would be good information for Kennedy to pass on to the sheriff. "How much is in here?" he asked Kennedy. "You could save us the trouble of countin' it."

"Save your necks while you still can" was all Kennedy would answer.

"Sorry you feel that way, but I reckon I understand how you're feelin' a little poorly about all this. Kinda like the way some of the small farmers and ranchers feel when you folks at the bank foreclose on 'em." He stood over the two trussed-up men for a few moments. "Oscar," he said then, "reach in his right-hand coat pocket and get that bunch of keys he's carryin'. We need to lock that back door when we leave, so nobody don't break in on 'em."

They carried their two sacks full of money out through the back door, then waited while Eli tried all the keys on the ring he found in Kennedy's coat pocket, until he found one that worked on the back door lock. Then he locked the door and they hooked their sacks of money on the pack-horse. After that, they checked on John Williams in the outhouse. Already wet with the sweat he generated trying to get out of his bonds, there was no evidence showing a gain on the escape situation.

"I'm gonna leave you the keys your boss was totin', so you can get back in the bank, if you ever get outta there," Eli told John. "Tell him I was much obliged." He hung the keys on a nail sticking out of the out-house door. "If I'm ever back to this part of Texas, I'll buy you a drink."

"Come on, Oscar," Casey said, already in the saddle. "We got a long ride before sup-per." Eli closed the outhouse door and turned the little wheel nailed to the outside of it with the words IN USE straight up. He climbed up on Biscuit and followed Casey and the packhorse down the alley behind the feed store and the barbershop.

Riding at a leisurely pace, so they wouldn't attract any attention, they rode out the trail they had come into town on. When only a little more than a mile from town, they came to the creek where they had stopped to change into their disguises on the way into town. They turned off the trail and rode down the creek to the same spot they had stopped at before. They stripped off their old men's outfits and took advantage of the creek to clean off all traces of their makeup. Satisfied they were Casey and Eli again, they started out for home.

CHAPTER 25

The one thing Colton Gray had been able to determine was that the two mysterious old bandits had evidently ridden into Mexia with no other purpose but to rob the train. It was evidently the first time they had been to the town, for no one there had ever seen them before that day. They had not inquired about the train schedule before, but they were there when it arrived, robbed the train, then disappeared. Colton had ridden to all the small settlements within a day's ride of Mexia. There was no evidence of the two men's existence. Finally he decided he was accomplishing nothing, and rode back to Waco to report his unsuccessful search.

When he walked into U.S. Marshal John Timmons's office, the marshal didn't look surprised to see him. "Colton Gray," Timmons announced. "I was wondering if you might show up here in Waco any day now."

Thinking his boss was complaining because he had been on this assignment a long time with no results, Colton had to protest. "You told me to stay out there as long as it took to run those two old bandits down. Well, I stayed after 'em till there wasn't anyplace else to look, and I ain't found the first clue about where they came from or where they are. So I came in to tell you I'm just wastin' my time. I don't know where to pick up their trail. They just disappeared."

Timmons pushed his chair back from his desk and propped one foot on the edge of it. "Well, maybe you could pick up their trail at the Waco Cattleman's Bank. They robbed it yesterday, right after closing time. Cleaned the safe out." He paused to let that sink in. "I'da been a lot more impressed if you had told me you got on their trail and followed 'em here, even though you got here too late to stop 'em from robbin' the bank."

Almost stunned, Colton did not respond at once. Timmons had been known to joke about some things from time to time. Finally Colton said, "If I had told you that, it woulda been a damn lie. They were here in Waco? Robbed the bank right here in Waco? Are you japin' me, boss?"

"I'm afraid this ain't no joking matter," Timmons told him. "Those two old buzzards came right here, where we live, and

444

robbed the bank."

"You sure it's the same two outlaws?"

"I think it is," Timmons insisted. "Thomas Kennedy spent a long time talking to them. We showed him the drawings of the two that robbed the bank in Wichita, and he said these two yesterday looked just like 'em. Leonard Crawford and John Williams said the same thing. They said the two old geezers had let their hair and their beards grow since those drawings were made. But it was definitely the same fellows." He paused when he could see Colton's mind working on it. "I know what you're thinking, but all three of them at the bank said there wasn't any doubt. These two really were old codgers who didn't give a flip if they got caught or got shot."

"Whaddaya want me to do now?" Colton asked.

"Whaddaya think?" Timmons responded. "You're still on the case. Go find 'em and arrest 'em."

"They might not show up anywhere again," Colton said. "If they cleaned that bank out, like you say, they oughta have enough money to last them for the rest of their lives."

"You'd think so, wouldn't you?" Timmons said. "As old as they are, the money from

445

the bank and train jobs they did before this one shoulda been enough to last 'em. The crazy old coots might be getting all pumped up over the success they've had. They're gonna show up again — that's what I think — and that money is gonna show up where there wasn't any before."

"If they don't just dig a hole in the ground and bury it," Colton said. "If they're as old as everybody says, they might forget where they buried it."

Following Timmons's instructions, Colton went to the bank to see if he could get any helpful information from Kennedy and his tellers. He found their testimony little different from what Timmons had already told him. The only hope he uncovered was when he learned that the old men had left their horses tied by the outhouse while they went into the bank. That was easily confirmed by the hoofprints he found. Since he had no better lead to follow, he decided to see if he could track them, and maybe at least find which way they left town. It was no problem to follow the tracks along the alley behind the buildings, for there were no others in the alley. When they left the alley, it became more of a guessing game for Colton, but he continued to follow tracks that were now mixed in with others on the backstreet. When the tracks he was betting on turned onto the trail, west to Fort Gates, he hesitated before deciding to continue, thinking he could be totally wrong.

"What the hell . . ." he mumbled, and started out again.

He had ridden only a mile or so when he came to a creek. When he started across, he realized he didn't see the tracks entering the water. He dismounted to take a closer look and discovered the tracks had left the trail and gone down the creek. Leading his horse, he walked along the creek bank until he came to the remains of a camp. He knew at once he had been following the wrong hoofprints. It didn't make any sense for the two he tracked to go into camp a mile from the bank they just robbed. *Unless,* he thought, *they were younger men anxious to get out of their disguises.* He knew he was the only one who considered that a possibility, but he wasn't ready to completely give it up.

In a few days, the D&T Ranch was back operating, as it had before when it was known as the Whitmore Brothers Ranch. The only difference was the absence of the two older cowhands, Casey and Eli, tending the cattle. They were now the ranch owners and managers, and their new status was accepted by the other men as a result of pure luck. Whereas the Whitmores were seldom seen outside the ranch headquarters, the new owners were seen almost every day. The cookhouse was in operation again, with Smiley there to do the cooking. It was a good time to be employed by the D&T.

"Who's this comin' here?" Casey asked when he saw Davey Springer talking to a man on horseback. The young teen was pointing toward the cookhouse, where Casey and Eli were having a cup of coffee with Smiley.

"Ain't got no idea," Smiley said. "But I expect he's lookin' for you and Eli. Don't you reckon?"

"I don't know, Smiley," Eli joked, "might be he's heard about your cookin', and he's come to try to hire you away from here." They waited and watched the man approach.

"Mr. Tubbs, Mr. Doolin," the stranger said when he stepped down from the saddle. "My name's Douglas Spencer. I own a little spread south of Joe Nicholson's ranch. Wonder if I could have a word with you?"

"About what?" Eli asked.

Spencer seemed reluctant to spit it out.

"About the cattle business," he said.

"Why, sure you can," Casey volunteered when he saw his reluctance. "I'm Casey Tubbs and this is Eli Doolin. We were just havin' a cup of coffee with Smiley, here. Can we offer you a cup?"

"I reckon not," Spencer said. "Thank ya just the same. I don't wanna take up your time, but I just thought I'd ask you a couple of questions, if you don't mind."

Casey realized then that Spencer was reluctant to talk with Smiley sitting there listening, so he suggested that the three of them walk back to the front porch to talk. "Smiley's been tryin' to get us out of his cookhouse, anyway. Come on, Eli."

They started back toward the front of the house, but Spencer didn't wait until they reached the porch. "Joe Nicholson told me what you fellows did for him. And I know that ain't none of my business, but times have gotten desperate all of a sudden for a lot of us. Just like Joe, I owe the bank money I ain't got. I made the mistake of borrowin' money when things were goin' pretty good, year before last, and I built a new barn and stable. I don't owe as much as Joe did. I can feed my family, but I can't pay off that loan." He didn't pause at all as he laid it all out for them, so they didn't interrupt. "The reason I'm here is because Joe said you were buyin' cows, and if you still are, I've got fifty head I'd love to sell you."

"Do you know what we paid Nicholson for his cattle?" Casey asked.

"Yes, sir, I do," Spencer said, "two dollars and fifty cents a head."

"How much will it take to pay off your debt to the bank?" Casey asked.

"Well, I owe the bank two hundred and twenty-five dollars," Spencer said.

"Two dollars a head wouldn't give you all of your payoff," Eli commented.

"I know that, but it would be a good piece of it," Spencer said. "My wife inherited her mother's old furniture and I'm hopin' to sell that and some guns and stuff I've got that might be worth a little."

They had reached the front steps by then, so Casey invited him to tie his horse and sit down on the porch, while he and Eli went inside to talk over his offer to sell his cows. "Juanita might have some coffee on the stove. You sure you don't want a cup?"

"No, thanks. My stomach's kinda actin' up. I don't think I'd better drink any," Spencer said.

"All right," Casey said. "We're a fifty-fifty partnership, me and Eli, so we have to talk over every decision. We'll be right back."

They went directly to the safe in Eli's room and made their decision. When they came back to the porch, Casey handed Spencer a small stack of bills. "We've decided to give you three hundred dollars for your cattle, and we'll send some of the boys over to get 'em next week."

Spencer was too stunned to speak at once, so it was several moments before he choked out his appreciation. "I never expected this much," he managed. "I don't know how I'll ever repay you for your kindness."

"You don't have to repay us anything," Casey told him. "Just don't tell anybody else about our deal."

"I d-don't know w-what to say," Spencer stammered. "I don't know what to s-say . . ."

"You don't have to say anything," Eli said. "I expect you'da done the same for us, if it was turned around the other way."

Anxious to tell his wife the amazing news, Spencer didn't stay any longer than it took to ask the Lord's blessings for them both.

They stood on the porch and watched him ride out the gate, and Casey was inspired to comment, "Partner, I got a feelin' we ain't gonna be able to retire from our professional business as soon as we thought we were."

"It looks that way, Elmer," Eli said.

ABOUT THE AUTHORS

William W. Johnstone is the #1 bestselling Western writer in America and the *New York Times* and *USA Today* bestselling author of hundreds of books, with over 50 million copies sold. Born in southern Missouri, he was raised with strong moral and family values by his minister father, and tutored by his schoolteacher mother. He left school at fifteen to work in a carnival and then as a deputy sheriff before serving in the army. He went on to become known as "the Greatest Western writer of the 21st Century." Visit him online at WilliamJohnstone.net.

J.A. Johnstone learned to write from the master himself, Uncle William W. Johnstone, who began tutoring J.A. at an early age. After-school hours were often spent retyping manuscripts or researching his massive American Western History library as well as the more modern wars and conflicts. J.A. worked hard and learned, later going on to become the co-author of William W. Johnstone's many bestselling westerns and thrillers. J.A. Johnstone lives on a ranch in Tennessee and more information is at WilliamJohnstone.net.

CPSIA information can be obtained
at www.ICGtesting.com
Printed in the USA
BVHW042308240523
664780BV00005B/5

9 798885 789592